M000280993

THE TASTE OF DESPAIR

THE MASTER OF PERCEPTIONS SERIES

THE SIGHT OF DEMONS
THE SOUND OF SUFFERING
THE TASTE OF DESPAIR

THE TASTE OF DESPAIR

THE MASTER OF PERCEPTIONS SERIES, BOOK 3

DARIN C. BROWN

The Taste of Despair
Copyright © 2020 by Darin C. Brown

All rights reserved. This book or any portion thereof may not be reproduced or used in any manner whatsoever without the express written permission of the publisher except for the use of brief quotations in a book review.

This book is a work of fiction. Names, characters, places, and incidents either are the products of the author's imagination or are used fictitiously. Any resemblance to actual events or locales, or persons, living or dead, is entirely coincidental.

Printed in the United States of America

Library of Congress Control Number: 2020920393

First Printing, November 2020

ISBN 13: 978-0-9995-031-33

Ebook: 978-0-9995-031-40

This book is dedicated to those who struggle with depression, as well as the steadfast professionals who provide advice, comfort and solace.

THE TASTE OF DESPAIR

PART I

CHAPTER 1

IT WAS 3:57 AM. An explosion hit me from beneath my bedroom floor like an atomic bomb, jolting me awake. Its concussive wave carried horrible colors, smells and textures, but among them floated a familiar purple. I sat up, shivering with revulsion while the aftershocks flowed over me. As I focused on the warm, sweet purple buried inside the frigid, choking grey, my eyes widened with recognition. Mom!

Once last year, Mom's aura had erupted with an expansive silver cloud in response to a comment I'd made. She'd hurried off to her genetics lab after praising me for inspiring her, although I had no idea why. What scientific insight could a thirteen-year-old boy possibly offer to a woman with a PhD?

This was different. The bitter wailing and gritty hissing felt ominous. It reminded me of the screaming I'd felt from Mrs. Ryan's aura, the sound that betrayed the teacher's suffering. Fortunately, I'd been able to help her by removing the source of her pain.

This chaotic blast left me confused and concerned.

At least she wasn't in immediate danger. Threats produced a progression of tingling, tapping, thumping, and, with mortal peril, incessant pounding. Nor did she feel fear, whose characteristic dirty laundry odor was unmistakable.

Instead, the grey cloud brought a hailstorm of agitation and sadness, along with a prickled redness suggesting a mixture of anger and pain. There was also a prominent green vortex tinted with black. If it hadn't been for the purple, I wouldn't have recognized it as coming from Mom.

What just happened?

Since Grandpa helped me discover the nature of my ability three years ago, I learned a tremendous amount about the combinations of sights, sounds, smells and tastes that made up people's auras, as well as ways to manipulate them.

Some sensations were easy to understand. For example, when people were lying, their auras would flow in waves, like the ocean. Males were easily identifiable by a distinct pink. I could tell if a woman was a mother because her aura contained purple, although how strong it was varied depending on circumstances. Pain appeared as a spicy redness. Happiness and sadness resulted in shades of yellow or grey, respectively. Fear was easy to recognize, as was danger.

When I perceived pink, purple, yellow, grey, waves, spiciness, or the smell of sweaty clothes, I knew exactly what it meant.

Most of the time, however, I felt a complicated mix. Emotions and other thoughts blended with traits that I described as "baseline" characteristics. My own baseline aura was a blue color that I thought implied a predilection for medicine. I'd seen it in the auras of many physicians, like Grandpa. I'd since discovered many shades of blue, and not all doctors had the same one. There were many other colors and sensations whose meanings I had yet to grasp, but I was learning.

I'd made great strides over the summer, thanks to my friend Ian. His father, a skilled reporter, taught him at an early age to read people. Like his father, Ian was especially adept at recognizing emotions and character traits based on a person's expressions or actions. I was hopeless at this, because I grew up isolated with autism until age ten. Fortunately, I didn't need to recognize expressions if I could interpret the auras.

From my practice with Ian, I understood that Mom was devastated by the news she'd received. I'd felt a similar pattern of greenish

swirls inside a thrumming grey once before, when our mutual friend
Allan found out he wouldn't be allowed to play laser tag because of
a family obligation. Ian explained how the wide-eyed frown, the
high pitched voice, and the pleading gesture allowed him to deduce
Allan's feelings about the matter. I filed the data away along with
dozens of other patterns I could recognize.

The magnitude of Mom's aura implied something shockingly horrible. Whatever happened was much worse than missing laser tag.
My mind raced with possibilities, making further sleep impossible.
To distract myself, I began planting spicy redness into my own aura,
resulting in a series of wounds opening up along my arms and legs.
I deftly healed them by replacing the redness with my normal blue
color, a skill I'd refined to perfection. Although it helped pass the time,
it didn't take my mind off Mom's distress. I desperately wanted to know
what happened, but I couldn't simply walk downstairs and ask.

I imagined how that conversation might go:

"*Mom, what made your aura blow up with wailing grey and
greenish swirls?*"

"*Hunter Miller, what are you talking about?*"

"*Your aura. It just went crazy! I saw it from my room.*"

"*Perhaps it's time to call Dr. Eisenberg again.*"

✶   ✶   ✶

Grandpa sternly warned me against telling *anyone* about my
ability. My skin prickled with caution when I considered opening
up to my parents, with whom I had something of a tempestuous
relationship. They let my psychiatrist, Dr. Eisenberg, lock me up in
a mental ward when I first mentioned seeing auras. Plus, they lied
to me about a number of things, including the nature of their work.
I could see the waves in their auras. I wished that I could trust my
parents with my secret, but somehow I knew I couldn't.

Dad was some kind of spy, and he spent his time flying all over
the world doing who-knows-what. I could understand him omitting details about his employment. Mom's job situation was more

puzzling. She was a geneticist, and her paycheck came from the University of Washington here in Seattle. But I knew better. She had another employer, but refused to tell me about it.

The biggest secret they tried to keep concerned my own origin. Dad wasn't my biological father. When I first realized this, I lapsed into a place I called "the void." This empty space was an escape from consciousness that I used when I was younger, when I thought the auras were demons. It was my safe place, but when I was there, I mentally checked out. Up until I was ten, I spent most of my time there because of my fears. It was only after I discovered the true nature of the sensations that I learned to control when I entered the void.

I became proficient at hiding everything about the auras from my parents. They had their secrets, and I had mine.

Fortunately, I had Grandpa. I felt closer to him than any other person on earth. His aura was uncannily similar to mine. He was a doctor, and I wanted to be one too. He was the one who explained that the demons were actually auras, and that each different sensation had meaning. It wasn't a curse, it was a gift. Not only that, he taught me how to use the signals to make changes, like healing myself from injury. I could also affect others by changing their auras, and I'd helped Grandpa by fixing his knees.

Once I learned to control the signals, I used my ability to stop a group of bullies from teasing me and my friends, and then I'd helped a teacher get away from her husband, a dirty cop who'd been abusing her.

Grandpa understood my situation. He told me about Dad's job, exposing that secret. He'd also saved my life last year when I went too far experimenting with auras. I'd lost myself in the void so badly that I ended up in the ICU, completely delirious. Grandpa figured out that low blood sugar kept me from controlling the auras, and cured me by giving me intravenous doses of glucose. Grandpa was the only person in the world whom I'd ever trust completely.

When I thought about him, I felt a pang of guilt. I hadn't spoken to him for nearly a month. He'd counseled me strongly against pursuing Orlando Ryan, the police officer who was abusing his wife.

I was attacked while spying on Ryan in the bad section of Seattle. Despite weighing only one-hundred pounds, I thought my minimal martial arts training would be enough to protect me in the dangerous neighborhood.

I'll never forget how the three thugs laughed when I told them I knew karate. They stopped laughing when I used my secret ability, along with a side-kick, to break the leader's leg. Unfortunately, his hulking partner punched me so hard I could barely breathe. If I hadn't been able to heal myself, it would've been all over right then. Instead, I pulled the huge man into the void, where he couldn't hurt anyone. Only after breaking a rib of the third man, who'd grabbed me and was about to crush my throat, did I finally escape.

I never told Grandpa the truth about that night; I felt guilty and embarrassed. I decided to wait until I could see him face-to-face, when he moved here this fall. Now that he was back in our lives, he'd decided to relocate to the West coast. According to Mom, he'd already received his Washington State medical license, and he'd applied to several small hospitals locally.

I'd visited him in Massachusetts three times. The first was when I'd broken my leg after being conned into climbing a huge tree by stupid bullies. During that visit, we discovered I could heal myself. The second was last August, when he took me to meet Faye the Mystic, a healer who used Reiki instead of regular medicine to fix people. The third was over Christmas break, when we met Grandpa's acupuncturist friend, Dr. Fukawara. Grandpa kept trying to help me figure out the nature of my talent. He wanted me to know exactly what I could do, and why. The last time we spoke, he mentioned some new information he found, and I couldn't wait to hear what it was.

As the sun poked above the horizon, I decided I'd call him. I couldn't bear avoiding him any longer. I'd have to accept his gentle but firm disapproval, and perhaps even endure a tongue lashing. It would be worth it.

I felt Mom's aura again, and my heart quivered with anticipation and dread as I hopped out of bed and headed downstairs to confront her.

CHAPTER 2

"HUNTER," MOM said. "Did you hear me?"

I studied Mom's aura again for any sense, any hint, any trace of waves. But there were none. There had to be waves.

"Hunter?"

"Say it again," I said.

Mom shook her head. I dissected the emotions in her aura, the way I'd practiced with Ian over the past few weeks. I saw concern, confusion, dismay, and guilt, the latter of which made no sense. Why would Mom feel guilty? Purple glowed more brightly than usual, but all of it was dominated by the hazy, grey sadness that had exploded earlier that morning.

"Grandpa passed away last night," she said quietly.

It was impossible.

Before Mrs. Collins, my 4th grade teacher, had died, her aura was ghastly thin. The same was true of other sick people like Fat Louie, the diabetic kid who reacted so badly after eating a bunch of candy bars that he had to go to the hospital. When I was in the ICU, I noticed the same waftiness in many of the patients' auras. Grandpa's aura was full and vibrant, like mine.

Mom's hands touched me, and I jumped. I'd never been one for physical contact, except for the occasional hug from Grandpa.

"It's OK, Hunter," Mom was saying.

But it wasn't. I wracked my brains for any reason that Grandpa might have suddenly taken ill. He taught me a lot about diseases, and he never mentioned having any of them himself. His wife, my grandmother, died of cancer. But he told me that cancer took months or even years to develop. If he had cancer, I'd have seen evidence of it in his aura, wouldn't I?

"What'd he die of?" I burst out.

Mom fell backward as though struck by my words. The stale, fern-colored vibrations in her aura reflected a cross between surprise and annoyance.

"Heart attack," she said, after a deliberate pause.

"No way."

"It's… the doctor…" Mom started, then trailed off.

Grandpa had been training for the Boston Marathon in April. After I'd fixed his knees, he began racing again, picking up where he left off several years before. He'd been a competitive athlete throughout high school and college, and as an older runner, he'd been one of the best in the country for his age. He easily ran a qualifying time for Boston's prestigious race last year, and he was looking forward to competing alongside some of the best runners in the world. From what he'd told me about heart disease, I simply couldn't believe Grandpa suffered from it. He didn't smoke, he wasn't overweight, and he ran daily. He took amazing care of himself.

"I think you should take the day off from school," Mom was saying.

"I want to see him," I said defiantly.

Mom flinched like she'd been slapped. She stammered slightly. "Um, I haven't made the funeral arrangements yet, but you'll have a chance to say goodbye."

"I don't want to say goodbye, I want to see him!" I demanded.

"I'm sorry, Hunter. He's gone."

"There's no way he's dead!" I yelled.

"I can't believe it either, but the police found him in his bedroom. Apparently he died in his sleep. He didn't suffer."

My aura suddenly hissed with a gritty maroon. "HE'S NOT DEAD!" I screamed, over and over. Mom's attempt to calm me down by hugging me only made me flail about. The pitch of my screams reached such a crescendo that I heard dogs barking outside. As I squealed, my aura blazed in a horrific arctic redness. I sought the place of solace that never abandoned me, no matter how despondent I'd become. I went to the void.

CHAPTER 3

MY LIFE had been going so well. I'd conspired with my two friends Allan and Ian, along with Ian's father, Roger Pierce, and Roger's compatriot, Pam Winston, to help put an evil man behind bars. We discovered corruption in the local police force, and used the local newspaper to expose what we'd learned to the Washington State Police. In the process, I'd saved the life of Mrs. Ryan, a teacher whom I'd only met in passing. We lamented our individual fates on the far side of the school's playing fields during our daily lunch breaks. Her aura screamed so loudly that I knew something was wrong, and I had to help.

Mrs. Ryan's aura screamed because of the man tormenting her, and only after he was arrested did it finally stop. Ian and the others had been instrumental in the adventure, but after our initial exploits failed, I ended up taking matters into my own hands.

After our success, my friendship with Ian grew, partly because Allan's parents rewarded him for his stellar school year by taking him to Hawaii on vacation, and I spent my time with Ian instead. Allan and Ian were my only true friends. I could tell Ian enjoyed that time together by the yellow buzzing in his aura. It reminded me of playing chess with Rob Friendly, the first kid at my school who was nice to me. Rob and his family moved to the other side of the country after bullies attacked the two of us, sending us to the hospital with our faces covered in dog doo.

Ian's skill at reading people greatly aided my understanding of aura combinations. It started on the first day of summer, when we went to the mall to get ice cream. Ice cream provided sugar, which helped me use my skills to their fullest. I paid careful attention as Ian watched people going about their business, decoding their facial expressions and gestures.

"See there, look!" he said.

"What am I looking at?"

"That couple is having a fight. Check out the clenched fist, the tightened jaw, and the upright stance of the guy. He's pissed."

I checked the aura, seeing first a rusty orange, probably the guy's baseline color, then a sizzling crimson that confirmed Ian's assessment. As I cleared away my own aura and focused, I could see a bitter, musty chestnut-brown coldness, amidst a bright green murmur. There was more going on.

"And that's why I think she's cheating on him," Ian concluded. I'd missed most of what he'd been saying.

"Cheating, right," I said, filling the suddenly empty space between us.

"Dude, how many times do I have to tell you—stop doing that!"

"What?"

"Phasing out like you aren't even here! I mean, when we're in public and you do that, it makes me look like I'm talking to myself. Cut it out!"

"Sorry," I mumbled.

"Don't be sorry, be better!"

"Come on, let's go to the clothes store and watch the girls try on summer dresses."

Ian could watch girls for hours. I didn't understand the attraction. Other than the lack of pink in their auras, I didn't see much difference between boys and girls. The mannerisms, expressions and emotions that Ian described were the same for either gender.

Ian's aura brightened with a satiny butterscotch when he

discussed the anatomic parts of several of the girls. He enjoyed watching them prance about in their new or soon-to-be-new purchases. When Kathy Smitzer emerged from a changing room with a rather tight skirt and blouse, Ian's aura flashed a light purple color—one I'd noticed in my parents' auras when I caught them kissing.

A warm, sweet purring emanated from Ian as he quickly jumped up. "Come on, let's go," he said. "I just remembered I have to meet my Dad for dinner."

He didn't wait for me as I stood staring after him in confusion. Ian explained everyone else's emotions very well, so I didn't mind that he avoided telling me about his own.

There was another advantage to being Ian's friend. Because he was somewhat popular, I was invited to participate in many new activities.

In addition to laser tag, a battle game that Allan brought me to last year, I played paint ball and miniature golf, and joined Ian at the lake. There, we swam, sat out on the beaches, listened to music, or threw the Frisbee with his pack of friends, most of whom were in lower grades. During quiet times, he'd sit next to me and describe what each of his "mates" were thinking about, or what talents they possessed. I'd reconcile what he said with the auras they displayed. I couldn't have asked for a better guide.

One of Ian's followers was Toby Gascoigne, a 6th grader with whom Ian spent little time, but whose aura intrigued me. It contained a deep blue and bright silver that occasionally blazed like the sun, but most of the time it was obscured by a syrupy brown that oozed weakness. The bits of porcelain with a cinnamon smell confused me. Since Ian didn't know much about Toby, I tried to speak to him on my own, hoping to correlate the nature of his personality with his aura.

That proved more difficult than anticipated, as the kid was more elusive than an eel. About the only thing I discovered was that he was a very talented chess player—a fact that made me want to connect with him even more.

I didn't understand why sometimes I felt drawn to Toby. His deep blue aura was the nearly same shade as my own, but he was younger than me and didn't speak much. He seemed unhappy much of the time. I shared his aura color with Grandpa, Rob Friendly, and Allan, three people to whom I'd felt closest.

Toby also displayed a bright silver, like Mom, although hers was usually overcome by a strong maternal purple. I'd seen that silver in a weird homeless man who called himself Vzee, and once back when I was at the University of Washington Autism Center, before I knew anything about the auras.

I was puzzled by the silver color, because I could see nothing at all in common with Mom, Vzee, Toby, and an autistic kid who couldn't communicate with others. It made no sense. I couldn't ask Ian without him becoming extremely suspicious, and one thing I knew for sure, I could *never* tell Ian about my gift. My skin crawled with buzzing electricity when I even considered it, even worse than when I thought about telling my parents. I took that internal warning sign very seriously.

My fruitless attempts to interact with Toby reminded me that my social status barely exceeded that of a leper. My buddies who helped me take down the school bully two years ago had moved on. During school, they might say hi to me in the hallways between classes, but that was it. With summer in full swing, I never saw or heard from them.

Still, I was much better off than I'd been at the Center. That place was a torture chamber. None of the kids could hold a conversation, myself included, and the auras around me exuded a toxic blend of smells and tastes that made me physically ill. It was so miserable that I spent most of my time in the void. At least now I had a couple of close friends, Allan and Ian. Plus there was Grandpa.

But, now there *wasn't* Grandpa!

*   *   *

My eyes jolted open. I hoped it was all a dream, but I knew it wasn't. I jumped out of bed, fighting the disorientation that comes from standing too quickly after a prolonged period of lying down. How long had it been?

I checked my watch to discover the bad news. Two days. I'd been in the void for two full days. Forty eight hours. Time I'd never get to spend the way I chose, and a major setback for my quest for normalcy. There was nothing worse than losing control.

No, Grandpa being dead was definitely worse. It wasn't even close.

I still didn't believe it. Not truly. It didn't make any sense. Mom must have heard wrong. After I steadied myself, I went downstairs and dialed his number. He'd answer the phone, clear up any misconceptions, and tell me when he was moving to Washington.

Five rings. Six. Seven. Eight.

He answered on the ninth ring and my heart leapt into my throat.

"Hello, you've reached Carlton Hayes. Please leave me a message, and I will get back to you as soon as humanly possible."

My heart sank back into my chest. His answering machine. Well, yes, of course. He's not home, he's a busy man. I'll need to call back later.

Mom's car was in the garage, but she wasn't here. Perhaps she'd gone for a walk. I had the place to myself. Dad was out on another mission, and I never knew when he'd return. Sometimes I thought it would be cool to be a super-secret agent, like him, but I always dreamt about becoming a doctor, like Grandpa. After all, I could heal myself completely from any injury, and by removing the cloudy, spicy redness from auras, I could heal others just as easily. I'd have to go to medical school to learn about diseases, but once I understood the basics, I'd be the best doctor ever.

I mused about healing for a while, and even played the old game where I imagined I had a huge cut on my leg, picturing the way my aura would look. Then, I made it happen. Poof! Then, before any blood spilled onto my sheets, I restored my aura to its baseline blue color, and *voila!* the laceration was gone.

I spent years thinking this ability was a curse. Time wasted. I should have been learning how to use it. When I was younger, I thought the sights and sounds all around me were demons. I needed the void to escape them. Since Grandpa helped me discover their true nature, I learned to control the auras as well as my trips to the void.

Finding out that Dad wasn't my biological parent last year shocked me so badly that I lost control, and found myself involuntarily in the void. That had been the last time I'd collapsed until I heard Mom's news last week.

Which, by the way, I knew to be false.

I tried Grandpa's number again and again. I kept trying for an hour until Mom came back inside, carrying a small box.

"Hello, Hunter. Good to see you up. Who are you calling? Allan?"

"No, I was trying to get Grandpa."

Her face fell, and her aura buzzed with a cloudy grey.

"Grandpa's dead, Hunter. I'm sorry. He's not coming back."

She approached me as though to give me an embrace, but I ran back upstairs. At least I didn't fall into the void. Instead, I turned and went to the garage, where I pummeled the punching bag until so much sweat rained down that I slipped in the puddle it made on the concrete floor.

"HE'S NOT DEAD!" I yelled angrily, to no one in particular. I righted myself and began thrashing the bag anew. I didn't even notice the red drops falling from my fists, which were swollen, bruised and bloodied beyond recognition.

CHAPTER 4

THE FLIGHT east was mind-numbingly boring. Dad met us at the airport in Boston, apparently aware of Grandpa's supposed fate. After a brief mini-family-reunion, we drove together to a hotel near Grandpa's house. On the long car ride from the airport, I listened blankly as my parents discussed Grandpa's affairs. They decided to rent a storage facility for his furniture and other items until they could figure out what to do with it.

"He's gonna need his stuff!" I yelled.

Mom and Dad shook their heads and quietly resumed their conversation.

I checked my aura, which wasn't emitting waves. I must be right. Grandpa wasn't dead. If I was lying, I'd see waves. Of this I was certain.

"Have you spoken to the real estate agent yet?" Dad asked.

"We'll be meeting up with her after the service," Mom replied.

"The place is in a very nice neighborhood, it'll be snapped right up. If we're lucky, we can take care of this quickly before heading back to Seattle. I'm only cleared to be away for today and tomorrow, so I'm sorry, but you'll have to handle the rest of the details on your own."

"No problem. Oh, is that the hotel?" Mom asked, pointing to a large Marriott sign in front of a monstrous building.

"Oh, look, Hunter, they have a pool. Won't that be nice?" Dad added.

How could they just move on, like Grandpa didn't even exist anymore? Didn't they understand? What were they thinking?

I punched the seat in front of me, reopening the wounds on my knuckles. I hadn't bothered to heal them.

"HUNTER!" Mom yelled.

"Everyone deals with grief differently," Dad said soothingly. "It's going to be OK, Hunter. You'll get through this."

"Nobody believes me, Dad. But I know Grandpa's not dead!"

"Listen to me, Hunter. There's nothing strange going on here. Grandpa had a heart attack. He passed away. He's gone, and he'd want you to be strong for him. He'd want you to be a doctor and save lives, like he did."

I opened my mouth to object, but he put his hand up and continued.

"When I first started doing the work I do, I realized I'd have to face death far more than the average person. Sometimes, the people I'm fighting against die. Occasionally, a friend or colleague will die. We have a special place where we remember each and every one who passes away in service to our country. That's to make sure that we, the ones left behind, never forget the patriotic work they accomplished.

"I want more than anything for your grandfather to be alive, but the only way to honor him now is by keeping his memory strong in your heart, and doing the things he'd wished for you. Anything else is a dishonor to his memory. Do you understand?"

This was the first time Dad opened up to me about his work. I understood his words, and appreciated his effort to explain the situation from his perspective, but I could tell he didn't get it. If this was a battle I had to fight alone, so be it.

When I didn't respond, Dad continued again.

"Tomorrow we're going to honor Grandpa's memory. We're

going to bury his body and say a few words. I'm sure that wherever Grandpa is, he'd very much like it if you said the words that you feel about him in your heart. I guarantee that he'll hear them and appreciate the sentiment, as will everyone else at the funeral. We need to remember him in our own way. You more than most. Please consider what I'm saying. Turn your emotions into your ally, or they will get the better of you. Always remember that!"

I had just enough presence of mind to check his aura. No waves.

I put my head into my hands and teetered on the edge of the void, barely holding onto reality until a thought occurred to me. I'd see Grandpa tomorrow as they tried to lower him into the ground. I'd simply heal him, and that would be that. I used that realization to maintain the upper hand with my battle against the void through the rest of the evening. I fell asleep in my hotel bed, confident that I'd solve everything tomorrow.

*   *   *

The next morning, after a quick breakfast in the hotel lobby, we loaded into the rental car and drove to downtown Holyoke. We parked outside a giant stone building that looked like a misplaced castle, looming ominously over a modern city. The only thing that was missing was a moat. There were towers on either side of the main section that would provide excellent lookout posts for archers, and a giant central crest with a humongous symbol on top. Instead of a family crest, this centerpiece resembled a rounded weather vane with a Y-shaped base. There were three arches over the ground floor entrance, and an A-frame section containing an expansive window. As we exited the car, I spotted colorful windows providing contrast against the weathered stone.

I'd never been to a church before, but I'd read about them. I expected to see a cross, but the weathervane looked more like a massive hatchet. I got the feeling that this fortress was capable of sustaining an attack from any of the devil's minions.

The three of us entered through the doorway beneath the middle arch and were immediately accosted by a robed man who flowed into our path to express his sympathies. I lost interest immediately, wondering where Grandpa was. After pontificating briefly about death, the robed man described the history of the building and congregation. I heard very little of his speech, which sounded rehearsed, as I was still trying to get my bearings inside this behemoth of a structure.

St. Paul's Church, I was uninterested to learn, had been around since the 1860's and was established by the same folks who founded the town. A cotton magnate paid for the land and construction, and one of their early ministers spoke during the memorial service for President Lincoln. Fascinatingly irrelevant. I needed to see Grandpa.

I extricated myself from my parents and the bishop, or whatever he was, choosing instead to explore the church on my own. Ian's voice whispered "observe your surroundings," and I kept my eyes open instead of focusing on auras. I saw several impressive features.

The first was a series of colorful stained glass paintings on the massive windows. The largest, corresponding to the window visible from the outside, included Jesus and a group of children, or maybe angels. I couldn't tell which. In the next, Jesus was sitting on a throne with rays of sunshine behind him, giving the appearance of a glorified crown. Men before him all bowed their heads into their hands, while Jesus basked in their praise. A massive stone sculpture erupted from the floor below, this time with Jesus reading from a book, which I imagined to be the Bible.

The smaller windows contained intricate works of art, including ornate columns, buildings surrounded by palm trees in a Middle-Eastern style, and a scene with a teacher herding small children like a flock. A statue of Jesus stood inside a garden with rocks, trees and sand, calling out for all his children to bask in divine comfort.

A relief of Jesus, surrounded by angels, watched everything from a far wall. Closer stood a powerful angel with oversized wings, praying with her eyes closed. Perhaps she could read auras and didn't need regular vision?

Candles were everywhere, and in several places I saw an interesting coat of arms. It consisted of a red shield divided into four quadrants, all of which were empty except the upper left. That contained a series of crosses arranged into an X, all inlaid in blue. I didn't understand the symbolism until I rearranged the picture mentally to see it was a cross that divided the shield into quadrants. Once I identified that pattern, I saw crosses everywhere throughout the interior. It reminded me of the picture of triangles within a triangle that Mr. Lajoie, my sixth grade teacher, showed us when we were working on geometry.

Several flags were raised along the back wall. I recognized the American flag immediately, but there were two others whose significance I didn't know. Despite all of these incredible sights, the most impressive was the series of pipes, all of differing heights and widths, running near the piano adjacent to the flags.

I was so enthralled that I didn't notice the electric blue aura next to me until it spoke.

"You like the organ?" it said.

"Huh?"

"The pipe organ. It's really quite incredible. James, the organist, makes it sing in glorious harmonies. He'll be playing later today."

"Oh," I said, not knowing what else to say.

"Forgive me, I haven't introduced myself. I'm Reverend Sanderson, the rector at St. Paul's. I've been speaking with your parents, but you wandered off before I had a chance to say hello. I'll be delivering the eulogy for your grandfather."

"So you must know where he is?" I said.

"Um, yes. You'll be able to say your final good-bye at the cemetery. He reserved a plot, and we'll be saying a few more words after the funeral here. I must say, your grandfather had quite a large support system. We anticipate several hundred people coming to the ceremony, so we are setting up speakers in the smaller rooms in case the main auditorium overflows."

"I need to see him!" I implored.

"I'm sorry, Hunter, is it?"

"Yes."

"Your parents told me your name. I take it you were very close to your grandfather."

"Yes, and that's how I know he isn't dead!" I bellowed.

"Hmm. Tell me about the connection you have with him."

I was stuck. Obviously I couldn't describe the similarity of our auras, which was the first thing that popped into my head.

Seeing my dismay, Reverend Sanderson bailed me out. "He was the one person in the world who truly understood you?"

"YES!" I agreed. "That's exactly it."

"Well, don't worry that his death will stop that connection," he said.

"What do you mean?"

"There are forces in the world much stronger than death. The special relationship you two have is assuredly one such entity. If you ever despair about missing your grandfather, remember this: he is with you. He will always be with you."

"Reverend," a woman called out, gesticulating wildly.

"Oh, excuse me, Miss Abernathy requires my urgent assistance. Chin up, Hunter," he said, as he hefted his bulky body toward the frantic woman.

*   *   *

People collected inside the church before the service, dividing themselves into discrete sections. I avoided everyone, but from afar, I noticed similarities within the different groups.

I could easily identify the largest group, the doctors and nurses, by their conversations and auras. Because of my autism and general carelessness, I'd been around medical people my whole life. When I was very young, the only times I left the house were to see Dr. Stonington, my primary care doctor, or to visit the emergency room to take care of my latest mishap. I learned to recognize the characteristics in their auras. They felt "right" to me.

I'd never seen so many health care workers outside a hospital before, and the effect was powerful. The people swam through the ocean of blue, with sparkles of yellow shimmering in the grey sadness as one of the mourners recounted an amusing anecdote about Grandpa. I understood why I'd thought blue implied being a doctor. Nearly everyone in the pool added some shade of blue to the milieu. By the warmth and sweet smell, I could tell these people all truly cared about Grandpa. I wanted be part of this tribe.

Standing closer to the doorway were a section of athletes, probably Grandpa's running buddies. The strength and density of their auras boasted their physical fitness. They were all thin, like Grandpa, and they spoke about upcoming races and other events. I expected medical people would have the healthiest auras, but the reality was nearly the opposite. From this limited sample, I concluded that doctors didn't take care of themselves, only others. Strange.

Mom and Dad spent most of their time interacting with the group of family members. Grandpa's parents had long since passed, as had his only sibling. However, she had been prolific, having half a dozen children, most of whom lived on Cape Cod. They had traveled en masse to Holyoke to pay their respects. I watched as the young children of Mom's cousins milled around the outskirts of the group. I could see the family resemblance in the auras, which were so similar that I couldn't tell which child corresponded to which cousin. I didn't really care much. I stayed well away from all of them.

The last cluster was where Reverend Sanderson spent most of his morning, although he had circulated among the groups. The people in this section possessed cooler auras laced with blue and gold, but with an irritated redness smelling of bad breath. The grey shared by the rest of the mourners was absent. They didn't want to be here, which made no sense. Why go to a funeral of someone you didn't care about? The prickly pungence made me want to avoid them even more. For the millionth time, I wished Grandpa were here to explain who these people were, and why their auras were so nasty.

* * *

At the request of the Reverend, we all filed into the main auditorium and took our seats. Mom, Dad and I sat in the front row,
much to my chagrin. After some welcoming comments, he looked
straight at me and spoke.

"Let us pray.

"God grant us the serenity to accept the things we cannot
change, the courage to change the things we can, and the wisdom
to know the difference between the two.

"Living one day at a time, enjoying one moment at a time,
accepting hardships as the pathway to peace. Taking, as He did,
this sinful world as it is, not as we would have it, trusting that He
will make all things right if we surrender to His will. Trusting that
we will be reasonably happy in this life and supremely happy with
Him forever in the next. Amen."

After some sad organ music, a few hymns, and a long sermon
on how God has a plan for all of his children, the Reverend invited
attendees to come to the pulpit to give testimony to the life of this
great man.

I watched the auras as a parade of individuals spoke about
Grandpa's life. He spent it saving lives, relieving suffering, helping
those in need, volunteering with local agencies, donating to worthy
causes, brightening the days of the sick or needy and always smiling
and speaking well of others. Aside from occasional flashes of yellow,
woolen grey sadness permeated the event. After a while, I stopped
listening and counted the moments until I could get to the cemetery. I'd find Grandpa, heal his body, and return things to normal.
All of these people would see the terrible mistake they'd made.

* * *

The cemetery was only a short drive, although traffic on
Northampton Street was very slow. Apparently this road had some

significance for Mom, as she smiled and glowed yellow briefly when Dad mentioned it. However, I was far more interested in finally getting to see Grandpa.

As we pulled up in our limousine, I could no longer restrain myself, and I opened the door while the vehicle was still moving.

"Hunter!" Mom and Dad yelled simultaneously, as I leapt from the open door onto the grass.

"Where is he?" I spurted.

"His plot is over there," Mom said. "At least I assume it is, given the new hole in the ground. He bought it years ago and I never…"

I took off running toward the open hole and the small crowd of people who'd already begun to arrive. I recognized Reverend Sanderson, and made a beeline for him.

"Reverend!" I puffed.

"Why, hello, Hunter."

"Where is he?"

"Your grandfather's ashes are already in the casket, but you'll be able to say a few words just before we lower it into the ground."

"Ashes?" I said, dumbfounded.

"Yes, strange, I know. He'd purchased a plot years ago but for some reason he was cremated. Not sure why; he'd been an organ donor, but apparently they cremated him immediately, even before harv—"

The sickly look on my face stopped the Reverend from completing the sentence.

"Apologies, son. I didn't mean to sound insensitive. I know you never really got a chance to say goodbye, so let me clear out these people and give you a moment alone."

He looked over to where my parents had stopped a few feet away. Mom and Dad both nodded as the pastor stepped away. I still didn't quite comprehend what had happened. I raised my hand and glanced at them.

"Mom, what does cremate mean?"

Mom's aura soured, and she looked like she was barely able to speak. Dad piped up, "Hunter, when someone's dead, their body isn't important anymore. The part of them that you remember is inside your head, not in any physical place."

"What does cremate mean?" I asked again, my voice shrill and tense.

"They reduce the body to ash," Dad said stiffly.

"Someone BURNED him alive?"

"No, Hunter," Dad said calmly. "His heart and brain had stopped, and the person that he had been, was gone."

"Fritzcloves!" I shrieked.

"Hunter, language!" Mom said.

I couldn't believe it. Someone had killed him. He was murdered by these people who burn corpses. I started screaming, then running, then wailing, and then, for the second time in a week, I lost myself to the void.

CHAPTER 5

I AWOKE in my own bed.

I glanced at my wrist for the time, but my watch was gone. A clock on my bedside table read 9:34 AM. I felt panic rising as I saw an intravenous line dripping fluids into my arm. I must have been unconscious for a while to require such a measure. The last time I'd had one of those, I was in the Intensive Care Unit at the Children's Hospital in Seattle, having nearly died.

I tried to call out for Mom, but my voice didn't respond. I could only produce a gurgling noise that resembled a drowning hamster. My throat ached. That was stranger than my inability to speak, because I hadn't experienced pain since I'd gained control of the auras.

At least I wasn't restrained, like when I was in the ICU. I tried to sit up, but my head felt like it was full of bubbles, and I fell back into the bed, almost passing out. A black box that I didn't recognize sat adjacent to the clock on the table. It had a flashing red light and a small display screen. As I leaned over and grabbed it, the box made a loud chirping, which frightened me and made me drop the box onto the floor. As if on cue, I heard footsteps tromping through the house.

"I'm coming, Hunter!" the unfamiliar voice called.

A slim, brunette woman in a white outfit strode quickly into the room.

"Who are you?" I tried to say. My vocalization sounded like a duck in a blender, which I thought was a considerable improvement over the hamster noise.

"You're awake! Wonderful! Dr. Eisenberg had no idea how long you'd be out, but she wanted to make sure someone was here when you woke up."

I struggled mightily to sit forward or to make a coherent sound, but she put her hand on my chest gently, saying, "Easy, now, Hunter. Just relax. If you're not careful, you'll rip your IV out. Everything's OK. You're at home, and nobody's going to get you."

I stopped thrashing long enough to make a face. Ian always called me "an open book," because my emotions were so easy to read. Since I couldn't speak, I hoped to convey the proper message. "Who is this insane person in my room?" my features said. It worked.

"Right, I'm Cathy Shaw. I'm your nurse this morning."

I had many questions, but I couldn't ask any of them.

"One second," she said. "Wait right here."

I shook my head and took a deep breath. Where was I going to go? Nurse Cathy reappeared shortly with a glass of water, which I accepted greedily. After feeling the cool liquid soak my parched throat, I felt substantially better.

"Thanks," I managed.

"You're very welcome," she said, in a sing-song voice.

"Could I have some more, please?" I asked, shocked by my own manners.

"Certainly. Coming right up!"

She brought in a pitcher and refilled my glass. I inventoried my situation. The last thing I remembered was… oh, yes. Grandpa! The funeral service and burial in Holyoke. I'd lost it when—the unwanted thought flooded my head like a river in a hurricane. They burned him!

I grabbed the sheets and squeezed, crumpling them up and untucking them from the foot of the bed. Nurse Cathy's facial expression turned to concern. I felt myself slipping back into the void and I fought it despite my severely limited strength. I'd wake up in the looney bin if I went out again. Think. Think!

Curiosity kept me in the moment. "How long?" I croaked.

"Pardon?" she answered.

"My watch," I hissed, as now the duck turned into a snake. I pointed to my wrist to make my point. "Do you know where it is?"

"Oh, I'm not sure. Did you have it when you came back from the hospital?"

How the heck should I know? Where did they find these nurses?

"Well, today is Thursday the 23rd, and it's just before ten in the morning," she said.

I felt the air escape from my lungs so completely that I doubted I'd ever breathe again.

"Are you all right?" she asked.

I looked back at her. There were no waves. She was telling the truth. But something was wrong. Very wrong. The auras were— wrong. There was no other word for it.

"Hunter?" Nurse Cathy said, rather loudly, as though she'd been repeating herself.

"Yes?"

"I thought I'd lost you again. I promised to call your Mom when you woke up, so I'd better do that. Do you need anything else?"

I felt like I needed to urinate, but was suddenly aghast to realize there was some kind of tube inside me, down there.

Reading my thoughts like the open book that I was, Nurse Cathy immediately understood my concern.

"I'll get the catheter out right away. So sorry, but you were unable to, you know, on your own."

I stoically endured the humiliation of having the tube removed. The procedure was painful, but I felt tremendous relief once it was out.

"Let me know when you need to go the bathroom, and I'll walk you there. You're not safe to be on your feet just yet. I've got to call your Mom, though. I'll be right back."

Between the shock over missing three weeks submerged in the void, the emotional discord at the thoughts of Grandpa getting burned up in an incinerator, the unusual aura that Nurse Cathy displayed, and the strange aches and pains I kept feeling, I hadn't noticed that I was famished. The moment I had the thought, I grew even more concerned, as I'd rarely felt sensations like hunger. I knew I had to eat when I manipulated the auras, but I'd never experienced cravings for food. My body had undergone serious changes while I was comatose.

"Can I get some food?" I called out. Nurse Cathy was evidently on the phone with Mom, so I waited for her to return. I couldn't get up anyway. She'd been right about that. I felt like a one-hundred pound weight was lying on my chest. I could barely sit up.

"Your Mom's on her way. She wants to make sure you're OK. She's been very worried about you!"

"Can I have something to eat?" I reiterated.

"Of course. Hope you like Jello. It's the best thing when you haven't had anything in your stomach in a while. Very easy to digest, and a tasty treat. I'll bring some from the kitchen."

While waiting for her to reappear with my treat, I decided to access my aura, primarily to check for signs of physical damage. I remembered the spicy redness of my broken leg, and hoped not to find anything like that today. Instead of the powerful cool blue, my brain perceived a cloudy, thin, muddled, greying quagmire. I could barely detect the pink strands that identified me as a male. I *knew* something was wrong with the auras. I hadn't had anything to eat in a while, so I concluded it was hypoglycemia, like before. Once I ate I'd be fine.

The raspberry flavored goop did little to assuage my fears. My stomach rumbled like a thunderstorm as I consumed the gelatinous material. The nurse made a face as I finished the entire container in less than a minute.

"Hungry, are we?" she said, not even trying to conceal the sweet sarcasm.

"Starved!" I said. In this case, it was literally true.

"Let's give your stomach a little rest, and I'll bring you something else after your Mom arrives. I don't want you throwing up because we fed you too quickly."

I felt much better, despite the persistent growling. Surprisingly, the world around me appeared confusingly normal. I could hardly see Cathy's aura, and I didn't feel Mom's warm purple embrace until her body covered mine on the bed.

"Hunter," she began, but she didn't finish the thought.

Ordinarily, I didn't care for hugs, except for those from Grandpa, but the warmth of Mom's body felt like her aura, and I found that reassuring. Instead of pulling away, I returned the gesture, and didn't let up until I noticed that Mom was crying.

"Are you OK?" I asked.

"Mfft... me?" she responded quizzically. "Yes, I'm good. Are YOU OK? You've been unconscious for weeks!"

"Oh, sorry, I lost it when—well, you know."

"Don't apologize, it's not your fault. I'm just glad you're awake. I know how close you and Grandpa were. You've always had trouble with crowds, so when all of those folks were there, at the funeral, well, we shouldn't have put you in that situation. I'm sorry, Hunter."

Another thought hit me. "How did I get back home?"

Mom paused. "When you passed out, we thought it was because of the stress of, well, everything. Dad and I assumed that given time, you'd simply wake up, like in the past. So instead of bringing you to the hospital, we rented a car and drove home. It was a long trip, but Dad drove the first half, and I drove the rest of the way. When you still hadn't come to by the time we made it to Seattle, I called Dr. Stonington and Dr. Eisenberg, who both agreed this was a psychological problem, but we needed to keep you hydrated until you awoke. Instead of keeping you in the hospital, we agreed to keep you here. Dr. Stonington and the nurses, Cathy and Mary, have been watching over you ever since."

Nurse Cathy had squirreled out of the room when Mom arrived, but she returned with a steaming bowl.

"All right if he eats some broth?" she asked.

"Certainly, Cathy, thanks. Let's get the boy fed."

"I had Jello," I said.

"The ultimate food for the recovering patient," Mom said with a smile.

Cathy brought in a tray so that I didn't need to get out of bed, and I slurped down a large bowl of chicken noodle soup. Mom watched until I had nearly finished.

"Your Dad's back at work," she said.

I glanced briefly at Cathy, who didn't react.

"OK," I said.

"I'd better call Dr. Stonington. He said he'd come out and visit when you woke up."

I nodded and tossed the bowl back, waggling my tongue to catch the last few noodles and remaining broth from the bowl. Mom's face scrunched slightly at the uncouth display, but she continued.

"I also promised Dr. Eisenberg that I'd bring you into the office when you came out of it, so let's plan on seeing her tomorrow. She says it's not unusual for someone like you to have episodes under situations of extreme emotion."

What was that supposed to mean? How many people "like me" were there?

Mom changed her tone. "Anyway, let me call the office and see what time she can squeeze you in."

"And I'll take out that catheter," Cathy said.

I froze, checking down toward my pants with trepidation.

"No, Hunter, the IV line in your arm."

I sighed audibly with relief.

"Now that you're eating normally, we won't be needing that any longer. It's better to get it out as soon as possible so it doesn't get infected."

I wasn't worried about any infection; I'd fix my aura if I started getting one. I wanted the catheter out, though, so I held out my hand. She took off the dressing and quickly removed the plastic piece, covering the wound with a small bandage.

By evening, my strength returned, and I could stand and go to the bathroom unaided. Dr. Stonington visited briefly, checking my vital signs, listening to my heart and lungs, pinching my skin and pushing on my stomach before pronouncing me fine.

"Don't try to run a marathon right away," he joked. "But seriously," he said to Mom, "he should be fine. Call me if anything comes up." With that, he left.

I ate ravenously, which sated my hunger, but not the strange feeling that something was amiss with my body. I managed to sleep a few hours before waking to a horrible nightmare where I was being burned alive. I soaked my pajamas with sweat. Thoughts of Grandpa kept me awake the rest of the night, so I was exhausted when Mom came to get me.

"Hunter, time to get up," she said quietly, after knocking on my door.

"I'm awake," I groaned.

"We have to leave in twenty minutes. Let's get ready quickly, please."

I rubbed my face with my hands, hoping to wipe away the horrible feeling I couldn't shake.

Nineteen minutes later, I was dressed and waiting in the garage for Mom, who had a last-minute phone call that distracted her. Fortunately, she was able to placate the person on the other end of the line. The delay almost made us late for my appointment, despite Mom's aggressive driving, which included whipping into a parking space very close to the entrance that was marked "reserved".

The receptionist at Dr. Eisenberg's office was familiar, so I ignored her in favor of checking my surroundings. I was very bad at it, but the memory of Ian's voice poking fun at my lack of observational skills kept me motivated to improve.

The space had a large window where Mom spoke to the registration clerk, who typed my information into a computer. A series of uncomfortable-looking, thinly-padded wooden chairs were set up back-to-back in a central aisle, creating a miniature maze that led to the offices. In addition to Dr. Eisenberg's room, there was another door with a nameplate that read *Dr. Jenkins*. No other windows were visible, and the floor was carpeted with a soft, thick material. The cream colored walls reminded me of the aura color I associated with someone who was helpful to others. I silently wondered if other people saw the auras but chose not to speak about them. Maybe they painted the walls this helpful color to make patients more comfortable.

"Hunter!" Mom called, apparently not for the first time.

"Uh, yeah, Mom," I mumbled.

"She's ready for you."

I wasn't in the void, but I wasn't paying attention either. I shook myself mentally and wandered past the chairs into Dr. Eisenberg's office. She stood behind her desk, speaking quietly with Mom.

"Good morning, Hunter," she said congenially.

"Who's Dr. Jenkins?" I said.

Mom stared at me using a facial expression I should've been able to identify, but couldn't. I stared back dumbly.

"She said 'good morning, Hunter,'" Mom whispered, through clenched lips.

I looked at Dr. Eisenberg, whose mask of a face never changed, and realized my mistake. "Oh, hi, Dr. Eisenberg. Who's Dr. Jenkins?"

"Dr. Jenkins is my partner. He's been here for six months. He covers for my patients when I'm unavailable."

I nodded knowingly. Right! Like when Orlando Ryan had his goons beat you up. My appointments kept getting postponed or cancelled. Well, fortunately all of those men were behind bars now, thanks to me.

"Hunter, I'm going to let the two of you talk. I'll be outside. I don't have to go into the office, so I'll be here in case you need anything."

Mom walked out and closed the door after a nod from Dr. Eisenberg. It was odd that Mom decided to wait—she always went back to work during my appointments. The good news was that I'd get home quickly once we were done.

Dr. Eisenberg smiled sourly. "I'm so sorry for your loss, Hunter. I know you were very close to your grandfather."

The weight of her simple statement pulled me like an anchor under water. Grandpa was gone. Dead. Murdered by flame. Destroyed, never to be heard from again. My trusted friend, my only real confidant, departed from this world. I felt a horrendous taste in my mouth and then vomited my breakfast onto the rug. I spewed my stomach contents so completely that further heaving only brought up a few dribbles of saliva.

The daylight that had previously surrounded my body turned black as night, and I nearly fell into the void as oppressive sensations pummeled my brain. I retched again, producing another small bit of liquid. I was vaguely aware of the doctor scrambling to get towels and throwing them onto the mess. Shortly after, Mom appeared and touched my back, making me convulse.

"Let's get you home, Hunter," Mom said.

I was in no position to argue. Dark grey morass bathed my every motion. Chunks of congealed milk stuck to my shoe as I walked through the vomit. Mom grabbed my hand and redirected me, and the hasty change of course nearly made me erupt again. All the while, a disturbing taste gripped at my tongue.

Dr. Eisenberg groaned a bit as I tracked slop through her office, and finally grabbed my foot and toweled it off.

"I'll reschedule you for tomorrow, Marissa," she said.

"Thanks. Sorry about the—"

"It's all right. Fortunately I have some time before my next session. Get him home and into a safe environment."

My head spun as we drove home, and this continued well past the time I got back into my room. At least I'd stopped puking.

I had no idea what happened. One minute I was documenting the color of the wall paint, and the next, I felt like the world had ended. The crushing weight I'd experienced eased slightly, but didn't resolve. I felt like I was lying in a thick pool of grey fog, and it smelled worse than anything I'd ever breathed before, with the possible exception of the emotions of the kids at the University of Washington Autism Center. As that thought crossed my mind, I realized it was quite similar. Perhaps it was the vomit I'd stepped in.

I pulled my pillow over my head in an unsuccessful attempt to stop the room from swirling and to block the horrid smell. I basked in misery until Mom brought me a glass of water and helped me shed my soiled clothes.

After a while, the feelings began to wane. I curled up into a ball on my bed and tried to imagine how life could get any worse. I thought about Grandpa again, and suddenly all of the horrid sensations recurred with a vengeance. My stomach danced somersaults, but at least this time, I didn't throw up. There was nothing left, as I'd barely sipped the water Mom brought.

I couldn't take it any longer. I left my body for the serenity of the void.

CHAPTER 6

I REGAINED my senses long enough to go to the bathroom, eat oatmeal, drink diluted juice, and wash my face, which was still encrusted with my former stomach contents. I swam through the thick, smelly, greyish ocean of pressure toward nowhere.

I had no idea how anyone could expect me to live like this. Mom tried to get me out of bed, to no avail.

"You have an appointment with Dr. Eisenberg. Come on, Hunter, you really need to get up and get moving," she pleaded.

I pulled the blanket back over my pounding head to hide from the pressure and the smell.

"All right, I'll reschedule," Mom conceded, leaving me to my internal swamp.

This routine continued. My days and nights were haunted by snippets of Grandpa. The first moment I saw his aura. The salvation I felt when he revived me in the ICU. Healing his knees and receiving the warmest hug ever. Mistaking the smell of sweat from his dirty gym clothes as a sign of fear, and panicking. Learning CPR—how to do chest compressions and mouth-to-mouth—even though I assured him that I'd never need it. Hearing the news he was moving to Seattle to be closer to us.

Playing hours of chess. Beating him at poker while using his aura to discern whether he was bluffing or not. Watching scores of people at the park near his home in Holyoke. The memories flowed in no particular order, and each one sent me reeling toward the void.

Mom reassured me dozens of times.

"Hunter, it's going to get better."

But it didn't.

My birthday came, and when Mom and Dad sang "Happy Birthday," I barely had the strength to sit up.

After the song, Dad said, "Remember last year, when you had Allan over and we ate sloppy joes? That was fun, right?"

A small ray of sunlight shone through the open window next to my bed. I nodded. Allan had always been a good friend.

"And what about your new buddy, Ian?" Mom said. "Maybe we can invite them both over tomorrow, and they can eat the leftover cake with you?"

For the first time in nearly two weeks, the weight lifted slightly from my shoulders. "Yeah, that would be good," I said. I ate my slice of cake and felt the sugar's energy surge through me. The fog parted and I was able to walk to the bathroom and take a shower. Mom changed my sheets.

"Getting a little ripe in here," she said. "About time you took a shower."

*   *   *

True to her word, Mom invited Ian and Allan over the next afternoon. They brought me presents. They insisted that I didn't need to have my birthday party on the actual day, which made the whole thing rather silly. If you could celebrate any day, why not treat every day like your birthday? Obviously life wasn't like that. It was still uplifting to see them.

"Hey, buddy," Allan said. "How're you holding up?"

"I'm OK," I lied. Ian nodded knowingly.

"Did you hear that we have a new teacher?" Allan asked.

"Of course we have a new teacher, we get one every year," Ian quipped.

"No, stupid, I mean there's a new teacher coming from somewhere else, Georgia, I think, and she's going to take over the 8th grade HCC," Allan said, referring to the acronym for our class, the highly capable cohort.

Allan whacked Ian on the arm to make his point. Ian tried to jab him back, but Allan blocked it away with his lightning reflexes.

"Oho… so that's how it is," Ian said.

Allan smiled and shrugged. "Anyway, you probably didn't see the packet, but she sent a reading list. Here—open this."

He handed me one of the gift-wrapped packages off the table. I opened it, and inside was a new copy of *The Hobbit* by J.R.R. Tolkein.

"Cool!" I said.

"Read it later," Ian said. "We've got cake to eat!"

"What's the new teacher's name?" I asked.

"Mrs. Burnell. You'll meet her tomorrow," Allan said.

"What? How? Why?" I sputtered. "Does she come for home visits?"

"No," Ian said. "School starts tomorrow, silly goon."

It took a moment for me to process this, and by the time I had, Mom had returned.

"Are you all right?" she asked.

"Uh, yeah. Allan just told me school starts tomorrow."

"That's true," Mom said. "You wouldn't want to miss the first day, would you?"

"I guess not," I lied.

"That's the spirit, mate!" said Ian jovially. "Now let's get into this cake your Mom promised us. We don't have all day, you know!"

Allan frowned at Ian, who ignored him and made a beeline for the cake on the kitchen table. Ian picked up the knife and cut himself a huge slice, then proceeded to eat it without a plate or fork, showering the floor with crumbs.

"Very smooth, Ace," said Allan, who used a plate for his piece.

After the cake, I opened my other presents. In addition to the book, Allan got me a very small punching bag.

"It's called a speed bag," he said. "It's for boxers, mostly. You get into a rhythm, punching it away and then hitting it again when it comes back. My Dad got me one and I liked it a lot, so I found one for you."

"And I got you this!" Ian announced, retrieving a smaller package and handing it to me. I hastily ripped off the newspaper he'd used to wrap the gift and discovered a multicolored, six-sided object with little obvious use.

"What is it?" I asked.

"A Rubik's cube. Perfect for your crazy genius brain. The tiles on this side are all white, and if you turn it over, they're all blue. All the other sides are the same too. This is how it looks when it's solved. Here's how it works. You turn one row like this," he demonstrated. "If you make a bunch of random turns, it mixes it up. When you want to solve it, you rotate each side so all the colors line up like when we started."

He made a few more turns and rotations, and all the colors aligned again.

"Wow, cool," I said. "You're really good at it. You solved it right away!"

"He just undid the moves he used to mix it up, in the opposite order," Allan explained.

"Did not!" Ian said.

"Oh, really? Let me see it."

He swiped the toy out of Ian's hand, turned his back, and mixed it so that each of the six colors was evenly distributed on every face.

"Solve it now!" he challenged.

"Well, it *is* Hunter's present, now isn't it? Let him play with it."

"That's what I thought," Allan said.

After about ten minutes of experimenting, I figured out how to relocate tiles from one place to another using a series of basic turns. Five minutes later, I'd solved it.

"Holy canoli!" Ian said. "You really did solve it!"

"Do that again," Allan said, and he mixed it up completely.

This time, I solved it in about ninety seconds.

"Freakin' geekazoid," Ian muttered.

"Your turn, genius," Allan said to him.

"Nah, I think we've had enough of that. How about going outside?"

We went outside and talked for a few hours while walking around the neighborhood. As we returned home, they both noticed the time and said they had to be going. I suddenly realized that neither one mentioned anything about Grandpa.

"Grandpa's dead," I blurted.

"Yeah, we know, so sorry, Hunter," Allan said quietly.

"Sorry," Ian mumbled.

I looked at them.

"Your Mom told us not to say anything about it," Ian added, apologetically.

A horn sounded out in front of the house.

"My Dad's here," said Ian. "I gotta go."

I nodded.

"See you tomorrow?" Ian said.

I nodded again. He tapped me lightly on the arm and jogged to the front door.

Allan said "My mother is gonna be here in a few minutes too. Are you coming back to karate anytime soon? We have that tournament coming up, and I really want you to watch me win this year."

"I don't know," I said hesitantly.

"It's all right. Take your time. If you ever need to talk, I'm here."

Mom came in shortly after. "Allan, your Mom's out front."

Allan nodded at me and hustled out the door.

"Did you have a good time?" Mom asked.

"Yes," I said honestly.

"Show me that cube thing," she said.

"Oh, it's pretty easy, here, I'll mix it up and show you."

I solved it in a few moments, as the solution came into my head almost instantly. It took more time to rotate and twist the cube than to figure out which way it needed to go.

"I'm sure anyone can do it," I said.

"I wouldn't bet on it. I have no idea how you just did that," she said. "I'm glad you had a good time. Let's have dinner and maybe you can read your new book before bedtime."

"OK," I said.

*   *   *

Unfortunately, my thoughts drifted to Grandpa, so I couldn't fall asleep. I tossed and turned until the wee hours of the morning. When my alarm went off, I didn't hear it. Mom shook me awake and forced me to get out of bed. I mechanically slogged through dressing, eating, washing, and heading to the bus stop. In addition to everything else, I had to deal with sleep deprivation for my first day back at school.

Once the bus arrived, Allan found me and directed me toward our new classroom.

Ian's energetic form whizzed by as he bolted through the open doorway in front of us. "Hunter, my man, sit over here!" he said.

I looked at Allan, who'd been my desk partner for the past two years.

"It's all right," he said. "I'll sit with Bob. Unless she rearranges us in alphabetical order, in which case I'll be right back with you."

I plopped down next to Ian, who seemed quite ready for mischief. He bounced around like he was on fire.

Like Ian, my other classmates were all in high spirits. Davis Blovat, Bob Deluca, Don Schmelling, Mickey Murphy and Brady Patrick—the guys that helped Allan and me embarrass the school bully two years ago—chatted loudly on their way in. Mike Giovanni, Glenn King, Charlie Ramsfield and PJ Wasciewicz were all smiles as well.

"We're gonna rule the school!" Davis was saying, as he walked past our desk.

"Top of the food chain, baby!" replied Mickey, who, with his baby face and slight build, was unlikely to be the top of anything except a cheerleader pyramid.

The girls, Patty Owens, Christy Johnson, Amy Mullens, Anne Altavista, Kristen Worthy, Nicole Oliver and Elaine Farrar, swarmed in like bees. They all looked different than last year. More—something.

"Those are *girls*," Ian whispered into my ear.

"Yeah, I know!" I said, so loudly that several girls turned their heads in my direction. After a brief disapproving glance, they resumed the march to preferred seating, befitting their regal status.

"Piece of advice, mate. Easy on the staring."

"I wasn't staring," I protested.

"Uh-huh. And you don't have a secret crush on Patty Owens either," he said quietly.

"What? I don't have a crush on Patty Owens!"

Patty turned my way and smiled wryly.

"You're welcome," Ian said.

I closed my eyes on the sights of the world. On top of everything else, Ian was making a fool of me again. It was just like last year when he put the "kick me" sign onto my back. I shouldn't have sat with him.

A complete hush blanketed the room, and the silence was so deafening I had to open my eyes to see what happened.

"Oh my gosh, I'm in love," Bob said softly to Allan, who sat right behind me.

I turned to look back at him, and he motioned to the front of the room, where flowing locks of light reddish hair covered the head of a pale, freckle faced teacher. Tall and athletic, the young woman had a disarming smile, a pink sweater, white pants and black shoes with high heels. I silently thanked Ian for encouraging me to mind my surroundings.

"Good morning, y'all," she said, drawling her words in a fashion I'd never heard before. "I'm Miss Burnell. I'll be your new teacher for 8th grade."

A murmur of acknowledgement rose from the class, punctuated by Bob's suddenly shrill voice. "Good morning, Miss Burnell!"

"Now that's the kind of reaction I expect from the HCC contingent," she said encouragingly. "Y'are supposed to be highly capable, after all. How 'bout the rest of y'all?"

"Good morning, Miss Burnell," came a disjointed cacophony.

"We'll work on that, I guess," she said, and I noticed that each word took longer for her to speak than any normal voice. She somehow stretched the word "that" to three syllables.

"In case you hadn't figured it, I'm from Atlanta, Georgia. I felt the need for a change of scenery, and I moved out here to teach in your fine city. I like soccer, country music, and dogs, 'cept those little ones that bark all the time. Now, I've told something about me, let's hear something 'bout all y'all."

She pointed to Patty, in the front row.

"I like cheerleading and my friends," she bubbled, gesturing to her flock as she spoke.

Miss Burnell continued on down the line. I was reminded of when Allan spoke up for me when I was asked the same question on my first day at Madrona, exactly two years ago. When my turn came, I was ready.

"I'm Hunter, I like chess and karate," I said quickly, and sat back down.

"Hopefully not at the same time," the teacher quipped.

I looked at Ian. "A joke," he whispered. I never got the jokes.

When Bob stood up, he said, "I'm Bob Deluca. Are you married?"

"Well, that's just none of your business, young man," she answered angrily.

"It's just that, you said, it's Miss Burnell, so I figured you aren't. How old are you?" he persisted. Allan whacked him hard on the arm.

"Manners, Mr. Deluca. It's wholly impolite to ask a woman her age. But this once I'll oblige with an answer. I'm 28. Now, something about yourself, if you please?"

"I like soccer, country music and dogs," he proclaimed.

"Wonderful," she said sarcastically. "Next!"

My classmates finished up the introductions and we started into lessons. The excitement of meeting the new teacher and seeing all my classmates wore off quickly, and the fatigue of a poor night's sleep began taking its toll. Eighth grade was more-or-less a continuation of seventh. Unfortunately, I'd avoided school work last year in deference to my quest to save Mrs. Ryan. Despite missing the required reading, I wasn't far behind the rest of the group, and I survived the early morning without any embarrassing moments.

Instead of recess, we had physical education, or PE, in the late morning. We'd done this last year as well, and I'd hated it. Allan informed me the true goal of PE, which was to help the coaches find new players for their respective athletic teams. Football was a very big deal at Garfield High, and the best players often came from Madrona, including last year's star quarterback.

The worst part about PE was the number of students. Instead of just the HCC, PE involved the entire 8th grade class. Normally I would ignore everyone else, except to occasionally check their auras. Because of this, I was always among the last picked for any teams. Nobody wanted the weirdo on their team. I wasn't good at any sports, either. The only athletic talent I possessed was for karate, and even though I'd been working on it for eighteen months, I was still only mediocre.

September was football season, so the PE teacher, Mr. Groves, brought the flag belts with him to the recess field.

"We're going to play flag football today," he announced, as if there could be any doubt.

The guys all cheered.

"Go Seahawks!" somebody yelled.

"They suck!" came an answer.

"You suck!" proclaimed the first.

"All right, enough! Let's get four captains to pick teams," Mr. Groves commanded.

As usual, the best athletes in the class divvied up the talent, taking Ian, Allan, Davis, Bob, and Mike fairly early, leaving Mickey, me, and a few girls to the very end.

Kenny Logan picked me second to last. "OK, him," he said forlornly, as his choice was between me and a skinny girl who—wait, I recognized her.

"I guess I get Betsy," the last captain said. "Team 4, huddle up over here!"

Betsy! That was her name. Wasn't she in 9th grade this year?

"Yo, doofus, let's go!" one of my teammates said, as the rest of my group headed to the opposite side of the field. I jogged after him.

"I'll be quarterback. Kristen, you hike me the ball and then be the outlet receiver if everyone is covered. Ian, you and John are the wide receivers. I'll probably be throwing you guys the ball, so make sure you get open. Alan, you and Dennis play running backs. Alan, keep your big body between me and any of the rushers, and Dennis, you can be my other outlet receiver. Anne, and you... uh, what's your name?"

"He's Hunter," Ian said.

"Yeah, you two, um, block. OK?"

"Think quick!" John said, and he tossed the ball at my head. It collided with a loud thump.

John, Dennis and Kenny laughed. "Great, you catch like my Grandmother," John said.

A wave of thick sadness washed over me. Grandpa!

"No, Grandma," said John, as evidently I spoke aloud.

"I can't believe you picked the freak," John said.

"It was either him or Miss Depresso over there," Kenny replied, waving his hand at Betsy. "Never mind. OK, here's what we're gonna do on defense," he continued. However, I lost track of the conversation. Grandpa was dead. I was never going to see him again. I had no one. How was I supposed to continue on?

CHAPTER 7

WHEN REALITY returned, I felt a rock-hard cot underneath me and noticed a familiar medicinal smell. I knew exactly where I was. I recognized the eye chart, the picture of a creepy old doctor on the wall, and the jars on the counter from which the peculiar odor emanated. I'd been here previously after losing control of the auras. I was in the nurse's office at Madrona. This was much better than finding myself in an ambulance on the way to the hospital, like when I realized Dad wasn't my biological father.

I checked my watch. It had only been about twenty minutes since the embarrassing episode. Anger, bitterness and fear coursed through me as I replayed the event in my mind. Why did they have to be so mean? Why did it bother me so? Why couldn't I control myself?

I'd spent months battling the void when I thought the auras were demons. I'd finally conquered them, thanks primarily to Grandpa, who was now lost to me forever. Without him, would I just regress back to the autistic kid who couldn't even speak?

An unfamiliar frame suddenly loomed in the doorway of the nurse's office.

"Hunter?" she said cautiously.

"Yes, ma'am," I said, as calmly and politely as I could muster. I couldn't risk having the school nurse thinking I was crazy.

"Ah, you're awake. Hi, I'm Ms. Bohrman, How are you feeling?"

"I'm better now," I said.

"I see here in your file that you passed out on your way into school two years ago, and my predecessor noted that you were stressed because it was your first time on the bus."

I remembered the short, squat woman who'd dismissed me without calling Mom. "What happened to her?" I blurted.

"Oh, she retired. I came from the University Hospital where I worked in the ER. It was alright for a while, but lately we've been overrun with frequent flyers. 'Can I have a sandwich? I need cab fare with my Percocet! Pretty please?' Yeah. Fourteen years of that. Enough is enough."

"Um, OK," I replied.

"Anyway, the chart says you're autistic. What's that like?"

"Uh," I stammered.

"Well, I guess you don't really have anything to compare it to. Never mind. Are you all right? The other kids said you hit your head. Any headache?"

"No," I said.

"Nausea, weakness, tingling?"

"Nope."

"And this is the same as last time, right? You passed out for a bit and then you were fine?"

"Yes," I said succinctly.

"This happen at home too?"

"Not really," I replied.

"Well, being a teenager can be very stressful. I have a teenage son and he gets down all the time, so I understand. With your history, I think this is probably par for the course; wouldn't you agree?"

"Most definitely," I said. I didn't want her to call Mom, or worse, Dr. Eisenberg.

Reading my thoughts, she frowned, and said, "I'm going to give your mother a quick call, and if she says it's OK, I'll let you head back to class."

"NO!" I yelled.

"I'm sorry, I really must. It's required by the state, and all that. Besides, if you have any kind of head injury, you should be examined by a doctor."

"I don't need a doctor, I'm just upset because Grandpa is dead!" I shouted.

She nodded thoughtfully. "I'm so sorry for your loss," she added.

"Mom knows," I said. "And like you saw in the file, it happens every now and again, because I'm, uh, autistic. So really it's no big deal. If I have any problems the rest of the day, I promise I'll come back and you can call Mom. I don't want her to worry.

"Well aren't you the concerned son," she said. "Very well, just a few more questions. Do you know where you are right now?"

"Madrona."

I responded to few more questions, wiggled all of my body parts to her satisfaction, and jumped up and down in place before she agreed to let me go back to class.

"Remember, if anything changes, like a headache, feeling sick to your stomach, or dizzy, come back here immediately," she warned.

"I will," I said, as I bolted out the door.

$$*\qquad*\qquad*$$

I went to the wrong room and saw my old teacher, Miss Preneta, teaching the new seventh grade class. She waved, and I stupidly ducked away hoping she wouldn't see me. When I finally made it to the right place, the teacher was just dismissing everyone for lunch. Instead of going in, I waited outside the door as the rest of the group exited.

"Hey, bud," said Allan. "You all right?"

"Yeah," I answered glumly.

"Hey, don't sweat what happened," Ian said. He made a move to touch my back, but I dodged his hand and started toward the cafeteria.

"You need your space, right mate?" Ian said.

"Let's get some food," Allan added.

The two of them flanked me all the way to the lunch room.

I joined the line to buy milk, with Allan and a few others from my class. Ian went to save us a table.

Kenny Logan appeared, along with several of his friends. He walked up and stood next to me in the line.

"Hey, stupid! We lost the flag football game because we were a player short. Not that you'd have done any good anyway."

It took a few moments for me to register that he was speaking to me.

"Leave him alone," Allan said menacingly. He strategically placed himself between me and the much larger boy.

"What're you gonna do, beanpole? That little freak ruined my game!" Kenny said, pointing his finger at me.

Quick as a flash, Allan grabbed the extended finger and twisted it in a way in which it clearly wasn't designed to go. Kenny cried out and buckled to his knees.

Allan bent down and whispered into Kenny's ear. "You're going to leave him alone."

Kenny struggled briefly and Allan increased the pressure.

"OK! I'll leave him alone," he acquiesced.

Allan released the finger and grabbed Kenny's wrist, pulling him up quickly to his feet.

"What's going on over here?" Mr. Parziale said, approaching from the far corner of the cafeteria.

"Kenny lost his contact lens. Found it now, everything's fine," Allan said.

The teacher looked at Kenny expectantly.

"Uh, yeah, I found it."

"Oh, do you need some solution? I think we have some in the staff lounge."

"No, it's OK. I've got some. I can wear my glasses."

"Very well. Let me know if you change your mind. Carry on," he said, turning to leave.

After we paid, Allan and I joined Ian at his table.

"What was that all about?" Ian asked.

"That douchebag was blaming Hunter for losing the football game."

"Are you kidding me? I was wide open EVERY PLAY and he couldn't get the ball to me. He was intercepted like five times! It was totally his fault we lost. The only reason we were even close was that I scored a touchdown on defense. That guy…"

"I know, I was there," Allan said.

"So you used your Ninja skills on him?" Ian said.

"Karate," Allan corrected.

I ate my sandwich quietly and wondered how I was ever going to make it through the rest of the day.

*   *   *

Fortunately, I managed to avoid any relapses, and Mom was waiting for me when I got off the bus at home.

"How was your day?" she asked.

"It was OK."

"That's it? What happened? Do you have a new teacher? Are all of your friends back this year?"

"Yeah, Ian sat next to me, and Allan was there."

"You seem pretty down. Are you sure everything is all right?"

The football episode replayed in my mind. Mom's gaze bore down upon me as if I were a prisoner and she was waiting for my confession. I didn't want to talk about it, but I couldn't stop the words from spilling out.

"Well, one of the kids from school called me stupid because I didn't catch the football."

"Was this kid named Albert?" Mom asked.

"No, it was Kenny."

"Listen. Unless Albert Einstein is at your school, you're the smartest one there. Look how fast you solved the Rubik's cube. I bet none of your classmates can even solve it at all, let alone in under a minute. And… what's 316 times 128?"

I paused for a moment. "40,448."

"I guarantee that nobody in your school can do that either. Stupid? Forget about it."

With my spirits lifted, I told her about Miss Burnell and how Bob seemed to act like an idiot around her. The story made Mom laugh. Her laughter made me smile, and for a few minutes, everything was all right.

CHAPTER 8

DAD LEFT on another mission, or whatever he did, which meant Mom and I were alone in the house. She tried to engage me in conversation during dinner, but thoughts of Grandpa crept into my head. Once they started, I couldn't stop them. I excused myself early and barricaded myself in my room. Unable to read or complete any of the homework I'd been given, I eventually gave up and went to bed.

That proved useless too, as I kicked and tossed all night long. I fell asleep long enough to have another nightmare about having my partially burned ashes spread over the football field, with Kenny Logan and his friends laughing all the while.

When my alarm went off, I dragged myself out of bed and got ready for school, feeling miserable. It was the worst I'd felt in my life, with the possible exception of my first years at the Autism Center. At least I could speak, and I had Mom, Dad, Ian and Allan. Perhaps having Grandpa and losing him was worse than having nobody. I wasn't sure.

Slogging my way downstairs for breakfast, I nearly ran into Mom heading into the kitchen.

"Whoa!" she said, dodging my aimless mass to avoid a collision.

I kept trudging along.

"Hunter, what's going on?" she asked.

My head was being compressed by a vice. An oily, smelly vice. I shook my head instead of answering.

"You look like you haven't slept."

I gazed at her sharp eyes, unable to disguise my exhaustion.

"You can't go to school like that. Just go back to bed. I'll make an appointment for you to see Dr. Eisenberg this afternoon."

I followed her command, and fell soundly asleep upon hitting the pillow.

∗   ∗   ∗

True to her word, Mom contacted my psychiatrist and set up a time for my visit. Shortly after lunch, we traveled to her office near the hospital.

"You need to be honest with Dr. Eisenberg," Mom said.

Fortunately, she was paying attention to the road and missed my scowl. I couldn't be honest with anyone, least of all Dr. Eisenberg, the woman who'd locked me up.

Our relationship started two years ago while I was at the University of Washington's Autism Center. When I told Mom about the demons, she brought me to the doctor, who prescribed prolixin, a medicine used to treat psychosis. I had such a strong desire to rid myself of the demons, I took too many pills and ended up admitted to the psychiatric ward. Everyone assumed I'd tried to kill myself with the overdose. I had to convince Dr. Eisenberg that I wasn't a danger to myself before she would let me go home. I also had to convince her that I no longer saw the demons, which I now knew to be auras. Only when she was fully satisfied had she released me.

Then last year, I lost control of the auras and ran headlong into traffic in broad daylight, nearly killing myself again. With a second suicide attempt on my record, I had trouble making the case for my own sanity. I couldn't speak about the powerful auras I'd felt, because that would only make it worse. Plus, I'd thrashed about while in the void, injuring several staff members in the ICU, so they had to immobilize me with chemical and physical restraints. It wasn't until Grandpa gave me sugar in the intravenous line that I snapped out of it.

Dr. Eisenberg suspected something else was going on, but she discharged me with the requirement that I continue to see her periodically. On a follow up visit, I voiced concern about Mrs. Ryan, the teacher whose husband was abusing her. Dr. Eisenberg checked out my story, causing Orlando Ryan to send thugs to beat her up and to intimidate her into discontinuing her investigation. When I pressed Dr. Eisenberg about the attack, she grew suspicious. Mom had been in a hurry due to a work emergency, and took me home before we could delve into that any further.

I realized, much to my horror, that I hadn't actually talked with Dr. Eisenberg since I'd revealed to her that I'd spoken to prostitutes while searching for evidence about Ryan. She might still want to revisit that topic.

I panicked. "Look, Mom, I don't want to see Dr. Eisenberg."

"What?" she answered. "We're almost there. Besides, you need to talk about Grandpa. I know how much you loved him and miss him. It's normal to grieve, but you are a special boy, and it's harder for you than for others."

I thought hard, but my brain was incapable of inventing any plausible excuse for avoiding the appointment.

Perhaps she'd forgotten all about it. It had been several months, after all, and the official reports gave the credit to Ian's father, Roger Pierce.

I'd nearly convinced myself that I'd be fine, when Mom announced, "We're here. Let's go inside."

We left the car and walked slowly across the parking lot, entering the building alongside a brown haired man wearing dark rimmed glasses. He held the door for us, and we proceeded to the waiting area. The man was of medium height and build, and he had on a white coat over his dress shirt. He followed us all the way to Dr. Eisenberg's office.

"Hello, young man," he said pleasantly.

"You're not Dr. Eisenberg," I observed.

"No, sir. I'm Dr. Jenkins, Dr. Eisenberg's partner."

The name triggered the memory of my most recent visit when I'd vomited all over the place. I felt a wave of nausea return.

"You all right, son?" Dr. Jenkins asked.

"Hello, Dr. Jenkins. Marissa Miller. Nice to meet you," Mom said, intervening and shaking hands with the concerned fellow.

"Pleasure. I hope Dr. Eisenberg can help you feel better," he said, looking squarely at me. "She's a highly skilled provider."

I inclined my head weakly in reply. He nodded back and proceeded through the door to his office.

Mom diverted me to the receptionist window, where we checked in. The woman behind the desk took down our information, then motioned toward the uncomfortable chairs, where we sat, waiting to be called. I felt my insides knotting up again, recalling the discomfort I'd felt when Dr. Eisenberg had asked me about Grandpa. I doubted I could keep it together. Mom seemed to sense this.

"Do you want me to come in with you?" she asked.

I nodded. I needed support or I'd surely revisit the void.

Instead of the reception lady calling out, the tall, thin, brunette form of Dr. Eisenberg emerged from the offices and met us in the waiting room. She'd never done that before.

"Hello, Hunter," she said. "Do you think you'll be able to talk today?"

I nodded. Suddenly I understood. She didn't want me throwing up all over her office again. If I was going to blow chunks, she'd prefer it to be out here so her private area didn't stink.

"Um, sorry about puking on your carpet," I said. "I think I'll be fine today."

"Then let's get you back," she said. "I've got Hunter," she called out to the receptionist, who assented with a quick head movement.

"Would you mind if I joined in, at least for the start of the session?" Mom asked.

"Of course not. A fine idea," she agreed.

As we stepped into the office, Dr. Eisenberg grabbed an extra chair from among a half-dozen sitting against the wall, and set it up for Mom. I sat in my usual seat and braced myself for questions about Grandpa.

"How is school?" she asked, throwing me for a loop.

"Uh, OK?" I said.

"Just OK?"

The gym class fiasco replayed in my brain for the tenth time. I ignored it. "It's only been a few days," I added.

"Tell her about the present that Ian got you," Mom offered.

I brightened. "Oh, yeah, I got a Rubik's cube!" I said proudly.

"Ah yes, I've seen those. My nephew has one. Hasn't been able to solve it entirely, but he's completed two full faces. How's your progress?"

I was surprised by her comments. How could he not solve it? It was easy.

"Hunter solved it the first day," Mom boasted.

"Is that right," Dr. Eisenberg asked.

I nodded my head in the affirmative, smiling broadly for the first time in weeks.

"That's very interesting," she said. "Well, now, you have your friend Ian, who gave you the cube. Do you have any other friends?"

"Sure," I said. "Allan. He was my desk partner all last year. I mentioned him before."

"Yes, I remember. He does karate with you, correct?"

"He's a black belt. But I haven't been back since…"

My mouth suddenly filled with concrete, and I couldn't speak.

"Listen, Hunter, I know it's been difficult. You were very close to your grandfather. I understand, believe me. But we need to talk about it. You have to open up. Grieving is a process, and the first step is to talk about your feelings," she said.

My feelings? What was she thinking? Hadn't she ever lost anyone? This was ridiculous. Grandpa was GONE! And she wanted me to talk about feelings? That wasn't going to bring him back. I wanted to pick up the chair and hurl it at her. I wanted to use my best karate moves on her. I smelled burning flesh as the fury flamed inside me. I opened my eyes, expecting to find myself inside a raging volcano with my clothes and hair on fire, but instead, I was sitting in a cool office building.

"I can't help him if he won't open up," a voice said.

"I know, but he needs more time," Mom answered.

"All right, we can try again tomorrow. But if this keeps up, we may need to hospitalize him."

"That won't be necessary, Dr. Eisenberg," Mom said.

"You'll have to make an appointment out front. Tell Jess to squeeze him in. I'm sorry. There's another patient waiting, and I have a full schedule today."

"Of course. I'm sorry." Mom looked back at me quizzically. "Hunter?"

"What?" I said.

"It's time to go."

"OK," I said, and stood up to leave. The flames had died away and I felt confused. Noticing the psychiatrist staring sternly in my direction, I added, "Goodbye, Dr. Eisenberg."

"See you soon, Hunter," she said flatly.

As we walked to the car, I shook my head, trying to make sense of what happened.

"That was a pretty short appointment," I said.

"Hunter, you sat and stared at her for nearly thirty minutes without saying a word. We're all trying to help you get through this, but you need to talk eventually. You can't tune the world out every time something bad happens. Life doesn't work that way."

Fritzcloves! I'd lost time again. Angry with myself, I silently vowed to beat this thing. Whatever it was.

CHAPTER 9

MOM DROPPED me off at school, and I went to the office to sign in before heading to class. When I entered Miss Burnell's room, Ian nodded, and I skulked to my seat next to him.

"Been off to the shrink?" he whispered.

"How'd you…" I started.

"Open book, remember?" he answered quietly.

"What are…" I began.

In response, he picked up and waggled his beaten up copy of *The Hobbit*. I'd started reading it, but gave up when I found myself re-reading the same paragraph over and over. Unable to follow the conversation about the book, I ignored it and tried to figure out what was wrong with me.

I felt Ian's elbow in my ribs.

"Hey!" I yelled.

He motioned with his head toward the teacher and rubbed his eyes with his fingers to hide his gesture.

"Hunter?" Miss Burnell said.

"What?" I said, somewhat defiantly. I was angry with Ian for jabbing me.

"Well, what is your opinion?" she drawled.

"I don't think people should smack each other in the ribs!" I said.

This brought a torrent of laughter from my classmates.

"That'd be a very nice bumper sticker," the teacher said. "But what's that got to do with the question I asked?"

"What question?" I said, with an irritated tone.

"Look, son," she said. "I know you're dealing with a painful situation, and I sympathize. But that doesn't give you the right to ignore me and be disruptive to the class."

I had no idea what she was talking about, and my patience was running out.

"I'm not doing anything!" I yelled.

"And that, young man, is precisely my point. Off to the principal with you."

When I made no attempt to move, she raised her voice both in pitch and volume. "Now!"

I stood up so quickly the desk flipped forward, and all of Ian's things flew into the two girls in front of us.

"Hey!" they yelled simultaneously, as debris pelted them in the back.

"Sorry," I mumbled.

"Shoo shoo," the teacher said, waving her finger at the door.

I clenched my fists and kicked my chair backwards, hitting Allan's desk and making him jump. Then I plowed through the door, slamming it so hard that it bounced back open.

"What's with him?" I heard Kristen say.

"He's got a screw loose," said one of the boys.

"Oye! He just lost his Gramps. They were really close!" Ian defended.

"Psycho!" said another of the girls.

"That's enough!" said Miss Burnell firmly. "Let's get back to work, the show's over."

I stormed off to the main office, swung open the door, and loudly plopped myself onto the chair in front of the secretary.

Mrs. Frechette, a short woman with long blonde hair tied

severely back into a bun, poked her head out from her inner sanctum.

"Hunter!" she said, surprised. "I assume you have a good reason for getting yourself sent to see me? Come on back."

I scowled, stood up and followed her into the private room. She reclaimed her seat behind the large desk. Stacks of files and papers overwhelmed the smallish woman, to the point where she nearly disappeared behind the clutter.

"Close the door," she said, and I did.

"It's not fair!" I blurted.

"Oh," she answered, confused. "Why don't you start from the beginning?"

I huffed. She nodded her head expectantly.

The words rushed out so quickly I couldn't really control them. "Mom made me see the shrink this morning, and then yelled at me because I wouldn't talk to her, but it's not my fault! I don't know what happened! And then I get here and everyone is making fun of me, and I just want to scream!"

By the end, I was practically shouting.

"I see," she said.

I didn't really care what she saw. Instead of replying, I looked around for something to smash.

"Is there anything you'd like to talk to me about?" she asked.

"Yeah! Why is Grandpa dead?" I stood up. "ARRRGGGH-HHHH!!" I began screaming, pounding my fists onto her desk, and sending several files onto the floor.

"Are you through?" she asked calmly.

I could only stare.

"Look, Hunter, you're one of the brightest kids I've ever met, and I'm very sorry for your loss. But you can't be here until you get yourself under control. I'm calling your mother to pick you up."

The secretary opened the door a crack and said, "Everything OK, Mrs. Frechette?"

"Yes, Blanche, we're fine. Can you get Marissa Miller on the phone for me please? Her number's in Hunter's file."

"Yes ma'am, of course."

Seeing that I was about to do something stupid, the principal cut me off. "Hunter. Sit down. Now."

I looked at her and obeyed.

"Very good. Your Mom will be here soon, you can wait right there until she arrives."

Mom spoke with the principal for several minutes while I waited in the outer office. She gave me a frustrated look as we stepped out of Mrs. Frechette's office.

"What am I going to do with you, Hunter?" Mom said, as we headed to the parking lot.

I was still fuming, but Mom's quiet tone diffused my bitterness.

The answer to Mom's question was to keep me out of school until after my next appointment with Dr. Eisenberg, which was the following Monday.

After wasting the weekend moping around the house, I was relieved to have something—anything—to do, even seeing the shrink. I'd rehearsed my answer to her inevitable questions about my feelings, because Mom informed me I wouldn't be attending school until I was "cleared" by the doctor. I had to perform better than last time. By Monday afternoon, I was ready.

After the preliminaries of signing in, waiting a bit, and getting called back to the office, I steeled myself for an intense session. As I entered her office, I was shocked to find the room overflowing with people. In addition to Dr. Eisenberg, there were seven kids, three of whom I recognized, and a smattering of adults, including Mom, all crammed into the relatively small space.

Noticing my confusion, Dr. Eisenberg directed her voice at me. "Welcome to group therapy."

Group therapy? What the heck?

"Parents, please help arrange the chairs, and then I'm going to have you all wait outside as usual. Before we start, I want to introduce a new friend, Hunter."

She pointed at me. I was welcomed to the group by a collective but disjointed mutter of "helloooo, Hunter," which trailed off.

"What's going on?" I said to Mom. With all of these people around, I'd never make it through my speech about my feelings.

"Do your best to get involved. Everyone here has problems of their own, and you can help each other while you help yourselves," Mom said.

I stared blankly.

"Now get in your seat."

The chairs were arranged in a circle, and I wriggled my way between two of them and sat down. Dr. Eisenberg sat in the circle as well, and the other kids hefted themselves into seats as the parents filed toward the exit. I sat next to Betsy, the girl from gym class who got picked after me. Next to her was Toby, Ian's acolyte who liked to play chess. Across from me, I recognized a thin girl who used to ride my bus. I didn't know any of the others.

"Time to start," the doctor said. "For Hunter's benefit, let's go around and introduce ourselves. As you all know, I'm Dr. Eisenberg." She nodded to her left.

"Suzanne Potter," the girl said. She was nearly as thin as the blonde next to her. The two of them shared a connection that Ian would've been able to identify, but which escaped me.

"Denise Stahl," said the girl from my bus. I didn't recognize her name. She was older than me, so I never would have heard it.

"Kayleigh Richards," said the next girl. Like Denise, she had long blonde hair, but her body frame was on the opposite end of the spectrum.

"Toby Gascoigne," said Toby. I nodded his way slightly. He showed no evidence of recognition.

"Betsy Knopf," said Betsy, whose last name I'd never heard before.

I was so lost in the process that I didn't realize it was my turn until Dr. Eisenberg prompted me with a throaty noise.

"Oh, Hunter Miller," I said.

"Lynn Jermaine," said the last girl.

"Very good," said the doctor. "Now, let's remind everyone of the ground rules. This is a safe place, and what's shared here can't be disclosed outside these walls. We're here to support one another and to help the healing process. If anyone breaks these rules they'll be immediately expelled from my practice. Understood?"

A murmur of assent echoed off the walls.

"Who would like to start?" she asked. When nobody responded, she forced the issue. "Suzanne?"

The young woman growled and shifted in her seat. Dr. Eisenberg stared at her until she began speaking.

"Fine, whatever. I can't believe my father keeps making me come to these stupid sessions!" the girl spouted, clearly conveying her annoyance.

"Suzanne, remember what we talked about last time."

"Sorry, Dr. Eisenberg. It's just that, you know, I don't have anything in common with these," she paused and pointed her finger around the room, including at me. "People," she said, making her voice drop to emphasize how inhuman she considered the rest of the group.

Dr. Eisenberg rubbed her thumb and forefinger on her forehead. The others seemed entirely unaffected by this insulting outburst.

"That's enough of that. I need you to apologize to the group before we can continue."

"Sorry," she said blandly. She mouthed "losers," while facing away from Dr. Eisenberg.

"You're going to improve your attitude, or I'll be forced to remove you from the group and recommend inpatient care."

A strange look passed across Suzanne's face. "No!" she said, visibly shaken.

"Then do you have something to say to the group?"

"I'm really sorry I called you losers," she said, and this time, she turned her face toward the apex of the circle. "I want to help us all get better."

"Very good. Let's move on, and you can reflect on what we talked about over the last two weeks."

After a nod in her direction, Denise began.

"I haven't thrown up in four days."

"Very good," said the doctor, who looked around the room. With prompting, the other kids mumbled positive comments.

"I have an appointment with my doctor on Wednesday and the nutritionist on Thursday."

"Go on."

"I don't know why I never want to eat. And even when I'm hungry, I can only eat a bite or two before I get sick," she said. "I'm hoping the nutritionist can figure out why, because so far the doctors don't know anything. The worst part is Coach Daniels told me I'm going to be kicked off the soccer team if I lose any more weight. That's just not fair!"

Kayleigh piped in, "I wish I had your problem. No matter how little I eat, I still gain weight."

"People have different physiology," Dr. Eisenberg said. "Each of us has to live with the genes we were born with. Denise, I hope the nutritionist can recommend some healthy foods, but there is a component of behavior here too. For both of you, in fact." She alternated her gaze between the two of them. "That's the element we are hoping to address here. Both of you are unhappy and have a problem with food intake. But it's not entirely food that's the problem. You two have more in common than you think."

"She's a twig, and I'm a blob!" Kayleigh said.

Dr. Eisenberg held up a hand, but Denise interrupted. "It's bad enough that others call us names, we certainly don't need any of that here," she said.

"Yeah, I hate it when people call us stuff," Toby said. "The cool kids call me geek, dork, freak, and all sorts of stuff every day. I don't know why they take such pleasure in tormenting me."

I nodded, as did the others except Suzanne, who, I got the feeling, dispensed the nicknames rather than received them.

"Hunter?" Dr. Eisenberg said. "Care to share?"

"Well, I got called 'freak' and 'doofus,' at gym class. They called Betsy 'Miss Depresso' too."

"Who?" said Betsy.

"That Kenny kid."

"Jerk!"

The animated conversation that followed devolved into a series of name calling, until Dr. Eisenberg reined the group back in.

"Betsy, let's hear from you. How are things at home?"

Everyone grew quiet.

"Well, Dad's gone, and Mom totally doesn't understand me."

Sitting right next to her, I felt a strange connection. Her father had died, so she at least understood what I was going through. She spoke about her troubles, including bad grades, absent friends and no support network, and how she missed her father. I realized that if I could answer questions the way she did, I'd be able to get out of this group. The moment I had this revelation, we moved on to Lynn's problems.

"I just don't have any reason to live," Lynn said. "There's no point in even getting out of bed most of the time."

Dr. Eisenberg answered quickly. "I know it seems that way sometimes, but you have to be strong when those sensations come along. Things will get better."

She continued on with reasons why things would get better, but I went adrift with thoughts of Grandpa. If he was truly dead, a fact of which I wasn't entirely certain, how could his situation ever get better? Or mine? If only I'd been there with him when he had his heart attack. I'd have healed him, and he'd be fine now. He'd be right here in Seattle with me, Mom and Dad, and we'd have a normal family.

But no, he wasn't ever going to speak to me again. There was so much I still needed to learn, and he was the only one who could help!

Dr. Eisenberg clapped her hands.

"OK, everyone, that's all the time we have. We had a few break-throughs today. Please consider what we discussed throughout this week. We'll meet again at the same time next Monday. Remember to fold your chairs and put them back against the wall."

The clatter drowned out my thoughts as I followed everyone else and brought my seat to the side of the room.

CHAPTER 10

DESPITE HER initial trepidation, Mom sent me to school on Tuesday. When I arrived, I said hi to Allan and sat quietly in my seat. I didn't want anyone asking me where I'd been the day before.

Moments before class was supposed to start, Ian barreled into the room, creating a ruckus as he dropped his bag and plopped loudly into his chair. He gave me an open-mouthed grin that revealed an orange peel covering his upper teeth. I couldn't help but smile.

Miss Burnell smiled too, but hers was villainous, as she announced, "Pop quiz today!"

The class collectively groaned.

Mercifully, the subject was math, so even though I'd missed all of the lessons, I still knew the answers. After I put down my pencil, Ian made a quiet coughing noise. I looked at him.

"What?" I whispered.

"Let me see your answers. I just want to make sure I got them all right," he whispered back.

The quiz was easy enough, so I let him see my paper. He scribbled furiously as Miss Burnell said, "two more minutes."

The rest of the day was another blur. I didn't pay attention in class, as I couldn't focus on the material. News of my meltdown had spread, so everyone knew about Grandpa. A few of the guys wanted to express sympathy, but Allan and Ian kept people from talking to me. "He needs space," they'd say, and it worked. Everyone left me alone instead of trying to tell me how sorry they were for my loss.

On Friday, we had another quiz, but this time in language arts. It consisted of several short answer questions, followed by a full paragraph essay on one of three themes in *The Hobbit*. I hadn't even finished the first chapter, so I took wild guesses at the multiple choice and wrote a paragraph about how novels were too long and should be condensed to a few pages to make it easier on the reader. Ian coughed again, and I showed him my answers.

After we handed them in, Ian said, "Dude, your answers were crap!"

"I know. I didn't finish the assigned reading."

"How the heck am I supposed to ace this stuff if you haven't read the book? Come on man!"

I looked at him incredulously, unsure if he was serious.

He saw my expression and said, "Yeah, grieving, I know. It's fine. But you need to come back to reality soon or we're both gonna flunk!"

I ignored his advice, and everything else, and went home from school feeling as though I didn't learn a single thing all week.

I found myself paradoxically looking forward to group therapy. Once I learned from Betsy how I was supposed to feel about Grandpa's death, I could be free of Dr. Eisenberg. I frittered away the weekend, morosely enduring the slow passage of time before my next session.

Monday morning, Mom woke me up at the usual time.

"Let's go, Hunter. You need to get ready for school."

"But we have group therapy today," I protested.

"That's not until four pm. You can go to school and then see Dr. Eisenberg. That's why she has the session so late, so you don't have to miss classes."

I hopped off the bus more irritated than usual, and even Allan avoided my scowling face. I saw Betsy at gym class and waved at her, and she responded in kind. I discovered where she ate lunch, at a table behind the witch girls. I didn't think they were truly witches, but that's what everyone called them because they wore dark wigs and black dresses every day.

When I arrived home, I barely had time to walk in the door before Mom herded me into the vehicle to take me to my group session. She dropped me off at Dr. Eisenberg's building and left, planning to return in an hour. She no longer felt she needed to wait, nor did most of the other parents. I felt more relaxed since I knew what was going to happen, and I even helped set up the chairs as the others arrived.

"Thank you, Hunter," said the doctor.

We used the same seating arrangement as last time, with Suzanne and Lynn closest to the therapist's chair, me next to Becky, and Denise, Kayleigh and Toby on the opposite side of the circle.

"Since everyone knows each other, let's get right to work. We'll start with you, Lynn," Dr. Eisenberg said, inclining her head toward the sad girl on my left.

"Why me?" she said glumly. "I've got nothing to say."

"That's not true. Last week you opened up quite nicely. We made definite progress."

"Whatever," she answered. Her voice had such a sour intonation that I felt depressed listening to her speak.

"Tell us about your day, Lynn."

"Ok, fine. When I woke up, I wanted to shoot myself. Except I don't have a gun. So I thought I might take all of my pills, but since my overdose, they only give me a week's worth at a time. That's not enough to do any real damage. I'd get a little sick and that's it. No point. Worthless waste of time. Like everything in my life."

I was taken aback, but Dr. Eisenberg showed no emotion whatsoever. "But you didn't try to kill yourself. What things about your life made you want to continue on?"

"Nothing. There's literally no point to any of it."

"A lot of people feel that way, but we all manage to find something in life that gives us pleasure—something to look forward to. What can you look forward to, Lynn?"

"Getting out of here," she said. I almost laughed, but nobody else did, so I stifled it.

"You enjoy your music, right?" Dr. Eisenberg prompted.

"Yeah, I guess," Lynn answered.

"I have an assignment for you for next time. Write us a poem that you can turn into a song. Something that expresses how you feel about yourself and the people around you. Do you think you can do that?"

"I don't want to share my music with these," she paused. "With anyone," she concluded.

"You don't have to share it with the group if you don't want to. Write the song, or the poem, or even just the tune. Sing it or play it for yourself. It will be yours, and yours alone."

Lynn perked up slightly. "I can do that."

"Very good," said Dr. Eisenberg. There was a quiet murmur that smacked of positivity as the rest of the group readjusted their bottoms in their seats.

"Hunter?"

"I can't write music," I said.

"That's not what I meant. Tell us about your day."

Although I should have known I'd be next, I had nothing in mind to say. I really just wanted to hear from Betsy.

"I didn't do anything. Just went to school."

"Is there something in your life you look forward to?"

"I looked forward to coming here," I said.

Dr. Eisenberg's face betrayed some hint of emotion, but lacking Ian's eagle-eye perception skills, I had no idea which one. "Really," she said.

"Um, yeah."

"And why, precisely, is that?"

Left with nothing but the truth, I answered. "I want to hear what Betsy has to say."

The therapist nodded slowly. "Very good. In fact, that's excellent. Betsy?"

"Yes?"

"Tell us about your day."

Betsy looked like a deer in headlights. "I, uh," she stammered.

"Go ahead," prompted the therapist.

"I wanted to hear what Hunter had to say," she said.

"Ooooh!" said Suzanne. "Young love!"

Dr. Eisenberg looked sternly to her left. Suzanne froze and quieted her cooing.

"Are you sure you're not just saying that because that's all Hunter had to say to get me to move on?"

Betsy looked shocked again.

"Busted!" said Toby.

"No, I… I sort of do want to hear what Hunter has to say," she said, this time with something of a pleading in her voice. She may have been trying to convince herself.

She smiled at me. I'd never seen her smile. Up to that point, I'd been convinced that she'd never once smiled in her entire life. I had no idea how to react, so I did nothing.

Dr. Eisenberg, who was watching this interaction like a hawk, surprisingly said, "Very good. Thank you so much for opening up."

And with that, we moved on to Toby. We continued through Kayleigh, Denise, and Suzanne, who again managed to insult each and every one of us so thoroughly that an exasperated Dr. Eisenberg cut the session short.

"That's enough for today. We'll see you all next Monday. Keep up the good work."

We bolted for the door, but were stopped by the therapist's booming voice. "Chairs!"

After folding and putting away our chairs, the seven of us made a collective beeline for freedom, clambering over each other to escape. Since Mom wasn't there yet, it didn't matter that I was the last one out. I had to wait in the lobby for her to return. So did Betsy.

"Did you mean what you said in there?" she asked.

"Yes," I said simply.

"Why did you want to hear what I have to say?"

"I don't know," I lied.

"OK," she answered, apparently quite satisfied with that answer. "Join me at the table for lunch tomorrow?" she said.

I nodded. She smiled again. I was lost, but fortunately, her mother arrived at precisely that moment. "Betsy, let's go," she called.

"Gotta go," Betsy said, and she turned and followed her mother to the parking lot.

CHAPTER 11

ON TUESDAY morning, Miss Burnell began class with a physics experiment. One at a time, she picked up and showed us a chalk board eraser, a huge dictionary she referenced when there was a question on the meaning or spelling of a word, and a small safety pin.

"OK, everyone, now tell me. Which of these objects will hit the floor first if I drop them simultaneously?"

"The book, it's the heaviest," said Patty, confidently.

The class responded with general agreement. Davis mumbled "know-it-all," causing a slight titter on that side of the room.

"So everyone agrees? If I drop the book and the safety pin, the book will hit first?"

"Definitely."

"Sure."

"Of course," said others.

"And if I drop the eraser and the book together? Same?"

Again there were no dissents. But it didn't seem right to me. Grandpa taught me about this when I was visiting him in Connecticut. He explained that all objects experience the same gravitational force, and when you work through the math, the weight cancels out. With limited exceptions, everything falls at the same speed.

I raised my hand.

"Hunter? You have something to say?"

"Won't they hit the ground together?"

The class went dead quiet.

"He SPEAKS!" said Glenn, punctuating the silence and evoking laughter from those around him.

Of course I could speak. I'd been able to talk since I was nine. What did he mean? I hadn't known any of these people then.

"So, you think all three would fall at the same speed, Hunter?" the teacher drawled. "Now, why on earth might that be?" she added sweetly.

"I'm not sure exactly. Grandpa told me that weight doesn't matter when you are talking about the pull of gravity."

"Well, now, are you saying that you could pick up a school bus just as easily as this safety pin?"

"Uh, no, that's not what I meant," I stumbled.

"Your Grandpa is a complete idiot!" Glenn said.

I exploded. "He's the smartest man I've ever met! Way smarter than you!"

"Settle!" yelled the teacher, but it was too late. Our shouts devolved into creative name-calling until I closed my eyes to block the sounds.

*   *   *

Moments later, Allan tapped me on the shoulder. "Hey, let's go. Lunch."

I stood up to leave. Everyone else was gone.

"You OK?" he asked.

I didn't answer.

"Your grandfather was really bright. And so are you, Hunter. Don't let people get to you."

I nodded sullenly and collected myself, rising to go to the cafeteria with Allan.

When I got there, I suddenly remembered Betsy, who caught my eye from her table in the far corner with an imperceptible wave. I moved toward her.

"Hey, where're you going?" Allan said.

"Um, I promised Betsy I would sit with her at lunch."

He nodded slowly. "All right. Fair enough. Good luck!"

I didn't know what he meant by that, but I negotiated my way through the busy cafeteria to the far side, dodging youngsters and ignoring the sounds of mass feeding.

Betsy turned to face me as I sat in the closest available seat, right next to her.

Despite the din, I heard her soft voice clearly. "Hello, Hunter. How are you today?"

I didn't dare admit that I'd spent the entire morning in the void. She'd think I was crazy and never speak to me again. I summarized my morning by blaming everything on Glenn.

"One of the kids in my class called Grandpa an idiot."

At first, she didn't respond. After a few moments, she said "Why would he say that?"

I reiterated the story of how I embarrassed myself, making the mistake about gravity.

"You're totally right," she said. "Well, mostly correct, anyway. When two objects fall, they both have the same velocity, unless there's a lot of air resistance, like with a feather or something. Otherwise, yeah, they hit the ground at the same time. Galileo did a famous experiment dropping stuff out of the Leaning Tower of Pisa in the 1500's."

"Really?"

"Well, probably not, but that's the story. Anyway, the math works out that way."

"How do you know?"

"I had the same stuff last year."

"What?" I said, confused. "They teach the same things over and over?"

Her features dropped. For a moment, I didn't think she was going to continue speaking, so I ate my food quietly.

"I got held back last year," she said.

"What do you mean, held back?"

It took longer for her to answer, and this time her face held a pained expression when she finally did.

"My mother didn't let me go into ninth grade. She made me repeat eighth. She said I was doing too poorly and wanted to make sure I'd get into a good college. 'Better to repeat a grade now when it doesn't count on your official transcript,' she said. I didn't have any choice in the matter."

I could hear the bitterness in her voice.

"Never mind about that. How do you plan to get back at Glenn?"

"What do you mean?"

"He called your grandfather an idiot. Your grandfather isn't an idiot, I take it?"

"No, he's a doctor!"

"Certainly a bright individual then. So how do you get back at Glenn?"

"I don't know. Glenn's not so bad. I'd rather get back at that Kenny kid. Except he's way stronger than me and I've got no idea how to do it."

"I've got an idea. Let's meet after school and I'll show you something."

"OK," I said. "Where do you live? Maybe Mom will let me ride my bike to your house." I used to ride to Ian's last year all the time, so I was pretty sure she'd let me go.

"Where's your house?" she countered.

I told her my address, and she told me hers. After a few minutes of coordinating landmarks, we figured out how to get to one another's houses without using a map. Since lunchtime was nearly over, I agreed to call her when I got home and we'd set up a time to meet. We exchanged numbers, and I headed back to class.

Allan met me half way there.

"How'd it go?" he asked.

"Good," I said hesitantly.

"You get her number?"

"Um, yeah. I'm going to call her later and we are going to meet up. She said she had something to show me."

"Well done, buddy!" he said. He was clearly excited, slapping me on the back.

The feeling of plodding through foul-smelling mud that I'd experienced for the last few weeks lifted slightly. I went to my seat, and noticed Ian wasn't there. I assumed he'd been sent to the office for some mischief. Good to see he was up to his old tricks. By the end of the day, he still hadn't returned, which was odd. Maybe Principal Frechette sent him home. Too bad—he'd surely have some choice comments about me talking to a girl.

I tried to listen to our afternoon lecture, but I was so far behind that none of it made sense. I hadn't heard anything Miss Burnell had said for weeks. I didn't know what chapter of the book we were on. Without Ian, I had nobody to ask, so I gave up. It didn't matter. The teacher never called on me. She directed most of her questions to Patty.

I passed the time mentally solving my Rubik's cube, then thinking about chess. I hadn't played in months. Not even on the computer at home. Maybe I could get Toby to play. It felt good to ponder something other than Grandpa's death. Unfortunately, as soon as I thought about Grandpa, the grey stench rapidly returned, overpowering everything else. Soon I was back to abject misery. By the time class ended, I could barely get out of my chair. Even my upcoming meeting with Betsy couldn't lighten my mood.

At the end of class, Allan stayed behind and collected me. "Let's go bud. Time to catch the bus."

I nodded and allowed him to drag me to the parking lot. He pointed to my bus and gave me a small shove. I rode home in silence.

This was no way to live.

When we got to my stop, the driver had to remind me to exit the vehicle. Mom was waiting.

"Hunter?" Mom said. I barely registered her presence.

I looked up without speaking.

"Let's get you inside."

We walked to the front door without conversation, but once

inside, she said, "Your teacher called me and told me she was very worried about you. Except for math, you've failed every quiz, and you never offer anything in the way of class participation."

I didn't know what to say, so I said nothing.

"Look, it's tough, I know. But the only way you're going to move forward is to talk about it. You've got to get it all out there. That's what the group is for."

A thought relating to the group whispered around me, like a leaf on the wind that I couldn't quite catch, but I couldn't remember what it was. Mom stared at me, and I knew I had to say something or I'd be stuck in this position forever.

"All right, Mom," was all it took.

I moped up the stairs to my room, went inside and closed the door, opting for the cushy bean bag chair instead of my bed. Mom brought me *The Hobbit*, and I started to read page three again, but lost myself in nothingness. Other than a brief break for dinner and for Mom to show me some physics problems that the teacher had mentioned, my evening simply passed by.

CHAPTER 12

WHEN I got to school the next morning, I sat alone at my desk, listening to Miss Burnell talk to the rest of the class about variables and how to solve for x. She put an equation on the board:

$$5 (x + 4) = -7 (4 - 3x)$$

I looked at it. Fearing more reprisals from my mother, I decided to participate.

"X equals 3," I said, much to the general surprise of everyone.

"Hunter?" Miss Burnell appeared to be calling on me, belatedly.

"X is 3," I repeated.

"Why, that's correct," she drawled. "Mind telling the class how you solved the equation?"

"It's obvious," I said.

The teacher made a face. "Just the same, perhaps you could explain to the mere mortals how you arrived at the answer?"

This wasn't going as I expected.

"You multiply the 5 and -7 through and get $5x + 20 = 21x - 28$. Subtract 5x and add 28 and you get $48 = 16x$, and divide by 16. $X = 3$."

"He's right," agreed Patty, as though there might be some question.

"I know he's right, sugar. I thought he might have guessed," said the teacher sweetly. To me she added, "Very good, Hunter. Apparently you're not completely without grey matter."

She demonstrated on the board, adding a few unnecessary steps, and the class slowly caught on. She erased the previous problem and replaced it with a new one. I solved it immediately, but this time, she hushed me when I tried to say the answer.

"Let's have someone else answer, Hunter."

I didn't get it. Mom told me I was in trouble for not participating, and here I was, calling out the answers to easy questions and being told to stop. It was just like everything else. Not fair. I retreated inside my own world again, ignoring everything around me. I didn't speak or move until it was time for gym class.

When I saw Betsy, I knew something was wrong. Fritzcloves! I'd completely forgotten about calling her! I strode purposefully in her direction, but she ran away to the other half of the field. I tried to follow, but the teacher corralled me back to the proper side. We started our game, and I made no effort whatsoever, merely stepping aside when the ball or others came near. They disregarded me and enjoyed themselves. My misery compounded.

When the coast was clear, I wandered to the edge of the field.

"Nurse's office," I said to the teacher, whose name I couldn't remember despite being in the class for several weeks.

"OK, Hunter, sure," he said. He'd probably jump at any opportunity to get rid of me.

I spent half an hour with Ms. Bohrman, until she was sick of me and sent me back to class to fester. On the way back, I felt the urge to use the bathroom, so I followed a younger boy into the closest one.

"What are you doing?" she said.

"I need to use the bathroom," I replied.

"This is the girls' room!" she said, indignant.

"What?" I said, stunned. Like lies, determining gender was an area where the auras were never wrong.

"The boys' room is over there," she continued, pointing to the correct place.

"Oh, sorry," I said. What was going on with the auras? I turned and went to the correct doorway, relieved that nobody else saw my latest blunder. Then I heard the voices.

"That eighth grader doesn't know he's a boy," a younger child was saying. The small crowd cackled with high pitched laughter.

Great.

In addition to losing time, getting in trouble for not participating, then participating too much, forgetting to call Betsy, who wouldn't even talk to me, and having the auras fail me, I'd had to deal with the humiliation of nearly going into the wrong restroom. What was next, an asteroid hitting me on the way home?

*   *   *

School wasn't even a consideration on Thursday. Mom understood and didn't press the issue. I told her what happened with Betsy.

"You need to apologize," she said. "A girl likes to hear an apology."

"I tried. She ran away and wouldn't listen!"

"You obviously didn't try hard enough," she answered.

"What am I supposed to do, follow her around until she listens to me?"

"If that's what it takes. You made a mistake. Now you have to fix it. And simply saying 'I'm sorry' won't cut it. You have to do more."

"Like what?" I asked.

"That depends on the person. You have to tailor your apology to Betsy. Explain exactly what you did wrong and what you are going to do to make it up to her. That's how these things work."

I understood Mom's words, but I'd be more likely to walk on the moon than achieve what she'd asked. Nonetheless, I welcomed the distraction. At least now I had a task—something to think about other than my own misery. But it was useless. Despite spending the entire day considering clever ways to apologize, the best I could come up with was "I'm sorry I forgot to call you. I had a lot on my mind."

On Friday, Mom agreed to let me stay home if I promised to work on the assignments she'd collected from my teacher. I busied myself with reading, science, math and social studies through the weekend. It took ten times longer than usual to accomplish anything, but I made progress. Ian would be happy—he'd be able to cheat off me again. More importantly, Mom helped me compose an apology for Betsy.

✳   ✳   ✳

By Monday morning, I felt like I'd be able to get through the day without losing time. I'd survived the weekend and completed all of the homework despite my severely limited attention span. Every few minutes, some intrusive thought about Grandpa made me stop. Nonetheless, I'd finished *The Hobbit*, read the assignments on physics and world history, and finished the math problems. Even at ten percent capacity I could do the math quickly.

When I got to school, I was disappointed to find Ian absent. Perhaps he was ill. We didn't have any quizzes, which was unfortunate, because I could've aced any topic. Allan wasn't there either, so I tried to sit with Betsy at lunch. She was cold as ice, refusing to acknowledge my presence. I wasn't able to deliver the apology that Mom and I spent an hour crafting. However, I knew I'd have another chance later, after group therapy, so I gave up and ate quietly by myself. Instead of mending my new relationship, I focused on surviving the school day without another meltdown.

✳   ✳   ✳

When I arrived for our session, I helped position the chairs in a circle inside the cramped office. We took our seats, and Dr. Eisenberg surprised me by asking Betsy to begin the session.

"I think people should do what they say they're gonna do!" she said pointedly. She didn't look my way, but the words were clearly aimed at me.

She whipped her head around in my direction, glared, and added, "Don'tcha think?"

I held up my hands in surrender. "I'm sorry! I had a bit of a breakdown and wasn't able to call. I feel horrible! Please forgive me."

I spouted the well-rehearsed lines in front of the entire group, and instantly regretted it.

"Oooooh, lover's tiff!" said Suzanne, rubbing her hands together in glee, as though this juicy gossip completely made her day.

"Get a room," said Toby.

"You and her?" said Denise, flabbergasted.

"Calm down!" Dr. Eisenberg said loudly, quieting the crowd. "Hunter, do you have anything else to add?"

Fritzcloves! Not only did I embarrass myself with a public apology, I was still center stage. I had to share even more information about my day. The group waited patiently, all eyes on me.

With no other option, I gave in and began speaking. "It was stupid," I started. "Mom said my teacher called her because I was flunking my quizzes and not participating. So I answered an easy question in class. Then, when I tried to answer another, the teacher told me to be quiet and let the others answer. Which is it? Am I supposed to talk or not?"

By the end I was practically yelling, and my skin was on fire.

"What's that got to do with you not calling me?" Betsy said, dousing the flames with mud.

"I… lost it," I said quietly.

The collective nods of the group implied that they'd all been there, in exactly that place. Even Suzanne commiserated.

Dr. Eisenberg let the silence hang for almost a full minute. "Very good, Hunter. Betsy, do you have anything to say back?"

"Apology accepted," she said softly.

Suzanne reverted to her normal behavior, applauding raucously and startling the group. "Bravo, well done. You may be getting some after all!"

"Enough, Suzanne," said Dr. Eisenberg. "Let's move on. Forgiveness is a very important thing. I'm sure each of you has someone to forgive, and maybe someone to whom you owe an apology. Toby? Can you tell us about someone you need to apologize to or forgive?"

The room fell silent as Toby formulated his reply. His jaw muscles worked without sound as he wrestled internally with words. When he finally spoke, the boy's confession left me confused.

"I'd like to apologize to my Mom for putting her through all that I did."

Dr. Eisenberg nodded knowingly. "That's very good," she said softly. "Do you think you can say that to her?"

Toby put his face in his hands and started crying. Betsy and Kayleigh both reached over and put their hands on his shoulders and head, gently massaging. Suzanne started to speak, but icicles blazed from Dr. Eisenberg's eyes. Suzanne wisely let her comments die in her throat.

We spent the rest of the session comforting Toby and congratulating him for his wonderful breakthrough. By the end, even Suzanne nodded in his direction. I couldn't guess what he'd done, but it wasn't anything good. Afterwards, I shared a brief glance with Betsy while we packed up the chairs.

"See you at lunch tomorrow?" she said.

"Yes," I mustered. She smiled as we both exited to the lobby.

CHAPTER 13

NEITHER IAN nor Allan were at school again on Tuesday, so I figured they'd both contracted the flu. Nobody else in the entire HCC class spoke to me, so I kept to myself and waited until lunch. Betsy beamed when I arrived at her table.

"Hi," I said.

"Glad you could make it," she said.

"How come you're always here before me? We both get out at the same time."

"My classroom is right next to the cafeteria, dummy," she said, smiling.

She'd smiled three times since we'd begun talking. Perhaps I'd truly made another friend. I wondered if now was the right time to ask her how to escape group therapy sessions. I didn't get the chance.

"So why are you in group? I've got the others figured out, but you don't make any sense."

I countered with a question of my own. "What did Toby do to his mother?"

"Oh, yeah. He tried to kill himself. Took a bunch of pills. Left a note and everything. Was in the hospital for a while. From what I heard, he was almost successful."

I could only stare back, stunned. The scenario hit close to home. I'd taken too much prolixin and nearly died, but I wasn't trying to kill myself.

"Wait, why would he need to apologize to his mother? She didn't force him to take the pills, did she?"

Ignoring my illogical question, she answered quickly. "Unlike SOME parents, his mother loves him. You can tell when he mentions her. When he nearly died, she was wrecked. This is the first time he's talked about it, even though he's been in the group a long time."

Her explanation stirred up thoughts about my mom, who also loved me. I was sure of it, because of the strong purple hue in her aura. She must have been upset when I nearly died, first from the pills, then when I ran in front of the truck. Neither of them were my fault. I was just trying to… I don't know, fix myself. I was definitely broken in some way. Even more so since Grandpa was gone.

The feeling of Betsy's hand on my face caused me to jerk my body backwards into the table, knocking over several glasses on the far side.

"Hey, cut that out, spaz!" yelled a dripping wet boy.

"Why do you do that?" Betsy asked.

"I… you surprised me," I stammered.

"No, I mean why do you just sit there and stare at nothing?"

I checked my watch. The lunch period was more than halfway over. Fritzcloves! I'd lost more time. "I don't know," I said. "It just happens sometimes."

"Eat your sandwich," she said. "We've only got a few more minutes before we have to go back to class. How about this time, you actually call me?"

"OK," I said sheepishly.

We wolfed down the remainder of our meals in silence. I resumed the school day, feeling better about my interaction with Betsy, yet not well enough to pay attention to the teacher.

*   *   *

When I got home, I told Mom what happened.

"You'd better call her this time," she said. "No girl is going to accept a second blunder. If you want some privacy, you can use the phone in my office."

I dug the paper with her phone number out of my pocket, went upstairs to Mom's room and shut the door. I picked up the receiver and felt the blood drain from my face. What if I screwed up again? A sharp noise from the phone punctuated the silence, and I slammed the phone down.

Mom knocked on the door. "Everything OK?" she called out.

"I'm not sure I can do this," I said.

"Just pick up the phone and call. It's like talking to Allan or Ian. No big deal."

Yeah. No big deal. Just like talking to Allan. No problem.

Before I lost my nerve again, I picked up the phone and dialed as fast as my fingers would allow.

A masculine voice with an Italian accent growled from the other end. "Hello?"

"Is Betsy there?"

"Yo. Who's this?"

"This is Hunter."

"Do I sound like a Betsy to you, Hunter?"

"Uh, no, uh, sir," I spluttered.

"Damn straight! Check the damn number you little piece of—" the voice said.

I hung up before I learned what I was a piece of.

Considerably rattled, I tried again, this time pushing the buttons more carefully. I was used to the rotary phone downstairs, and I must have pressed one of the buttons twice, or accidentally hit an extra one.

When the phone rang on the other end, I felt my heart jump into my throat. Why did it feel different than talking to Allan or Ian?

"Hello?" came the soft voice.

"Betsy?" I said.

"One moment, I'll get her. May I ask who's calling?"

"Hunter," I said, with as much confidence as I could muster. At least I dialed the correct number, even if I didn't get the right person.

"Hi, Hunter," came a slightly quieter voice with similar intonation.

"Betsy?"

"Yes, it's me. Thanks for calling. I was starting to get worried that you'd mess up again."

"I did," I admitted. I told her about the wrong number and the Italian guy.

"I can't really talk here," she said. "How about meeting me?"

"I don't know, I have to ask Mom," I said.

"Well, if it's OK, meet me at the Madrona Beach Park. We can talk there."

"Give me a second," I said.

I opened the door to the office and called downstairs. "Mom! Can I meet Betsy at the Beach Park?"

"Sure, it's nice outside, you can ride your bike," she answered.

I ran back to the phone. "Mom says it's OK."

"Great, I'll meet you there in twenty minutes," she said, and gave me the precise location of the bike racks on the southwest side.

"OK."

"OK, bye!" she said, and hung up.

*   *   *

My leg muscles screamed as I pedaled up the small incline leading to the park. Most of the way had been downhill, and I shuddered to think about the return trip. I'd probably have to stop and walk. I'd lost my strength after weeks of inactivity. I'd have to restart karate with Allan. Once I'd convinced Dr. Eisenberg that I wasn't a danger to myself, I'd be able to reclaim my old life.

I reached my destination and chained my bike to the rack. While I waited, I stretched my legs and tried to shake that exhausted feeling that had been my constant companion recently.

Betsy waved as she arrived, and I studied her as she locked her bike next to mine. Her short black hair was completely covered by a pink hat, and although she usually wore glasses, she didn't have them on. Her thin face didn't wear its usual scowl, either. I was surprised to find her wearing a fluffy, rainbow colored sweater along with her blue jeans. The bright colors didn't seem natural on her, and the bulky sweater made her appear twice her normal size.

"I want to show you something," she said. "Come on."

I followed her down a trail into the woods. The giant canopies blotted out the sun, restricting growth on the forest floor. The trail was littered with dead leaves and pine needles, a scattering of tiny plants, and an occasional small sapling. After ten minutes on the well-traveled path, we took a series of quick turns and entered a small clearing interspersed with a few large rocks. I remembered Grandpa telling me about glaciers and pictured massive sections of ice spreading these boulders like pebbles.

Betsy took my hand and broke my reverie.

"Look here."

Nature had created a small triangular cave, bounded by a rock wall on one side, a wayward pine on another, and a buildup of dirt, roots, and forest detritus on the third.

"Sometimes I come here to think. It's my special spot," she said. She stopped suddenly, held her hand up, and added, "Promise me that you'll never tell another soul about this place."

"I promise." I said.

"Swear!"

"I swear!" I said emphatically.

She dropped to the ground and positioned herself flat inside the small alcove. "Good. Come on in," she said, patting the ground next to her.

I wriggled beside her. There wasn't room for me to be completely covered by the pine, but I found the accommodations quite relaxing. Normally, being so close to another person would be troubling, unless it was Grandpa, but not today.

"So, Hunter Miller, tell me your story."

"What story?"

"The story of you. How did you end up the person you are today?"

"I don't know," I said.

"I get it. I'll make it easier for you. I'll tell you mine."

"OK," I replied, unsure what else to say. I hoped she'd reveal what she told Dr. Eisenberg about the death of her father. I still had no idea how to respond to questions about Grandpa, other than my carefully rehearsed speech: "it's been a shock and I miss him." Betsy held the key to my freedom.

"Everything was great up until last year," she began. "I was in the 8th grade HCC class with Mrs. Fowler, the teacher who left to spend more time with her family. I think the whole thing with Mrs. Ryan might have had something to do with her leaving. Did you hear about that?"

"Yeah," I said tersely, not wishing to divulge my own involvement.

"Well, my Dad and I were always really close. But he decided to have an affair with a lady from work, and Mom found out and had a fit. She hired a nasty lawyer, divorced Dad, and got full custody of me. Because the divorce was his fault, he didn't get visitation rights. He's not restricted from talking to me or anything, but he can't come to the house, and Mom won't let me go to his either. The result is the same.

"They didn't even ask my opinion," she continued, her voice rising. "I totally wanted to stay with Dad, but NO! I'm stuck with Mom, who's a complete psycho half the time. She stays out late almost every night, ignores me unless it's a complete emergency, and sometimes I find her asleep on the floor in the living room or kitchen, still in her clothes from the night before."

I made a non-committal noise, shocked at the depth of her revelation.

"I don't know why she hasn't been fired. She's always late to everything, including work, and she never listens to anything I say. I can't stand it!"

"So then, on top of that, your father died?" I asked.

I could barely see her in this limited lighting, but her features changed. "He's not dead," she said, almost angrily.

"I thought…" I said, and trailed off.

"No, he just moved to California. Can't see me anyway, so why stay here? His boss found out about the affair and transferred him to another office."

"Oh," was all I could manage.

"So last year, I messed up in school and stopped doing my work. I tried to talk to my friends, you know, but they didn't listen. They told me to deal with it. We'd all been so close, too. We did everything together. Went to the mall, the beach, the movies, the ice-cream store, the outlets, everything! But they continued having a grand old time with their wonderful lives, while mine totally fell apart."

I was processing the information slowly, but a memory hit me like it was yesterday. Ian and I watching four girls in a clothing store, then him taking pictures for his scrapbook. He was going to make a montage for one of them. I wracked my brain for a moment.

"Kathy Smitzer," I mumbled.

"Yes," she said, surprised. "You know her? And Maureen and Michele?"

"Uh, no, not really."

"What do you mean?" she was suddenly very interested and slid closer to me, if that was possible.

I had to tell her about how Ian tricked me into getting sent to the principal's office. It was a bit humiliating, but she'd shared the details of her life, so I supposed I owed her something in return. "I got sent to the principal for lifting up her skirt."

She shoved me halfway out of the shelter.

"Hey!" I yelled.

"Pervert!" she yelled back "Let me out of here."

"I didn't do it!" I said defensively, scrambling along the ground while she pummeled me sideways, trying to move me aside and stand up at the same time.

"Ian did it, and blamed it on me!" I said, feeling guilty about betraying one of my only friends.

She stopped shoving me. "Ian Pierce?" she said.

I nodded.

"Oh," she said, deflating. "Yeah, that sounds like him. He's had a crush on Kathy for a long time."

This time it was my turn for shock and disbelief. "Really?" I said.

"Pretty obvious, don'tcha think? He followed her around like a lost puppy, taking pictures and stuff. A bit creepy. But he never did anything like lift up her skirt, as far as I knew."

I couldn't help but tell the truth, with Ian's honor at risk. "That was actually my fault. I wanted to talk to Principal Frechette, so Ian was doing me a favor."

"Any favor you do for Ian probably has strings attached," she said.

"He's been really nice to me. He and Allan are my only real friends," I said.

"Oh, Allan Marks? He's pretty nice looking," she said dreamily. I didn't know how to answer that, so I left it alone. I was glad she stopped speaking poorly about Ian.

She returned to her regular voice. "So what happened to you?"

I was on the spot again, but I realized the obvious answer to her question.

"I've got autism," I said.

She nodded. "Is that why you phase out every now and then?"

Did everyone know about my losing time? What else did people know about me that I didn't want them to know? Ian always said I was an open book, but he was very perceptive. He was always able to tell me what lots of other people were thinking and feeling. Mom, Dr. Eisenberg, and Ian's father, Roger, all seemed to know what I was thinking before I spoke. Was it really that easy?

"See, you're doing it now," Betsy said.

"Sorry," I answered. I glanced quickly at my watch. It had only been a few moments. "I guess it just happens."

"What else?" she demanded.

I was uncomfortable talking about myself at all, but discussing my psychiatric history struck a nerve, so I held my tongue.

"What happened when you ran in front of the truck at the mall?"

I shook my head.

"It's all right," she said. "You don't have to talk about it. I'm just being nosey. Don't worry about it." She reached up and touched me on the shoulder, and I reflexively shuddered away.

"Let's just go," she said.

"OK," I said, mollified.

We remained silent on the walk back. We passed several other people on the trails, all smiling and laughing. I felt more like screaming. My heart was racing and I wanted to punch something.

We got to the rack and unlocked our bikes. "See you tomorrow at lunch?" she said hesitantly.

"Yeah, OK," I answered glumly.

"OK, it's a date," she said, hopping onto her bike and scooting away.

I took off toward home, and as I feared, got stuck going up the larger hills. I had to get off my bike and walk. How fitting. My entire life was one giant uphill battle. Too bad I couldn't stop the world and take a break.

CHAPTER 14

WE WERE nearly finished with our discussion on *The Hobbit*, but since I'd finally read the book, I was able to follow along during Wednesday's class.

"Tell me about the contrasting feelings the dwarves had when they were in Smaug's lair," Miss Burnell said.

Several hands went up, mine decidedly not among them. "Christy?" the teacher called.

"When Bilbo stole the cup and proved he was a thief, they were all excited and elated. But when they realized they were trapped inside the mountain, they felt sad and scared," she said.

"It was more than just sad and scared," Patty chimed.

"How so," asked the teacher.

"It was despair. They had no way out, and even if they did find a way out, they were going to be eaten by the dragon. Their lives were over."

Despair, I thought. No escape, and if there were an exit, it was to a fate worse than being trapped. That's how I'd felt when I was fighting the demons. I couldn't show myself to them, so I stayed hidden in the void. With Grandpa dead, I was again lost—fading into the void and losing time, unable to function.

Was that how Toby felt when he tried to kill himself by taking the pills? Was that how Betsy lost control of her life, failed at school and had to be held back, leaving herself doomed to group therapy?

And what about Lynn? She kept saying in group that she had nothing to live for. That level of depression described how I was feeling most of the time.

My enemy had a name. Despair.

I mused until gym class. We started playing basketball, another sport at which I had no skill. Fortunately, I only had to step onto the court for a few minutes at a time. The good players preferred to let me sit on the bench so they wouldn't lose the game as a result of my horrible play. That suited me. I smiled at Betsy across the gym, but she was on another team, so I didn't get to speak to her.

On the way back to class, I caught a glimpse of Allan. He hadn't been playing basketball, even though he was ordinarily quite capable. Something was wrong with his face, too. I didn't know what was going on, as I hadn't talked to him in several days, but I hoped to ask him about it at lunch.

After we were released to the cafeteria, I sidled up to Allan and saw that his eye was black and blue, as though he'd lost a fight. I tried to check his aura, thinking I might be able to heal him, but instead of the sharp, glistening blue, sweet cinnamon and porcelain, I only detected a sloppy, oily sludge that smelled horrible. Aside from Grandpa's, Allan's aura was the closest match to mine of anyone I knew. I couldn't detect any spicy redness to extract to heal his wound. That didn't make any sense.

"Hey," he said, seeing me approach him.

"What happened?" I asked.

"You'd have known if you were paying attention," he chided.

I didn't say anything. Obviously I'd lost time during a prior conversation. We walked soundlessly until we got to the cafeteria.

"Karate tournament?" he said, expecting me to know what that meant.

Slowly, it came to me. Every September, Allan competed at the Washington State Z-Ultimate Karate Tournament in Everett. I'd accompanied him two years ago when he came in second amongst brown belts in the sparring section. Last year, he was second again in the first degree black belt competition. Judging by his sullen attitude, he hadn't won this year like he'd hoped.

"What happened?" I asked again.

"Seavey. Beat me good."

Derek Seavey, from Fall River. He'd been the winner each of the past two years as well. "Did you get second?" I asked.

"Well, yeah, but I wanted to win," he said, his frustration evident.

"What happened to your face?"

"He got me on a double kick. Knocked me out, if you must know."

"Isn't that illegal?"

"Yeah, it was, but since I had to forfeit, I lost anyway. I hate that kid. He's such a jerk!"

We went through the line and I got milk to go with my sandwich. I waved at Betsy when I saw her, but she noticed Allan and seemed to understand that I wanted to sit with my other friend today.

"Next year I promise I'll come and watch you win," I said, as we found our table.

"Yeah, OK," Allan said. He stopped, turned, and said, "Hey, I'm gonna hold you to that."

He perked up, and we started talking about me coming back to karate lessons. Allan was going to test for his second *dan*, the next level of black belt. I'd have to work out with the orange belts. Recalling my inability to pedal up the hill by my house, I decided to ask Mom about it that night. I wasn't even close to normal, but if I started doing regular activities, maybe I'd get there faster.

Even though I felt a little better over the next few days, I couldn't help feeling that something was seriously wrong. A bubbling, steaming mass of wretchedness lived just beneath the surface of my existence, waiting to burst forth at the most inopportune time.

On Saturday, I met Betsy at her special place again. She didn't press me about my life story, as she called it, so it was tolerable. She told me about Kathy Smitzer and her other friends, and I felt guilty about how she disliked Ian. I wanted to talk to him about it, but he hadn't returned to school, so I didn't get the chance.

Home life resumed a sense of normalcy, as Mom returned to full time work. Dad was still off on a mission, so I was briefly alone after school. Mom made it a point to be home for dinner every day, and we began talking more. I told her about Allan's tournament loss, my class discussion of *The Hobbit,* and spending time with Betsy, although I omitted the details of her special place. One thing I was an expert at was keeping a secret.

Whenever I thought about Grandpa, though, I regressed. Mom stopped me on Sunday, grabbing my arm while I poured milk into my bowl.

"What are you doing?" she gasped.

"I like milk on my cereal," I said defensively.

"Those are French fries," Mom replied.

Fortunately, those episodes were becoming less frequent. On the other hand, the auras still weren't working properly. What could be wrong? I began to wonder if Grandpa's passing had disrupted them permanently. After all, he was the only other person who knew about them. After spending hours considering this point, I finally gave up and went to bed.

*   *   *

Monday's group therapy session started with the seven of us arranging our chairs and Dr. Eisenberg welcoming us.

"Good afternoon, everyone. Does anyone want to start? Maybe tell us about your day?" she asked.

When no one volunteered, she selected for us. "Denise? How was your week?"

Denise glared angrily at Dr. Eisenberg, clearly not wishing to be first, but she began nonetheless. "Coach won't let me play in the league tournament," she said, making no attempt to conceal her bitterness.

"Why is that?" Dr. Eisenberg asked.

"He says he's worried about my ankle," Denise said, raising her leg and displaying a plastic cast on her right lower leg. "But I know it's because he thinks I'm too..." she stopped.

"What happened to your ankle?"

"I sprained it during soccer practice on Thursday. Tripped over Donna Metcalf. She was trying to take me out because we both play the same position. We were doing two person drills and she stuck her foot out so that I'd fall over it. It hurts, but I'm fine," she said.

"Did you get it checked out?"

"Yeah, I went to the doctor, they took x-rays and then gave me this splint to wear. He said nothing was broken, and if it felt better I could start back in a week. But the tournament starts on Wednesday. Close enough, though right? Six days is almost a week, right? I should be allowed to play. It's not because of the ankle though."

"Why do you think he won't let you play?" Dr. Eisenberg asked.

Denise paused, then exploded. "He thinks I'm crazy. Everybody thinks I'm crazy. I go to group therapy, so I must be crazy!"

"Screaming like that doesn't help your cause," said Suzanne.

Denise stood up to take a swing at her, but Dr. Eisenberg was lightning quick out of her chair and grabbed Denise before she could do any damage. "That's enough," she said. "Sit back down, please."

Denise struggled for a second and then sat back down. "Why do you have to be such a bitch?" she bristled at Suzanne.

"Just my nature," Suzanne answered.

"Suzanne, leave it alone," Dr. Eisenberg said, still trying to calm Denise down. When it seemed safe, she resumed her seat, but addressed Denise directly. "Why do you assume everyone thinks you're crazy?"

"Because they all say it. 'She's crazy,' or 'nutjob' or 'wacko' or whatever. I hear it from lots of people. And that's just the ones that say it out loud. Everyone else thinks it for sure."

"Listen, it's bad enough the number of real battles in your lives. There's no call for adding imagined ones on top." Dr. Eisenberg said. "Kids can be cruel. They say things to get a reaction. They want to feel that they're better than you, so they try to hurt you with words. But that's all they are, words. You don't need to internalize them and give them power."

The seven of us listened intently, barely breathing.

"Do you think that you're crazy?" Dr. Eisenberg continued, speaking directly to Denise.

"No, I just want to play," she answered.

Dr. Eisenberg leaned back. "I know we've talked about this before, but it's a very important point. Have any of the rest of you had people call you names?"

The place erupted.

"Sure. Geek, toad, tool, shrimp, garlic toast, weenie, jerkwad, useless waste of protoplasm," said Toby.

"Blob, cow, whale, whale that ate a cow, fatty, porker, lard-ass, fatso," said Kayleigh.

"Bitch is what I get most," said Suzanne.

"Freak, nobody, sad-sack, loser," said Betsy.

I recalled the verbal drubbings I'd received, and added to the list. "Retard, dummy, spaz, psycho, moron," I said.

Dr. Eisenberg held up her hands amidst the onslaught. "Yes, exactly. And how do you feel when they say things like this to you?"

"Horrible!"

"Angry!"

"Sad."

"I want to get even," I said.

"Of course, yes," Dr. Eisenberg agreed as the kids listed their emotions. She stopped at my words.

"Hunter, what do you mean?"

"I hate bullies. Like when Bruce Davis used to ruin my chess games with my friend Rob. And one time he punched me in the face. And Tommy LaChance and his stupid friends tricked me into climbing a tree and breaking my leg. But I got back at him."

"How so?" she asked.

Panic flowed through me as I realized I was about to take credit for what we'd done to Tommy and his friends two years ago. So far, nobody knew who did it, and I wasn't even a suspect. So many other kids had been bullied by their gang; half the school had motive. The principal's office never followed up because his exposure, so to speak, turned out to be a good thing for the school.

I thought fast. "I realized that I could stand up to him and he'd stop bothering me. So I took karate lessons, and since then, nobody's been bullying me."

The nods from around the room suggested I'd scored some points, and Dr. Eisenberg seemed satisfied with the answer. "Yes," she said. "Except for physical abuse, like punching in the face, which you should report to the teachers, everything else they do is just a test. Treat it like that. You don't have to let their words bother you. Ignore them. They're trying to feel superior. It's much easier to be superior when the words have effect. It's up to each of you to be strong and not let words hurt."

The class nodded again.

"But," she added. "Don't worry about revenge," her words were directed at me, though she didn't make eye contact. "Nothing good can come from trying to 'get back' at the other kids. They have their problems, and we have ours. We can't solve their issues, but we must always work on our own. That's where the focus must lie."

I knew better than to voice my disagreement.

"One thing, though, before we move on."

The class looked at her curiously.

"Someone called you 'garlic toast'?" she said, looking at Toby.

"Yeah, I didn't get it either," he answered.

CHAPTER 15

I ASKED Mom about karate, but she nipped that idea in the bud.

"You're not ready, Hunter," she said. "If you have another episode you'll end up back in the hospital. All the progress you've made will be for naught. How about practicing your exercises and punching the bag in the garage?"

I ruefully accepted her logic. When I started hitting the bag the way Dad showed me, she interrupted and forced me to wear the gloves Allan gave me. She didn't want me to scrape up my hands. I'd beaten them bloody before, and she was worried I'd hurt myself. Silly. I could heal them any time I wanted. Besides, part of the goal of using the bag was to toughen up my skin. She wouldn't relent, so I obliged and wore them. I also resumed calisthenics, forms, one-step moves, and combination strikes. They might come in handy if Kenny bothered me again.

Mom encouraged me to visit Betsy in the park. She was thrilled I was spending time with a girl, a prospect clearly more dangerous than fighting any number of black belts. I didn't protest, as I needed Betsy's help to convince Dr. Eisenberg I wasn't crazy.

At Betsy's special place, we talked about our past. Her life was completely miserable—father out of the picture, mother uninvolved, academic life disrupted by failing a grade, and friends abandoning her. Losing her support group was the worst, but it wasn't entirely their fault. Ninth graders attended Garfield High, and Madrona only went to eighth. Her prior classmates were at another school, making it nearly impossible to maintain close friendships.

Betsy no longer had much in common with her high school counterparts. When they saw her outside school, they eyed her with awkward pity. Not wanting to be seen with an eighth grader, they shunned her. For Betsy's part, they reminded her of what she'd lost, so she avoided them, too. The whole situation was a living nightmare.

I told my story, starting with the Autism Center, and moving to Madrona's special education class. She liked the part where I impressed Mrs. Barrett, the substitute teacher, with my math talent, earning a chance at Principal Frechette's placement test. I ended up in the "highly capable cohort," where I met Allan and the others.

Betsy had been in the HCC too, but since flunking, she'd been relegated to the regular section. The classwork was boring, so she gave up on everything. I understood, having been through the same thing. Hearing her words reminded me of Lynn, from the therapy group. Nothing to live for. The story was horribly depressing.

She asked about Grandpa, but I couldn't talk about him, so I dodged her questions. I cycled between guilt and anger whenever I thought about his death. Had I been there, I could've healed him, and I wanted to eviscerate the butchers who tossed him into the furnace. His loss shrouded me in a billowy cloak of despair that flared violently whenever I thought about him. The only way forward was to suppress all memories of Grandpa. Curiously, I felt closer to Betsy when she brought up his death, even if I never spoke about it.

We met routinely after school at her special place. We also ate lunch together, with Allan's encouragement. At first I thought he was trying to get rid of me, but he'd proven his friendship time and time again, so I knew that wasn't the case. He always smiled when he saw me with Betsy, and I believed he was genuinely happy for me. I tried to check his aura to clarify, but like before, it was mostly a brownish oily mess, like Betsy's.

Reading the auras made me confused and lightheaded, and I wasn't able to learn anything. I kept a ton of candy in my jacket pockets out of habit, but even loaded up on sugar, I couldn't read them properly. I yearned for Grandpa's counsel, but thinking about him made it worse. It was easier to ignore the auras, like everything else.

Ian hadn't returned, and I wondered if he'd taken a vacation with his Dad, or if he was helping with another investigative journalism project, like last year. During our search for evidence about Orlando Ryan, we never missed school, so the latter was less likely. I missed him. It felt a bit like when Rob Friendly, my chess-playing buddy from sixth grade, moved to New York with his family after getting bullied by Bruce Davis.

On the upside, my scholastic career took a turn for the better. I had several quizzes during the week, and I aced the math, scored highly on the science and history, and performed relatively well on the French, which for me meant anything other than a zero. On Thursday, Miss Burnell went so far as to pay me a compliment.

"Well, Mr. Miller, I reckon there may indeed be a brain behind those freaky dark eyes. I was beginning to wonder how you became a member of this fine HCC class." Despite the thinly veiled insults, it was nice to hear positive commentary about my schoolwork.

I told Mom about it when I got home.

"Guess what," I said.

"What?" she answered, apparently not keen to guess.

"Miss Burnell told me I may have a brain after all," I said.

"Did she now?" Mom said, bemused.

"Yep. I scored pretty well on three of my four quizzes this week."

"Well, that's excellent. Maybe we should celebrate."

We had cake and ice cream after dinner, like on my birthday. I'd never really enjoyed the taste of food, although I recognized its value as an energy source. Somehow, though, cake and ice cream with Mom made me happy. I was slowly regaining my concentration. I started reading the next Asimov book in the series Mom had given me for Christmas. I even played a chess game on my computer before I zonked to sleep.

I went to school Friday in relatively high spirits. Even Kenny's lame attempt to belittle me during gym left me undaunted. After locking away all memories of Grandpa, I was slowly rejoining the world of the living. Grandpa was gone, it hurt like anything, and I missed him horribly, but there wasn't anything I could do about it.

I mused about my progress during Miss Burnell's discussion of algebra. Discussing Betsy's plight in great detail helped and, much as I hated to admit it, hearing the misery of the other members of my therapy session left me better equipped to deal with my own. I'd lost my closest confidant, but he hadn't left me on purpose. I decided that I'd learned enough to talk my way out of group therapy. I had Betsy to thank, though it wasn't for the reason that I'd anticipated when I'd befriended her.

She grabbed me by the shoulder as I entered the cafeteria, then dragged me to her usual table instead of letting me wait in line to get milk. I fought the urge to swat her hand away and allowed her to lead me to the back of the room. She didn't sit. Something was different, but I had no idea what.

"It's getting worse at home. Mom didn't get back from the bar last night until almost six in the morning. I heard her come in. She smashed the glass table in the front room into millions of pieces. I think she fell onto it."

"Was she hurt?" I asked.

"She didn't seem to be. Got up and dusted off the shards, then told me to go back to bed. I asked if she wanted to talk, and she said 'What could I learn from a little piece of crap like you?' Can you believe that?"

I shook my head. I couldn't imagine Mom, Allan's Mom, or any mother I'd ever met, saying something like that to her child.

"I can't take it anymore!" she wailed.

I struggled for something supportive to say.

"At least I have you. Hunter, you're so wonderful!"

She pulled me into her arms with a huge embrace. I reflexively recoiled, pulling my face from her shoulder and accidentally lining up nose to nose with her. She leaned in with her mouth like she was about to bite me. I shoved back in terror, sending her crashing into the table and creating a carnage of flying silverware, dishes, and stray hunks of food. The room fell momentarily silent.

"Gee, that's just great. Wonderful. Thanks for nothing!" She ran out of the room crying.

"I'm sorry!" I called back. The younger kids sitting at the table next to ours tried to recover their spilled food, and they blamed me for wasting their meal money. Others from around the room looked curiously at the mess. A few raucous eighth graders applauded.

Mrs. Weiss came from the hallway to investigate. "What's going on here?" she asked, pointing to the disorderly jumble that had previously been a lunch table.

"We, uh, bumped into each other, and she fell into the table," I said.

"You shoved her into the table," a smaller boy said.

"She tried to kiss him," one of the others added.

"Is this true?" the teacher said.

"No, not at all. We're friends!" My voice was high and shaky.

"To the office with you," she said. "Mrs. Frechette will sort it out."

No amount of protesting would change her mind, so I walked to the office, munching my sandwich along the way. I hadn't had a chance to eat because Betsy hijacked me at the beginning of the lunch period.

"No eating in here," said Blanche, the office secretary.

"So I should go back to the cafeteria?" I said hopefully.

"Finish the sandwich in the hallway," she demanded.

I retreated to the hall to finish, and after stuffing the remaining bites into my mouth, I stuck my head back into the office. "Gumph enumph?" I said.

"Fine. Wait in that chair and I'll tell her you're here, Mr. Miller."

I was shocked she knew my name. How many times had I been

to the office?

Moments later, she said, "Come on back."

I swallowed the last bit of dry sandwich, wishing I'd had my milk.

"Hunter, what's going on?" Mrs. Frechette said.

"I… she…" I hadn't thought about my story and had no idea what to say.

"A girl, Hunter?"

I nodded my head in the affirmative.

"What happened?"

"We were talking, and she tried…." She'd tried to kiss me, one of the kids had said. Why would she do that?

"Why, Hunter, are you blushing?"

I had no answer to that.

"Never mind. How did you end up getting sent to me?"

"She fell into the table and sent the dishes flying. Mrs. Weiss told me to come here."

"Who's the girl? Is she OK?"

I'd forgotten about Betsy. "She ran out of the cafeteria. I guess she went back to class."

"Which girl?"

"Oh, Betsy Knopf."

"OK. I'll check with her teacher. Nobody else was injured?"

"A few kids lunches, maybe, but that's it. I'm sorry," I said.

"Go ahead and finish your lunch period, and then go back to class."

*   *   *

Thirty minutes later, Miss Burnell sent me back to the principal's office. Blanche escorted me right in.

"Betsy Knopf?" Mrs. Frechette said.

"Yes?" I asked, now a bit concerned as to her state.

"She never went back to class."

"Did you try her house?" I asked.

"I called, but nobody answered the phone," she said. "Do you know where she went? Did she say anything as she was leaving?"

She'd probably gone to the park to think, but I couldn't say that. I wouldn't betray her trust—she made me swear not to tell anyone about her special spot.

"She said, 'thanks for nothing' and started crying," I said.

"What did you do to her?" she asked, looking sternly at me.

"She tried to hug me and I don't know, I panicked. I pushed her away and she hit the table. I didn't mean it, I don't like people touching me. Never have," I blurted.

Mrs. Frechette nodded slowly. "OK, Hunter, thanks. Hopefully she found her way home. I'll have Blanche keep trying her number. Dismissed," she said, waving her hand toward the door.

*   *   *

I went back to class and spent the last hour completely preoccupied with Betsy's fate. She'd been extremely upset, and shoving her into the table hadn't helped one iota. She didn't normally skip class, and I hoped she was all right. I had to get to her spot as soon as possible to apologize. Time dragged on, and I felt increasingly anxious as I waited for the school day to end. When the final bell rang, I ran for the bus and was the first one on.

The ride took forever, and I sprinted from the bus stop to my front door, barging through as Mom was exiting.

"What's the hurry?" she said, stopping me in my tracks.

"I, uh, is it OK if I go to see Betsy?"

"Of course. Just be back before dark. And bring your jacket— it's supposed to be a chilly evening."

I pedaled furiously to the park, making it in record time. I racked my bike and jogged into the clearing on jello legs, but Betsy wasn't there. I poked around to other recesses, and scouted the path for other possible locations before returning to the entrance. I went up and down several other trails, calling out her name until the sun started getting low on the horizon. She had to be there, but I checked everywhere and couldn't find her.

I figured she'd gone home. I should have called first instead of coming here directly. Now I'd have to wait until morning to talk to her. At least she was safe.

CHAPTER 16

I TOSSED in bed most of the night, unable to shake the uncomfortable feeling that something was wrong. Even though it was Saturday, I got up an hour before the usual time and went downstairs. Mom was drinking coffee and reading the newspaper.

"Good morning, Hunter. You're up early. Did you sleep well?"

"Not really," I said.

"Are you all right?" she asked.

"I'm OK, just worried about Betsy."

"Why don't you bike over to her house? You can't apologize appropriately by phone."

Mom knew a lot more about girls than I did, so I took her advice. The chill morning air blasted at my face the moment I stepped outside, so I was glad Mom had encouraged me to wear a jacket again. I stuffed the pockets full of candy, as my legs were still fatigued from yesterday's rigorous ride to the park, and I figured I'd need extra energy.

When I arrived at the Knopf's, I saw blue lights rotating on the roof of a car in the driveway. Since I'd discovered Orlando Ryan was a corrupt cop, I'd lost my faith in the police, so I approached the house cautiously and unseen. I waited and watched for fifteen minutes before concluding with sudden horror that the police were probably there because something had happened to Betsy.

The moment I made the decision to go to the door, a solitary officer appeared from it, escorting an older, bedraggled woman from the house. She'd dressed hastily with a rumpled blouse that was buttoned incorrectly, jeans, and two different shoes. Her hair pointed in every direction, and her makeup job was better suited for a Halloween costume. She looked decidedly miserable.

Though I'd never seen her before, I could tell it was Betsy's mother. The two had roughly the same height and build, and Betsy's description matched this disheveled menace. I could easily imagine this woman calling her own daughter "a piece of crap." She obviously couldn't take care of herself, let alone any offspring.

"We found your car wrapped around a telephone pole down the road," the tall, male officer was saying. "With your Breathalyzer this high now, I can't imagine what it must have been last night when you drove off the road. Hope you've got a good lawyer."

He stuffed her head ungraciously into the back of the cruiser and locked her inside with a slam. I ducked out of sight and waited for him to leave. Then I ran to the front entrance, opened the screen, and banged on the wooden door, which was partially open. It pushed inward under my pounding, so I crept quickly inside, calling out for Betsy.

She didn't answer.

I doubted Betsy could remain asleep while her mother was being dragged away in handcuffs, but I wanted to find her bedroom to make sure. The house was a shambles. Dirty dishes, take-out boxes, spoiled food, papers and clothes littered the common area. Two garbage cans sat on the ground sideways, spilling their contents, and the entire area was covered in a layer of dirt and grime that may have dated back to the turn of the century. An odd odor permeated the area, making me pull my shirt up over my nose to avoid getting sick.

I discovered the source of the smell outside of a bathroom. A smattering of vomit streaked the wall and congealed into a pool on the floor, as though the person responsible tried to make it inside the room, but settled with the wall outside. It was mostly clear liquid, but several hotdog chunks verified that it had been stomach contents.

"Betsy?" I called again.

No response.

I immediately replaced my shirt over my nose and mouth. I understood why she met me out front and brought me to the park instead of inviting me inside. The place was disgusting. Living in a pig sty certainly contributed to her misery.

I kept looking for her bedroom until I saw a poster of a band Betsy liked on a door. This must be it. I knocked softly, and hearing nothing, turned the doorknob and poked my head inside.

A haven of cleanliness appeared inside, in stark contrast with the rest of the house. The books were all organized on shelves, the clothes were put away in the drawers or closet, there were no food crumbs or dishes, and the floor and dressers were neat and tidy. The only thing out of place was a small scrap of paper on the perfectly made bed.

I crept into the room, feeling guilty about invading her privacy.

"Betsy?" I said quietly, although I could see she wasn't there.

The paper called ominously to me. I picked it up, unfolded it and stared in disbelief. It contained only two words.

"I'm sorry."

The words pierced my heart with icy dread. I knew exactly what it meant. Like Toby, she'd chosen to attempt suicide, and she wanted to apologize to her mother, the woman who'd been carried away by the police.

It was my fault. If I hadn't shoved her away.... If I had said something constructive, if I had hugged her back, anything other than what I did, she'd be alive right now.

But where had she gone? I'd checked her special place yesterday afternoon and it was empty. She wasn't in her room, and judging by the revolting appearance of the rest of the place, she wouldn't be caught dead in another part of the house, so to speak. I groaned internally at my twisted pun.

Still, I had to check. I ran all over the house, avoiding disease-ridden dishware, moldy food, soiled clothing, and of course, the puddle of puke. I called her name, but I knew it was useless. It was a single level home, and it only took a few minutes to open every door and inspect every nook and cranny. She wasn't here.

I realized my stupidity with a jolt. Fritzcloves! She'd obviously gone *home* first, written the note, and *then* went to her private location in the woods!

But how did she plan to kill herself? She could impale herself on a tree branch or throw herself into the lake, but then she could've gone directly to the woods. She must have needed something from the house. Maybe a knife to cut her wrists, or…

I scrambled through the house again with a new aim, finding her weapon. To my horror, I found exactly what I'd feared. It was on the floor of the bathroom befouled by the pooled slop. An empty pill bottle.

I bolted out of the house, pocketing the container. The crisp, cool air buffeted my face as I jumped astride my bicycle and pedaled ferociously toward the park. I nearly wiped out on the huge downhill because of excessive speed, but I needed to find Betsy before it was too late, if it wasn't already.

The sun emerged from behind a thick cloud cover as I found the park entrance and tossed my bike next to the rack without bothering to lock it. Although breathing heavily already, I sprinted to the alcove, scraping my exposed skin on tree branches. I kept slipping on wet leaves, nearly falling several times. When I burst into the clearing, the sight of Betsy's unmoving body temporarily stopped my own heart.

She was pale and cold to the touch.

Waves of guilt toppled me, and I fell to the ground next to her. I nearly vomited, experiencing that same horrific taste that made me spew in Dr. Eisenberg's office. It had a burning quality to it this time, and I felt a pulsating howl.

This was all my fault. I might as well have killed her myself. I pushed her away when she needed a friend, and now, there was nothing I could do. Just like Grandpa.

Wait.

I'd been castigating myself for not being there for Grandpa. How many times had I told myself that I'd have healed him if I were there when he had his heart attack? Now here I was, lamenting the loss of my friend before trying to help her. I rolled up onto my elbows and looked at Betsy's icy face. Her eyes were closed. Her clothes were rumpled and pulled in toward her, as though she'd been huddling for warmth. She'd picked the coldest night of the year to be outside.

I knew what I had to do.

I rifled through my jacket pockets and found several full packages of candy, a small apple, and various other snacks. I ate everything, scarfing with a savagery that would have impressed a jackal. I felt the energy course through me as the sugar revived my hope and my spirits.

Fully loaded, I reached for her aura.

The taste, which had dominated my senses moments ago, faded slightly and was replaced by the feel of cold brown sludge, like I was trapped inside a barrel of used motor oil. An eerie black folded its way through the darkness of the slimy morass. Her aura was disgusting, like her house had been. I felt sick simply contacting it, and fought the inescapable urge to block it out completely. I pressed on nonetheless, fully aware that my failure to act would result in another death.

Two things didn't make any sense. Her aura was thick and full. It was very dense and powerful, not disintegrated like I'd seen in Mrs. Collins right before she died. And it contained a pink color, one particular to males.

There was another presence—a tiny shadow outside the sludge. A sensation slightly beyond my reach. It reminded me of the first time I cleared my aura, when the eruption from thousands of auras blasted me. I'd fallen so hard into the void that I ended up in the ICU and it took Grandpa's trick of IV sugar to bring me back.

Fritzcloves! It wasn't Betsy's aura that was so revolting.

It was my own.

Instantly, I knew it to be true. I'd been suppressing my own aura ever since Grandpa died. That unbearable taste. It was as though nothing in the world could ever be the same. Nothing was worth doing. Nothing was worth living for. It was… despair.

I understood. My enemy had both a name and a taste. Despair.

I knew what needed to happen. I had to beat it. I had to force my deep depression to take a back seat, or else Betsy would be lost forever. I could save her. Hunter could save her. But I needed to be Hunter, I needed to be myself.

I reached out again to the aura, my aura, and felt the desperation. I struggled mightily, but it was no use. I was stuck in my morass and it was inescapable. I wasn't going to be able to heal Betsy if I couldn't access her aura.

Another thought struck me. Grandpa saved people all the time. He didn't need supernatural abilities. He… did CPR!

My soul lightened as I realized I could help her. I rolled her body flat, like Grandpa taught me. I swept my finger inside her cold mouth to make sure her breathing passage was open, and I placed my mouth on hers, carefully pinching her nose, and breathed life into her lungs.

She stirred, sputtered a cough, and opened her eyes.

"Now you kiss me?" she said, so weakly I could barely hear her.

"You're ALIVE!" I screamed.

She made a noncommittal gesture and closed her eyes again. I pulled the pill bottle from my pocket. "Did you take all these pills?" I said, my voice shrill with terror.

She slowly reopened her eyes. "Yes."

"I've got to get you to the hospital!"

"Thanks," she said, again so faintly I could barely understand.

"For what?" I asked.

"For trying to save me. I knew you would. I hoped…" her voice trailed off as she lapsed back into unconsciousness.

I remembered Grandpa's CPR lesson, and realized I'd never checked for a pulse. I put my index finger on her neck, right where the big artery was supposed to be, and felt a thin, almost ghostly beat. I put my finger on my own neck, calibrating to what normal should be, and repeated the process on her. Far slower, far weaker, and fading. She was dying in front of me.

This was worse than before. Now it was undeniable that she was about to die if I didn't do something! It was as if five minutes ago was just a dress rehearsal, and I'd get to watch her die in my arms for real.

I grasped for my aura but felt nothing except the same suffocating mire, resolutely immutable. I had to break through my own aura just to get to hers, yet that was impossible. And the only person who could help me, Grandpa, was dead and gone. I felt the despair closing in, stinking and pounding so badly that I could barely breathe. The depression was literally killing me.

"HELP!" I bawled. "I need HELP!"

Nobody answered. The park was deserted. And who could help me anyway? I was suffering in a trap of my own design. I searched my brain for anything that could be of value.

Reverend Sanderson's deep voice reverberated from nowhere. "He's with you. He will always be with you," it said.

"Grandpa!" I called out, to no avail.

I started to panic. Another voice said, "Turn your emotions into your ally, or they will get the better of you."

Dad.

Yes, Dad saved people too. He was a secret agent. He told me he'd saved lives, and there were no waves, so I knew he'd spoken the truth.

I took several deep breaths, and calmed down, trying to master my emotion.

"Grandpa," I whispered. And I sought him out.

I poked at the abyss which was my own aura. As I slowed my breathing and thought about Dad's words, I felt the weight lift slightly. Encouraged, I thought about Mom. The way she tried to comfort me after I heard about Grandpa. The way she stayed with me through the group therapy, karate lessons, and at home. She brought me cake and ice cream. She gave hugs, but only so much that it didn't drive me crazy. True conversation. Love. The mass lightened more.

Allan. He was always there for me. When everyone else abandoned me, he remained. My true friend. Willing to take me back into his life at a moment's notice. Working with me to take down the bullies. Protecting me from enemies. Sharing my birthday. Helping teach me karate. Lighter and lighter.

Others. Miss Barrett, the substitute teacher who rescued me from the special education class and helped me enroll in the HCC group where I met Allan. Principal Frechette, who remained on my side and helped me with my quest against Orlando Ryan. Ian, who taught me to mind my surroundings, and his father Roger, without whom I'd never have learned photography or investigative journalism. Bob, Brady, Mickey and Davis, the guys who helped me take down Tommy Lachance. Miss Preneta, my 7th grade teacher who'd been so understanding and helpful, and Mr. Lajoie, from 6th grade, whose mathlete cup awards brightened my days.

I kept remembering people who'd affected my life in a positive way. Everyone from Faye the Mystic and Dr. Fukawara, the acupuncturist, to Mr. Wales, the head of the Autism center. I took them all in, and returned to Grandpa. He was always with me.

I reached out again and felt the ray of cool blue break through the mire. I picked at it, opening a doorway for Grandpa's aura. He'd come back. Or he'd never left. He knew I was in trouble and sent his aura to help.

I drank in the cool blue, bathing in the familiar smell, taste, and feel. It soothed me and bolstered me. I felt the strength of half a dozen candy bars coursing through me as I cleared Grandpa's aura, no—*my* aura. The onslaught of information from the outside shocked me as much as it had the first time I'd cleared my aura.

This time, however, I knew exactly what was going on, and I channeled the unnecessary sensations away. I utilized the sugar for strength, and the motivation of helping Betsy as a powerful ally. *Use the emotion.*

I reached out and felt the extremely frail aura right next to me.

Betsy was indeed dying. Percolating spicy redness ate away at her being from the inside. She, too, tasted like despair, the oily morass slopping through her ghostly, black-tinged aura.

I had no idea about her baseline traits. I'd never experienced them. The only thing I could do was remove the parts that didn't belong, like healing my spicy red lacerations during practice. I teased away the horrible tasting blackness, pulling with it much of the repulsive oily junk, leaving behind brownish shards amidst periwinkle blue, orange and shafts of silver.

I fell backward. Her skin was still cold and pale, but when I checked her pulse, it beat more strongly. Unfortunately, the frail nature persisted. No matter what I tried, I couldn't beef that up. Instead, I felt my own aura weaken. I'd done all I could.

I checked my watch. It was 2:30 pm. I'd been in this alcove for hours. My stomach rumbled, a terrifying thought, because I only felt hunger when I was completely famished and near passing out. I rummaged through my pockets again, finding only a small box of raisins amidst the empty pill bottle and some trash. Time to go.

I hauled Betsy over my shoulder and stumbled toward the park entrance. A young adult couple, walking hand-in-hand in the sunshine, ran over when they saw us.

"Are you OK?" asked the woman breathlessly.

"No, she took pills," I said, collapsing to the ground under Betsy's weight.

"What's your name?" the man asked Betsy. When she didn't answer, he said "We need to get her to the hospital." His aura and facial features echoed concern.

He picked up Betsy like a sack of potatoes and walked quickly to his car, which was parked near the same entrance as my bike.

"How did you get here?" the woman asked, as we followed her husband out of the park.

I pointed at my bike, sprawled next to the rack.

"Why don't you lock it up and come in the car with us," she said, as the man flopped Betsy's helpless body into the back seat.

"Thanks," I said, and hopped in, putting her head into my lap.

CHAPTER 17

THE GOOD Samaritans brought us across town to the University of Washington Hospital. The man carried Betsy's limp and nearly lifeless body into the emergency room. The familiar bustle of people, many in need of care and many there to deliver, was a welcome relief, as I knew Betsy could finally get the help she needed. I drank in the smells and textures of the auras as I walked quickly beside the man, who showed no signs of tiring.

A nurse met us at the doorway to the department. "Have your wife register her at the desk," she said. She was unbelievably calm, pulling a stretcher from the hallway as though nothing was wrong.

"She took pills," I said, my voice straining with urgency.

"What kind," the nurse asked, suddenly interested in me.

I held out the bottle.

"We've got an OD!" she called out, taking the bottle from me.

Half a dozen people converged around the stretcher as the man gently lowered Betsy onto it. The sudden activity had a certain beauty to it, as though a giant multi-headed organism had come to life. Its tentacles surrounded Betsy from every angle in a giant, loving embrace.

Nurses attached monitors for blood pressure, heart rate and oxygen content, then established intravenous lines, and drew blood samples into tubes. A specialist from respiratory put a tube into her nose, and a technologist attached EKG wires to her arms, legs, and chest. I was shunted away as they wheeled her into a private room.

The man joined me in the hallway, followed by his wife, who had been talking with the registration clerk. "We don't know her name or any of the information," she said. "Do you know her?"

"Yes, I know her name," I said.

"Come with me then," she said, pulling me back toward the entrance.

"Do you know the patient's information?" the woman at the desk asked.

"Yes," I said.

"Take a seat. I have some questions for you."

Before I sat down, I turned to the couple. "Thank you so much!" I said.

"You're welcome," said the man.

"I hope she's OK," said the woman.

They left quietly, and I plopped down into the reception chair.

"Name?" the secretary asked,

"Hunter," I said.

She looked up. "Patient's name?" she said, in the same deadpan tone.

"Oh, Betsy Knopf. K-N-O-P-F."

I provided her address and phone number, both of which I knew, but stumbled at date of birth.

Just then, one of the nurses appeared behind me.

"We need permission to treat, if possible. The guy who dropped her off didn't know her name. Given her clinical state, we can use implied consent, but it's important that we talk to her parents as soon as possible," she said.

"She lives with her mother. Her father is in California."

"Betsy Knopf," the secretary said to the nurse.

"Wait, Knopf?" the nurse asked. "We had another Knopf this morning getting medical clearance," she said.

"Do you know her mother's name?" she asked me.

"I don't know her name, but I doubt she's here. I saw the cops taking her away this morning."

"Hmm. Stay here," she said to me. "Can you check if it's the same family, Phyllis?" she said to the secretary.

I sat nervously, waiting to answer other questions, but all the while wishing to see Betsy.

Meanwhile, Phyllis started clicking buttons on her computer. Then she picked up her telephone and made a call.

"Yeah, I got it. Leslie Knopf has the same address. That's probably her mother." The voice on the other end spoke for a few moments. "OK, I'll put her in under that. Thanks."

She hung up.

"We've got all we need, thank you Hunter."

"Can I see Betsy?" I asked.

"Why don't you go out to the waiting room, and I'll have the nurse get you when you can see her."

Suddenly I realized I was stuck at the hospital with no ride home.

"Can I use your phone? I have to call my Mom."

I called Mom, and she arrived twenty minutes later.

"Are you all right?" she asked.

"Fine. But Betsy took pills," I said.

I told her the whole story, and when I finished, I was getting lightheaded. "Do you have anything to eat?" I asked.

We bought junk food from the vending machines and I ate like a starved coyote. Mom looked at me sideways but didn't say anything. We waited in silence for the nurses to let us visit Betsy. Rejuvenated by food, I opened up to the auras.

My own blue was infected with buzzing, muddled sadness, but no longer overwhelmed by darkened pressurized globs of hopelessness. I could breathe in my own sensations again, and I could access the auras of those around me. Mom's maternal purple and thumping concern were soothingly familiar, and I was happy that she wasn't worried about me for a change. Or maybe she was. Either way, it was good to be me again.

When they allowed us back, Betsy was awake, with IV fluids travelling into her veins, but most of the other monitors had been removed.

"Mrs. Knopf?" the new nurse asked.

"No, I'm Dr. Marissa Miller. I'm Hunter's mother. This is Hunter, Betsy's friend."

I bypassed the conversation and went directly to the bedside, but didn't say anything.

"Hello, Hunter."

"Uh, hi," I said awkwardly.

"It's OK, I'm not going to die. Or bite."

I felt for her aura. It was easier than asking how she was feeling. I was surprised to find bright periwinkle blue, cinnamon flavored brown, and gritty, vibrating anxiousness only mildly clouded over with charcoal grey depression. Strands of yellow and light purple meant she was happy to see me. Or happy to be alive, and able to see anyone.

"You need to stop doing that," she said. I stared at her, confused.

"Never mind. Thank you for saving me," she said. "The nurses told me that a boy and two adults dropped me off, and if they hadn't, I'd be dead. I don't really want to be dead. I want to be alive. But not stuck with my mother."

"I don't think you're going to have to worry about that. The police took her away in handcuffs. She's probably going to jail."

"No, she's going to rehab. Dad's coming up to take care of me for a little while."

I understood the yellow now. This was what she'd wanted all along. Too bad she had to attempt suicide to get it. Hmm.

"Hunter!"

"What?" I said, jumping slightly.

"Come here," she said, reaching out with her arms. I shuddered.

"Don't worry, I'm not going to try to kiss you. Even though you kissed me," she said.

"I was doing CPR!" I yelled defensively.

Mom and the nurse jumped at my outburst, looked at me briefly, and then resumed their quiet conversation in the doorway.

"Sure you were," Betsy said. "Come here."

I bent down and she gave me a hug. I didn't pull away.

PART TWO

CHAPTER 18

ON THE car ride home from the hospital, Mom's aura beamed with purple and yellow. Being reacquainted with the auras, I realized how much I had missed them. They were part of me. They were Hunter.

"What happened in the woods?" she asked, her voice recalling me to the present.

"I told you," I said. "Betsy ran off and—"

"Not with Betsy. With you."

I stared at her while she watched the road. I could feel her attention on me, although she wasn't looking.

"What do you mean?"

"You're better. I can see it in your eyes," she said.

I nodded. "Yes, I think I am."

She smiled, and I swam in the soothing warmth of her colors. I couldn't help but grin back.

"It's called acceptance," she said.

I remembered Grandpa telling me about the stages of grief. It took two months for me to experience them all. Denial, anger, bargaining, sadness, and acceptance. Now here I was. On the other side.

"Kubler-Ross," I said, recalling the woman Grandpa credited with developing this theory.

"Yes, exactly. You're an amazing young man," she said, her aura beaming with a sharp, salty, cool sensation alongside the bright yellow happiness.

I saw another unknown configuration, also cool and sharp, but golden colored and distinct from the other one. I still had a lot of work to do. There were many patterns and textures I didn't understand. I couldn't yet look at a face and determine emotion or other characteristics, but with Ian's help, I'd soon learn how. It was time to get back to the cataloguing process.

I rode home quietly watching Mom's aura, marveling at its complexity. I thoroughly enjoyed experiencing the sensations. It was like being released after weeks in captivity.

Safely back in my room, I resumed my old exercises. It took a few moments, but soon I was able to pop open a wound on my hand by adding the requisite redness and discord, then heal it by replacing the cool blue. I repeated the process all over my body, fixing whatever damage I caused. It was fun. I took care not to spill any blood onto my sheets or clothes—Mom would freak if she discovered what I was doing.

I loaded my pockets with food, smiling to myself as this habit had saved me in the woods. Without the burst of sugar, I surely would've lost myself to the void. I went to sleep Sunday night eager for the following school day. I had so much to learn, and I couldn't wait to see Ian and get started.

*   *   *

When I arrived in our classroom, Ian wasn't there. For the third week, I was alone at my desk. This time, however, I was acutely aware of his absence.

I paid attention in class, though the math was so boring I could barely stay awake. I even answered one of Miss Burnell's questions. Allan smiled at me when I raised my hand. I didn't have to look at him to tell. Cool.

Betsy wasn't at gym class, which bothered me until I realized that she couldn't possibly be out of the hospital after her suicide attempt. I knew that from firsthand experience. I remember pleading with Dr. Blake to let me go home, to no avail. He had admitted me to the psychiatric floor after I woke up, and I stayed for several days.

✶   ✶   ✶

Today was basketball again. Even with the teacher's attempts to get me involved, I mostly stood around and dodged the other players. Despite my skill with math or science, the only role I served during gym class was as a target for Kenny's teasing.

"Get out of the way, you moron!" he yelled as he dribbled up the court, nearly colliding with me. I watched the clock and counted the minutes until gym ended.

When lunch period came, I approached Allan on the way out of the classroom.

"Hey, buddy, you look good. What's going on?"

"I'm wondering where Ian is. Have you seen him?"

He stopped walking and grabbed me by the shoulder, forcing me to look directly into his eyes. I didn't care much for face-to-face contact, and I shuddered slightly.

"He's gone. He left the country a couple weeks ago. I thought you knew."

"What?" I said, feeling the forest-green doubt wrapping my aura. Iron-grey dismay replaced the green as I saw no waves in Allan's aura. He was telling the truth.

"Yeah, his Dad got a job back in England. You were out of school for a couple of days, sick I think. Ian really wanted to say goodbye, but his Dad said something about a lead that needed immediate attention. They packed up for the plane ride and hired a moving company to get the rest of their stuff."

"Fritzcloves!" I yelled.

"Someday you'll have to tell me what that means," Allan replied as he released me.

*   *   *

I finished my school day rocked by the news of Ian. It was part of a conspiracy to remove those closest to me. Rob Friendly, Grandpa, Ian, all gone. When I got home, Mom provided more bad news.

"Are you ready to go to your therapy session?"

"Do I still have to go? I don't need it anymore," I said.

She looked at me and nodded slowly. "I think you're probably right. Let's go one more time so Dr. Eisenberg can see your progress. If she doesn't release you, I'll talk to her myself."

I begrudgingly agreed to the terms and trudged to the car. When we got to the parking lot, I moped toward the building, but Mom stopped me before we entered.

"Hunter, listen to me. I know you don't want to be here, but you can't go in there like that."

"Like what?"

"Like you dropped your ice cream cone onto the floor and it was carried away by ants."

"What?" I said, confused.

"If you're going to show improvement, you have to behave like before, not like you're unhappy. She's not going to believe that the reason you're depressed is because you're being forced to go to group therapy. She's going to think you haven't achieved acceptance. Do you understand?"

I nodded. "Yes, you're right. Thanks, Mom."

"One more thing. Your father is coming back tonight. He should be home in time for dinner."

"Great!" I said, suddenly excited by the first piece of good news I'd received all day.

"I'll pick you up after the session," she said.

"OK," I answered, heading through the door. "Bye, Mom."

She started to leave, but Kayleigh appeared and Mom held the door for her. I watched her as she went past. Despite her large size, her aura was weaker than most—powder blue and brown, slimy and itchy with a trace of silver and bronze. It smelled of cinnamon. I tried to process the sensations but was distracted by her voice.

"Aren't you coming?" she said.

"Uh, yeah." I followed her into the waiting area where the others had collected, all except Betsy.

"C'mon back," Dr. Eisenberg said, motioning to her office. She wore a jacket and had entered through a separate door.

We set up the chairs as usual and sat in our circle, leaving the seat on my right empty.

"Betsy won't be joining us," the doctor said. Toby jumped up and removed the extra chair, clanking it into the wall as he folded it.

She scanned the group. I stared back into her eyes as they met mine.

"Hunter. Why don't we start with you."

I recalled Mom's words and began. "I feel better. Mom and I had a discussion about acceptance. I was angry and sad about Grandpa's death, but now I realize it's just something I have to live with. I'm ready to move on."

Dr. Eisenberg's face betrayed nothing. But her aura swirled a forest-green murmuring doubt that resolved quickly into a salty, humming yellow that I assumed meant she'd bought my story.

"Very good, Hunter," she said. "Very, very, good."

Relieved of the need for further discourse, I was able to study the auras of my fellow members. With Betsy gone, the next on my right was Toby, the scrawny kid with the high pitched voice. Being younger, his aura was less firmly developed, but even taking that into account, it was more fragile than other sixth graders. I noted the familiar deep blue that flashed bright silver, the carrot-orange, the cool, syrupy, porcelain-white, and the requisite pink belying his gender. I'd seen it before, but it had been buried in an ugly malodorous brown that had since grown faint. I hadn't yet figured him out, but I knew he'd taken pills in a suicide attempt, like Betsy.

On the left, between me and Dr. Eisenberg, sat Lynn. As I focused on her, I spasmodically jerked away, causing the conversation to stop abruptly.

"Hunter?" said Dr. Eisenberg.

"Sorry," I said. "Can I use the bathroom?"

This was an old trick I'd first used in elementary school to get away from the odors of the auras that made me shudder, or if I was simply bored.

"Is it an emergency?" she asked.

"Sort of," I admitted. I did feel nauseated.

"Yes, but please go straight there and return right away. I can't have you wandering around. It's the last door on the right when you leave my office."

"Sorry," I said again, as I rose from my chair and evaded Lynn to get to the doorway.

As I walked out, I considered how Lynn's aura sparked a memory. It was desperation. Lynn was on the edge of an abyss. I'd caught a faint glimmer of a cool, slimy, sweaty grey, dominated by a brownish fetid smell. A cyan blue swirled ghostly in the background, a color I recognized in those with musical talent. I recalled Dr. Eisenberg asking her to write a song. Somehow, she recognized that hidden talent—Dr. Eisenberg was indeed highly skilled.

The primary taste and colors reminded me of the Autism Center. After a few minutes of introspection, I finally put two and two together. The locked-in kids reeked of the same despair. I felt horrible for them. They couldn't convey their feelings because they lacked the ability to communicate, even on the most basic level. At least Lynn, Toby, Betsy and the others could talk about their problems. The severely developmentally delayed kids suffered in silence. I understood. I had been just like them.

This insight made me depressed, and I tried to shake the feeling. Perhaps I could alter the auras and heal minds, like I did with bodies. I could become a psychiatrist like Dr. Eisenberg. I pondered this thought for a while in the bathroom stall. Checking my watch, I realized I'd better get back or I might not get released from the group.

I sneaked in and quietly reclaimed my seat, with a brief nod from the doctor. Denise was speaking.

"I went to all my appointments, and my blood tests were all good, but I still don't get my period. Dr. Stonington says I work out too much, but how am I supposed to make the high school team as a freshman if I don't work hard? I need to stay fit, and I can't afford to gain weight, or I won't be good enough. If the coach doesn't let me play, I don't know what I'll do."

I didn't know what she meant by her period, but I understood her wanting to work hard to achieve her goal. Her aura was surprisingly dense, tawny brown with a medium blue shading, a gamey smell, and amber streaks. Though she was thin as a rail, her aura showed unexpected strength. A greyish fume bathed her when she finished her speech, echoing the depressed sentiment.

I missed Dr. Eisenberg's reply, and I kicked myself mentally. I had to remain present, especially here, during what was hopefully my last group session.

We moved on to Suzanne. I wasn't sure what I expected from her aura, but it wasn't this. The same medium blue as Denise, also fairly dense, but with powerful gold and silver, a tenacious orange, and a cold, rancid blackness. My working hypothesis of blackness involved either evil or death, and Suzanne was definitely evil. She was malicious to the rest of the group, and probably to everyone she'd ever met. Yet she had many strong qualities. As far as I could tell from my summer work with Ian, the blue, silver, gold and orange all represented positive traits, like intelligence, creativity, leadership and fearlessness. The other properties reminded me of bullies like Trigger, who'd tried to beat me to death. I was glad she was a girl, although that probably didn't matter much.

It didn't take long for Dr. Eisenberg to stop the discussion, as Suzanne provoked a tirade from the others with a series of personal insults.

"One more comment like that and I'll revoke your conditional discharge, Suzanne," the psychiatrist said quietly, but with a threatening tone that I'd never heard her use.

The cacophony died instantly.

"You need to think about what you are trying to accomplish here, and be prepared next week to interact appropriately," she added, her aura flush with maroon anger.

"All right, that's enough for today," she said, after a pause to let her previous remarks sink in. "Please put your chairs away. And Hunter, stick around a moment, won't you?"

I froze midway between standing and collecting my chair. "Yes. Sure," I said. I hoped it meant good news.

After everyone left, I waited inside the office while she called Mom in from the waiting area.

"Dr. Miller, I think Hunter has made tremendous progress in the past two weeks."

"I think so too," Mom concurred.

"I'd like to meet with him one more time in an individual session next week, and if that goes well, he could follow up in three months, if you agree."

Mom nodded her assent.

"Yes!" I said triumphantly.

"Before you go, can I speak to you about another matter?" she asked.

"Certainly," replied Mom.

"Alone?" said the doctor.

"Of course," agreed Mom.

"Hunter, would you please wait in the waiting room? It won't take long," said Dr. Eisenberg.

"OK, no problem," I said, quite excited about not having to go back.

I waited longer than I'd expected, but I passed the time looking at the auras of the woman behind the desk and the patient that left Dr. Jenkins' office.

When she was finished with her meeting, Mom collected me, and I practically ran to the car. Free at last!

CHAPTER 19

DAD MET us at the door as we arrived home.

"Hunter! How are you?" he greeted.

"I'm doing much better," I told him.

"How's school going?"

"I've caught up with my studies, but I won't be top of the class this year. It's gonna be Patty Owens."

"How about karate?"

I'd forgotten about that. "Oh, Mom, can I start again?"

"I suppose so. We'll have to sign up again. I can call Mr. Nam and ask about it tomorrow. You might be able to go Wednesday."

"Cool!"

During dinner, we discussed my recovery and what happened with Betsy. I asked Dad about his work, but he deftly redirected the conversation. The golden portion of his aura swirled and vibrated, almost making waves, but not quite. He was nearly lying, but hadn't crossed the threshold. It was a very interesting pattern.

I liked talking with my parents, especially while examining their auras. I hadn't felt happiness in a while, and I noticed a dramatic contrast between my daily dreariness and this sense of enjoyment. Accepting Grandpa's death turned my entire life around. Getting out of bed wasn't a chore. I didn't struggle to perform everyday activities like brushing my teeth or eating dinner, and my brain functioned like it had previously.

After all the pain and sadness, I felt a new appreciation for many aspects of my life, particularly the people in it. Allan was always there for me, and I was looking forward to seeing him during karate. I counted Betsy as a new friend. I'd grown closer to Mom during my crisis, and although he hadn't been there, it had been Dad's words that stopped my panic at the critical moment in the woods.

"Turn your emotions into your ally, or they will get the better of you," he'd said.

Without those words, I couldn't have rescued Betsy. If she had died, the blame would have rested squarely on my shoulders, first for fighting with her and driving her to take the pills, then for failing to use my gift to heal her. Dad, and everyone else in my life, had helped me through that dark hour, and I felt gratitude toward all of them.

I still missed Grandpa. However I accepted his absence, and I knew that I'd carry a part of him with me forever.

I went to bed content, and for the first time in weeks, slept comfortably all night long.

*   *   *

I returned from school the next day to find a letter from Ian on the kitchen table. I ripped open the envelope and read it hungrily. It was short and direct, like Ian.

> *Hey mate,*
> *Sorry I had to leave without saying goodbye. Dad heard from one of his friends here in the UK about an opportunity at a magazine that was just too good to pass up. Said it was in the bag. Big increase in pay, lots of benefits, a great new job. But he had to act right away. You missed school for a couple of days, so I didn't get a chance to see you before I left. We moved out so quickly that we hired a service to pack up and ship our stuff. We were living out of a hotel room with a week's worth of clothes and a single camera!*

It was the day after the funeral service for Dad's friend, that lady from the news. You remember Pam Winston? I guess she had a car crash or something. It was sad. Dad was really upset. I think he had a thing for her, and that's part of the reason we took off so quickly. I mean, why not at least wait until the end of the school year?

I really miss you and the gang, but I'm making a bunch of new friends. I hope to visit you sometime and if you are ever travelling overseas, obviously you'll need to stop by jolly old England.

Write me back if you feel like it. It would be great to hear from you.

Your friend,
Ian

I was so excited to hear from my friend that I grabbed paper and pen and scratched an immediate reply.

Dear Ian,

I'm sorry you had to move away. I really miss you too. I doubt I'll be in England any time soon, but I'll let you know if that changes.

I'm sorry to hear about Pam Winston's death. She was nice. It sounds like your Dad lost a friend, and I know what that's like.

I'm going to start karate again with Allan. I'm looking forward to that.

School is the same. At least that kid Kenny hasn't been bothering me recently.

I met your friend Toby. I hope I can talk him into playing chess. Feel free to write me any time!

Your friend,
Hunter

It was lame. Regardless, I sent it without editing. Mom helped me with the envelope and postage. It took a while to reconstruct his return address, because I'd ripped it to shreds while opening the letter. The address was strange, with extra lines of information and a zip code containing letters and numbers. Mom told me to write "Air Mail" on the envelope, although it seemed perfectly obvious to me. How else would it get there, by boat?

We put the letter in the mailbox and pulled up the flag so the postman would know to collect it. I went to bed that night feeling even better than the night before. I had a friend close enough to write me a letter!

*   *   *

Betsy remained absent the next day, so I sat with Allan at lunch and told him about the letter.

"Hey, that's cool," he said. "Sorry to hear about Pam Winston, though. I liked her. She was instrumental in getting Orlando Ryan off the street. I know she was good friends with Mr. Pierce."

"Yeah, it really sucks to have someone die on you," I said.

Allan remained momentarily silent, allowing me to reflect on Grandpa.

"I'm glad you're feeling better, though," he said after a while. "It's important for you to move on."

"I wonder how Betsy is going to do it," I said idly. "Her mother got arrested and sent to rehab."

When Allan's aura burst into a bright fizzing green, I realized I'd divulged private information. Dr. Eisenberg warned us against betraying confidence, and I cringed thinking about what others probably said about me.

"You can't repeat that," I said quickly. "I only know that because I was in the hospital when she found out. Please don't spread any rumors."

"I promise I won't say anything," Allan replied solemnly.

We finished our meals in silence. I could always count on Allan to keep a secret. A sign of a true friend.

*   *   *

In our afternoon classes, I noticed a puzzling pattern. When Miss Burnell asked a question, she called on Patty Owens, Christy Johnson, or maybe Kristen Worthy. Every once in a while she'd ask Allan, Glenn, Charlie, or one of the other girls, but she almost never called on Bob, Davis, Brady, Mickey, or me. I knew Bob and Davis were pretty smart, because they were Mr. Lajoie's Mathlete champions in 6th grade before Allan and I started winning.

With nothing better to do and a full supply of snacks in my pockets, I studied the teacher's aura to determine the cause of this anomaly. I had to tease away the emotions to get to her baseline—a sweet, lemony-white, slithering through a warm, dense, sky-blue that felt vaguely familiar. Where had I seen that before? I turned my mind's eye to Patty, repeating the exercise. Her aura also glowed with light blue as well as several of the other traits. There were key differences, like a darker shade of white, much less gold, and a bronze color that replaced the orange I saw in Miss Burnell's aura, but the overall structure and colors were very similar.

Like Archimedes discovering buoyancy in his bathtub, I felt like standing up and yelling, "Eureka!"

The more two people's auras matched, the closer they were destined to become! I knew this instinctively from the moment I met Grandpa—his aura pulled me toward him like a giant beacon. Allan's aura had many traits similar to mine, as did Rob Friendly. Naturally these were the people to whom I gravitated.

Immediately I questioned my conclusion, as I knew Toby's aura, although weaker, contained the same deep blue. It took me most of the morning to figure out that for the past two months, mine had been stained by abject depression. Instead of being drawn to Toby, I was drawn to… Betsy. Someone close to despair.

Armed with this information, I double checked my break-through by looking at the auras of my other classmates. I focused first on the lighter shade shared by Patty and Miss Burnell. I snacked a bit to provide the necessary energy, then cleared my aura carefully to observe the entire group. Sure enough, Kristen and Christy had the same baseline blue. So did someone behind me. This aura contained pink, indicating it belonged to a male. When I turned around to see the owner, my aura buzzed with a confused green.

It was Bob.

Miss Burnell hated Bob. She never called on him, and she ignored everything he said during class. That didn't make sense.

But, Bob *had* really liked Miss Burnell. Freakishly. The first day of school he humiliated himself trying to get her attention. Somehow Bob reacted to a similarity of their baseline auras, but she didn't have the same response. Perhaps she had another emotion distorting hers, like I had the grey sadness obscuring mine. Maybe there was more to it.

Even so, I knew I'd discovered something with major implications. I wondered for years why I felt so much closer to Grandpa than to my own parents. Their auras were nothing like his or mine. This also explained my discord at the Autism Center, where all of the kids had brownish, frustrated and depressed auras. The smell and taste made me shiver with nausea because of the dissimilarity. But I was autistic too—how could our auras be so different?

I let my brain percolate on this through the afternoon and the bus ride home. I bet the auras held more secrets and power than I could imagine.

CHAPTER 20

MOM SURPRISED me at the door.

"Guess what, Hunter," she said.

Her aura sparkled with soothing butterscotch. I felt the eagerness in her aura, and tried to match it to her facial expression, to no avail.

Taking my silence as an inability to guess, she revealed her secret. "I signed you up for karate! I'll take you myself tonight, but hopefully you can ride with Allan like last year. Isn't that exciting?"

"That's great, Mom, thanks!" I said.

"Get your clothes ready. We'll be eating as soon as Dad gets here. It shouldn't be much longer."

After a nice family dinner, Mom brought me to the *dojo* for practice. I changed in the locker room along with several familiar faces, like Josh Felton and Scott Cerano, who both said hi. Allan was in the gym when I arrived, and I waved at him as Sensei Nam called us to opening bows.

I wore my orange belt, but I was so out of practice that I hid in the back, trying in vain to keep up. I was horrible, but the others didn't make fun of me. They were supportive.

"Hey, good to see you back, Hunter," Josh said. "Don't worry about those kicks, it'll all come back to you fast."

Kim Anders and Nicola D'Onofrio smiled and gave me a thumbs up too.

After the session, Allan met me on the way to the locker room. "Nice job today!"

"I was terrible. I can't do a front kick without falling over," I said dejectedly.

"Hey, I'll help you get back into shape. I know the low belt exercises because I've been helping Sensei Nam."

"Cool!" I said. I'd get to hang out with Allan and learn karate. I secretly wanted to use it on Kenny during gym class.

"Let's meet after school on Tuesdays and Thursdays. You'll come back faster if you practice every day. Besides, I work out anyway and I can show you the cool moves I'm learning for my next level of black belt."

"Awesome!" I agreed.

Mom was talking with Allan's mother about ride-sharing when we came outside. In addition to having us ride to practice together, they agreed that I could work out with Allan five days a week instead of three.

*   *   *

With Betsy still out of school, and my scholastics under control, I focused exclusively on karate. My aggressive training paid rapid dividends. Within a week, my skills rivaled my orange belt counterparts.

The biggest challenge was the *kata*, a complicated series of moves against invisible opponents. The white and yellow belt *katas* had been simple, but as students progressed, the respective forms increased in complexity and vigor. Allan spent several hours on Thursday demonstrating the parries and strikes, putting emphasis on how to stand and how to flow between the moves.

Because of his careful attention to detail, I had no trouble performing the entire routine. I lacked Allan's grace and style, but since I knew the sequence well, I no longer had to hide in the back. On Friday evening, we began with a common session, including calisthenics, warm-up, stretching, and meditation, and then we broke up into individual belt groups. I stood next to Josh during practice, so I became familiar with his aura. It was a warm, medium-blue, with bronze, white, and a few other speckled colors. The clean and salty combination contrasted with a sweaty smell, but that might not have been his aura. We were exercising intensely.

Ian's voice reminded me to note Josh's physical appearance, which was similar to mine, except his skin was black. He was tall, scrawny, and gangly, but his muscles well-toned. One major difference between us was during physical contact. My aura fizzed with a sticky red when I had to touch others, but neither Josh nor the rest of my classmates experienced any such discomfort. I never understood why I found physical contact so torturous, but I assumed it related to my autism. Being different made me… different.

After our breakout group work, Sensei Nam called us together.

"We have a demonstration today," he said. "Mr. Marks, front and center!"

Allan took his position in front of the group, and bowed to Sensei Nam. Then Allan began a complicated series of moves including punches, kicks, spins, parries and blocks that were so physically challenging that I knew I could never execute such things. Some of them reminded me of Master Jung, the seventh degree black belt who'd done a demonstration last year. We all applauded when, after a series of triple kicks, Allan landed in a crouching posture with one knee on the floor, the other leg bent, and both hands held palm-forward on either side of his body.

"That was absolutely amazing!" I told him as we were getting changed. "I could never do anything like that in a million years."

"Try seven. Remember, I've been at this a while. Besides, I don't stop every few months to break for insanity, depressive episodes or suicide attempts."

He was only partially kidding, but then he grabbed me by the head and pulled me into a quick hug.

He was right, though. I'd spent most of my life either institutionalized, recently released, or on the verge of re-entry. However, karate made me feel like I was finally on the path to normalcy.

*   *   *

Dad set up the speed bag Allan had given me for my birthday, and we practiced over the weekend. Dad's aura glimmered with the same medium blue as Josh's, but it was much colder, sharper, and laced with gold and tiger-orange. Hidden in the recesses of the colors and textures lurked an ominous black. I'd learned to associate black auras with evil people, but seeing it in Dad's aura assured me that "evil" wasn't the proper interpretation. That color combination reminded me of Suzanne Potter from group therapy, but in her case, the black *did* seem evil.

I'd seen Dad's shade of blue a number of times. Obsessed with trying to discern its meaning, I spent Sunday night making a list of people with that baseline color. In addition to Dad, Suzanne, Josh, and Sensei Nam, the list included Kenny Logan, Master Jung, Denise from group, and, unless my memory was tricking me, Tommy Lachance. I hadn't seen him in over two years, but I had studied his aura, and I was pretty sure he belonged on the list.

I tried to make sense of the names. Three of the group were karate black belts, and two were bullies. Suzanne was a girl, and Josh reminded me of myself, except with a medium blue aura. One was my father!

Neither Allan nor Mr. Jani, the other black belt at our *dojo,* were on the list, so being highly skilled at karate couldn't be the defining characteristic. I didn't know anything about my instructors, or, for that matter, Dad. Perhaps they were all bullies when they were younger?

Kenny and Tommy were surely bullies. But I vividly recalled Trigger, Tommy's number two, and his aura contained no blue whatsoever. I reflexively shook at the memory of the huge boy who had punched through the glass window of the administration office in an attempt to decapitate me. The profound black in his aura felt undeniably evil.

But what about the other bullies in Tommy's gang—Simon and Fat Louie? Also Mark Gilbert, and the thugs from Orlando Ryan's posse. None of them shared this blue. But Ryan himself? Yes, I'd forgotten. Orlando Ryan's aura was medium blue. I'd mentally blocked him. He certainly qualified as a bully, abusing his wife and using his position as a police officer to run a prostitution ring for money.

I tried to put pieces together, like gold, black and medium blue, which was Dad, but also Tommy Lachance and Suzanne Potter. Without the black, it was Kenny Logan, Sensei Nam, Master Jung and Josh. I tried mixing traits like coldness, tiger-orange, and sharpness, but no matter how I recombined the different attributes, it always ended up nonsense. The only conclusion that I could draw was medium blue had something to do with a knack for fighting. Most of the group fought with their fists, but Suzanne fought with words.

Perhaps that was it?

I missed Grandpa so much at this moment. I needed someone in whom I could confide. After all this time, and despite my "acceptance" of his death, I still didn't entirely believe he was gone.

I fell asleep fending off the oily brownish stench of depression.

CHAPTER 21

BETSY RETURNED to school the following Monday. Outwardly, she showed no evidence of her suicide attempt and hospitalization. She smiled at me in gym class, but I didn't get to talk to her. The boys started wrestling, another sport in which I had absolutely zero interest, and the girls were doing gymnastics on the other side of the gymnasium.

My next lesson was math, leaving me the opportunity to ignore the didactics and consider Betsy's life. Her parents had divorced, her mother turned to alcohol, and her father left. I never saw her mom's aura, but it probably reeked of the brownish gunk of depression. Her house was a pigsty, and Betsy was abandoned like the trash lining its floors. She had no friends or family, and the one person she trusted shoved her into a table instead of allowing intimate contact. No wonder she tried to kill herself.

Then there was me. I had two parents who loved me. I knew because of the purple coloring. They provided me with anything money could buy—new books, nice clothes, a great watch, an expensive bike, karate lessons, and a beautiful home in which to live. I had friends like Allan who stayed by me through thick and thin. What right did I have to be depressed?

Yet Grandpa's death had nearly destroyed me. I'd spent months wallowing in self-pity, wondering how I could continue to live. It was truly surprising that I hadn't caused permanent damage to my life or to my relationships. Perhaps I had and didn't realize it. The period ended, and the tromping feet of mass exodus jolted me back to awareness.

Lunch break provided my first opportunity to speak with Betsy. I looked quizzically at Allan as we walked together toward the cafeteria.

"Is it OK if I sit with Betsy?" I said.

"Yes, go!" he said, clearly understanding my need to see her. "I'll catch you later at karate," he reminded.

As I approached the back table, I focused on Betsy's aura, hoping to identify any changes since the last time we'd been together. I braced myself for the horrid taste of despair.

Forearmed, I parried the greyish morass of depression and focused on her baseline colors, truly experiencing them for the first time. Absent the repulsive components, I drank in the sensations around her in as much detail as possible, teasing away any rapidly changing emotions.

The primary component was a trusting/dependent orange. It was the trait I'd exploited in Simon, the bully pack member from two years ago, making him confess something he hadn't done. Interspersed lay a loose, cloudy, gritty brown, with layers of light-blue and silver. The stench covered a clean cinnamon flavor. Dangerous vibrations ensconced in the greyish unhappiness made me nervous, but there wasn't any black. Although I knew the color wasn't evil, I thought its presence was related to her prior suicidality. While its density had improved, her aura still lacked the fullness of the other kids around us.

A burst of sunny, lemony happiness smothered the grey, and I opened my eyes to find her clambering out of her chair toward me.

"Hunter!" she called enthusiastically.

I dodged back slightly as she approached.

"Don't worry, I'm not going to kiss you," she said. Her aura wavered as if she were telling a white lie, like Dad's had done when I asked about his work. That threw me for a loop.

"You're staring, cut it out!" she said.

"Oh sorry," I said. "How're you doing?"

"Actually, much better. My Dad came home, which is nice, but he brought his new girlfriend, which is awkward, to say the least. He was so revolted by the state of the place that he hired professional cleaners to fix it up. He complains all the time because he pays for Mom's rehab. But it's still nice to have him back."

"That's good," I said.

"How about you? How're you doing? You going to group this afternoon?"

My mood brightened. "No!" I said excitedly. "I mean, I don't have to go anymore. Dr. Eisenberg released me because I'm better."

"Oh," she said, the greyness returning in full force.

"I brought my lunch over. Can we sit down and eat?" I asked, hoping to assuage my own guilt. I was making her depressed.

"Yeah, sure," she said glumly.

The greyish stink from her aura made me lose my appetite. Then a thought struck me. I'd spent years healing myself in a variety of ways. I practiced all the time on my self-inflicted lacerations—all I had to do was eliminate the spicy redness, and *voila,* the cuts were gone. What would happen if I removed Betsy's malodorous gunk? Perhaps I could eliminate her depression the same way I'd fixed Grandpa's knees.

It was a fantastic idea. I'd need calories, but fortuitously, it was lunch time. I crammed my peanut butter and jelly sandwich into my mouth and sidled up to Betsy while she chewed silently. It was best to be as close as possible for this to work.

As I had done earlier, I dissected her aura thoroughly, this time locating the depressing colors and tastes and squeezing them away. I knew immediately it worked, because as she started speaking, her voice changed from a dull, unhappy mourning into a chipper song.

"I still have to go, and I probably won't get out of there for the rest of the year at the earliest. I'll have to listen to Suzanne bitch about how she's so much better than the rest of us, and… hey, do you feel that?"

I knew exactly what she felt—depression being lifted away from her aura. My own aura responded with satisfied happiness and relief. I wished I could take the credit, but I couldn't do so without exposing my ability.

"Feel what?"

"I don't know," she said. "The world just feels lighter somehow."

"Maybe it's your turkey sandwich?" I suggested. "I always feel better when I eat."

"Maybe," she agreed. She went on to tell me how things weren't so bad after all. I smiled, gratified with the results of my newest skill.

⋆　　⋆　　⋆

Later, I took the bus to Allan's house so we could go to karate together. Although it had been several hours, I was still unable to contain my exuberance.

"What's got you all revved up?" he asked.

I deflated as I realized I couldn't explain the reason behind my triumphant attitude. I invented a suitable lie, quivering as my aura waved with deceit.

"I'm happy to be done with group therapy," I said, trying to sound convincing.

"Yeah, must have been a real pain in the butt. You seem much better, though."

I nodded my agreement.

"How's Betsy?" he asked.

"Um, good," I said.

"Are you sure your newfound happiness has nothing to do with her?"

"What do you mean?" I said defensively.

"Easy, gunner. She seems nice, and she's the first girl you've ever talked to without fumbling all over yourself. She's good for you."

"How...why...wha..." I stumbled stupidly.

"It's OK, buddy," he reassured, patting me lightly on the shoulder. He knew not to get too close. Such a good friend.

We spent the afternoon goofing around, and they fed me dinner.

His Mom dropped us off at karate with a goodbye wave, and we went to the locker room to change. Josh arrived and came over to use the locker next to mine.

"Hey, Josh, this is my friend Allan. He's a black belt," I said.

"I know," he replied. "You're really good," he said to Allan.

"Thanks," Allan said, shaking hands with Josh.

"He's been helping me prepare for the green belt test," I added.

"Wow, that's so cool!" Josh said. "Maybe you could help me with breaking stuff. I always worry that I'm gonna hurt myself on the wood."

"The key is to punch through. You won't hurt your hand if it ends up on the other side of the plank," Allan said.

"I know that in my head, but I'm still afraid," Josh admitted.

"C'mon, we'd better get out there," I said.

"Yep, don't want to be late," Allan agreed.

At the end of practice, Sensei Nam announced that belt tests started next week. I hadn't tried breaking boards yet, though this was a requirement for advancement. Unlike Josh, I wasn't concerned about getting hurt, because I could easily heal myself. I was worried about failure.

Allan saw the consternation in my face as we left the gym for Mom's car.

"You worried about the test?"

"Yeah. I think I have the moves down, thanks to you. But we have to break two boards, one with a punch and one with a kick. I missed all of the sessions on breaking stuff. What if I can't do it?"

"Not to fear, I am here!" he said with a confident smile, opening the car door to allow me inside. We both sat in the back.

"All set?" Mom asked.

"Yeah," I answered.

"Why so morose?" she said.

"He's worried about the belt test next week. But it's no big deal," Allan said.

"No big deal for you, you can break bricks," I complained.

"I already told you the secret. You have to strike through. We can practice on the bag in your garage later this week."

"Ok," I said, unconvinced.

*   *   *

I had an appointment with the psychiatrist Tuesday after school that was supposed to be a quick visit, but she was running late, so Mom and I were forced to sit in the waiting room for almost an hour. When we finally got called inside, Dr. Eisenberg's aura buzzed with discord.

"Sorry to keep you waiting so long," she said.

"No problem, you're obviously busy," Mom replied.

I told her about resuming karate classes, catching up in school, and Dad returning home. I mentioned Betsy briefly, but didn't speak about my efforts to squash the discolorations from her aura.

"Sounds fantastic, Hunter. I think we made the right decision. Let's have one more session in a few weeks, and if all is well, you won't have to see me anymore unless something changes. Sound good?"

"You bet!" I agreed, far too enthusiastically.

*   *   *

Allan came over after dinner, and as promised, he spent two hours showing me how to focus while striking.

"Watch me," he said. "The bag isn't going to move until after I hit it, but once I make contact, it starts to push in the direction of the strike." He stood on his left leg and cocked his right and kicked slowly, touching the bag slightly and then pulling his leg back. The bag barely budged.

"Now, when I kick for real, I'm not aiming at the first point of contact," he showed me again with a soft, fake kick. "I'm focusing the force well past, so when my leg is here," he kicked slowly through the bag, "I'm still building up energy rather than letting it fizzle out. Now watch full speed."

He swung his leg and the bag went flying, just like when Dad hit it.

"See where my leg ends up after the kick?"

He did it again, and I saw how far past the bag his leg traveled before the bag returned.

"That's where your focus needs to be."

I tried several times, but I didn't have the strength to move the bag in the same way.

"You're getting there," he encouraged. "Let's try it with a punch."

I followed his lead and struck the bag again with my fist.

"No, you're hitting the bag where it is, not where it's going to be," he said.

He punched again, and I saw how his fist, like before with his foot, continued well past the point where it initially hit the bag.

"Now you," he said.

This time when I struck, the bag moved much further.

"YES!" Allan said. "You've got it!"

We repeated the lesson with kicks, and although it wasn't quite as successful, I still felt like I'd made major progress. It was another week before my test, and Allan was sure I could pass. I wasn't entirely convinced, but at least now I had a chance.

"Allan's mother's here," Mom yelled into the garage.

"Thanks!" I said fervently. "I'd never be able to do this without you."

"What are friends for?" he replied, grabbing his bag and heading to the door. "See you tomorrow."

"Thanks again," I said, nodding.

He went out and Mom walked in. "Practice going well?" she asked.

"Yeah… he's teaching me how to punch through."

"Show me," she said.

"All right," I said proudly.

I went to the bag and blasted it with my fist, focusing on the far side of the bag. Then, for good measure, I kicked like I'd been taught.

"Very good!" she said. "You'll get your green belt next week for sure."

"Thanks, Mom," I said.

"You'll have to show your father when he gets back. He had to go on a business trip for a few days... he won't be gone quite as long this time, though."

I felt the raspberry irritation in my aura reacting to the waves in Mom's. I really wish she'd tell me the truth.

CHAPTER 22

IN GYM class on Wednesday, I was paired with PJ Wasciewicz for wrestling. His aura was dominated by a fearless orange, and supported by traits I identified as warmth, generosity and leadership. Bright yellow happiness danced frequently with the baseline colors, and he smiled a lot. I didn't know him well, but he never picked on me.

Physically, he was six inches shorter than me but stocky, and we weighed about the same. Mr. Groves said that wrestlers were matched by weight regardless of strength, and PJ could pick me up off the ground like I was a sack of flour. I had no chance.

I learned in our first match that once I was pinned to the mat, the contest was over. Given my distaste of physical contact, I wished to avoid a prolonged bout. So from then on, the moment the whistle sounded, I sprawled my body flat and face-up such that PJ only had to lay on top of me briefly and I was pinned. By the third time, he put his hands on my shoulders briefly and then let me up.

"Not much for wrestling, are you, Hunter?" he asked.

"I really don't like people touching me," I said.

He nodded. "No problem. I'd like to practice the moves on somebody though. Do you mind if I switch partners?"

"Not at all," I said. I could fake wrestle anyone.

The first pair we encountered was Glenn King and Alan Paul. Both boys outweighed PJ by fifty pounds, so we kept moving. Bob Deluca was wrestling Allan, Mickey Murphy tangled with Brady Patrick, and Mike Giovanni and Kenny Logan were paired together. We stopped at Mike and Kenny. Mike was very close in build to PJ, short and stocky. Kenny was pinning him as we got there.

The whistle blew again. "Change up! Whoever was down is now up, and vice versa," came the call from Mr. Groves, who was on the other side of the gym working with the girls.

PJ approached the pair. "Hey, Mike, do you mind switching?" he asked.

"Let me have one more crack at Kenny," Mike answered. "I'm up this time," he said to Kenny, who obliged by getting down on all fours.

"Get out of the way," Kenny barked.

The whistle blew and we watched Kenny grab Mike's hand and twist it back, then swing his legs around and completely reverse their positions. His momentum propelled Mike hard onto his back, making him grunt loudly. Mike tried to flex his legs, but Kenny caught him with both arms behind Mike's legs, and pinned him to the mat. It was over almost as quickly as it started.

"Wow, nice!" commented PJ.

"You guys didn't go," Kenny said. "Let's see what the retarded dork can do."

The whistle blew again. "Switch!"

This time, Kenny and Mike watched us.

I got on all fours, and when the whistle blew, I used my flop technique and PJ landed on top of me. I slapped the mat indicating a pin, and PJ jumped off quickly.

"What is that, Polish wrestling?" Kenny scoffed.

"What do you mean?" PJ asked.

"Ha!" Kenny said. "The retard turned over and pinned himself! Like a Polack."

PJ's normally happy aura steamed red. Despite giving up several inches in height and a few pounds, he sprang toward Kenny like a runaway freight train, driving his arms into Kenny's chest. He shoved him so hard that Kenny flew backwards, landing in a heap near Mickey and Brady, who both jumped out of the way. Kenny rose slowly, making a show of dusting himself off.

"Do you have any idea what you just did?" he said menacingly.

"Bring it on, big boy," said PJ.

Kenny covered the distance to PJ in three strides, then launched himself like a rocket. PJ anticipated this and ducked into a crouch. At impact, PJ gave ground, went down onto his back and extended his legs, using the other boy's momentum to catapult him high into the air. This time, although Kenny's body landed on the corner of the mat, his head struck the hard, wooden gym floor with a loud "thunk."

The whistle blew again. Mr. Groves appeared. "What's going on?" he called.

"PJ and Kenny were wrestling and Kenny hit his head," Mike said.

"Is that right?" the gym teacher asked.

I saw waves tumbling over all three boys as they hastily agreed to the blatant lie.

"Are you OK?" the teacher asked Kenny.

"Fine," he spat.

"I thought I paired you up with Mike," Mr. Groves said to Kenny.

"Oh, yeah, that's my fault. I wanted to switch," said PJ.

"You were paired with… oh, I see," he said, looking at me. His aura emitted a salty, fuzzy murmur. "OK, Mike and PJ, you can pair up for now. Kenny, why don't you and Hunter take a break. You two can pair up next time."

He blew his whistle again and spoke to the class as a whole. "Five more minutes. Switch again!"

He waited a few moments and blew the whistle again. Mike and PJ went at it, as did the other pairs. I stood with Kenny, whose aura crackled with sharp maroon. He was pissed.

"So now I gotta wrestle the retard?" he said, after Mr. Groves was out of earshot.

Mr. Groves returned after everyone else started wrestling again and looked at Kenny's head.

"Are you OK? That's gonna swell up. Why don't you go to the nurse's office and get some ice?"

"I told you, I'm fine," Kenny said again bitterly.

"Just the same, why don't you call it quits for today. You don't mind, do you Hunter?"

I shook my head. I was perfectly happy not wrestling Kenny.

The period ended, and I went back to Miss Burnell's room, where she'd set up an experiment. She rolled a series of balls down a ramp, using variations in the height and slope of the ramp. I'd read the chapter and knew the equations, so I didn't bother paying attention. I passed the time studying auras instead.

I couldn't wait for lunch, as I looked forward to seeing Betsy again. I'd sat with Allan yesterday, and only waved at her from our table. I wanted to experience her aura without the greyish slop. I knew her baseline, and since I understood her personality, I thought I'd be able to distinguish the meanings of her different colors and textures.

Once released, I bolted to the cafeteria, making my way quickly to the far side where Betsy sat. I sought her aura amid the half dozen kids at her table. The taste and smell froze me in my tracks. I couldn't believe it. Instead of the pretty periwinkle blue or the blazing orange, all I could sense was a greyish brown stench. I felt yellow streaks cascade briefly through the stink when she saw me, but the overriding discordant sadness remained.

"What's going on? Are you OK?" I asked.

"Same as always," Betsy replied. "You?"

There were no waves—she wasn't lying.

"But I thought…," I started. I had to stop when I realized what I was going to say. I clearly hadn't healed her depression.

"That's your mistake," she said. Seeing my confusion, she explained her witticism. "Thinking. That's your mistake."

I had no idea what she was talking about.

"Never mind. How was your karate class?"

"Great!" I said, relieved by the change of topic. "I'm testing for green belt next week. Allan's helping me. I have to learn how to break two boards with a front punch and a side kick."

I tore into my sandwich and listened to her talk without hearing a word. What had happened? I was sure I'd completely removed her depression on Monday. It had returned as though I hadn't done a thing.

I ate my lunch, puzzling over what I might have done wrong. Rejuvenated by the calories, I reached into her aura and squished away the smelly grey goop. When the orange shined brightly, she looked at me and gasped.

"There it is again!" she said.

Despite my aura pouring waves, I acted surprised and confused. "There's what?"

"It's a *deja-vu* feeling. I don't know. I feel different. Better. Same as Monday."

"Great!" I said, truly enthusiastic. I must have corrected whatever mistake I'd made.

"I think it's you," she said.

My own aura soured and I tasted my peanut butter sandwich again. Had she figured out my secret?

"Drink your milk," she said, noticing my expression.

I obliged.

We finished our lunch, and I was relieved that she didn't discuss further what had happened. I relished in the thrill of having helped my friend. I didn't know why her aura reverted to the ugly sprawling grey, but I was sure that this time, I'd truly fixed it.

✳   ✳   ✳

I took the bus home and met Mom in the doorway as I entered the house.

"How was school today?" she said.

The episode from gym class replayed in my head.

"What's a Polack?" I asked in reply.

"Where did you hear that?"

"A kid at school called me one."

Mom's aura flared angrily. "It's a very impolite slur. Please don't ever use that word again."

"But what's it mean?"

She stared at me. "It's slang for someone of Polish descent, and the implication is a lower level of intelligence," she said dryly.

"Are Polish people different from others?"

"Not at all."

"Then why would he call me a Polack?"

"Why indeed," she answered. We sat in silence for a few minutes, pondering the reason.

"Mom?"

"Yes?"

"Why would my friend PJ be angry at Kenny for calling me a Polack?"

"What's PJ's last name?"

"Wasciewicz," I said.

"That's a Polish name."

Mom stared at me. I thought for a few moments.

"Oh, I get it," I said, nodding my head.

I understood quite well. Kenny was a jerk who didn't care who he hurt. No wonder I didn't like him.

CHAPTER 23

WEDNESDAY'S KARATE practice began with bows, warm-up, stretching, calisthenics, and drills. Then Sensei Nam announced that all belts higher than yellow would practice breaking techniques.

By way of demonstration, Allan crashed through six boards at once with a flying side kick. The crowd gasped with amazement. Another black belt, Mohinder Jani, whirled and kicked a board almost two feet over his head.

Finally, Sensei Nam stood in the midst of four upper belts, each of whom held boards at varying heights in front, back, and on both sides of him. He struck four times, with his head, elbow, fist and foot, splintering all the wood around him in under a second.

We broke into applause, unable to contain our admiration.

"Now, form up by rank!" he said, and we assembled ourselves into groups. The three black belts, Allan, Mohinder, and the Sensei, distributed themselves among us, demonstrating the proper strikes required for each of our advancement tests.

"Cool!" said Josh, who had been worried about the test and wanted to practice breaking boards. At that moment, our instructor appeared with a dozen boards.

"You first," said the dark-skinned man, pointing at Josh. We usually called him Mo, but since he was acting as our instructor, we had to call him Mr. Jani, or sir, as a sign of respect.

"Yes, sir, Mr. Jani," said Josh, making no mistake, as he did not want to do push-ups before breaking the boards.

The black belt then waggled his finger at Kim, one of my classmates, who jumped to attention, bowed nervously, and approached.

"You hold firmly, like this, Ms. Anders," Mo said, showing Kim the proper technique. Then, he picked up another board and held it at a forty-five degree angle to Josh, setting up for the second strike.

"Ready?"

"Yes, Mr. Jani," said Josh.

"Begin!"

Josh took a few moments to collect himself, then punched the board held by Kim. His fist collided with a dull thud, but the board didn't break.

"Continue!"

Josh struck with his foot, and this time, the board broke easily.

"Remember to punch through. OK, next. You!" he said, pointing to me.

"Yes sir!" I said, hopping quickly into position.

"Mr. Felton, your turn to hold. Mr. Miller, are you ready?"

"Yes," I said. They held the boards exactly as before.

"Begin!" he commanded.

I punched through the first board easily, my fist going so far that I nearly hit Josh. I continued as Allan had showed me, and kicked through the second board held by Mr. Jani.

"Good!" he said. "Your turn to hold. Remember to hold firm."

I held the next board as Kim tried to break. She failed on both attempts. I felt bad, but there was nothing I could do about it, so I took my seat. Kim held for her friend, Nicola, who broke both boards easily, as did Scott, the other orange belt. We rotated through until everyone had a second chance, and I succeeded again with both strikes, as did Josh, Nicola and Scott. Kim, however, simply couldn't do it. Her hand was red from impacting the board.

Mo made her try again, but I could see she had no chance. Her aura sagged. The third time was not the charm, despite Mo's quip that it would be.

"Must be some bad boards. You know, knots or something," Josh said, his aura covered in waves. He was obviously hoping to make Kim feel better.

Mo tossed each up in the air, breaking them in half before they hit the ground.

"Boards are fine," he concluded, picking up the pieces from the floor. So much for preserving feelings.

We moved on to one-step moves, then finished up with a group warm-down and final bows. On our way to the locker room. Josh, Scott and Nicola gave each other high-fives, all feeling relatively confident about the upcoming test. I was also excited. Green belts began sparring, which was sure to be fun, as long as nobody tried any wrestling moves on me.

"How'd it go?" Allan asked, as we got changed.

"Great!" I said. "I broke both boards twice, no problem."

"Good job. How are you with the *kata*?"

"I think I have it down. And we went over the one-steps today, so I should get my green belt before Thanksgiving!"

"That's cool. Do you mind if I don't come over tomorrow? My Mom wants me to help clean the house because we have relatives coming next week."

"OK," I said.

"Besides, you've got this. You don't need any more extra help."

His Mom arrived, and she drove us home. Allan said he'd see me at school, and I went in and told Mom about the session. She was excited for me and reassured me that I'd pass the test.

I finished my eventful day by reading several chapters of an Isaac Asimov novel, then went to bed.

*   *   *

The major upside to Thursday was that we didn't have gym, which meant no wrestling. The downside was that we had French class, which I despised. I'd never caught up from my three year deficit, as everyone else started French in first grade. Losing the better part of two months as a result of my battle with depression didn't help. I was bombing.

M. Poirer wasn't particularly nice about it, either. He called on me periodically, though I never raised my hand, and forced me to speak in French. He inevitably responded with the same refrain.

"No, no, *NO!*"

He then criticized my accent, pronunciation, and effort. It was like a game.

Meanwhile, Glenn and Amy could have a fluent conversation in French, while the teacher listened in ecstasy to his native language spoken properly. I couldn't wait until ninth grade, when French would no longer be a requirement.

Still, this was better than wrestling, a sentiment I shared with Allan on the way to lunch.

"Yeah, I'm no good at French either," he confessed. "But what's so bad about wrestling?"

"I don't like people touching me," I said.

He nodded. "Some of the best martial arts involve wrestling moves though. Like *jiu jitsu*. It's more grappling than kicking. Same with judo and *hapkido*."

"Well, I'm sticking with karate. I don't mind punching someone, but I really hate the idea of grabbing."

We both sat down at a table near the cafeteria entrance after procuring milk from the line. I looked across the room at Betsy, and focused on her aura, which had reverted to the same as before. She waved at me, and I waved back, trying to hide my shock and dismay.

"Yeah, I get it," Allan was saying. "You've always been like that. Makes sense. Hey, how's Betsy doing? How come you didn't go over to her table?"

I shuddered slightly with guilt.

"She always seems depressed, no matter what I do."

"I don't know," Allan said. "She perks up around you. I think she likes you."

"How come she never comes over to sit with us at lunch then?" I asked.

Allan pointed to Brady, Bob, Mickey and Don, all of whom sat around our table. "Would you approach these guys if you were a girl?"

"Bring on the girls!" yelled Don.

"Girls! Yes!" echoed Mickey.

Brady made rude gestures and feigned having a large chest.

"Guess not," I conceded. Secretly, I was afraid of that smelly grey aura. Why did it keep coming back? "I'll eat with you today and sit with her tomorrow," I said.

"Cool," he said.

"Hey guys, anyone up for laser tag on Saturday?" Bob said.

The boys erupted with cheers and excitement.

"Hunter, you in?" Allan said to me.

"Yeah, that'd be cool," I replied.

"I'll see if Mom will let me go. My grandparents are arriving on Sunday and staying the whole week, so I have to…" Allan trailed off.

As he stopped, I smelled fear in his aura. I put it together quickly—he was afraid I'd think about Grandpa and lose my mind.

"I miss Grandpa, but I'm OK," I said.

The fear abated. "Yeah, sorry. Anyway, I hope I can go too. I'll let you know tomorrow."

I ate my lunch feeling melancholy, thoughts of Grandpa swirling uncontrollably in my brain.

CHAPTER 24

WHILE I found French annoying, at least it didn't involve people touching me. I was not looking forward to wrestling on Friday. After Kenny and PJ's fight on Wednesday, Mr. Groves kept them far apart. The unfortunate consequence was that I partnered with Kenny again, and this time, the end-of-class bell wasn't going to save me.

After the teacher demonstrated three escape techniques and two head locks, we divided up into our pairs.

"You're gross. I don't want to touch you," Kenny said to me.

"I don't want to touch you either," I replied honestly. "I'll be down first."

"Fine," he said, although nothing about his tone or his aura suggested he was "fine."

The whistle blew, and I flopped onto my back so quickly that he didn't have time to react. He was left standing over me while I behaved like a dog looking to get his belly rubbed.

"What the hell?" he said.

I slapped the mat. "You win."

He stood there, reds and greens swirling in his aura. We waited until the whistle sounded, and I rose from the mat and looked at him. I tried to pick apart the rancid taste, putrid smell and blaring seaweed green from the prickly raspberry annoyance. The odor of bad breath and the salty hum were sensations I'd felt before, but I was unsure exactly what they represented.

I heard a shrill noise and found my legs yanked out from under me. Mysterious arms wrapped around my neck and right thigh, and I belatedly realized that the whistle had blown and the next match had started.

Kenny's aura had engulfed mine, a rather sickening feeling. I yanked it into the void to clear away the disgusting odors, and his body fell limply on top of me.

I used one of the escape techniques Mr. Groves covered earlier, shoving Kenny's lifeless body off me. I sat next to him until the teacher approached. Without thinking, I leapt on top of Kenny, effectively pinning him to the ground.

He blew the whistle.

"Nice job, Hunter!" he praised. His aura murmured a sticky green disbelief. "You pinned him!"

I replaced Kenny's medium blue, filling in holes with spicy redness out of spite.

"Oww!" he yelled, tossing me off. "What happened?"

"Hunter pinned you," said Mr. Groves.

Kenny swore loudly. "This twerp? No way!"

"Office!" said Mr. Groves, pointing to the door. "We don't tolerate that language, Mr. Logan!"

Kenny took a step toward me and found his way barred by the teacher, who redirected him to the exit. "Now, son!"

Kenny gazed in my direction with a facial expression that matched his angry red aura. I nodded, making mental note of the grimace and the colors surrounding him. I'd learned a lot today.

"Take five, Hunter," the teacher said to me. He blew the whistle, and the remainder of the class resumed their grappling. After a few more rounds, Mr. Groves finished class with a few pointers on takedowns. Allan came over as we headed back to change out of our gym clothes.

"What happened?" he asked.

"Kenny swore at me and Mr. Groves sent him to the office," I summarized.

"Sorry, dude. He's a jerk. How come you aren't paired with PJ?"

"Long story."

Mr. Groves called out to the class, "Have a great weekend. See you all Monday!"

I wasn't looking forward to dealing with Kenny next week.

✳   ✳   ✳

I didn't have to wait until Monday, though. After vocabulary and grammar, Allan and I were confronted by Kenny in the hallway near the cafeteria. He wasn't supposed to be in our lunch period, but he appeared anyway.

He cornered us in the corridor, out of sight of the lunch proctor.

"You and me, right now!" he demanded.

Allan inserted himself between us. "Back off!" he threatened.

"Or what? You'll tell your mommy?"

Allan simply glared, unmoving.

"C'mon, wimp! Or does your boyfriend here do all your talking for you?"

"Just move along," said Allan, a hint of malice in his voice.

"Step aside, string bean," Kenny said. He tried to give Allan a shove out of the way, and found himself face-first into a set of lockers, with Allan holding his wrist behind his back.

"Let it go," Allan whispered. He motioned with his head for me to continue on to the cafeteria, so I did. Allan joined me shortly after.

"Making friends, again, are we?" he said.

"It wasn't my fault!" I protested.

"Don't worry, Hunter. I don't think he'll be bothering you anytime soon."

We entered the cafeteria, and I went through the line to get milk. Before Allan went over to sit with the guys, he said, "By the way, my Mom wants me home Saturday, so I'm gonna see if we can go to PlayDate next weekend instead. OK with you?"

"Yeah, cool," I said.

"Good. See you after lunch. Say hi to Betsy."

I nodded and navigated toward the far tables, fearing what Betsy's aura would reveal.

She turned and smiled when I arrived, generating a waft of yellow inside the sea of dingy grey. The depression had returned with a vengeance.

"Hi, Betsy," I said.

"Why so glum?"

It annoyed me that she could interpret my facial expressions as easily as I could read her aura.

I wanted to tell her the real reason I was unhappy—I couldn't heal her depression. That was out of the question, so I revealed something else that bothered me.

"Got into a fight, kinda."

"With who?"

"Whom," I said.

"I don't know," she said, confused.

"Oh, no, I mean it's with whom. You have to use the objective case after a preposition. We covered it in grammar today."

"Excuse me, Mr. Shakespeare. With whom did you enter a tussle?"

I smiled. A joke, and I got it.

"Kenny."

"Oh that *jerk*!" she said. "I hope you kicked his butt!"

"Me?" I said, incredulous.

"You know karate!"

"Allan's the black belt. He did a cool move and shoved Kenny into the lockers. He told me not to worry. I think he said something to Kenny after I left."

"It's wonderful that you have such a good friend," she said. A cold, earthy murmur of jealousy pierced her aura.

"How is the rest of the group? I forgot to ask you the other day," I asked, hoping to change the subject.

"The same. Suzanne's a bitch, Toby is a weenie, Lynn is borderline suicidal and Denise and Kayleigh can't figure out their diets. I don't think the sessions do anything."

"I got better," I said.

"You only had situational depression. I looked it up. See, real depression doesn't get better. You have to deal with it every day. I know you were sad because your grandfather died, but it's not the same thing. People like Lynn, Toby and me, we don't get better. We just get by."

I considered her words carefully and took a few bites of my sandwich so I wouldn't have to say anything. She was right. It explained why nothing I did to her aura ever stuck. The grey clouds returned because they were part of her baseline. What a depressing thought.

"It's all right, Hunter. Don't feel guilty that you're not sick like me."

My face must have been giving away my feelings again, because that's exactly how I felt. I was powerless to fix it.

We ate the rest of our food without further discussion. As the lunch period wound down, I decided to give it one more shot. I reached in, pulled away the grey, and watched her as she suddenly perked up.

"Any plans for Thanksgiving?" she asked.

"I don't know," I said.

"My Dad and his girlfriend are making turkey dinner at my house. He didn't think it would be wise to take me to visit his family in California, although I get the feeling he wants to go. From the moment he left, it's not been the same, you know?"

I didn't know, but I nodded anyway.

"Well, have a good weekend. Lunch Monday?" she asked.

"OK," I said.

"You don't have to if you don't want to," she replied, again seeing something in my face.

"No, it's OK."

"Gee, thanks," she said.

I started getting flustered.

"Hunter, relax. I'm playing with you. I'll see you here Monday. Enjoy your weekend!" she said again.

I wondered if I'd ever understand girls.

CHAPTER 25

FRIDAY'S KARATE practice focused on preparing for the promotion tests. We separated into groups quickly and went over all of the required skills, making sure we had everything down. Allan, who was not testing, spent most of his time with my group. I felt confident, as did Josh and Scott. Nicola worked through the *kata* while the rest of us watched.

"I can't wait to start sparring," said Josh.

"Yeah, it looks like fun when the upper belts do it," agreed Scott.

"I don't think I'm gonna pass," bemoaned Kim.

"Why not?" asked Scott. "You've got the form down pat, and the one steps are easy."

"I can't break the boards," she confessed. She was right. We all knew it.

"Allan told me the key was to punch through," I offered.

"I'm just not strong enough," she said.

Allan had finished with Nicola and overheard Kim's comment.

"It's not about strength, it's about technique," he said. "Watch."

He demonstrated the punch very slowly, snapping his fist at the last instant. "The point at which I make contact is the key. See how my hand is positioned? Make your fist look like this."

She did.

"Now, very slowly and smoothly, and with exactly the same technique, strike at the center of my hand."

He held up his hand, and she punched it.

"No. Hold on. You didn't keep your fist straight. If you don't have the correct technique, it won't work no matter how strong you are. But if you do, it will be fine."

He repositioned her hand and they repeated the process while we all watched. Allan cajoled her each time, making minor corrections. On the sixth try, they both smiled.

"That's it!" Allan said. "Now for the kick. The holder mustn't present an edge, and the grain needs to be correct, so only black belts will hold for the test. We have the hard part. You only need to execute the kick."

He kicked slowly, demonstrating as he had with the punch.

"Now you," he said.

Kim copied him, and they went over it until she performed the strike properly. I watched Allan's blue aura shine brightly, along with several other colors and sensations. Allan usually smelled of cinnamon, but today, I detected a warm, minty flavor that reminded me of Miss Amanda, a woman Mom hired to watch me years ago. Supportive. I nodded internally at the connection.

"OK, Orange belts, great job. Hope you look good in green, because come Monday, you're all going to have a new color to wear!"

We gave ourselves a round of high-fives as warm, fragrant humming emanated from Kim in particular.

"Thanks, Mr. Marks," she said, and the others all echoed her.

"No problem," said Allan. "Make me proud!"

Sensei Nam called the class back together for stretching and bows, and when we left, all five of us felt fully prepared for our impending advancement. I could see the change in our auras, which became enshrined in a solid, clear vanilla with gold flecks. Confidence. My hard work and practice were paying off, both with karate and with reading the auras!

*   *   *

"That was so cool, what you did with Kim," I told Allan as we walked out to his mother's car.

"I like teaching. It's fun."

On the ride home, I bragged to his mother about how he taught our entire group. "You should have seen him, Mrs. Marks. He was awesome!"

"That's my boy," she replied.

I caught a hint of bad breath in her aura, and a salty coolness inside the bright maternal purple. I was completely confused. What were salty coolness and bad smells doing in her aura right now? It made no sense! She should be happy, right? Fritzcloves! My interpretation skills weren't anywhere near as good as I thought.

*   *   *

When I got home, Mom asked me to show her everything, including the form, the one-step moves, and the breaking strikes. She nodded her approval at each one, and I sensed the same salty coolness and odd odor. She was happy for me, though. The bright yellow confirmed it. Frustration mounted, and I couldn't take it.

"How do you feel right now, Mom?" I said.

"Very proud, of course," she answered. "Why do you ask?"

Pride? Salty and stinky? Maybe. I thought stinky things were more like fear or despair, yet pride was a good emotion.

My internal debate raged on, as I heard an external sound.

"Hunter?" Mom repeated.

"Oh, I'm trying to figure out expressions. Since Ian left, nobody is helping me to compare people's facial features to their feelings."

Mom's aura fizzed with several different shades and sensations, creating an unidentifiable complexity.

"Yes, of course," she said. "A common difficulty autistic people face is the inability to recognize non-verbal cues." She paused. "Is that what you're doing when you stare at me?"

"I guess," I said. I didn't know I was staring.

"Interesting," she continued. "We should work on that. I should have realized… I'm sorry I never thought to help you with this. You wouldn't have been able to ask, because it would be normal for you."

She mumbled the last words more to herself than to me.

Her usual purple contained a strong navy-blue which buzzed through a cloud of silver.

I recognized that shade of blue from my classmate Davis. His was nowhere near as thick, nor did it possess any silver. I knew Davis pretty well, but I hadn't figured out that color yet.

"You should come grocery shopping with me tomorrow," she offered. "With Thanksgiving next week, I want to shop before the stores get crowded. I know you don't like being around people, but you can watch them while we shop. You can look at their expressions and try to identify the related feelings. If you have questions, I'll be there to ask."

"Great!" I said. What better person to help read people than Mom? Ian always hid his own feelings, and Mom wouldn't do that. She always told me the truth. Well, as long as we didn't discuss her job, Dad's spying, or who my real father was.

✳   ✳   ✳

The next day at the store, everything started out well. Mom was perceptive, like Ian. She pointed out a girl with puffy eyes, smeared make-up, a downturned face and bowed shoulders. I saw the grey murk smothering her bluish-orange baseline, and easily felt her sadness. I listened with rapt attention as Mom described the physical features that went along with sadness, but once I saw the aura a few times, the physical characteristics took on little importance. I *knew* what she felt.

We saw a couple arguing with one another in the pasta aisle. The raspberry auras gave away their irritation, but again Mom pointed out a dozen little mannerisms that I could never imagine appreciating. Pursed lips, crossed arms, deep frowns, grand head movements, hands placed confrontationally on hips. The raised voices, rattling sour taste, and other sensations blended together in my head. I began having trouble processing all the information.

"Are you all right?" Mom asked.

"Yeah, it's just a lot to take in," I said.

"It's OK, Hunter. We'll stop for today. We can practice whenever we go out. It will help your relationships at school if you can identify what other people are feeling."

I nodded in agreement. She paid for the groceries, and I grabbed a newly purchased apple as we loaded the car.

Mom eyed me appraisingly. "We ate breakfast right before we left."

"Looking at people makes me hungry," I said.

"Is that why you load your pockets with all that junk food?"

I had no idea she knew about that.

"Guilty!" she called out.

I felt a dry, grating chestnut color muddling my blue aura. OK, so that is guilt. But how did *she* know?

"Curious as to how I knew?"

My aura rattled a bluish green curiosity, then rustled with a tart middle green, the color of grass.

"Impressed, are we?" she added.

"YES!" I said. This thirty seconds provided more value than the entire hour we'd spent shopping.

"Well, you wear your emotions on your sleeve," she said.

I looked at my shirt.

"No, Hunter, that's just a metaphor. But that, right there!" she said.

"What?" I asked.

"Your eyes widened, you touched your face right here," she pointed to my eyebrow on the right, "and your mouth opened a little. Also, your face turned a little pale. Those are all signs that you are confused.

"OK," I said.

"And before, when I mentioned loading your pockets, you turned your head away with your chin dipped toward your chest. You didn't want to make eye contact, and your posture drooped, like you didn't want to be discovered. Your face turned a little red there, too, I think, but it was hard to see because you turned away."

This is why Ian always said I was an open book. He could read every single expression, like Mom!

"Wow, Mom, you're really good at this," I said. "I used to think you were reading my mind."

"You should see your father. He's remarkable."

"So why am I so bad at it then?" I asked, not realizing the full ramifications of my question until Mom's aura crackled with a sour rose color. I stared at her face, looking for all of the signs of guilt that she had mentioned, but she demonstrated none of them.

She answered without missing a beat. "Your autism makes it hard for you to recognize emotions, Hunter. It's just part of who you are. Besides, hiding your feelings isn't all that it's cracked up to be. Sometimes I wish people could be honest all the time, like you."

We jumped into the car, and I ate my apple.

She looked at my face, probably seeing the flash of guilt. Thankfully she didn't say anything this time. If she knew about loading my pockets, how many other secrets of mine did she know?

CHAPTER 26

I FELT great heading into school Monday, after spending the weekend relaxing. Mom worked with me on recognition of emotions, and I continued to make progress. When alone, I practiced cutting and healing myself, a skill I hadn't needed recently but wanted to keep sharp.

Miss Burnell's lectures, while dry and uninspiring, didn't dampen my mood, but things changed when I went to gym class. Kenny's sharp maroon bitterness reminded me that all was not well in my world. His aura hissed with chilly grittiness, and I noted the raised chin, flaring nostrils and sweeping hand gestures that Mom taught me to look for to confirm anger.

Fortunately, Mr. Groves kept us far apart, and I wrestled with Mike Giovanni rather than Kenny. I purposefully flopped, but Mike didn't make a big deal out of it, and I made it to lunch without any skirmishes with Kenny.

Betsy's aura had returned to the horrible grey, and I found myself depressed just to see it. Nonetheless, she smiled when she saw me, and the happy canary streaks contrasted brightly with the underlying misery. Despite the futility, I pulled away the grey again while eating, leaving her in much better spirits than when she first saw me. By this point I had no delusions that I could fix her, but

I didn't enjoy being around her when her aura was so discordant with mine.

By late afternoon, I wanted school to be over so badly that I phased out completely. I ran through the moves for the green belt test in my head. My aura vibrated and sizzled with butterscotch anticipation. I put that into the memory bank along with the other sensations I'd learned over the weekend.

When school was finally over, Allan caught me on the way to the bus.

"You ready for the test?"

"Yeah!" I said excitedly.

"Remember that your Mom is taking us tonight, OK? And I have to be back home as soon as it's over."

"Yep, Mom knows."

"Are you nervous?" he asked.

I checked my aura for the green, dry, sizzling and sweaty smell that would suggest nervousness.

"Not really," I concluded.

"Good. There's no reason to be. You'll do fine. I'll see you in a bit," he said, heading off to his own bus.

*   *   *

Mom dropped us off at the *dojo* and promised to return promptly, assuaging Allan's fears.

"You're more nervous than I am," I observed.

"My mom didn't even want me to go tonight. Her parents are visiting and I need to be respectful, she says. I don't know what the big deal is. They're here all through Thanksgiving. I'll have plenty of time with them."

I didn't know how to respond, so I didn't say anything. Instead, we talked about the belt test while getting changed.

After the bows, the white belts began the testing process by performing their *kata*. I recognized it from my own yellow belt test. The new students mostly nailed it, with a few minor mistakes like turning the wrong way between punches. They continued on with their testing, with Sensei Nam issuing a series of commands, which they followed flawlessly. It was clear that they were all going to advance.

The yellows were next, and they were excellent. I could see the crispness in the forms, the increased confidence in the strikes, and the higher complexity of the moves. They too, all appeared to pass with flying colors. I could feel my nervous energy building as Sensei Nam called my section onto the floor.

All five of us lined up in a row, and he called for us to begin. I'd repeated the moves so many times that I didn't need to think. My body flowed freely, and it was over in no time. The entire group performed perfectly. We then went up individually, and when it was my turn, I listened carefully as Allan called out one-steps. I responded with the proper block and strike. Again, my colleagues and I were flawless.

Then came the board breaking, and I could feel Kim's anxiety rise as her aura vibrated with a sour tackiness. Josh went first, with Mr. Jani holding the board for him to punch, and Sensei Nam holding the one for him to kick.

It was over in seconds. Bam, bam! Both boards broken.

"Mr. Miller!" Sensei Nam called. I assumed my place as the black belts picked up fresh boards. "Begin!"

Bam, bam! Two boards broken. I bowed, and the instructor called, "Ms. Anders!"

As Kim walked past me, her aura sizzled so violently with sweaty fright that I knew she was going to mess up. The holders grabbed new boards, and when she was in position, Sensei Nam called out, "Begin!"

Thunk! Her fist hit the unyielding board as though it was a brick wall. Her anxiety and fear morphed into a dry, slate grey disappointment.

"Again!" yelled Sensei Nam, causing the apprehension to resurface in abundance.

I knew she could do it, but not if she was this fearful. I closed my eyes, reached out to her aura and soothed away the unpleasant banging and other aspects of her fears.

Bam, bam!

A collective sigh of relief came from the four of us. She'd done it. We all wanted to applaud, but knew that would get us push-ups, so we kept quiet as Kim returned, smiling, to our group.

"Ms. D'Onofrio!" came the call, and Nicola and then Scott both broke the boards without issue. We'd all passed!

The three green belts trying to advance to blue all performed well. They had considerably more complicated forms and three boards to break. A short girl, whose name I didn't know, missed on the spin kick, but otherwise they all did very well. The five of us rocked back and forth with exhilaration, barely noticing the blue test. I realized how stupid that was the moment they'd finished. We'd have to do the same test for our next belt. Even so, it didn't detract from the relief and excitement we shared.

Time ran out, so the Sensei called us together and congratulated everyone for our wonderful performances. Only then did we receive a round of applause from the upper belts. I noticed Allan as he motioned anxiously with his head for me to get to the locker room. He had to leave. I patted my compatriots on the back and excused myself.

"Sorry, dude, I know you wanted to celebrate."

"It's OK," I said, getting dressed quickly.

"Good job, though," he added.

"Thanks."

Mom was waiting in the parking lot. "Congratulations!" she said immediately.

"I passed!" I said, belatedly realizing that she'd already congratulated me.

"I had no doubt," she replied.

"How did you know?" I asked.

"High chin, laughing with wide smile, sparkling eyes and you practically ran out the door. All signs of success."

"Nice!" commented Allan.

"Yeah, Mom's helping me like Ian did."

"That's very cool, Mrs. Miller."

"Thank you, Allan. I like to be thought of as 'very cool.'"

Mom drove Allan home as I recapped the testing procedure. We dropped him off and said our goodbyes. Mom put the car in reverse and I sat back in my seat, while Allan walked toward his house. I had a good feeling that things were finally starting to go my way.

CHAPTER 27

THE GOOD feeling passed immediately. Before we pulled out of Allan's driveway, I sensed a thumping danger and another aura, banging with agitation and blackness. Someone else was out there, and with bad intent. It reminded me of the time I was attacked by the three thugs downtown.

But this was a suburban neighborhood. What could happen here?

As Mom put the car in gear and pulled away, I reached out for Allan's aura. He had been heading toward his front door, but never made it out of the driveway. I jolted in my seat as spicy redness splashed over his pristine blue.

"STOP!" I yelled.

Mom slammed the brakes and the tires screeched the vehicle to a halt, only a few hundred feet from Allan's house.

"What is it?" she said.

A motorbike fired up its engine and sped off, the lone rider a blur in the dark night. I didn't get a feel for the aura that occupied the seat, but it had been the source of the blackness I'd felt immediately before.

"Take us back to Allan's!" I yelled.

Mom obliged, returning the car to the driveway. I undid my

belt and leapt out of the car, plunging through the darkness toward the damaged aura that belonged to my best friend. I heard Mom's car door slam as I found Allan, with blood pouring from the back of his head.

I had no idea what to do. Light silhouetted several people in the house's doorway who'd been drawn by the screeching of Mom's brakes. Allan's mother emerged, calling out, "Allan? Is that you?"

Mom's aura exploded in shock and disbelief. She shoved me out of the way and put her finger on Allan's neck.

Satisfied with the strength of Allan's pulse, she ran her hands over his head. The blood, along with something else she felt, made her aura bang loudly.

Allan's mother appeared beside us, rattling with a confused olive green. "What's going on?" she asked.

"Call 911," Mom said. "Your son's been attacked by a mugger," she said.

Mrs. Marks ignored the request. "What?" she cried. She bent down onto her knees and looked at Allan's limp body.

"Oh my god!" she yelled. "Help! Help!"

"Go in the house and call 911," repeated Mom. She was remarkably calm. I was completely freaked out, as was Allan's mother.

"Hold your hand here," Mom said to me, indicating the wounded area on the back of his head. "We need to stop the bleeding."

Mrs. Marks was paralyzed with fear, and her aura reeked. Mom stood up and spoke directly into her face. "I'm going inside to use your phone to call 911."

Allan's mom collapsed next to him on the ground, and she began blubbering incoherently and grabbing at his bloody head while I pressed on the wound.

Stop the bleeding, Mom had said. What was I thinking? I *knew* how to stop bleeding. I took a deep breath, accessed Allan's aura, and squished away the spicy redness. There was more damage than a simple cut, however. Something happened inside his head that was much worse than anything I'd ever experienced. I felt Mom's aura returning as I swept away the cloudy mess from his brain. Fortunately, I knew Allan's aura very well, so it didn't take long to return it to the normal state.

"Ambulance is on the way," Mom said.

Allan stirred. His mother continued crying, her head on Allan's chest.

"Hold his neck still," Mom said urgently. "There could be a fracture."

There was no fracture. Even if there had been, I would have healed it. I felt a different tingling sensation, another danger. Mom had felt the cut and the lump on Allan's head. I took it away completely. Plus, there was blood everywhere. It would be obvious that I'd done something to fix Allan if there wasn't a scratch on him!

Reluctantly, I popped open a medium sized cut, and raised a lump around it by adding the proper redness and cloudiness to Allan's aura. I kept the brain clear, though, fearing the opaque blotch caused by the attacker's blow.

"What happened?" said Allen.

"Just relax and sit still. Someone hit you on the head," Mom said.

"Are you OK, baby?" said his mother, her words barely discernable amidst her sobs.

Allan reached up to feel the lump on his head, and made contact with my hand instead.

"Hunter?" he said.

"Yeah, I'm here," I said.

"Are you OK?" repeated his mother.

"Yeah, Mom, I'm all right. Just a little bump."

"I think the bleeding stopped," I said.

"Really?" Mom said. She didn't believe it.

"Yeah, I think so," I insisted. She looked at my face, confused.

Allan rubbed his head.

"Wait, you'll make it bleed again," Mom said. "Hold still and we'll let the medics take a look before we do anything else."

*   *   *

I felt Paramedic Phil's aura as he jumped out of his ambulance and joined us next to Allan.

"Hi, I'm Phil," he said, gazing at Mom, who shook his hand.

"Marissa Miller. This is Abigail Marks, and her son, Allan. He's been struck in the back of the head with a blunt object causing a laceration and brief loss of consciousness. The bleeding is controlled right now."

"Thanks, ma'am," Phil said. He looked at me.

"And this is my son, Hunter," Mom added.

"I thought you looked familiar. Hard to see in the poor lighting," he said quickly. Then he moved to a position behind Allan, donning plastic gloves.

"So, Allan, do you remember what happened?"

"No," Allan said. "I was walking into the house and something hit me in the back of the head, and the next thing I knew, I was here on the ground with blood all over the place and a huge lump back there."

"Any neck pain?"

"No," Allan said.

Phil asked several other questions and felt Allan's head and neck, then put a gauze dressing over the cut. He wrapped it with material that ran around the front of Allan's face, using enough to make him look like a mummy.

"Let's get you to the hospital. If you got hit hard enough to get knocked out, they'll probably want to do some xrays, and they'll have to sew up that cut."

I grimaced at the unnecessary transport, but I couldn't prevent it.

Allan's mother slowly regained her self-control, but she was still sniffling as Phil's partner brought a stretcher. Allan insisted he could walk. They tried to put a collar around his neck, but Allan resisted that too. Phil pushed on each of the bones of Allan's neck again to make sure they weren't injured, and finally relented.

A police car showed up moments later.

"I'm Officer Metz," said the dark-haired man wearing a Seattle PD uniform. I drank in his baseline aura, a mixture of a blue that was almost purple, a strong bronze and buttermilk white, and a warm cheesy taste.

Mom introduced everyone again.

"What happened here?" said the policeman.

Mom reiterated the story as Allan had told us, adding that we had dropped him off from karate practice moments before the attack, and that she'd heard a motorcycle drive off afterwards.

"Anyone else hurt?"

"No, he left immediately," Mom replied.

"Did anyone see the assailant?" he asked.

"No," said Allan, his mother, and Mom.

"How about his bike?"

"I didn't see it, but it was small. A one-twenty-five horse engine maybe. He gunned it out of here, but it took several seconds to accelerate," Mom recounted.

"Interesting," said officer Metz. The lime stripe in his aura suggested he'd made an internal connection of some kind.

"How so?" I asked.

"We've had a few other beatings like this, and nobody's quite sure exactly why."

"But you have a theory?" I said.

His aura confirmed that he did, and that he was amazed that I suspected such. Also, he wasn't going to tell me. I didn't need to see his face to figure any of this out.

"As I said, nobody is sure."

"All right if I take him?" Phil asked.

"Yes, that's fine," the officer said. "Would you mind coming down to the station to file a complete report?" he asked Mrs. Marks.

"I need to go to the hospital," she replied.

"Tomorrow, then?"

She paused, perhaps considering her guests. "Of course," she said finally. "What time?"

"Say nine AM?"

"Fine," she replied.

"Thanks very much for your time, everyone. And I'll see you tomorrow," he added to Allan's mother.

*   *   *

Mom and I had no choice but to go home. I wanted to join Allan and his mother at the hospital, but Mom refused to take me.

"Nothing else we can do," she said.

There was nothing *she* could do, but I could fix his head. If only I'd reacted right away, I could've stopped the bleeding and removed the whole lump before she knew it was there. Allan wouldn't need the hospital. I felt the slimy, burning guilt course through my aura.

More concerning, however, was the reason for the attack. Officer Metz knew something, but refused to share. I'd have to go to the police station myself and figure it out. No way I'd let someone hit my friend and get away with it. Not after everything he'd done for me.

I went to bed and tried to sleep, but instead kicked the sheets around most of the night, upset by the evening's events. Gone was the elation at passing my green belt test.

When I finally fell asleep, I dreamed about finding the assailant and yanking him into the void so hard that he never came out.

CHAPTER 28

MOM HAD to bang on my door to wake me up for school the next morning. I felt groggy, but I managed to drag myself through my morning routine.

I arrived at school barely registering people around me, other than to note that Allan wasn't there. Fortunately, Miss Burnell left me alone during geography and spelling, as did M. Poirer during French. Since we didn't have gym class, I didn't have to deal with Kenny, which was a relief. I ignored the rest of my classmates, none of whom seemed to have noticed Allan's absence, and at lunch, I ran immediately over to Betsy's table.

"What happened?" she asked.

The trickle of irritation I felt about openly displaying my feelings became rapidly engulfed by a river of red hot anger over Allan's fate. I could feel the thrumming lavender in Betsy's aura, and it calmed me slightly. She was concerned about me.

The news about Allan had been building inside my head all morning, and it exploded at the first person who cared.

"Allan got beaten up!"

"Oh no!" she gasped. "When? Where? Is he all right?"

I told her the story, omitting the details of my involvement, but including the hesitancy of Officer Metz.

"So you think the cop knows something but isn't saying?" she asked.

"Yeah, but I have no idea what."

"For all you know, he may have done it himself."

I considered her remark carefully. A corrupt cop in Seattle? After Orlando Ryan, it certainly was a possibility. But Officer Metz had nothing but concern in his aura—no guilt or evil that I could see. He wasn't the guy. Betsy interrupted my thoughts by whacking me on the arm.

"I was kidding!" she said.

Belatedly, I recognized that her aura had been emitting waves which stopped with her latest comment.

"Well, it wasn't all that ridiculous," I said. "After all, you know about Orlando Ryan, right?"

"Of course. He was married to Mrs. Ryan, the teacher from last year. She left because of all the stuff she was going through. And then he got arrested and died in prison. But just because one cop was bad, doesn't mean the whole police force is dirty."

"Wait, what?" I said, puzzled.

"Just because one cop beat his wife and stuff, you can't assume that the rest of the police force is out there beating up teenage boys!"

"No, about dying in prison," I said.

"Oh, that. Serves him right, if you ask me."

"How do you know he died in prison?" I asked.

"It was all over the news a few weeks back. 'Former local police officer found dead in his cell from apparent suicide,' was the headline. Or something like that. It was on TV too. They said he was involved in a regional prostitution ring, and was also convicted of domestic abuse. I guess he couldn't hack it in prison and took his own life."

I thought about it for a moment. Here was a guy who spent his life putting people in jail, and now he found himself among the criminals.

"Are you sure he committed suicide?" I asked.

"I would have, I'm sure," she said blithely.

Despite the cavalier nature of her words, her aura hissed with sour and bitter iciness that made me uncomfortable.

"It's just that he was a cop. Maybe someone he arrested wanted revenge and killed him."

She looked blankly at me for a moment, and then agreed. "Yeah, I guess being a cop wouldn't make him too popular in jail. I guess we'll never know. Anyway, assuming Officer Metz isn't guilty, who do you suppose tried to split Allan's skull?"

One face popped into my head immediately, and Betsy could tell. "Who?" she prompted.

"Kenny Logan," I spat.

She nodded in agreement. "Yeah, he's just the sort that would do something like this. But he's only fourteen. You said the guy rode away on a motorcycle. You think Kenny is old enough to drive one?"

"I don't know. Maybe," I said. "It's certainly worth asking him."

"He's not going to just tell you!" she retorted.

"Oh, he'll tell me," I said. A faint buzzing reminded me that I'd better watch what I said.

"You think he's going to brag? I doubt it. All you have to do is tell the cops he did it and they'll arrest him. Then they'll search his house for the bike, plus whatever he used to hit Allan in the head. If they find something, he'll get sent to juvi like Suzanne."

"What's 'juvi'?" I asked.

"Juvenile Detention. Prison for kids."

"Suzanne was in prison?" I asked.

"Yeah, once. She beat up another kid. Her parents ended up saying she was nuts, and that's how she got sent to the psych hospital. She really doesn't want to go back, so she's effectively on parole."

"Wow," I said. I'd never known any of that.

"So what are you gonna do?" she asked.

"What do you mean?"

"Are you really going to ask Kenny if he did it?"

I considered the problem. If he lied, the waves would confirm that he hit Allan, but I wouldn't be able to prove it. At least I'd know. Perhaps I'd take care of it myself.

"You'd better not be thinking of doing something to Kenny," she said, interrupting my deliberation of that exact thought. "Then *you'll* be the one the cops send to juvi!"

I nodded. Being imprisoned reminded me of the lockdown in the hospital, where I freaked out at being restrained. That simply wouldn't do. I needed a plan. It was another chess match, I concluded, and the game was on!

CHAPTER 29

I CALLED Allan's house after school.

"I'm fine," he said, after our initial pleasantries. "They put some staples in the back of my head which hurt when I lay on them, but otherwise I can hardly tell that I was attacked. They said I have a concussion, but I don't have any of the symptoms of one. Not even a headache."

I nodded internally. So *that* was what the muddled redness inside Allan's brain meant. Concussion. At least I was able to make that go away without exposing my ability.

"Any idea who did it?"

"Mom went to the police station and left me here with her parents. The trip was a complete waste, though. Officer Metz said something about local biker gangs, but didn't elaborate. Mom was still pretty upset and didn't press the issue."

"What about Kenny?" I asked.

"Kenny Logan? What makes you think he had anything to do with it?" he said.

"Makes more sense than a random gang. Whoever it was knows you, because he was waiting outside your house. And Kenny was pissed because of what happened outside the lunch room."

"I thought of that, but does he drive a motorcycle?"

We talked for a bit longer. I kept trying to blame Kenny, but Allan countered with a number of different arguments. Kenny could've picked a fight at school, like he did with me. He didn't have a motorcycle, as he was underage. He certainly didn't have a license to drive one. He wasn't in any biker gang, and Officer Metz felt that a gang member was the most likely suspect.

Still, I wanted it to be Kenny because then I could make him pay.

*   *   *

The next morning, instead of class, we watched kids from the younger grades perform a play based on the first Thanksgiving. They dressed as Pilgrims and Native Americans, acting out scenes depicted in history books. The plot seemed farfetched, given that the colonists virtually wiped out the indigenous population with war and disease, but the children had fun acting out the parts.

Perhaps it was a lesson in how our ancestors should have interacted.

Since we didn't have gym, and school let out early, I never saw Kenny. I was frustrated because I wanted to prove to myself that he wasn't involved. After my discussion with Allan, I begrudgingly agreed that the perpetrator was probably someone else.

Karate class focused on upper level belt tests. I watched with rapt attention as the blue, red and brown belts performed high level *katas*, sparring demonstrations, and breaks. The tests increased in complexity, and I wondered if I'd ever be able to perform the moves necessary to advance. I doubted it. It looked to me like everyone who tested advanced, some to new colors, and others only added "tips" to their belts. These were like half-belts, marked by tape on the end of the existing color. The blue belts tested for "red tip" first, then red-tip blue belts tested for full red. We didn't have them for yellow, orange or green, only the higher levels.

We applauded the new accomplishments, and closed out the session with bows.

I was surprised to find Dad waiting for me in the parking lot.

"Hunter!" he said, pulling me into an embrace.

Dad was one of the few people whose hugs I could tolerate.

"You're back?" I said.

"Brilliant use of your observational skills," he joked. "I got time off for Thanksgiving. Let's get you home."

Dad congratulated me on the acquisition of my green belt, and we talked briefly about school, but eventually I steered the conversation to Allan's attack.

"So you think it was this Kenny character?" he concluded.

"Well, I thought so at first, but the cops think it has something to do with a biker gang," I said.

"Hmmm, I know there's a Hell's Angels contingent in Seattle. They're linked to the Vancouver group. But beating up teenagers in the suburbs doesn't sound like their style."

"Hell's Angels?" I asked.

"Yeah, they're the most famous biker group in the world. Started in California in the 40's or 50's, I think. Some members of the group were associated with drug dealing, extortion, murder, stuff like that. Pretty sure they're not your guys."

"Officer Metz didn't say anything about them. Is there another gang?"

"I'm not sure, but I can probably ask around without too much trouble. I have a friend who'd know about it."

"One of your super-secret agent friends?" I asked.

He stared at me without saying a word.

"Right, I know. No talking about that."

He continued to stare, and I held up my hands defensively. "All right! I promise. No more, ever!"

"Good. I'll see what I can find out. Now, let's talk about Thanksgiving turkey or something more positive."

*   *   *

Despite my efforts over the next two days, neither Mom nor Dad were willing to further discuss Allan's encounter. They insisted we enjoy a nice Thanksgiving dinner without such distractions. I brooded quietly about the problem, missing Grandpa for the millionth time, but by Thursday night, I was no closer to finding a solution.

Dad accidentally gave me an idea Friday morning.

"How's your friend Ian?" he asked.

"Moved away. Back to England," I said.

"Oh, that's unfortunate. He seemed like a good kid. Bit of a troublemaker, but otherwise a good boy. Did he say why he had to leave?"

"His Dad told him he needed to return for a job. He sent me a letter because he never got to say goodbye before he left."

"That's too bad, but I'm sure both of them are doing fine. How about some pie?"

"For breakfast?" I asked incredulously.

"Sure. As long as Mom says it's OK. It's not like the calories are going to hurt you. Think of it as the post-Thanksgiving day pie celebration."

I didn't mind eating pie for breakfast, and Dad clearly wanted it, so I joined him while Mom looked on disapprovingly. I knew the look because she announced it.

"This is my disapproving face!"

"Ease up, Marissa. How often does Hunter break the rules?"

Mom shook her head and served the pie.

My mind drifted to Ian, and his favorite pastime, investigative journalism.

Of course! I could check the newspaper archives for information about local biker gangs. Today was a holiday for me, but the paper was open. I could go in, ask to see the archives like Roger Pierce had, and find prior stories about gangs. Then I'd be able to understand what Officer Metz had been thinking but refused to share. I doubt my parents would let me go, so I needed an excuse to leave the house.

I sprang my plan on my parents while Dad coated his pie in whipped cream, creating a pile so high there was more whipped cream than pie. He smiled and raised his eyes at Mom, who shook her head.

"I'm going to go for a bike ride. Is it OK if I go down to the park?" I asked, trying to keep my voice as even as possible.

"Aha, is Betsy going to be there?" Mom asked.

"I don't know, maybe," I said. My aura fluttered wildly with evidence of my lies.

"Who's this Betsy?" Dad asked, causing him to drop a blob of whipped cream onto his plate, which he scooped up immediately as though it would run away if he didn't.

"Just a girl from school," I said. I filled my mouth with pie to avoid having to say anything else.

"Hunter's been spending some time with her," Mom said.

"Oh, very good," Dad said.

"She's been meeting him for lunch, and she's in his gym class. They've also met a few times at the park."

"Nice," Dad said.

I swallowed and cleared my throat. "So can I go?"

"Of course," Mom said. "Just be back before dark please."

"Have a good time!" Dad added.

I finished my unorthodox breakfast, packed my pockets with food, brought my jacket to the garage and freed my bike. I hadn't been to the newspaper building for a while, but I reviewed in my mind how to get there as I headed west toward downtown.

It was only about three miles, and the trip out was mostly downhill, so it didn't take long. I followed a one-way street for a bit, and I had to cross Route 5. Most of the cars were heading to the mall, although a few ventured toward the business districts. The cool wind whipped at me as I pedaled, and I noticed the clouds overhead, suggesting an imminent rain shower. It rained a lot in Seattle, but not usually for very long. Unless it was cold, the rain never bothered me.

I took a right turn onto Boren Avenue and parked my bike in the rack out in front of the *Times* building. It was an ugly brown two-toned structure that appeared to have only two stories if you came in the front, but it looked much larger from the back because the building was on a hill.

I saw a bronze statue near the entrance and noticed a couple of awards on the walls for Pulitzer prizes. I remembered how badly Ian's father, Roger, wanted one of those. One award plaque told the story about a professor cleared on communism charges, and the other displayed a photo of some firefighters. Interesting, but not helpful.

I looked around until I found a large desk with the word *Information* on the front. An older, heavyset man wearing a uniform sat behind it. He was balding on top, with whitish hair symmetrically growing above his ears. He was reading a newspaper, but stopped and put it down as I approached, giving me his full attention.

"I'd like to visit the archives, please," I said.

"Well, hello, son," said the man. "And just who may you be?"

"I'm a friend of Roger Pierce."

"And your name?" he said.

"Hunter. Hunter Miller."

"Well, Hunter Miller, Roger doesn't work here anymore. And only people who work here are allowed to view the archives."

"How am I supposed to find out about stuff that happened in the past?" I whined.

"You could try your library. They usually have old issues of the *Times*. Or perhaps you could ask Roger to give you the name of a colleague to speak with. One of our current reporters?"

"Roger moved to England," I said dejectedly.

"That's too bad," he answered.

"But you said I can find old papers in the library?"

"Sure you can. The Seattle Public Library keeps microfiche copies for up to ten years. What's this all about, anyway?" he asked.

"Biker gangs," I said.

"You're not planning on joining one, are you?" he asked.

"Me? No way! I think one of them beat up my friend."

The man changed his posture and his aura lit up with curiosity. "Your friend?" he asked.

"Yeah. He got hit in the head."

"With a baseball bat?" the man asked, his curiosity piqued.

"I don't know, I didn't see. But I guess it could have been a baseball bat. Something big and solid. Enough to give him a concussion."

The man nodded, and I could see that he, like Officer Metz, had drawn some type of conclusion.

"I read a story in the paper about people being injured like that. Police thought it was related to a gang. Could've been bikers, I suppose."

"The Hell's Angels?" I wondered out loud.

"No, I don't think so," he answered. "I'd have remembered that. Why don't you check the library? I'm sure you'll find the article, and maybe others."

"Where's the library?"

He pulled out a map from behind his information desk and laid it onto the surface, smoothing it out so I could see the different locations. "Fourth Avenue between Madison and Spring Street. Right here, see?"

I recognized the location and mentally plotted a course. It wasn't very far.

"Wow, thanks for the help," I said.

"No problem. Just be careful. You don't want to get your own head bashed in. These gang people can be serious folks."

"I will," I said. I was a pretty serious person too. Just ask Orlando Ryan!

CHAPTER 30

I LEFT the *Seattle Times* building armed with several pieces of new information. There were other attacks like Allan's, and no matter how much I still wanted to blame Kenny, it was virtually impossible that he was behind all of them. I'd have to resign myself to disliking Kenny because he was a jerk, not a gang-based thug.

The weapon was probably a baseball bat. Made sense. Easy to swing, easy to transport, and it matched the size of the wound on Allan's head.

And although I wasn't allowed to use the archives, Roger's preferred source for information, at least I'd found an easily accessible alternative: the library. That was my next destination, only a brief ride away.

I unlocked my bike and pushed off, staying on the sidewalks and traveling slowly. Although it was a short distance, the hills made for a difficult journey. I got lost at a big hotel and saw a bank and several bars that were supposed to be right next to the library, but I still couldn't locate it. In desperation, I summoned my courage and asked a woman who was passing by on foot.

"It's right down this street. Just keep walking and you can't miss it," she said. She pointed in the direction from which I had just come. There were no waves, so I retraced my steps and continued my search.

The reason I didn't recognize it was that it was a gigantic structure with huge windows with a recessed entrance. It wasn't until I saw the book drop slot that I finally recognized the building as a library. It looked nothing like the one at my school, which was tiny, containing only a few shelves and tables.

This monstrosity was large enough to accommodate every book ever written. I had no idea where to find the newspapers, and I felt completely lost. I wandered around the first floor until I found the circulation desk, where half a dozen patrons were waiting to check out titles. I watched as each of them in turn presented some type of identification, and the librarian stamped the books and handed them back.

I finally made it to the front of the line and confronted a plump brunette women with large glasses.

"Can I help you?" she asked politely.

"I'm looking for the newspapers."

"Today's copy of the *Seattle Times* is over there next to those chairs," she said. "You can find the *Washington Post* and *New York Times* nearby as well. Just be careful not to damage the newspapers."

"Um, thanks," I stammered. "But I was hoping to get old editions. The guy at the *Seattle Times* told me I could find archive copies here?" I said, more as a question than a statement.

"Do you have a library card?" she asked.

"What's that?" I asked. Immediately I knew the answer. That's what everyone had been showing to get their books checked out.

"It's a card that has your name and identifying information so that we can find you if your items don't get returned on time. We charge fees for overdue books and things. So the library card is like a credit card, in a sense. Do your parents have one? Perhaps you could use theirs."

"I'm sure they do, but I live over in Madrona so I'd have to bike all the way home to ask."

"We have a branch in Madrona," she said, as though this should have been common knowledge. "You could get access to the old papers there. They'd also be able to issue you your very own library card. You could peruse the literature at your convenience."

"Really? That would be great!"

She looked at my excited face and grimaced. "Let me help you out. Tell me what date of the newspaper you need, and I'll make sure the Station House Branch has it for you by Monday. You can order your library card there, and they'll give you a temporary version that will be sufficient until the laminated card arrives in the mail. How's that?"

"Great," I said. "Except one thing. I'm not sure which date I need."

"Well, that could be a problem," she said. "Do you think you could narrow it down any?"

I remembered what the deskman at the *Times* said about a story in the last two weeks.

"One of the articles I'm looking for was in the past two weeks," I said.

"Good news, then. They keep the most current week in the media room. I'll phone over and ask them to keep two weeks available before sending it to the microfiche. That way, you'll be able to read through them without needing to use the reader. Sound good?"

"Thank you so much!"

"You're very welcome. Have a great day," she said, and immediately took the library card and book from the next person in line.

*   *   *

I'd spent the entire morning chasing down old newspapers and hadn't even seen one yet. At least I was on the right track. After I'd left, I realized I'd forgotten to ask where the Madrona Library was, but I was sure Mom or Dad would know. There were any number of reasons to visit a library, so they wouldn't be concerned if I asked to go. But absent the location, I couldn't simply bike there.

Instead, I went home for lunch.

"How was the park?" asked Mom, upon my arrival.

"I didn't go to the park. I biked around a bit and ended up at the library. They told me I needed a library card," I said.

"So you didn't meet Betsy today?" she asked.

"No, I'll probably see her on Monday," I said. I didn't understand Mom's fascination with Betsy.

"Oh, before I forget, you have an appointment with Dr. Eisenberg on Tuesday. I switched it so you wouldn't have to miss karate."

The disappointment oozed so badly that I could feel the slate grey fizzing loudly all around me. The thought of seeing Dr. Eisenberg dredged up many other feelings as well.

"For heaven's sake, Hunter, it's just a thirty minute visit. You'll be fine! Now eat the sandwich I made for you."

The grey buzzed and prickled, encircled by a frustrated shade of mahogany. I needed to control my emotions better. I tore into the sandwich so violently that crumbs went flying off the plate and I splattered a huge wad of grape jelly onto the floor. Mom made a face in my direction, but didn't say anything while she cleaned up the mess. I drank my milk quietly and tried to calm down. Mom was right—why was I getting so upset?

I knew the answer. I missed Grandpa, and I felt guilty that I'd forgotten about him. His life was over, yet mine continued. The depression I'd experienced nearly cost Betsy her life, too. What's more, Allan got beaten up and I couldn't even figure out which biker gang was behind it. I felt the angst building. I needed to *do* something!

"Hunter!" Mom said, startling me a bit.

"I have an idea. Why don't you change your clothes and show me how that punching bag that Allan got you works."

I brightened up. "Yeah, OK. Thanks."

I put on shorts and a T-shirt, grabbed the hand and foot pads, and went out to the garage. I showed Mom a few strikes, and then started pounding away. I directed each series of blows at an individual issue. Grandpa's death, for starters. Punch, punch, front kick, reverse direction, back kick, whirl, knife-hand strike, front kick, rebalance, side kick, and then kick, kick, kick. It was like my own *kata* that I invented on the spot. I repeated the motions with more power and focus. I switched stances, and performed the same routine in reverse. Why did Grandpa have to die? Bam, bam, bam! I pummeled the bag repeatedly.

Then I thought about Allan. I changed up the strikes, starting with ten punches straight on, then a backhand punch each direction, then a series of kicks. I lost my balance and fell off to the side as the bag moved toward me while I was trying to kick it. I yelled a guttural *kiai* and started again, punching furiously. I could feel the sweat starting to drip down my face and onto my shirt.

I pictured Kenny's blonde face, and although I doubted he was behind Allan's attack, I still wanted to make him sorry for being such a jerk. Thwack! I landed a huge roundhouse kick, making the bag move. I spun and switched feet and whacked the bag again. Back and forth with kicks, catching the bag each time at the peak of its lateral movement.

I thought about Mom, Dad, Betsy, and the library. I recalled Sensei Nam yelling "Focus!" to our group. I considered Dr. Eisenberg, my classmates, the gym teacher, my inability to speak French, and dozens of other random thoughts as I mindlessly pounded the defenseless bag.

By the time I stopped, I was drenched. Despite all the crazy things in my brain, a memory from Grandpa's memorial service calmed me the most. It was part of the prayer by Reverend Sanderson. "God grant us the serenity to accept what we can't change, the courage to change what we can, and the wisdom to know the difference," he'd said. I couldn't do anything about Grandpa's death, and I couldn't undo Allan's injury any more than I had. But I could make sure it didn't happen again, and that's where I needed to concentrate my energy.

CHAPTER 31

BY THE time I returned to school on Monday, I recovered from my miniature bout of depression. I knew that's what it was, because my aura felt foggy, grey, muddled, and heavy, exactly like it had before. The sensations clouded my judgment, made me quick to anger, and wreaked havoc with my emotions. Beating the bag had given me clarity. I felt fortunate that I was able to manipulate the grey away, unlike Betsy, who was stuck with it. I couldn't imagine being forced to live my entire life under that overcast nightmare, and I felt sorry for her.

Allan recovered completely, with a small residual lump and an infinitesimal scar as the only reminders of his ordeal. The warm purple and yellow that my good friend displayed in his aura reflected in my own. It was a positive feedback loop, like we learned about in biology. I stopped him on the way into our room.

"Good to see you up and about," I said.

"Yes, it was a rough weekend. My grandparents kept making comments about the safety of Seattle, and they wanted my parents to move. They're pretty used to getting their way, too, so everyone was on edge. Fortunately, they're gone now and things can get back to normal."

"Did the police find out anything?" I asked.

THE TASTE OF DESPAIR

"Not as far as I know. Mom talked to that policeman, Officer Metz, but he only asked questions and didn't say much. He doubted I was a being specifically targeted, though. Apparently, several others were attacked all over the area, and there's nothing that ties any of the victims together. Mom is still upset, but I think she's feeling better now that she's convinced it was probably a random thing and I don't have to be concerned about them returning."

The bell rang unexpectedly, as we'd spent too much time chatting. We bolted into the classroom and scurried for our seats.

"That's one tardy for each of you, Mr. Miller and Mr. Marks. Two more and you'll have detention."

"What? We were right here, at the door, talking!" I said.

"You know the rules. In your seats by the time the bell rings, or it's a tardy," she replied stiffly.

I had no recollection of any such rule, but I'd been paying so little attention in class that I'd obviously missed it.

"Sorry, Miss Burnell, it won't happen again," said Allan.

"I expected better of you, Mr. Marks. See that it doesn't."

I felt somehow relieved that she didn't expect better of me. I prepared to ignore the morning math session, but Miss Burnell surprised me with a notification.

"As y'all know, in the spring, y'all usually create a science fair project as part of the 8th grade requirements. However, this year, I've decided to offer a civics option for those of you who might prefer the softer sciences."

She looked at Patty Owens, who smiled back. Then she continued.

"Rather than building an exploding volcano or some such ghastly construct, y'all can instead write a five to ten page paper on something related to the community. Maybe one of you young underachievers can interview the Mayor. Perhaps you want to be a fireman and can speak with the fire captain about what it takes to become one. Who knows? Anyway, the project will be due in May, but I'll need your ideas by the second week in January to make sure you're on the right track. I'm letting you know now so that you can have the Christmas break to think about it."

I hadn't known about the science fair, but I'd have a far easier time building something rather than talking to someone in the community. Patty must have feared a science project, because her aura spewed a heavy mustard smell, which I'd learned implied relief. I ignored both the news and the next hour of algebra. I tried to pay attention in history, but my mind wandered toward identifying the "random" person who attacked Allan.

I lagged behind on the way to PE, my mind still drifting. The gym was set up for volleyball, which was nice because it meant we were done with wrestling. Also, I could easily hide during volleyball games, either on the sideline or in the middle of the court. I'd just step out of the way and let the other kids hit the ball, much like when I played basketball.

∗   ∗   ∗

I walked by Kenny, and immediately recognized something had changed in his aura. Not the baseline blue, or the abrasive smell. The orange and white hues were grated with a slimy, muddled brown. Chestnut brown. I knew that color. Guilt. I stopped dead in my tracks as I realized the implication, and Mike Giovanni ran me over from behind, sending me tumbling to the floor.

"Sorry, dude," he said, as he held his hand out to help me up.

"Thanks," I said awkwardly, accepting the hand.

Allan appeared and asked, "Everything OK?"

"Yeah, fine. I ran into Mike by mistake," I said.

Mike nodded and walked on.

"Did you notice anything about Kenny?" I asked Allan.

"He's avoiding us. Not a huge surprise, since I 'talked to him' last week. Why? What do you see?"

"He's looking guilty," I said.

"Oh you're the expert in facial expressions now?"

"Uh… Mom's been helping me. There are a couple things I've learned," I said evasively. "Guilt is one of them."

"So you still think *Kenny* hit me and rode off on his motorcycle? Come on, man! We've been over this. He's fourteen years old!"

"I don't know," I said hesitantly. But I did know.

"Let's play some volleyball. It'll be fun!"

We started dividing up into teams, so I got to speak with Betsy while we waited to get picked.

"Hooray, volleyball!" she said sarcastically.

"At least it's not wrestling," I said.

"Sit with me at lunch?" she asked.

"Sure."

I got selected, leaving her last. I smiled wanly.

"Last again," she mouthed.

I really wished I could fix her.

⋆   ⋆   ⋆

After a period of playing volleyball, or, more accurately, dodging others while they clambered for the ball, I quickly left the gym. I waited for Kenny outside the doorway.

He appeared, accompanied by several of the boys from his class.

"Hey, Kenny," I called.

"What do *you* want," he said, leaving off his usual term-of-endearment, such as "twerp."

"Can I ask you something?"

"Beat it, geek," said Dennis, one of Kenny's friends.

"Later, then," I suggested.

"In your dreams," said Dennis, who pushed me to the side while Kenny walked by.

Allan and Betsy came out together, sharing a sense of concern that vibrated between their auras.

"What are you doing?" Allan asked.

"Just trying to figure something out," I said.

"He's gonna punch you out if you bother him," Allan said.

I didn't think so. My aura hadn't alerted me to any sign of impending danger. The tingling, banging or pounding, depending on the severity of my predicament, had returned in full force since I'd accepted Grandpa's death and regained full control of the auras.

Perhaps I'd been right about him after all. I was there, at Allan's house, and I bet Kenny knew it. He might think I saw him and would be able to identify him to the police.

"Let's get back to class," Allan offered. I nodded and we headed off toward our room.

"See you at lunch, Hunter," Betsy called over her shoulder as she started off in the other direction.

I had gone full circle on Kenny, first convinced he was responsible for Allan's attack, then, based primarily on what I'd heard from the man at the *Times*, fully confident of his innocence. Now, after reading the guilt in his aura, I was entirely sure he was to blame. I could find out easily enough. I merely needed to ask him. He'd lie, but that didn't matter. I'd see the waves. The problem was, I never interacted with him except in gym class, and he was avoiding me.

Despite the guilt, there was still the matter of the motorcycle. Did Kenny really ride one? And if so, would he be confident enough to ride one to commit a crime? He must, if he was the one who did it.

Lost in thought, I caught my hip on the door handle and nearly fell over as I entered the classroom. Allan caught me and a few of the kids laughed. I ignored them and shuffled to my seat.

"You all right?" he asked.

"Yeah," I said. I sat down and thought about anything but the vocabulary words the teacher had written on the blackboard.

*   *   *

Betsy agreed with Allan.

"No way Kenny has his own motorcycle," she said, after I told her my suspicions.

"Maybe he borrowed one," I suggested.

"Yeah, good one. 'Excuse me, large biker dude, but can you lend me your bike so I can bash another kid's head in and use it as a getaway vehicle?' I don't think so."

"Maybe he stole it," I said, grasping at straws.

"And then he what, brought it back? Unlikely!"

I had to admit, the motorcycle didn't make sense. Kenny would have either walked or ridden a bicycle.

"I could follow him," I mused.

"Brilliant. Because if you are right and he's a sociopath, *that's* going to work out well, don't ya think? And if you're *wrong*, which you almost certainly are, then you're going to get arrested for stalking. It's a lose-lose scenario. Forget it."

She wasn't helping. I needed a real plan.

My lack of insight bothered me throughout karate class, although working out made me feel better. It was cathartic, like hitting the bag the prior night. It allowed me to focus on my problems without directly thinking about them. No solution presented itself, however, and I went home dejected.

CHAPTER 32

TUESDAY OFFERED no chance to corner Kenny, but I had another idea. If he had stolen a motorcycle, there'd be a newspaper article about it. Besides, if I was on the wrong track, and someone else beat up Allan and the others, I could read about it in the *Seattle Times*.

I asked Allan where the library was during lunch.

"Are you kidding me? It's only a block away. Haven't you been there before?"

"No," I said.

"But you've read tons of books. Where did you get them?"

"Mom bought them for me," I said.

"Must be nice."

"So, you have a library card?" I asked.

"Yeah. All you have to do is give them your name, address and phone number and you can get one. It's no big deal. Then you can take out any books you want. I usually get books during the summer but you can get them anytime."

"Thanks," I said. I'd have to take the bus home and pick up my bike, otherwise I'd be stuck at the library.

✻   ✻   ✻

Unfortunately, when I arrived home, Mom reminded me of my appointment with Dr. Eisenberg.

"Don't even try to talk your way out of it," she said, evidently prompted by my facial expression.

"But, Mom!" I wailed.

"Listen, you knew this was coming. It's still a condition of your discharge, like she told you before. You have to go. It should be a breeze, though. You're doing so well. Except for the other day, you've been completely fine."

"Can I go to the library after?"

"Why? Is there a book you need?" she asked.

"I'm working on a project for school," I said.

"When's it due?"

"Oh, not for a while," I said.

"Then how about Thursday instead. You have this appointment today and karate tomorrow."

"OK," I agreed sullenly.

I reluctantly flopped into the front seat of Mom's car and moped all the way to Dr. Eisenberg's building. We didn't have to wait long once we arrived. Mom came into the back office with me.

"Hello, Hunter, and hello, Dr. Miller," the psychiatrist said, opening the door to allow entry. "Will you be sitting in?" she asked Mom.

"No. Just let me say he's been doing very well at home and in school, and he really didn't want to come. I hope you can clear him."

"Thank you, I appreciate the input," Dr. Eisenberg said. "Let's get to it, then, Hunter," she added, motioning me to my seat and waving to Mom as she closed the door.

I scanned her aura briefly, noticing nothing out of the ordinary. I still felt a bit guilty about her getting beaten up last year because I asked her to investigate Orlando Ryan for spousal abuse. Ryan enlisted Joseph Batapaglia and two other goons to teach her a lesson. Dr. Eisenberg needed surgery to get fixed. Fortunately, the wounds had healed very nicely, and you could hardly see the disfig-urement in her aura.

"Are you well?" she asked.

"Yes."

"You look much better," she observed.

"Thanks?" I said, slightly confused.

"Even when you came in a few weeks ago, you were still struggling, but I see now that you have regained all of your confidence and strength. How are your friends doing?"

I told her about Allan and Betsy.

"And that fellow, Ian?" she asked.

"Oh, he's gone back to England. I haven't seen him in months. I did get a letter from him though."

"Did you write him back?"

"Yes, but that was a while ago. He was helping me look at people's faces and see their expressions, and now Mom's showing me some things. She taught me that the autism makes it hard for me to fit in because I can't tell what people are thinking or feeling by looking at their faces."

I didn't know what prompted me to discuss this, but her aura told me that she was satisfied and a little proud.

We spent the rest of the session discussing unimportant details, and she concluded by saying I didn't have to come back unless I had a change in status. I couldn't stop the relief from showing, and Dr. Eisenberg smiled.

"It's OK, Hunter. Nobody *really* wants to see a psychiatrist. I'm not offended that you don't want to come any more."

"Great!" I said.

"You can wait for your mother in the common room. Good luck, Hunter," she said.

I left happily.

*   *   *

The next day, I was feeling good and I decided it was time to approach Kenny. I waited impatiently until gym class, then walked boldly up to him as we headed for the locker room door. Kenny's friends hurled insults.

"Dork alert!"

"Hey, the pipsqueak thinks he can speak!"

"Better move along, little boy, before something bad happens!"

Allan hoisted me away before I had a chance to ask my burning question.

"What are you doing?" Allan said. "The last thing you want to do is pick a fight with someone like that!"

"I wasn't going to fight," I said defensively.

"That doesn't mean he wasn't!" Allan retorted.

Talking to Kenny during school hours seemed increasingly unlikely, so I resigned myself to finding him outside of school. I spent the afternoon entertaining scenarios where I might casually run into Kenny. The mall? Maybe. The library? That would be ironic. I didn't know what someone like him did for fun. Laser tag?

Perhaps I could follow him to his house. First, I'd have to discover his home address, and he'd never tell me. Mrs. Frechette would know, but why would she tell me? What about Miss Tilton from the guidance office? Maybe I could get Blanche, the secretary to tell me. Each idea that popped into my head was even worse than the prior one, so I gave up and thought about my upcoming karate practice instead. It would be my first sparring session, and I was excited.

Allan's Mom dropped us off for practice, and after warm-ups and stretching, we broke up into groups to work on new blocks and strikes. Sensei Nam gave us special instructions, and we paired off for mock combat. I had fun sparring with Josh as we attacked with simple punches and kicks. Both of us were scared of hurting the other, so we ended up going half-speed, but it was still enjoyable. It might come in handy knowing how to fight, as an alternative to dumping someone's aura into the void. I was looking forward to practicing with Nicola, Kim and Scott, too. Scott was wiry and quick, and unlike Josh, he had no compunction about throwing hard punches and kicks. Though I liked karate, I still found myself distracted by my yearning to find Allan's attacker, whether it was Kenny or someone else.

✳   ✳   ✳

After school on Thursday, I took my bike back to the library, which, as Allan had said, was right on Union Street. It was a small, single floor brick building with a chimney on one side, a weird statue of some cats sitting on a rock out front, and a sign that read "Seattle Public Library." If not for the statue and sign, I would have assumed it was someone's house. It was nothing like the main library downtown.

I walked inside and heard a noise from a desk at the far end. The woman behind the desk looked up and smiled.

"How can I help you?" she said.

"I'm Hunter," I said while heading over to her.

"Very nice to meet you. I'm Miss Kessler, the librarian. Is there something you need?"

"I'd like to get my own library card," I said.

"Fantastic!" she said. "I can help you with that."

"And I want to see old copies of the *Seattle Times*, if you have them."

"Yes, we do. We don't have the archives like the main branch, but if you know what dates you want, I could obtain a copy of the microfiche and you could read them in the reader-room," she said. "But first things first. Let's get you a card."

She asked my full name and the other pertinent information and filled out the application. While she fiddled with the papers, she chatted vibrantly.

"Is this your first time here?"

"Yes," I said.

"So, did you know that this used to be a fire station?"

"No," I admitted.

"It's true. It was built around the turn of the century, and converted into a library a few years ago. It's not all flashy like downtown, but we can get any book you want via intra-library loan. We're really a full service branch."

"That's great," I said.

She finished puttering around with the application, and came out from behind the desk.

"Let me show you where the newspapers are kept."

I didn't see anyone else in the library, although there were two cars in the parking lot out front. I wondered to whom they belonged.

"We have story time every day at four pm," she was saying. "You're welcome to come and listen. The books target younger kids, but you might like them too," she added.

"Thanks," I said, not knowing what else to say.

"Here we are," she said, holding up a copy of today's paper, which was trapped by a long wooden device that kept it from being carried away. "I have the past two weeks' issues behind the desk. We had a request from Central to keep them on hand for a local patron," she said.

"Awesome!" I said, suddenly interested. "Let me start with this. Then can I look at the others?"

"Of course. Is there something you're looking for in particular?"

I hesitated, not sure how much I wanted to divulge. However, this woman had been nothing but enthusiastic and helpful, so I told her what I wanted.

"I'm looking for news articles about motorcycle-related crime," I summarized.

"Oh, yes, we have a lot of that in Seattle. Not out here in Madrona, but the *Seattle Times* has stories about stuff like that every week."

She opened up the paper and showed me a section.

"This is the police blotter," she explained. "Everything in here relates to a crime committed locally, or to an arrest made. You can find nasty stuff, like murder and rape, or petty stuff like traffic violations, and anything in between. If you want to see who got arrested, arraigned or accused, here's the section for you."

She continued, "I'll tell you what. I'll look through the headlines of the last two weeks and see if there are any major stories related to motorcycle gang violence or arrests. If I see something, I'll make a copy for you. Otherwise, you can start looking through this section to find what you want."

"Thank you so much," I said. "This is a tremendous help."

*   *   *

I spent the rest of the time looking at the police blotter. I had no idea the extent of the criminal activity in Seattle. I was overwhelmed by both the volume and the descriptions. Petit larceny, grand larceny, assault, assault and battery, manslaughter, murder in the first degree—the list went on and on. And those were the serious crimes, or felonies. Amidst them were the misdemeanors, as Miss Kessler called them, many having vague labels such as "failure to appear." It was fascinating, but confusing.

"You know what you need?" said the librarian.

"What?"

"You need a book to help decode all of this information for you, like a primer on criminal law. At least then you'll understand the definitions of all of the terms."

"Cool," I said, suitably impressed.

"I'll find something for you and give you a call. If there isn't anything here, it will have to come from downtown, but intra-library loans usually arrive within a few days at most."

"Wow, thanks," I said.

"I've got to get ready for story time, but I'll look forward to seeing you again," she said.

*   *   *

The next day just before gym class, I caught a break. I emerged from the bathroom as Kenny arrived. He tried to avoid me while I sensed his guilt. I needed a single question to confirm my suspicion, but I didn't want to be too confrontational.

I settled on, "Hey, Kenny, have you ever driven a motorcycle?"

He looked at me bitterly. Or, his aura tasted bitter, and he made a facial expression that matched.

"No, never," he said. No waves. "Now get out of my way."

I moved aside as he entered the bathroom. I didn't know what he felt guilty about, but it wasn't hitting Allan with a bat. Nobody thought it was him except for me, but I had confirmed I was wrong. It was a significant step forward, but the real work remained ahead.

After PE I caught up with Allan walking back to class. I told him about the newspapers and the librarian. He didn't seem to grasp the significance.

"We're gonna find who's responsible for smacking you," I said confidently.

"I don't know," he said.

"It obviously was someone who rides a motorcycle, right? And who is that going to be?"

"A motorcyclist?" he responded.

"Not just any motorcyclist, but someone who's also a criminal. All we need to do is find him."

When he didn't say anything, I answered for him.

"Well, how do we do that, you ask? So glad you inquired. We look in the daily police blotter for similar crimes. Think about it. It's a very specific charge. Bashing someone in the head and driving away on a bike. I spent a few hours yesterday looking at crimes, and there are tons of them. We have to find someone who got caught doing the same thing, and then you can accuse him and get him arrested."

"I don't know," he said again.

"What do you mean? Don't you want to catch this guy?"

"It's no big deal, really. It was just a bump on the head and a few stitches. Not like before," his voice trailed off. I understood the reference.

Years ago, he was beaten up by bullies. He'd undergone facial reconstructive surgery and was out of school for weeks. His parents made him take karate classes so he wouldn't get picked on any more. It had worked, but the scars he endured were more than physical.

Three years ago, we had publicly humiliated the boy responsible. He and his followers had also been hounding dozens of other kids, myself included. They had stolen lunch money, pushed and shoved smaller kids at will, and verbally abused anyone outside their tiny circle. But that had stopped because of us.

This was much worse. The concussion, or whatever the red muddled cloudiness in Allan's brain had been, was serious. It was more dangerous than Allan would ever know. We needed to make sure it didn't happen again. In order to do that, we needed to discover the perpetrator, and I'd devised a plan to accomplish this task.

Why wasn't he more supportive?

"I'd rather just forget about it and move on. You know, like you and your grandfather. I don't want to get stuck all depressed about it for months."

I felt like I'd been punched in the gut.

"Hey, man, I'm sorry," Allan said, noting my expression. "Come on, we need to get to class. If we get a second tardy in two days, Miss Burnell is going to skewer us."

CHAPTER 33

I WASN'T ready to give up my quest, though, so I went back to the library that afternoon. Miss Kessler delivered on her promise by supplying me with a hardcover book containing the definitions of legal terms. In addition to Latin words, there were ordinary words with specific legal meaning, and strange words that no person outside a courtroom would ever say, like abrogate or abeyance. She also promised she'd help me read through the crime sheets whenever she was available, so I added the library visits to my weekly routine. I had karate on Monday, Wednesday and Friday; I scoured the newspaper for insights into the criminal mind on Tuesday and Thursday.

Unfortunately, the bulk of the "news" was lame, ridiculous, or unrelated. Stolen cars, damaged boats, shooting victims, break-ins where thieves left their contraband behind, graffiti painting--you name it, people did it. Someone was arrested for leaving feces behind on a neighbor's porch. There were hundreds of traffic violations. Failure to pay child support, bad checks, indecent exposure—the list went on and on. There were some motorcycle related crimes, but they were all about theft or vandalism, not attacks.

After consulting the legal book, I decided I was looking for cases of assault and battery, or assault with a deadly weapon. The guy had hit Allan with a baseball bat, most likely, and that qualified as potentially lethal. Once I figured out the proper terms, I skimmed quickly. There were assaults, but most were either committed without a weapon, or with a knife or a gun. Some involved household items like a hammer or plumbing pipes, but I saw no baseball bats. After several trips to the library without success, I became disillusioned. At least Miss Kessler's aura bubbled with white helpfulness whenever I saw her.

Her baseline swirled with an electric blue, peppered with a fire-colored orange and patches of silver. The warm, clean, wholesome flavors matched her vibrant personality. The yellowish sparks of happiness glistened in her compact frame, and I thought she'd be a great person to speak with Betsy—perhaps she could puncture that dismal grey.

"Sorry you haven't been able to find what you are looking for," she said to me.

"Maybe next time," I replied. I hopped on my bike and headed home.

This went on for weeks until the holiday season, when I took a break from the library visits to study for my exams. I didn't need to study math, and the science was simple and required only limited effort. I could study French all day long, and it wouldn't matter; I'd never be good at it. The history test required extensive review, and I needed to complete the book we were reading, *The Lord of the Flies*. That story reminded me that I'd hate to be stranded anywhere with a group of my so-called peers.

I spent the bulk of my time reading and studying history. Much like hitting the bag had been a welcome distraction from my search for the motorcycle maniac, the possibility of academic failure provided incentive to switch my focus to cramming.

When the exams came, I found them easy, and I wished I hadn't wasted so much time preparing. I even passed French. I was fortunate that we had no assessment for gym class, as I would've failed. PE didn't count as part of our grades for the HCC program. Perhaps the people in charge understood that as geeks, we shouldn't be penalized for a lack of physical prowess.

*   *   *

"Would you like anything specific for Christmas, Hunter?" Mom asked me on the first day of vacation.

I couldn't think of anything, so I shrugged.

"I can always get you some new shoes. Maybe a puzzle or game?"

"Sure, OK," I said. What I really wanted was the name of the person who had hit Allan. I'd find him, too. It was only a matter of time.

"What's Allan doing for the holiday?" she asked.

"He's going to his grandparent's house," I said.

"How about Betsy?"

"Her Dad is staying with her. She doesn't really get along with her Mom, so for her that's a great present."

"Come into the living room. Dad brought home a surprise," she said.

"Ta-da!" they both said, pointing toward a large evergreen tree in a stand.

"A Christmas tree!" Mom said.

I didn't understand much about Christmas, as neither Mom nor Dad were religious, but I basked in the yellow aura that danced between my parents.

On Christmas Day, I opened my presents. Most of the gifts were practical items like shirts, shoes and pants, but I did get some books and two jigsaw puzzles, which I always enjoyed. Mom and Dad exchanged several items, smiling while they watched each other unwrap the gifts. The unique purple color their auras shared implied a different type of bond. It made me happy seeing them interact.

*   *   *

Dad stayed around after the holiday, and since formal karate sessions didn't resume until January, he helped me with one-on-one instruction. We dressed in our training uniforms, including hand and foot protectors, and started our session with warm-up exercises and drills, like regular practice. He asked me to demonstrate my *kata*, which he learned in a few minutes, and then we began sparring.

"The most important thing to learn is misdirection," he said.

"What do you mean?" I asked, thinking about waves in auras.

"If I want to punch you in the stomach, for example, how best can I accomplish that?"

"You are so fast that you could punch before I had a chance to react," I said.

"That's true enough, probably, but let me be more precise. Suppose you wanted to punch me in the stomach. What could you do?"

"Pretend to punch you somewhere else first?" I posited.

"Exactly. Misdirection. Make your opponent move his guard to a place where it isn't needed, and then attack the open location."

"Just like chess!" I said.

"Sure, if you like. You can use a feint, a sacrifice, or a bluff in chess in the same way you'd use a combination strike in karate. Watch this," he said, and he slowly picked up his left leg and came at my head from the side.

I ducked, just as slowly. He then pulled his leg back and extended it right at my stomach.

"Combination. You think I'm trying to throw a roundhouse to your head, but I'm really preparing for a sidekick to the midsection. And once you block, duck, or parry, your guard is unprepared for the next move. You'll either be off balance, out of position, or perhaps trying a counterstrike of your own that might leave you exposed. Watch at full speed now."

Even though I knew exactly what was coming, I threw my arm out to block his kick and partially ducked, so that when his foot approached my stomach, I had no capacity to avoid it.

"See what I mean?" he asked.

I did indeed.

He spent several hours teaching me combination strikes. They reminded me of the one-step moves we'd done before, except the one-steps were reactions to a single punch. These combinations were complicated techniques used to attack during a sparring match, designed to strike through a deliberately created opening. I was fascinated. The workouts dramatically improved my sparring, and I enjoyed spending time with Dad. He radiated a paternal purple along with happiness and satisfaction in his aura. He, too, enjoyed our time together.

✶   ✶   ✶

Just before the year's end, I got a phone call that I wasn't expecting. Mom answered, and handed me the receiver.

"Hello?" I said.

"Hunter?" the woman's disembodied voice asked. I was reminded that I hated the phone, because I had no idea what the auras were doing.

"Yes?" I said cautiously.

"Hello, Hunter, this is Miss Kessler from the library. How are you?"

"Oh, hi, Miss Kessler," I said.

"There was a newspaper article today that I think you might want to read. I know you've been looking for information about motorcycle-related crimes, and today's paper has a long article by Lloyd Jonas that you may find helpful. Do you want to stop by the library and read it? You can always buy a copy of the newspaper at the store; but if you want, I can hold a copy at the library for you."

"That would be fantastic!" I said. I could feel the excitement percolating through my aura. I could hardly contain myself.

Although it was chilly, the roads weren't covered in snow, so I could ride my bike over to the old Fire Station-turned library. "Let me ask my Mom if I can come right now," I said.

"I'll be here until five. You can stop by anytime until then."

"Thank you so much!" I said.

I hung up and ran out of the kitchen to ask Mom if I could go to the library.

"I guess so," she said. "But school's over. What's this all about?"

I had my answer ready. "There's a civics project that we are required to do as part of the HCC for eighth grade. I'm doing some research for it. I have to pick a topic by the first two weeks in January."

"Oh, very good," Mom said. "Let me know if you need any help."

"Cool, thanks, Mom!" I said.

I went to change and bike to the library. Finally, a lead!

∗   ∗   ∗

Miss Kessler met me as I entered the building, magically appearing at the front door at the precise moment I arrived.

"Hello, Hunter, so good to see you," she said.

"Hi, Miss Kessler. Thanks for calling. Can I see what you have?"

She handed me the paper and guided me to a table to read it.

"Some of this is scary and maybe outside of your level, but I thought there was plenty of useful information," she said.

I scanned the article. By the time I finished the first page, my hopes sagged. As I completed it, I could feel slate grey dryness permeating my aura. The librarian could sense it too.

"So this isn't what you wanted?" she asked.

"It's a start," I said. "Let me look at it carefully again, maybe there's some stuff I can use," I said.

"OK, sorry," she said.

The article discussed local gangs, but it didn't provide the names of any individual members. It was all a bunch of generalities about the makeup, location, and crimes allegedly committed by different groups. I got excited when I read about the "OMGs" or Outlaw Motorcycle Gangs, thinking it might be a breakthrough, but it didn't point me in any particular direction. There were national OMGs like the one Dad mentioned, the Hell's Angels, but they had limited presence locally. Interesting reading, but I was no closer to solving the mystery.

*   *   *

Two of the more active local gangs were the Low Riders and the Highlanders. The Low Riders were associated with drugs, using motorcycles to transport marijuana and sometimes prescription medications across state borders. I didn't see any connection there, other than motorcycles. The Highlanders were the main rival for the Low Riders, but they focused more on prostitution, which I thought was strange because that had been Orlando Ryan's racket, and he had had nothing to do with biker gangs. We had followed him all over the place and never once encountered a person on a motorcycle.

I needed more information. Precise information. I needed a name. Once I had a name, I would take care of the rest, the same way I took care of Ryan.

Miss Kessler interrupted my reverie.

"I have another idea," she said.

I jumped.

"Oh, sorry, Hunter. Didn't mean to surprise you," she said.

"No that's OK. What's your idea?"

"The author, Lloyd Jonas, writes a lot of articles for the *Times*," she said.

"Yes?"

"Maybe he knows a lot more about the motorcycle people than he put in this story," she said.

"Right," I said, finally catching her meaning. "I could speak with him directly!"

"There you go," she said, the cheerful brightness reappearing in her intonation and in her aura.

"Fantastic! Thanks!" I said, my own aura now mirroring her jingling enthusiasm.

"Have you been to the *Times* building before?"

"Yes, I have. I used to have a friend there, Roger Pierce."

"Oh, wow! He wrote that expose on the bad policeman several

months back! I haven't seen anything by him lately though. I wonder what he's working on. Any idea?"

"No," I said. "Actually, he moved back to England."

"Oh, that's too bad, I really liked his writing," she said. "Well, perhaps Mr. Jonas can help you."

"Thanks again, Miss Kessler. If you see anything else, let me know. This is great," I repeated. I put on my jacket stuffed the article into my backpack, and headed toward the exit.

"Goodbye," she called after me.

"See you," I answered. It was a lead after all!

$\star$ $\star$ $\star$

I pedaled downtown to the *Times* building and parked my bike in the rack I'd used before. When I went inside, I was struck by the dearth of people. I ran over to the hefty, balding information guy, who looked up from his paper as I approached.

"Hello, young man. How can I help you?" he asked.

"I'm here to see Lloyd Jonas," I said breathlessly.

"I can ring his office, but I don't think he's here today," the man answered.

"Why not?" I asked.

"Maybe he's working on a story. Maybe it's his day off. I don't know. All I know is I've been here all day and he never came in. But, I'll ring the office, hold on a minute."

He punched the number into his intercom phone, and received no reply. The man shook his head.

"I can leave him a message if you want," he said.

"Do you know when he'll be in?" I asked.

"Probably after the New Year would be my guess. You can make an appointment, or call ahead and see if he's here. He often takes meetings during the day."

"OK, thanks," I said, clearly disappointed.

It was getting late, and I needed to get home anyway, so I went back outside, unlocked my bike, and toiled home. The climb made for a challenging ride, and I resorted to eating some snacks out of my jacket pocket to maintain my energy. The news story hadn't been much help, and the trip downtown had been a complete waste of time, but at least I'd opened a new avenue for potential progress.

CHAPTER 34

THE NEXT morning, I called the *Seattle Times* and asked for Lloyd Jonas, but he still wasn't there. The operator asked if I wanted to leave a message, which I declined. The information guy was right, Mr. Jonas was probably out until the first of the year.

Dad caught me as I hung up the phone. "Got any New Year's resolutions?" he asked.

Finding Allan's attacker was my number one priority, but I didn't want to tell him that. "Doing well in school and getting to blue belt," I said.

"On that note, shall we practice sparring this afternoon? I don't have to go back to work until January 2nd."

"Yeah, that would be cool," I agreed. I wanted to learn more combination kicks so I could use them when the time came.

Dad introduced more new moves, each of which involved a feint or misdirection.

"Watch this," he said. He punched toward my head. There was no chance that the blow would connect, but I reflexively blocked with an overhead technique. Quick as lightning, he jabbed at my exposed ribs.

"Why did you try to block my strike?" he asked.

"I don't know. I didn't think you were going to hit me," I said.

"Exactly. I took advantage of your muscle memory. If you're sparring an opponent with training, you can use that against him. You create an opening by eliciting a targeted response. In this case, I know you can perform an overhead block, so I tricked you into doing so with a low energy feint, then BOOM! Strike for real into the ribs."

"Cool," I said.

After two hours of aggressive training, I felt like a new person. I wasn't particularly competent with the combinations, but Dad reassured me that, with practice, I'd improve. More importantly, the exercise had helped clear my head.

When I was alone, I wallowed in self-pity. The bitterness and angst about my lack of progress in finding Allan's foe crushed my soul. It was the same grey morass I'd felt when I was hopelessly depressed about losing Grandpa. While working up a sweat, I forgot about my shortcomings, and the fog lifted. Dad could sense these changes as we exercised. He smiled at me and nodded.

I smiled back.

✶   ✶   ✶

On New Year's Eve, Mom told me I could stay up late and watch the ball drop, a reference to the televised tradition that marked the onset of the upcoming year. I didn't feel like it, so I went to bed early instead. The reminder that January first was a holiday—a day I wasn't going to accomplish anything—bummed me out. At least I'd been able to practice more karate with Dad.

✶   ✶   ✶

When school resumed, I was surprised to find my schoolmates' auras dancing with yellow happiness. That made no sense. I was miserable returning to school, and I assumed everyone else would be too. The only thing I was excited about was having another opportunity to investigate my elusive quarry, but returning to the classroom held little draw. Why was everyone so happy?

Miss Burnell graded our exams, and, as anticipated, I performed well on everything but French. Patty Owens celebrated her top scores, and Allan, Bob, Davis and Brady all felt good about their grades. Others felt disappointment, anger, and even fear, which shocked me. What could they possibly be afraid of? Then I recalled Betsy, who'd been forced to repeat 8th grade, and I understood. I had been concerned last year when I missed several weeks while in the hospital, but I'd caught up. The same might not be said for the weaker students in my group.

During the breaks, everyone talked about the new items they'd received for Christmas. My classmates verbalized "oohs" and "aahs" hearing about the booty, whether it was games, toys, cash, the latest fashion accessories, or a bicycle. Nobody was impressed at my haul of jeans, sneakers, books and jigsaw puzzles, but I didn't care. I had different goals.

We returned to our coursework, essentially the same topics as the first term, math, science, history, language arts, French and PE. Miss Burnell reminded us about the project, either a science fair entry or a civics paper. At this point, nobody except Patty was interested in writing a ten-page paper.

I saw Betsy in gym and promised to sit with her at lunch. Allan wasn't interested in pursuing his attacker, so perhaps she could help. Maybe the search would distract her from her chronic misery.

"How was your Christmas?" she asked, as I arrived at her table with my lunch and milk.

"Good, I got some clothes and stuff," I said. I'd learned how lame my presents were by comparison, so I didn't try to impress her.

"Dad bought me a new backpack. I lost my other one. I think I left it at the park that day…" she trailed off. I knew which day she meant.

"So, listen," I started. "I want to find the guy who hit Allan in the head with a baseball bat. The librarian showed me an article in the *Seattle Times* by a writer who seems to be an expert on local gangs. I want to speak with him to see if he has insight into who might be responsible."

"Don't you think that's a matter for the police?" she asked.

"Do *you* trust the police?"

I could see her mind racing. The cops had carried her mother off in handcuffs and forced her into rehab. While this had probably been for the best, Betsy didn't see it that way. I saw her aura agreeing silently.

"Is it going to be dangerous?" she asked, avoiding my question.

"I'm not worried," I said.

"Because you're a superstar karate expert now?"

I felt a buzzing warning. My ego had taken me dangerously close to exposing my talent.

"I'm just asking questions, that's all. If I find anything, I'll tell Officer Metz. He's the guy who came to Allan's house when it happened."

"Why don't you start by asking *him* who might have done it? Maybe he already knows."

I had no response. That was a very good idea. I could tell he knew something, but how was I supposed to get a policeman to talk? A vision of Orlando Ryan lashed to a chair confessing his crimes arose unbidden, and I rejected the idea immediately. Officer Metz was one of the good guys. Ryan was a monster who got what he deserved.

"Hey, better finish your food," Betsy prompted.

"So, will you help me?" I asked.

"I'll certainly listen," she answered.

I smiled. Any help was better than none. She returned the smile, and we finished eating.

*   *   *

When I got home I called the newspaper again, and the female voice confirmed that Mr. Jonas wasn't in. She asked if I wanted to leave a message. I wished I could see the operator's aura, because I thought she might be lying. Since I wasn't making progress by calling every day, I left a message. I gave my name and phone number and asked if Mr. Jonas could call me back about an article he'd written.

∗   ∗   ∗

Karate class resumed, and it was our turn to drive. Mom spent the trip talking to Allan about his Christmas. She asked what his favorite present was.

"My grandparents gave me a check," he said.

"Very nice. Are you going to buy something with the money?"

"No, I'm going to save it. Mom helped me set up a new bank account."

"How very responsible of you," Mom said.

When we arrived, I could feel the energy as the students greeted one another before entering the *dojo*. Josh bragged about a particularly awesome gift he'd received—action figures relating to some famous space movie. The yellow belts were excited about their recent advances, and they encouraged the two new students, both preteen girls, who were our only white belts.

I remembered when Allan had convinced me to start lessons two years ago, and I was thankful to have such a close friend. Before karate, I had no social life. I still didn't have much of one, but it was better now, and Allan was responsible. The two white belt girls displayed the same bond of purple friendship that flowed between Allan and me. I hoped they relished their relationship as much as I did mine.

Sensei Nam began with bows, and when we broke into groups, we started learning the blue belt *kata*. Sensei Nam reviewed each of the steps with us carefully, and we practiced them before moving to sparring. While fighting with Scott, I tried out three of Dad's combinations. Although I set him up well, my strikes were awkward and didn't hit cleanly. Still, it was fun trying out the new moves.

Afterward, Allan and I got dressed while waiting for Mom to return. She was late.

"I saw you sparring. You used some combinations I've never

seen before. Where'd you learn them?" Allan asked.

"Dad showed me," I said, suddenly excited. "I didn't think anyone noticed."

"The concepts are very cool. Once you're able to execute them, you're going to be pretty good."

"Thanks!" I said.

"You're going to have to show them to me, of course," he said.

"Sure," I agreed. I'd never imagined being able to help Allan with karate.

We chatted about school, karate, the weather, and anything other than his attack, until Mom finally arrived. I thought again about how much I valued his friendship. I vowed to avenge his assault, no matter what I had to do.

CHAPTER 35

THURSDAY MORNING, the phone rang as I was getting ready for school.

"Hunter!" Mom called down. "It's for you. He says he's from the *Seattle Times*. Do you know anything about this?"

"I'll be right there!" I yelled back.

She handed me the receiver as I breathlessly reached for it. Her aura flowed with curiosity and concern.

"Hello, this is Hunter," I said.

"Lloyd Jonas. I'm returning your call. You wanted to speak with me about a newspaper article?"

I looked up. Mom was a statue. The truth wasn't going to work.

"Yes, I am doing a project for school. I'm wondering if I can ask you a few questions. Are you free this afternoon?"

"How old are you, son?"

"I'm fourteen. I can ride my bike down to your office," I offered.

"Very well," he said. "How about 4:30 pm?"

"Yes, that's great, thanks. I'll see you then."

I hung up the phone.

"What's this all about?" Mom asked.

"Remember that school project?" I said.

"A civics paper, if memory serves," Mom answered.

"I want to ask him some questions for it," I said.

Mom was unconvinced. I felt helpless, unable to stop her from reading my expression.

"I've got to get to the bus," I said quickly. "I'm going to miss it."

"We'll talk more about this later," she said. "Have a good day."

I ran out to the bus stop to escape Mom's inquisitive glare.

I could barely contain my excitement. I cornered Allan after our first block of classes and told him the news.

"I'm going to see the newspaper guy this afternoon!"

"What newspaper guy?" he asked.

"His name is Lloyd Jonas. He writes for the *Seattle Times*. He wrote an article about gangs in the Madrona area, and he might know who was responsible for hurting you."

"Hunter, I appreciate it. But like I said before, just let it go."

"You're kidding, right?" I asked.

"No, I'm serious. I don't want to go looking for trouble. It'll only get worse."

He sounded resolved.

"But I can—"

"No, Hunter, leave it alone," he said with finality.

No chance of that, but I couldn't tell him so.

"All right," I said.

I sat with Betsy at lunch, and after arguing internally about it, I decided to tell her as well.

"I'm going to see Lloyd Jonas this afternoon. He's a writer for the *Times*. He may know something about Allan's attacker. But Allan doesn't want me to keep looking for the guy. If we tell the police, the guy will get arrested, right?"

Betsy's aura darkened.

"It's not always that simple," she said.

"Of course it is. Good guys do good things, and bad guys get punished!"

"No, Hunter, it's not. Listen, if Allan doesn't want you to pursue it, maybe you should respect his wishes."

"NO!" I yelled.

The goth kids at the next table stared at me briefly, then resumed plotting the demise of civilization, or whatever they did.

"I know your heart is in the right place, Hunter, but you have to listen to Allan. Maybe there's a good reason why he asked you to stop. Think about it, OK?"

I shook my head. What could possibly make Allan, Betsy, or anyone else *not* want to catch the person responsible for giving Allan a concussion?

Once school ended, I took the bus home and went straight to the garage to get my bike. I wanted to be sure I arrived on time for my appointment.

Mom stopped me.

"Are you ready to go?" she asked, dangling the car keys in front of me.

"Yeah, I was going to take my bike," I said nervously.

"No need, I can give you a ride. I have to pick up groceries, and we can stop on the way back."

Seeing Mom's resolve, I nodded in agreement and went to the car.

"Don't you want to bring a notebook or something?"

It was a good suggestion. "Yeah, thanks, I do."

I went to my bedroom and grabbed a three-ring binder with extra loose-leaf pages and a pen, and tossed them into my backpack. I met Mom in the garage.

"How do you know this fellow from the paper? Friend of Roger Pierce?"

I paused. How did she know about Roger? What was up with all the questions?

"No, his name came up at the library while I was looking for articles. He wrote a bunch. The librarian, Miss Kessler, suggested he might be able to give me more information."

"For your civics paper?" she asked.

"Yeah," I agreed quickly.

"OK," she said. Her aura confirmed that she didn't believe what I was telling her.

*   *   *

Unlike riding the bike, which I could leave right at the building entrance, we had to park in one of the lots downtown and walk over, so it took almost the same amount of time to drive. Mom and I strode into the offices and right up to the information guy.

"Hello again, young man. I see you've brought a friend. A sister, perhaps?" the old balding guy said. His aura flowed with waves, as though he was a hundred percent sure that Mom was *not* my sister. What was the point of that lie?

"Very clever, sir. Hunter Miller to see Lloyd Jonas," Mom said sternly.

"Why yes, of course. Finally got back to you, did he?"

He gave us the office number, pointed to the elevator, and watched us get on and take it to the requisite floor. Mom said nothing, apparently processing the man's comments.

We knocked on the door, and a man's voice beckoned from within. "Come in!"

The man rose from behind his desk and extended his smallish hand. He was slightly shorter than me, with a round head, a plaid shirt and baggy pants. His aura exuded a curious mix of two light blues, a bright silver, and a fiery orange, along with a clean, scratchy tapping. Plus there was pink, naturally, and an ivory white with a gamey smell.

"Marissa Miller," Mom said, taking the proffered hand. "This is my son Hunter, with whom you spoke earlier."

He extended his hand again my way, and I shook it.

"Have a seat," he suggested, although there wasn't any place for our bottoms to safely land. The office was a mess.

He hastily tossed some papers aside, revealing two uncomfortable chairs.

"Now, what can I do for you?"

Mom stared at me sideways. "Hunter?"

I was trapped. Either I told Mom what I was doing, or I wasted my trip.

"Um, yeah," I started. "I read your article from last week."

"Which one?" he asked.

It was no use. I wanted to find out what he knew, and Mom wasn't going to allow it unless she was in the loop.

"About the motorcycle gangs."

Mom's aura flashed an irritated confirmation. She'd suspected why I was here.

"Yes, that," he said. "What in particular are you interested in?"

I thought fast. What had Miss Burnell said? Something about the Mayor, or a fire chief. Interviewing… something about the community.

"I want to learn about the police department. Maybe interview the Mayor." The idea formed while I spoke.

"Yeah… I want to have an issue to talk to the police about, and I decided to use gang violence as that issue. So can you help me learn about gangs? And do you know people at the police office I could interview for my paper?"

It made perfect sense. Mom's aura buzzed with disbelief and concern.

Mr. Jonas, however, swelled with pride.

"Well, now, son, a good reporter never reveals his sources! However, I happen to know that there's a fine young officer at SPD named Skeet who'll be happy to assist you. He's been working on the gang task force since its inception two years ago by Captain Beurline. Skeet investigates all gang related activity in the area, and he'll be very helpful, I think."

"Skeet?" Mom said.

"Right, Officer Metz." Mr. Jonas said. "I think his name is Michael, but everyone calls him Skeet. Something to do with a mosquito bite he sustained during his training, I guess. Perhaps he'll tell you the story if you ask."

I knew I'd made the right move!

Mom looked at me accusingly as we exited the office after thanking Mr. Jonas for his time.

"Have you heard that name before?" she asked. Her aura intimated that she knew the answer.

"Yes, actually. Isn't that the name of the Officer who came to help Allan?"

"I believe it is," she said carefully. "Come on. Let's go speak to him," she said.

⋆   ⋆   ⋆

Instead of picking up groceries, we stopped at the police station on the way home. The East Precinct was familiar, only a few blocks from our house, and right near Capitol Hill, one of the places that Orlando Ryan used to go when we were tailing him. Although I'd seen the place many times, I'd never been inside.

We entered the large glass building and checked in with the person on duty in front.

"Can I help you?" she asked, opening a plate glass window that separated us from her.

"We'd like to see Officer Metz," Mom said briskly.

"Do you have an appointment?" she asked.

"No."

"All right, let me see if he's available. Meanwhile, sign in here, please."

She slid the window closed again and communicated with someone while Mom added her name to the ones on the clipboard. Moments later, the lady opened the trapdoor and reclaimed the list. She nodded her head toward a doorway that led into the back, saying "He'll be right out."

Officer Metz appeared after a buzzing noise that preceded the door opening.

"Michael Metz, at your service," said the man. I reviewed the colors of his aura and tried to place the purple-blue baseline. It wasn't common.

Just like with Mr. Jonas, Mom extended her hand and introduced both of us. "Marissa Miller, and my son Hunter."

We all shook hands in turn.

"Now, what can I do you for?" he said, smiling broadly.

Mom's aura flashed irritation, at what I had no idea. She turned to me without letting her expression change one iota. I marveled. I needed to learn that skill!

"Hunter?" she said.

"Oh, right. I'm doing a civics paper and I was hoping I could interview you. I want to learn about police work."

"Oh, wow," he said. "I'm pretty busy, so I don't know," he added.

Mom touched the man's hand. "It would mean a great deal to me if you could help."

He looked stunned. "Of course. Yes. Civic duty. Sure. I can help. Just not this instant. How about making an appointment for Monday?"

"Tuesday would be better," Mom said.

"About four pm?" he suggested.

"Yes, that would be perfect."

"Great!" I said.

"Thank you very much for your time," Mom said, excusing the both of us. Officer Metz went back through the buzzing door, and we went on to the grocery store.

"Thanks, Mom!" I said earnestly as we left.

She looked at me suspiciously.

CHAPTER 36

I COULDN'T wait to interview the policeman. I spent my morning ignoring the teacher and considering how to phrase questions. The problem was twofold. First, I needed to convince Mom, Officer Metz, and probably Miss Burnell, that I was working on a civics paper. Therefore, I had to restrict my questions to those that would be relevant for such an assignment. I didn't really know how to write a paper, but that was immaterial. I could sort that out later. However, I needed to formulate questions before Tuesday.

The second part of the problem was that I needed to discern what the police knew about Allan's attacker. This meant I had to ask about gang violence, specifically in the Madrona area, and figure out names and affiliations of those most likely to beat up a kid in my neighborhood.

To make matters worse, Mom knew exactly when and where the appointment was, and she was unlikely to let me go alone. My questions were going to be scrutinized by two adults, both well experienced in human relations and interrogation, and I had a limited time frame.

My advantage was my unerring ability to detect lies. That was the key. I needed to make sure that my questions were innocent enough to pass through Mom and Officer Metz without rousing suspicion, yet pointed enough to give me details. No small task. I needed help.

Allan wasn't going to assist me in this—he'd made that quite clear. I wished Grandpa could help, but I squelched that thought before the grey morass could affect me. Betsy was also reluctant, for reasons I couldn't understand.

My next thought was Dad, but he'd tell Mom, and he was out of town anyway. Ian would be able to help, but he was in England. Mrs. Frechette would tell Mom and Dad, probably. Dr. Eisenberg still harbored questions about my dealings with Orlando Ryan. My classmates all regarded me as an outcast, especially after the depression episode.

Depression. Hmm. A stray thought coalesced inside my brain. What about someone from the therapy group? We bonded in our time together. Maybe one of them could help?

I considered each member in turn. The girls, other than Betsy, all went to Garfield High. Lynn was too depressed to function. Suzanne hated everyone and wouldn't even consider it. Neither Denise nor Kayleigh had the capacity or motivation to help, and Betsy was already out. But what about Toby? He was a chess player and an outcast, like me. Moreover, he went to school at Madrona, so he'd be easier to locate and speak with. He'd obviously been teased before, and he might understand exactly why I was doing this. I nodded to myself.

Even as I made the decision to ask Toby, I revisited another option. Ian. Though he wasn't around, I could still contact him. I resolved to use a two-pronged attack.

I'd write a letter to Ian, and tell him of my plight. Despite his somewhat selfish nature, he always treated me like a true friend. I bet he'd help. Unfortunately, I'd have to wait for his return letter to hear his advice, and that would be too late for this first meeting. I'd need a second meeting.

Meanwhile, I'd find Toby and see what he had to say. Maybe having a meaningful project would help his depression, and he'd be able to squeeze away the bitter, ash-colored moaning in his aura.

"Mr. Miller?" came the teacher's voice, right in my ear.

I hadn't noticed her aura approaching, but I felt it now, too close for comfort.

"What?" my voice went high and crackly, causing some of my classmates to laugh.

"Why y'all think you can sleep through the lectures is beyond me. If I'd have tried that, the nuns would have whacked me with a ruler so hard I'd be redder than a ripe tomato after harvest," she said.

"But y'all are supposed to be the smart, sensitive ones. And I'm supposed to stand up here and be supportive. Well, I've had just about enough out of you!" she said.

Her aura was fuming. My own tingled with danger. Something bad was about to happen, and I didn't need that right now. I had things to do. Her aura was so close. So close, I could practically touch it. So close, it wouldn't take much…

I reached out with my mind and pulled away the acidic maroon and replaced it with a light yellow warmth.

"Please give me another chance, Miss Burnell," I said. "I'm sorry I wasn't paying attention. I've been having trouble since my Grandpa died." This was quite true, so my aura didn't display any waves, thankfully.

The emotions in her aura morphed quickly from a buttery, chestnut flavor, through olive green confusion, to a lemony, buttermilk white.

"Very well," the teacher relented. "But if it happens again, it'll be straight to the principal's office with you, and you won't be allowed to return without written permission from her and your parents!"

Some of the redness had returned, but not nearly to the extent it had been before. She reclaimed her place at the front of the classroom, took a deep breath, and asked, apparently for the second or third time, "Can anyone tell me a metaphor used by Bradbury in the assigned chapters?"

She held up her copy of *Fahrenheit 451*, which I hadn't started.

Allan raised his hand from the table behind me.

"Mr. Marks?"

"The great python spits its venomous kerosene into the world," he said.

"Yes! Yes! And how is this a metaphor?"

"Bradbury compares the hose to a giant snake," Allan said. The teacher was thrilled. All had been forgotten, and class went on as before, except I had to follow the discussion. Giant waste of time, but I had no choice.

I turned and looked at Allan, who'd saved me for the hundredth time. He gave me a slight nod. I smiled my thanks. Then I turned my head forward quickly so as not to evoke the wrath of the woman who wished to turn my skin into an overripe tomato.

⋆   ⋆   ⋆

When we broke for lunch, I embarked upon my journey to locate Toby, but the tour of the cafeteria was for naught, as he wasn't in my lunch period. I endured the rest of the day stoically, paying enough attention to the subject matter to avert any disaster involving the principal or Mom. Then, at dismissal, I made a beeline for the exit and carefully surveyed the swarming kids, scouring the younger sections for the mousy character onto whom I'd attached my hopes.

Toby was the last one out of the sixth grade sections, and as I approached, I was reminded why he was in Dr. Eisenberg's group therapy. His aura reeked of depression. Although I knew it would have little lasting impact, I pushed away some of the bitter grey. I made sure to get very close before doing so, as I'd eaten much of my pocket food after the incident with Miss Burnell, and I didn't want to use up too much energy.

"Toby," I said calmly, hoping not to spook him any more than necessary.

"Hi, Hunter," he said brightly. I'd added too much canary yellow to his aura. It was strange to see him smiling. I doubted it would take long to wear off.

"Hey, Toby, I have a problem and I think you might be able to help."

"Me? What is it? Lost something underneath a rug and you need me to walk under and find it?"

"What?" I said, confused.

"Never mind," he said. The yellow was fading quickly.

"No, nothing to do with a rug. It's about Allan. The buses are here, so I don't have much time right now, but how about we meet tomorrow at the park? Say early afternoon? Like one pm?"

"It's awful cold out," he said hesitantly.

"OK, indoors then. Do you know where the library is?"

"Of course I know where the library is. I'm in sixth grade. Do you think I'm an idiot?" he retorted.

"I didn't know where the library was…" I said, my voice trailing off.

He stared at me curiously.

"Anyway, library, one pm?" I reiterated.

"I'll have to ask my parents," Toby said.

"Uh, sure. Ok. Let me have your phone number in case you can't make it."

We exchanged numbers, and he ran off to catch his bus, and I did the same.

When I got home, I initiated the second part of my two-tiered plan. A letter to Ian.

Dear Ian,

I'm having trouble and I could use your help.

Allan got hit in the head by somebody, probably with a baseball bat. Nobody knows who did it. The guy rode off on a motorcycle, and the police think he may be part of a gang.

Allan is OK. He had a cut on his head and a concussion. He doesn't want to find out who did this, but I do. I tried to do some investigative journalism, but without you and your Dad to help, I ran into trouble. I found old copies of newspapers in the library, and the librarian is helping me look up police blotter stories, but I still have no idea who is responsible. I even talked to a reporter, but he wasn't able to tell me much, only the name of the officer investigating the gangs.

I am scheduled to meet with the police officer in charge of

the case, but he won't tell me anything unless I ask the right
questions. That's where you come in. How do I get him to tell
me something he doesn't want to share?
Hope you are doing OK.

Your friend,
Hunter

I didn't even try to edit it, I simply folded it up and stuck it into an envelope. I located his address and wrote it in the proper place. I attached several stamps and dropped the letter into the mailbox for the postal carrier. I didn't know how long it would be until I got a reply, but I hoped he'd answer quickly. Ian knew how to do stuff like this, and I needed his help.

✳   ✳   ✳

Karate class helped me focus, and I felt reinvigorated afterward. Josh had been impressed by the combination kicks I'd tried, and I smiled, thinking of Dad's lessons. I found myself wishing he were around this week so I could ask his advice about Allan, but he was back on assignment. I had no idea when he'd return.

Toby called while I was at karate and left a message saying he'd meet me at the library like we planned. I figured I'd go early and check the police blotter in case anything turned up since last week. Other than the story by Mr. Jonas, the newspaper had been a bust so far, but I didn't want to give up on that angle just yet. The bald guy at the information desk had seen something in the paper, and until I found that, I knew there was more to learn.

CHAPTER 37

"I'M GOING to the library," I called to Mom as I stuffed a sandwich into my face and headed toward the garage to get my bike.

"Are you meeting anyone?" she asked, suddenly appearing in my path.

I stopped short and swallowed. "Yeah, my friend Toby."

"Oh," she said. "OK, have a good time."

I extricated myself from her presence, finished my hasty lunch and rode to the Fire Station branch of the Seattle Public Library.

As I walked in, Miss Kessler called loudly from her desk at the other side of the room. "Hello, Hunter!"

I had thought you were supposed to be quiet in a library.

"Hi, Miss Kessler," I replied, using a more subdued tone.

She waved, and I proceeded directly to the newspapers, scanning the latest ones for any interesting arrests. A few minutes later, the door rattled open, revealing a disheveled Toby.

"Hello, Toby," called the librarian. I guess she knew him, too.

He responded mutely, walking over to where I was waving.

"So what's this thing you need my help on," he said glumly.

I thought about altering his aura to make him more cheerful, but decided against it.

"OK, here's the thing," I started. "You know my friend Allan?"

He shook his head. "No."

"He's in my grade and in my karate class. Anyway, he got hit hard by some crazy guy on a motorcycle, and I want to find the man who did it. The policeman who investigated it and the information guy from the newspaper both think it has something to do with a motorcycle gang, but they won't tell me anything else."

"Yeah, what's that got to do with me?"

"Here's the thing. I'm meeting with the cop again Tuesday. I want to get him to tell me more, but I stink at asking questions. I was hoping you could help."

"Why me? I'm nobody."

He was right, of course.

I nearly responded by saying that I didn't have anyone else I could ask for help, which was the truth, but I changed my mind. After all, nobody is truly "nobody."

"You play chess, right?"

"Sure."

"Well, think of this as a chess match. We want to hunt down the opponent's king, and we have access to a rook. You know, this cop. He can lead me to the king, but I have to capture him first."

His aura perked up, followed quickly by his facial features.

"Yeah, OK," he said confidently.

"So you'll help?"

"Yeah. What do you know about the cop?" he asked.

"He's a good guy. At least, I think he is. And he's been around a while. He's on the gang task force. So he knows all the gangs."

"Well there you go. Start from that angle."

"How do you mean?"

"Have him explain something about the structure of the gangs. Keep it general," Toby said.

"Like what?"

"Ask him who's in charge of each gang. Then ask who the lieutenants are. Who holds the power? Who are the kings and queens, so to speak. Once you know who's in charge, you can look for more information in the newspaper and stuff."

"Wow, that's great!" I said excitedly.

We talked a bit more about unimportant things and I left shortly after, feeling much better about my meeting on Tuesday.

*   *   *

I wasted Sunday and Monday with academic pursuits. I had to read *Fahrenheit 451*, and then during school, I was forced to listen while Miss Burnell detailed extremely boring math, physical science data and historical trivia. Tuesday morning I was rewarded for my attentiveness, as we had a quiz on the material from Monday. I aced it.

"Well, well, Hunter Miller," said Miss Burnell, tossing my quiz onto my desk. "One hundred percent. Will miracles never cease?"

I accepted the paper with a blank expression, not because I had any control of my facial muscles, but because I had no idea how to respond. She moved on quickly, so I turned around to look at Allan, who shrugged.

I could barely contain myself as the day progressed, as I was so excited to meet with Officer Metz. I bolted to the bus and sat frozen with anticipation all the way home. Mom wasn't there, so I left immediately for the police station, hardly believing my luck. Not only did I have a great set of questions, I'd be free to mess with his aura to get the responses I needed without worrying about getting caught.

The unfriendly police station had features more in common with a prison than anywhere else. The cage that housed the only visible occupant made me edgy. It felt like they expected someone to come in and shoot up the place. Fortunately, I felt no tingling to suggest imminent danger, so I approached the officer in the pit.

"Name," she said bluntly, after opening the communication portal.

"Hunter Miller. Here to see Officer Metz. I have an appointment."

"Sign in," she said, her tone equally flat.

I accepted the clipboard and used the attached pen to write my name in the next open spot on the roster. I handed it back and she slammed the sliding glass shut without another word.

Officer Metz emerged from the buzzing door, smiling slightly. I ate a bunch of peanuts from my stash, in case I needed to manipulate his aura. I had to make sure I didn't run out of energy and fall into the void. That would be disastrous.

"Hello, young man," he said, extending his right arm toward me.

"Hunter," I said, shaking the proffered hand.

"Michael Metz. Follow me."

He signaled to the woman behind the desk, and the door buzzed again loudly. We entered the bowels of the police station, a dark, dirty and smelly place with tile floors that made Officer Metz's shoes clack with every step. We walked by two empty workspaces and arrived at a desk containing a set of files, a typewriter, stacks of forms, various writing utensils, a box of tissues, a can of cola, and scattered debris, including old Twinkie wrappers.

He extended his hand toward the only chair not covered in papers. "Have a seat," he said. "How can I help you?"

I'd rehearsed my speech expecting Mom to be there, but her absence didn't change anything, so I began.

"I'm doing a project for school and I want to learn about gang violence. Specifically, I want to know what information you can provide on local gangs. What gangs are located in Seattle? How do they operate? What is known about each of the leaders or high placed officers?"

I watched his eyebrows furrow and saw the greenish flare in his aura.

"And this is for a school paper?" he asked suspiciously.

I convinced myself that I was going to write a civics paper instead of doing a science fair project, so that when I replied "absolutely" there would be no waves. It worked.

"Cool. What year are you?"

"I'm in the eighth grade HCC program at Madrona."

"What's HCC?" he asked.

"It stands for highly capable cohort," I explained.

"Nice. The smart kids. I get it."

I nodded.

"OK, sure. I can give you some information. What do you know so far?" he asked.

"Not much, I'm afraid. I've heard about the Hell's Angels, but I'm hoping to focus on local gangs instead of that one."

It was his turn to nod. "Right," he said.

I could see the silver, blue and white in his aura accentuate. I was frustrated by my complete lack of understanding of its significance. He continued.

"Well, the two big local gangs are the Highlanders and the Low Riders. They have a couple of things in common, and a few things that make them distinct. For example, members of both ride motorcycles. In the case of the Low Riders, they use them to traffic drugs like marijuana in from Canada and then around town. They distribute to young people, not much older than you, and they take their business pretty seriously. If other people, like members of the Highlander gang, try to interfere, they're not above beating or even killing them."

He paused to let that sink in for a while. It sounded very much like the article written by Lloyd Jonas. He went on.

"The Highlanders weren't very popular until recently. Most of the gang had been locked up in prison, where they belong. Unfortunately, many of them were recently released as a result of a technicality. The arresting officer had charges filed against him for corruption, so the DA had to overturn the convictions because they were based on testimony of a felon."

I raised my hand, an old habit but a time-honored tradition of demonstrating a question. Metz looked at me. "What?"

"DA?"

"Oh, yeah. District Attorney. See, when we catch someone for a crime, we have to *prove* they are guilty in a court of law. Otherwise, they just go back out on the street. Presumed innocent, the law says. Horsesh—" He stopped.

"Anyway, if the DA can't make a case, or the evidence is questionable, the perp walks."

I raised my hand slightly.

"Perp. Perpetrator. Guilty party."

"Thanks," I said.

"So when Ryan went to jail, all his cases went under review, and rather than re-trying them all, the judge simply dismissed many of them. The streets were flooded with hoodlums. And then in a twist of irony, some of the ones left in jail killed Ryan. The warden reported it as a suicide, but I doubt that. Poor sap."

A blinding realization of burning chestnut muddled my aura beyond recognition. It was Orlando Ryan. By exposing him, I'd been responsible for putting those thugs on the street.

"You all right?" Officer Metz asked.

"Yes. It's just—all those criminals put back on the street because one cop got arrested?"

"One guilty cop. They found enough evidence on him to put him away for life. Even though his life only turned out to be a few months longer."

I barely regained my composure enough to ask the next question on my list. "So, who's in charge?" I mumbled.

"Of the Low Riders? That's easy. A fellow by the name of Munson. Roderick Munson. He's the shot-caller for the entire Seattle unit. We know it, he knows we know it, yet he stays a half step ahead of the cops all the time. If I didn't know better, I'd say he has an informant in the SPD."

"Informant?"

"Yeah, someone just like Ryan. A rat. An officer or other employee, maybe someone in the DA's office, who tips Munson off every time we try to make a bust. Before Ryan, I'd never have thought it possible. But now, who knows? Maybe there's more. Oh, but don't put any of that in your essay, OK?"

"My what?" I asked.

"Your paper. The civics paper you're writing?"

"Oh. No, of course not. Mum's the word," I said, putting my hand over my mouth to accentuate the promise.

"Thanks," he replied.

I carefully considered what he told me and refocused. "Let me get this straight. You know who's in charge, but the police can't do anything?"

"Exactly. I mean, we keep trying to build a case, but everything we do turns into a dead end one way or another."

"Do you know about any of his lieutenants?" I asked.

"Oh, military brat?" he asked.

"What?" I replied.

"Nothing. It's just that most kids don't say lieutenants. Sort of a military term. Never mind. Actually, Munson runs the show pretty tightly. He doesn't seem to delegate much. You think that'd make it easier to catch him, but it doesn't happen."

"Hmm," I said.

"You can say that again," said the officer.

"What?"

He held up his hand and laughed. The yellow in his aura indicated he'd told a joke, but I didn't get it. Not a surprise. I changed topics.

"What about the Highlanders?"

"What do you mean?"

"Who's in charge of that group?"

"That's even worse. We have no idea. We've seen no viable candidates in all of the arrests we've made."

"Someone's got to be the boss," I protested.

"I'm sure there is one, but we truly have no idea who it is. We have a huge list of parolees who are members, but none of them even know the management. We've interviewed them all—nothing."

"Parolees?"

"Yeah. Some of the jailed members took deals for parole, or early release, in exchange for not risking having their cases reopened. We can track them, in theory, because they have to meet with a parole officer periodically to make sure they aren't breaking any laws."

"How do you know they are members of the Highlanders?"

"Most of them get tats—tattoos—while in the slammer. That's actually another thing we can track. If someone with a Highlander tattoo gets released, we put it down under 'known associates' in their file."

A brilliant idea hit me.

"Can I see the list of Highlanders?"

Officer Metz turned pale. "Sorry, I can't share that information. It's not something you should be looking into, either," he said.

I watched his eyes dart to one of the files on his desk. I thought about pressing the issue, but his aura indicated that I was making him uncomfortable. I needed Ian's advice on how to pry information from the files.

"Oh, never mind that, then. I probably don't need it."

"Good," he said. The mustard yellow in his aura fizzed with obvious relief. Even so, he still didn't completely relax. "Well, I hope this has been helpful. I need to get back to work now. Did you have any other questions?"

"Yeah, one thing. The guy from the newspaper said you had a nickname. Skeet?"

"Ha, ha, ha, yes," he laughed. "That is sort of a funny story. I was at the range as a rookie, and I was nervous. I had to pass my certification to carry a service revolver. The moment I started the test, I got bitten by a mosquito, and my first shot was so bad that it hit the next target over. The guys gave me crap for a month, and started calling me Skeeter in honor of the bug. It sorta stuck. It doesn't bother me anymore, because I can hit the bullseye ten times out of ten now, and nobody questions my ability on the range."

"That's cool," I said, in awe.

"Anything else?"

"No, you've been very kind. Thank you very much!"

He stood up, shook my hand again, waved to the lady in the cage who hit a button, and then walked me through the buzzing door. I headed out to the street to bike home. I had a lot to consider.

CHAPTER 38

AS I rode home, I reviewed the interview in my head. I should have asked to see the tattoo pattern that marked members of the Highlanders. That might turn out to be helpful. But something even more useful occurred to me. When I queried Officer Metz about a list of gang members, although he didn't allow me access, he confirmed the existence of such a list. I'd have to find a way to see it. If there was one for the Highlanders, there was probably one for the Low Riders. I'd get a look at both if I played my cards right. Ian might have some insight.

In the meantime, I could research this Munson character. It sounded like he'd been arrested before, perhaps multiple times, so each event would be in the police blotter. Miss Kessler could get papers for the last year or so, and somewhere I'd find arrest reports for the leader of the Low Riders.

Mom was home when I returned.

"How was your meeting?" she asked. I could see the conflict in her aura. She'd wanted to come with me, but she'd missed it.

"It was good. I got some ideas for my paper."

She stared at me closely, like she was reading my aura.

Of course she couldn't do that! She was reading my face.

"Great," she said, without much of a pause. "What's your next step?"

"I'm hoping to go back for a second interview later. Maybe I could talk to someone higher up?" Officer Metz's boss might let me look at the lists of gang members, I reasoned.

Mom peered at me again, but smiled. "Sure, that could be helpful. What do you want for dinner?"

The subject change threw me. "I don't care," I said.

"How about pasta?"

"Sure," I agreed.

The next morning, Mom called the police station and asked if I could speak with Officer Metz's supervisor, a man named Lieutenant Herlihy. She was very convincing. They said they'd call her back when he was available.

"Thanks," I told Mom, who smiled.

I bided my time with my usual daily activities to avoid suspicion about my secret project. School and karate occupied Wednesday, so I waited until Thursday afternoon to make my next move, visiting the library.

Miss Kessler greeted me in her usual enthusiastic fashion, offering her assistance with anything I might need. She always cheered me up. How much nicer would the world be if everyone was so helpful and kind?

Today, I took her up on her offer.

"Thanks, Miss Kessler," I said. "I'm looking for something quite specific. Any articles on Roderick Munson. My contact at the police department gave me the name. He said Munson was in charge of the Low Riders. The police arrested him a few times, but weren't able to put him in jail because of someone called the District Attorney. I didn't understand that part. Anyway, I'd love to find out whatever I can from the old newspapers. Maybe going back up to a year."

"Of course, Hunter," she chimed. "But if you want to look at newspapers that old, you'll need to learn how to use the microfiche reader, and I'll have to order the files from the main campus downtown. It may take a few days. But I can show you the reader today, and that way, when the package comes, you can be all ready to look through the slides."

I agreed, and she took me into a small room. She grabbed a stack of small plastic cards with images on them. On the lone desk was a computer with a giant TV screen, with a slot in the front where she loaded one of the plastic cards. A bright microscope light beamed the images from the card onto the TV, and I could see writing magnified a zillion times.

"Wow, cool!" I said.

She explained how to shift the position of the card to view the entirety of the fiche by moving it around. Then she let me practice.

"So how do I know what's on the card?" I asked.

"Well, that's the tough part. Each day's paper will probably be on a single card, but there's no way of knowing which one will have the story you want. You have to look through them all. It'd be easier if you knew which date you needed, but if not, you have to keep scanning until you find it. It could take days."

"Great," I said, unenthusiastically.

"I'll let you know when the box comes in. When it does, I should be able to help you, depending on whether anyone else is here. But I have to go now and assist other patrons. See you soon?" she said, her voice rising at the end to make it a question.

"Yes, I'll be back," I confirmed. "Thanks again for your help."

✶   ✶   ✶

It was nearly a week later when Miss Kessler called and told me the package had arrived. I wanted to skip karate and go right to the library to start scanning papers, but I managed to control myself and continue my routine. Besides, I was enjoying karate immensely because of the sparring.

I took off on my bike to the library the moment I got home from school Thursday afternoon. Miss Kessler waved, but she was talking with some people at the desk, so I had to wait a brief eternity for her to set up the reader and bring the microfiche cards.

"If you look carefully, you can see the blotter with the naked eye," she pointed out. "The format for each newspaper is the same, so once you locate it with the microscope, you can put each subsequent card in exactly the same spot on the reader."

She was right. I started with the earliest date that the downtown branch included and plopped the card into the reader. It took a few tries to manipulate the arm of the machine so that I could find the section I was looking for, but eventually I found the blotter. I scanned through the names and crimes, and, discovering nothing interesting, switched out for the next card. If I put the card in exactly the same orientation, the blotter came instantly into focus. Still, it was painstakingly slow. I didn't make it through a month of newspapers before my stomach started rumbling.

"Try again tomorrow?" the librarian asked as I packed up to leave.

"Saturday," I answered.

"OK, see you then," she replied, her voice as cheerful as ever. Despite wasting several hours with no results, I felt a little better because of her attitude. Strange.

I spent three more sessions without getting anything useful. Part of the trouble, I realized after the fact, was the prior winter had been very chilly. I was looking for bikers, and cold weather might impact their activity. Who'd ride a motorcycle in freezing weather?

I did find a few biker-related crimes, but none of them involved Munson. There were no mentions of the Low Riders or the Highlanders. I began to have doubts that I'd ever find anything.

My hopes soared when Ian's letter appeared in the mail a couple of weeks after I'd sent mine. I savaged the envelope, smoothed out the contents, and devoured the letter with fascination.

Hey, Hunter,

Good to hear from you. I hope you're doing well, and I hope Allan is OK. Tell him I asked after him and I wish him the best.

I've got good news and better news. Dad finally got a job

here, and I started competing in track. It's really fun! I'm in a local club with a bunch of guys from my area. Even though I'm only fourteen, I'm racing against the kids in the comprehensive schools preparing for university, and I'm beating them! I've won nearly every race so far, and my coach told me that I'm one of the best sprinters he's ever seen! I'm hoping to get on the Junior Olympic team. The best part is the guys who throw the shot put and discus look out for me. Nobody messes with me now.

I told Dad what you said, and he suggested you use the archives at the newspaper to find what you're looking for. They're sorted so you can search to find specific articles. Use the name of someone who works there so you can get access. They won't let you in unless you're accompanied by a writer from the current staff. He suggested Mr. Jonas, who writes about crime in the Seattle area. Use Dad's name to get an introduction. Good luck! I'm sure you'll get your man.

As to what to ask the coppers, try to get on their side. Ask about why they became an officer in the first place. Give them an open ended question about their motivations. And then, try this: "describe a day that made it all worthwhile." I know you're not great at making friends, but if you want them to open up, give them a reason to do so. Trust me.

What I really want to know is, are you messing around with Patty Owens yet? Write back when you get a chance.

Take care, mate!
Your friend,
Ian

What?

I could use the newspaper's archives to search for Munson? If it worked for names, might it also work for subjects, like the Low Riders or Highlanders? Why didn't anyone tell me this before? I'd wasted so much time.

I ransacked the house looking for the number for Mr. Jonas, as I couldn't find it next to the phone where I'd left it. I started looking through the phone book before belatedly realizing that I had it up in my room. It was the same as Roger's number that I'd used last year.

I called immediately and asked the receptionist for Lloyd Jonas.

"I'll put you through," she said blankly.

He picked up on the first ring.

"Jonas," he said.

"Um, hi, I was looking for Mr. Jonas?"

"You got him. Who's this?"

"It's Hunter Miller. We met a few weeks ago?"

"The kid, right? Sure, I remember. How's it going? Did you meet with officer Metz? He any help? Get some good info?"

He ran his words together so quickly I didn't have a chance to respond.

"Yes," I said, when Mr. Jonas paused for air. "Actually, I was hoping to learn more, and my friend Roger Pierce suggested I use the archives to find old newspaper stories."

"Ah, Roger! How the hell is he?"

"He's good, he got a new job in England."

"I always wondered why he left here so quickly. Couldn't get out of town fast enough. Thought the mafia was after him or something. Ha! Can't imagine who he pissed off, right?"

Something sounded peculiar in the story of Roger's departure, but I didn't have time to think about it.

"He told me I can't use the archives without an active staff writer. Would you be able to help?"

"As long as I get first crack at the story when it breaks," he said, without missing a beat.

"Um, sure. Of course!" I said. The newspaper article that Roger wrote helped bring Orlando Ryan to justice, so why not use the same trick on whomever attacked Allan?

"I've got a deadline coming and then some meetings, but how 'bout you come down on Tuesday and we'll check through the archives. You're in school, right? What time works for you?"

We settled on four pm, and then I hung up. I felt reinvigorated, like I was soaring through the sky. I'd find something useful in the archives for sure!

CHAPTER 39

MISS BURNELL brought me crashing back to earth on Monday by forcibly dragging me back to the world of scholastic purgatory.

"Let's see a show of hands. Who's planning on doing a science fair experiment for your 8th grade project?"

Every person sent a hand into the air except for Patty and me.

"All, right. Please put the title of your experiment onto the signup sheet that I'm sending around."

She handed a clipboard to Christy Johnson in the front row. She scribbled something and dutifully passed it along.

"That leaves you and you." She pointed at Patty and then me. "What's the title of your civics paper?"

Patty stood up and proclaimed, "I'm volunteering for the special election campaign of a candidate for State Representative for the 43rd district!"

I could feel the teacher's aura turn sour and create a noise like the scratching of fingernails on a chalkboard. I winced badly.

"Oh, wonderful. Politics. My dear, you're only in 8th grade, you have the rest of your life to… Ah, yes, well, never mind. Sounds fantastic. I'm sure you'll do great. However, the title needs work. 'I'm volunteering for the election of a representative' doesn't have a great ring to it. Maybe something like 'Democracy in Action' or

'How to help the government steal tax money from the working people,' or, well, ya' know, something snappy.'

Patty, whose excited mannerisms often reminded me of Miss Kessler, collapsed noisily into her chair. She looked like someone whose new puppy had been hit by a train.

"And you?" she faced me. "What brilliant musings will you present to impress this humble public servant?"

I felt a wave of panic coming over me. If she didn't like her favorite student's project, she was going to hate mine.

"I'm interviewing police and newspaper reporters about local law enforcement," I said quietly.

"What?" she said, her aura brimming with a fern colored pricking that meant she was stunned.

"Um, yeah, I know, that's not a title."

Her expression changed and she walked right over to my seat. "See me at the break," she said. The sticky seaweed morphed into a lighter sizzling green, followed by a harsh, salmon color with darker streaks. I smelled fear amidst the weird compilation of emotional colors. I'd struck some kind of nerve.

Class went on until Miss Burnell released everyone for PE. I tried to bolt, but she called out to stop me.

"Hunter, hang on, please."

I went back to my desk and sat down. I couldn't decide if I was more scared of her oddly polite command, or the new set of strange colors pulsing around her aura.

"Does your mother know about your project?" she asked quietly.

I recognized concern, and… a soft purple color, like Mom's.

"Sure," I said. "She brought me to my interviews with the police officer and the newspaper writer."

"Why police?" she asked. It was obvious that she had a problem with my topic, but I had no idea what.

"I don't know," I lied.

She spotted the falsehood, like Mom. Fritzcloves!

"Does this have anything to do with what happened to Allan?"

I considered my options. Without the pretense of this paper, I wasn't going to be permitted to keep investigating. She'd know if I lied, so I needed to say something true.

"Yes, I suppose," I said. "I met Officer Metz the night Allan was attacked. He's the person I'm interviewing for my paper. I wanted to do something for Allan, so I started thinking about the police, and how they help people. I decided it would be a good project."

Miss Burnell stared at me like I was a bug under a microscope. After a few moments, she nodded slightly and relaxed.

"Very well. Off to gym class. Keep me posted on your progress. It's supposed to be a ten page paper, so you'll have to work hard on it."

"OK," I said, trying hard not to betray my relief. I ran off to gym.

Having cleared that hurdle, I kept my head down for the rest of the day and quietly bided my time until my meeting with Mr. Jonas.

✶   ✶   ✶

Mom again wasn't home on Tuesday afternoon, so I pedaled over to the *Times* building and locked my bicycle at the rack. I went inside toward the desk. The guard smiled and waved pleasantly.

"Hello, son, how are you today?"

"I'm great!" I said. "I've got an appointment with Mr. Jonas. We're going to look through the archives."

"Very good," he said. "You know where his office is located?"

I nodded, and he extended his hand toward the elevator. I hurried over and punched the button furiously. I leaped inside the moment the door opened with its characteristic "ding". I rode up alone, considering what I'd say to Mr. Jonas.

The writer approached me as I stepped out of the elevator on his floor.

"Mr. Jonas!" I said, surprised at meeting him in the hallway rather than his office.

He looked at me blankly.

"Are we going to the archives room?" I said.

"I'm sorry, who are you?" he said. No waves. He had no idea who I was.

"I'm Hunter Miller. We have a four o'clock appointment."

"Right!" he said, hastily checking his wristwatch. "Oh, yes! That's now. Gotcha. OK."

"Archives?" I said.

"Remind me," he said. "What are you searching for?"

The elevator chimed again as another employee exited and walked past. "Hey, Lloyd," the man said.

Mr. Jonas nodded but didn't reply. Instead, he looked at me.

"We were talking about the Highlanders and the Low Riders," I said.

"Yes, yes," he said. I could almost see the light bulb going on in his brain. "Yes," he said again. "Let's go to the basement and see what we can find."

We re-entered the elevator and traveled three floors down, exiting into a dark expanse with a large bank of computers on the far wall. I was surprised to find no guard or other security measures. Despite what I'd been told, I could've easily walked into this room and used the archives without Mr. Jonas.

We ambled over to the desk terminal, and he sat down in the chair and started typing on the keyboard. The process lasted several minutes, during which time the screen changed a number of times, but nothing resembling newspaper articles appeared.

"What are you doing?" I asked.

"I've got to log into the mainframe. Then we can access the archives."

After a few more keystrokes, he stopped typing and waited for the screen to change one more time. "There!" he said. "I'm in!"

He adjusted his chair and looked back at me. "Who do you want me to search for?"

"How about the head of the Low Riders?"

"Ah, yes, Roderick Munson. Sure. Good place as any to start," he said, while typing in the name.

Several citations appeared.

"OK, here we go. Yes, I wrote some of these. Local Kingpin accused of money laundering and racketeering. Oh, Munson acquitted. Yes. Of course. Munson investigated on drug related charges. Head of Low Riders sought in murder investigation. There's more. I can print a list and you can use the microfiche to read the stories," he said.

"OK," I replied. These were interesting, but didn't help. "What if you search for Low Riders instead?"

"You got it."

He punched in the keys and came up with another list, containing some of the same articles.

"You want me to print these out too?"

I nodded. He sent the file to the printer, which buzzed slowly as it recreated the information onto the green and white paper.

"Might as well try Highlanders, too," I said.

"OK, easy enough."

After putting that into the appropriate search field, only a few articles came up. Mr. Jonas read the titles, and one caught my ear. "Gang members released from prison on technicality."

"That one," I said energetically.

"Yes, I see how that one could be important. Let me write down the date, and we can go get the fiche."

The newspaper basement had a microfiche reader like the one at the library, and he thumbed through a huge set of old slides to locate the date we needed.

"Let's see," he mumbled, as he fiddled with the controls. "Ah, here we go. Found it!"

"Can you print it out?" I asked hopefully.

"No, wrong format. But we can read it and take notes. Let's see," he said again. "After police Sergeant Orlando Ryan's conviction, many of his own cases were reopened due to possible conflict of interest. Blah, blah, blah… Oh, here's a list of names."

He pushed his chair back to allow me access to the reader. I breezed through the names, not precisely sure what I was hoping to find. However, one name stuck out like a pink aura on a female. Logan. William Logan. Could he be related to Kenny?

"William Logan," I said.

"What about him?" Jonas asked.

"Can we search for him?" I asked.

"Of course."

We went back to the mainframe and he typed in the name. A few articles came up, and Jonas printed out the list. We walked over to the fiche collection, found the slide containing the first paper on the list, and attached it securely onto the reader.

"Here we go," Jonas said, finding the article. "Parolee detained on suspicion of assault. William 'Billy' Logan was arrested in connection with the alleged assault of a Seattle native on April 4. Logan, 40, was released on bail. He was not considered a flight risk because of his ties to the community. Originally arrested and convicted of grand theft, Logan was subsequently released on parole after it was discovered by defense counsel that the arresting officer, Orlando Ryan, was himself implicated on charges of murder and racketeering."

"What does the part about 'ties to the community' mean?" I asked.

"Oh, he probably has a family or something."

"Any way to figure out if he has kids?"

"If he had them here, sure. We may have to go back a little longer. How old would the kids be?"

"My age. Fourteen or so."

Jonas looked at the list. "Yeah, you're right. These two here," he showed me the list. "They're birth announcements. I recognize the format. Yeah, we have Daniel Duvall Logan. Looks like he'd be a little older than you. And the other is Kenneth Raines Logan. He'd be fourteen. Do you know him?"

My heart was racing. My skin was tingling, not from danger, but from a mix of excitement, anger and hope. Finally. The break I needed!

"Yes, I do." I said, barely able to contain myself. "Can I have these?" I asked, motioning toward the printouts.

"Sure."

"I've gotta go," I said.

"Hey, remember our deal," he said, stopping me.

"What deal?" I asked.

"You get the archives, I get the scoop!"

I tried to make a break for the elevator, but he grabbed my jacket and kept me in place. He was getting angry.

"Seriously, son. You need to tell me what this is all about!"

I stopped. I'd need his help anyway. Mom wasn't here, and Miss Burnell wouldn't know, so I made a decision.

"Look, I'll tell you, but you have to promise not to say anything to my teacher or my mother."

"Hey, like I said before, a good reporter never reveals his source!"

I didn't believe him at first, but his aura displayed no waves.

I told him about Allan getting hurt, the motorcycle, the police investigation leading nowhere, and the fact that Kenny and Allan just had a fight the day before the incident. Mr. Jonas listened intently, his aura betraying his interest. All semblance of irritation had disintegrated. He was hooked.

"So you think this mysterious assailant is Kenny?" he asked.

"I did at first, but I found out Kenny doesn't ride a motorcycle."

"So what do you think now?"

"I bet it was his father."

"Of course! A known felon, previously arrested for assault, out on parole. He'd stick to the shadows, do his thing and get away before being seen. And since he's a member of the Highlanders, he'd ride a motorcycle for sure. You make a pretty good case. But there's one thing you don't have."

"What?"

"Proof!"

"What do you mean?" I asked, even though I knew exactly what he meant.

"I can't print a story until I have verification, otherwise it's just slander. And the cops can't arrest him without proof either, or he'd walk without standing trial. How do you intend to get proof?"

"I don't know yet," I said. "But I'll think of something. Promise me you won't tell anyone about this?"

"I won't say anything, but you be careful. This guy is nobody to mess with."

"I know. He could've killed my friend. I'll be careful."

"It's more than that. Hold on a minute. Let me print out a couple of stories I've written over the last few months."

He went back to the computer and worked for another ten minutes, periodically causing the printer to spit out hard copies of prior newspaper articles.

He collected the printed pages and handed them to me. "Take a look at these. It's probably a good idea that you know the sort of person you're dealing with."

"Thanks," I said. "And thanks for all the help today, too."

"You got it, kid. Keep me updated on your progress."

I nodded, stuffed the pages into my backpack, and joined him for the short elevator ride to the ground floor.

"See you soon," he said, as I made a beeline to the entrance. "And don't do anything stupid!" he added.

I waved quickly, went out to unlock my bike, and pedaled furiously toward Madrona.

CHAPTER 40

WHEN I got home, I barricaded myself in my room. I barely ate dinner. All I could think about was how I'd be getting my revenge. I told Mom I wasn't feeling well. I knew she'd be able to figure out I was up to something if she saw my face, so I hid. I knew. I *knew* who'd beaten up Allan, and although the newspaper required proof, I didn't. I only needed to get the man alone in a room to make him confess and pay for his crime.

I seethed all night long, but finally dozed off right before my alarm went off. I'd rested my body, but my brain remained on fire. The adrenaline rushed through my veins as I got ready for school and boarded the bus. Finally. An answer.

I arrived at school and saw Kenny as I was heading into the building. My aura sizzled with a cold, prickly hatred. I felt possessed. Since it was Wednesday, I'd see him at gym class. I made the decision to confront him. He'd soon tell me all about his father.

I could barely contain my explosive energy, and when I entered my classroom, I kicked my chair savagely.

"Mr. Miller, please stop attacking that poor defenseless chair," drawled Miss Burnell. "Do I need to send you to the principal's office today?" she added sweetly.

I flushed. "No!" I said angrily.

"Well, see that you pay attention and behave, then," she retorted.

I took her threat seriously. She never liked me, and she'd send me to Mrs. Frechette's office just to avoid hearing my voice. I quietly endured the morning session, using all of my resolve to listen to her drone about today's physics topic—torque. The moment I saw the mathematical equations, I understood it perfectly. Force, angles, mass, velocity, yep. Got it. But despite the monumentally boring monologue, I forced myself to listen. I had a goal to accomplish, and I wasn't about to fail by being sent to the office.

When the time came for PE, I blasted out the door toward the gymnasium. I wanted to get to Kenny right away, before we began whatever exercise or game the teacher planned.

Unfortunately, Mr. Groves shunted me outside.

"Dodgeball today! Should be fun!" he said. I groaned internally. I hated dodgeball.

As the others arrived, he continued, "Let's get out there and start picking up teams. You know the drill. The usual captains. I'll be out soon with the balls."

I had no choice but to go outside and wait for Kenny. He arrived soon after, along with two of his friends, walking toward the dodge ball area. I approached them resolutely.

"Hey!" I yelled, still a few feet away.

His aura soured. "What do *you* want?" he asked. He looked at his friends, whispered something, and all three of them laughed.

"Your Dad is a biker, isn't he?" I asked heatedly.

"What of it?" he replied, now suddenly focused on me and ignoring the others.

There were no waves in his aura, so that was all the confirmation I needed. The tingling began, but I ignored it.

"*He's* the one who beat up Allan, isn't he?"

In answer, Kenny punched me in the face so hard I flew backwards several feet. I could feel my eye start to swell up. I should have seen it coming and blocked the punch, but it was too late for that. I took a moment to stand back up, and I could feel the massive surprise in Kenny's aura as I boldly closed the distance between us.

He quickly recovered and rocked back to swing again, but I launched my right foot toward his face. He saw it and started to duck, exactly as I expected. I completed the combination kick by hooking my foot back, colliding forcibly with the back of his head. The blow was so violent that Kenny's spittle flew sideways into the face of Dennis, who'd been standing too close to Kenny. He scrambled to wipe it away.

I tried to follow up with a triple front punch, but only the first two landed before strong arms grabbed me from behind. I recognized the aura instantly, and felt horribly conflicted. I wanted to keep pummeling Kenny, who had since fallen to the ground, but I'd have to break the hold of my best friend in order to do so.

Allan yanked me from my feet like a sack of potatoes, and hauled me away from my enemy and his two friends, who were encouraging him to get back up and kick my butt.

"What are you doing?" Allan demanded, setting me down a few feet away. "You're going to get in trouble!"

"What's going on over there?" sounded Mr. Groves' booming baritone.

"Hunter was beating up Kenny!" said Patty, whose aura simultaneously showed a spectacular combination of amazement, pride and revulsion.

Mr. Groves nodded and grabbed each of us by the forearm and marched us back inside. "Let's go, you two," he said firmly. "The rest of you, go ahead and start picking up teams. I'll be right back."

I yearned to continue what I'd started in the playground, but the gym teacher's strong grip kept me in line. Besides, it was Kenny's father who had earned my wrath, not Kenny. Sure, he was a jerk, but I needed to calm down and bide my time.

Mrs. Frechette was in her office, so the three of us walked past the secretary and Mr. Groves deposited us inside.

"Fighting," he said.

"Thank you, Mr. Groves. I'll take it from here."

He nodded and left.

Mrs. Frechette stared at me with her penetrating eyes. I could feel the disappointment. She glanced briefly at Kenny and her mouth twitched slightly. I tried to figure out the color and smell of her aura, but it was very confusing. When she spoke, I jumped in surprise.

"Mr. Miller," she started, but stopped at my profound flinching. "Are you all right?"

"Yes, I'm OK," I said. She nodded, her aura expressing disbelief.

"What happened?"

"He jumped me!" said Kenny, drawing her attention to him.

"Is that so?" she said.

"Yeah, he just started kicking and punching me! I tried to get away. I fell to the ground and he kept coming after me! I didn't want to hurt him, so I didn't strike back. He's so scrawny I didn't even bother defending myself, either. I let him hit me until that tall kid pulled him away."

The waves flowed over his river of lies.

"Then how did Hunter get that shiner?" she asked, pointing to my right eye, which was swollen, black and blue. I'd forgotten to heal it.

"He had that already!" Kenny insisted, again clearly lying. Even Mrs. Frechette could see the deceit.

"Hunter?"

"He punched me first," I said.

"BS!" Kenny yelled. The principal's gaze pierced Kenny and the feigned indignation melted away. "All right, I hit him," Kenny admitted.

"Why did you hit him?" she asked.

"He said something about my Dad!" Kenny erupted.

The principal's gaze swung back toward me. I didn't like it.

"What did you say?" she asked.

I thought for a moment. I'd already told Mr. Jonas my theory. I might as well tell Mrs. Frechette too. She'd know if I lied anyway.

"His father is the one who beat up Allan and drove away on a motorcycle. He's a member of the Highlanders, and Allan got beaten up the day after Kenny and I had our last fight. His father's been arrested for assault a bunch of times and he was in jail."

Kenny stiffened. I could feel the anger and bitterness. It was extremely unpleasant.

"Is this true?" she asked Kenny. He didn't answer.

"Well, then, I think this is a matter for the police!"

She instructed us to sit in her office and wait.

Neither one of us spoke. We both stared straight ahead. I thought about ways to hurt Kenny and his father. Kenny's aura betrayed a combination of guilt, embarrassment, anger and frustration that made me even more confident about my conclusion.

After less than twenty minutes, Officer Metz appeared on the heels of Principal Frechette. His eyes flashed with recognition when they fell upon me. Moments later, Mom entered the room, along with another woman I didn't know.

"Mom?!" Kenny and I both said simultaneously.

We looked at each other for the first time since the incident, with surprise dominating the jangled mess of both of our auras.

There wasn't enough space in the small office, so Mrs. Frechette stood behind her desk, while Kenny and I turned our chairs toward the three newcomers. The principal made introductions, pointing to each of us as she said our names.

"Hunter, Kenny, Officer Metz, Mrs. Logan, and Mrs. Miller. Thank you for coming so quickly," she added, looking up to the adults.

"We have a situation here. Hunter says that he believes that Kenny's father is the one who beat up Allan Marks, another student here. He suggested this to Kenny, who took umbrage and struck Hunter, as you can see." She pointed to my raccoon eye, which was swollen so badly that I was having some trouble seeing clearly through it.

She continued after a brief pause. "Young Mr. Miller reacted violently. Although clearly overmatched, he struck Mr. Logan several times. Fortunately, he didn't seem to cause any significant injury."

I scanned Kenny's aura, and noticed no sign of physical damage. I'd thought my kick and punches landed pretty well, but, as Mrs. Frechette noticed, they didn't do anything. I realized belatedly that I should've added my own brand of injury on top of the karate moves. No matter. I could always do it later. Plus, I reminded myself, it was his father who deserved the punishment.

Mrs. Frechette continued. "Given the nature of the accusation, I felt it was imperative that we consult with law enforcement. Officer Metz, do you have information on this topic?"

The policeman shifted from one foot to the other. "I'm not supposed to divulge information relating to a criminal investigation. However, Mrs. Logan can speak freely on the topic. To avert any further malice on the part of the children, perhaps you could mention Mr. Logan's iron-clad alibi for the night of the attack of Mr. Marks?"

All eyes turned toward the woman I'd never seen before. Her light blue aura had a warm, minty feel, with the clean, bright purple that implied a supportive and conscientious mother. She was nervous and agitated, and her aura confirmed a sour, nutty blush of embarrassment, much like Kenny's.

"He was in jail," she said quietly.

Kenny's aura acted as if he'd been slapped. My own burst with confusion and disbelief.

"What?" I said, nearly jumping out of my chair.

"It's true," Officer Metz agreed. The word *true* kickstarted my brain. I'd be the judge of the truth!

Much to my chagrin, there were no waves coming from either Mrs. Logan or Officer Metz. They weren't covering anything up.

"Maybe he snuck out!" I postulated.

"You can't just 'sneak out' of jail," Mom said calmly. Again, no waves.

"But…" I sputtered. I'd been so sure. Everything pointed to Kenny's father. He was a motorcycle gang member with prior arrests for assault. It happened right after Kenny and I fought. Kenny's aura showed the exact same signs that I'd expect to see if his father had done it. But it was simply impossible, according to Officer Metz.

"I think you owe someone an apology," Mrs. Frechette said, breaking my train of thought.

"Who?" I asked indignantly.

She inclined her head at Kenny.

"Him?" I yelled. "You want me to apologize to Kenny?"

"It would be the right thing to do," Mom said calmly.

I could feel my emotions swirling about me like a tornado. I was closer to losing control than I'd been in a long time. I pictured Grandpa, remembering how he always helped me to regain my wits. "Think about it logically," his voice boomed in my head. "Kenny's father could NOT be the one. You already knew it wasn't Kenny. Your mother is right, you should apologize."

I turned to look at Kenny, whose aura burned with nearly as many conflicting emotions as my own. Taking Grandpa's advice, I spoke.

"Sorry."

He only nodded.

"Well, good. Now we don't have to suspend you both," said Mrs. Frechette. "However, one more shove, punch, kick, or even so much as an overly aggressive tap on the shoulder and you both are gone for a week. Understood?"

She looked at each of us in turn, and we both silently confirmed our acceptance. She then gazed at our mothers, who similarly nodded agreement.

"Very well. Back to class then."

When we didn't start for the door, she added, "Let's go boys!" We both hurried out the door, Kenny in the lead. I looked back to see her shut the door, with the three other adults still in the room. I thought about the implications. They were not good. My cover story was completely blown. Mom was never going to let me pursue Allan's attacker now.

Not that it made any difference. I had absolutely no idea who was responsible. As I trudged back to class, I felt the life flow out of me like air from a punctured tire. I'd blown it. Not only had I got myself into serious trouble, but I'd destroyed any chance of discovering Allan's assailant. The grey sludge of depression waited for me like a long lost friend.

CHAPTER 41

I AMBLED slowly outside to the field. I didn't want to play dodge ball. Nobody cared. I was terrible and neither side wanted me. I stood next to the teacher and waited for him to assign me a team, even though class was almost over. Betsy saw me and gave a small wave. I looked away. I couldn't face her right now.

"Why don't you go and see the nurse," Mr. Groves said. "She can get you some ice for your face."

That suited me just fine, so I went back inside.

"Whoa!" Mrs. Bohrman said, seeing my eye. "How's the other guy looking?"

"He didn't have a scratch on him," I replied dejectedly.

"Did you at least get off a few shots?" she asked.

I smiled slightly.

"Aha! Well done," she said.

I found myself feeling strangely fond of the nurse.

She pushed on my face, all around my eye, and made sure nothing was broken. Then she applied ice and let me rest on the cot. Moments later, I awoke to find Mom's aura nearby.

I jumped at the sound of Mrs. Bohrman's voice, not sure where I was.

"Oh, sorry to startle you, Hunter. You're mother's here to take you home."

I dreaded speaking to Mom about today's events, but I had no choice.

"Let's go, dear," she said reassuringly. When I stood up, she looked carefully at my face, like the nurse had. "Are you OK?"

"I'm fine, Mom," I said.

She nodded, and we walked to her car. School wasn't over, but apparently I was going home anyway.

I silently prayed that she'd leave me in peace on the ride home. No such luck.

"Mind telling me what that was all about?" she asked.

"I'm sorry, Mom," I said. "I thought Kenny's dad was the one. He was a motorcycle gang member, and Kenny hates me."

She paused for a moment.

"Let me get this straight. You figured that your classmate begged his father to exact revenge because he doesn't like you. The father, being the lawbreaker that he is, drove his motorcycle to Allan's house and whacked him in the back of the head?"

"Um, yeah." I said glumly.

"Why didn't Kenny beat you up himself? He's twice your size. Why be so oblique and ask his dad to hit your friend?"

"Allan stopped Kenny from hitting me!" I said, trying desperately to defend my thoroughly discredited theory.

"Uh-huh," Mom said.

I understood her point. I hadn't thought it through. I'd drawn a conclusion based on weak evidence because it fit my desired script. I'd behaved stupidly.

"I'm sorry," I said again.

"I'm disappointed on so many levels," Mom said. "Mostly, I'm glad you're OK. But I want you to understand that you can't go around picking fights. It's not the way to handle things. Plus it's dangerous."

"I know," I said.

"Your karate instructor is going to be upset with you too."

She was right. Sensei Nam said we must not use karate outside the *dojo* except for defense in life-threatening situations. I'd attacked someone. He could throw me out for that. My situation kept getting worse.

"Do we have to tell him?" I implored.

Mom looked at me briefly before returning her gaze to the road. For once, I was glad she could read my face like a book.

"I suppose not. But let's keep you out of karate for a couple of days so he doesn't see that shiner."

I nodded. A small price to pay.

*   *   *

The next morning I tried to make amends with Allan while on the way to the cafeteria.

"Look, I told you to leave it alone, and you couldn't do that," he said, his voice edgy and his aura annoyed.

"I'm sorry," I replied.

"Kenny and his buddies really have it out for me now. They all want to fight me. The whole reason my parents started me in karate was to *avoid* getting into fights. If my parents find out, they might make me quit karate!"

I was aghast.

"I can explain…"

"No, you can't. The more you stick your nose into things, the worse they become. Just leave it alone!" he said. The anger oozed from his pores.

"But Allan," I pleaded.

He held his arms out, palms extended. "Just think about what I said, OK? I'm going to eat."

He turned and left me there. I followed at a distance. We were going to the same place.

Allan made it clear I wasn't welcome at his table, so I sat with Betsy. I didn't mind the greyish muck surrounding her aura today.

"Allan's mad at you," she surmised.

"Yeah."

"Well, it's all over the school. You and Kenny got into it."

"I thought his Dad was the one. I was stupid. Now Allan's worried about his parents taking him out of karate because Kenny and his friends want to fight him."

"He asked you not to pursue it," she said quietly.

"Yeah, I know. But what am I supposed to do? Let whoever did this get away with it?" I yelled.

My loud voice attracted attention, but only briefly, as nobody truly cared what gibberish I spouted.

"Sometimes stuff happens, and we can't do anything about it," she said.

"I don't believe that!" I insisted.

"Get used to it. It's called life."

I ate my food quietly, fuming even more.

$$* \quad * \quad *$$

When I calmed down, I realized Betsy was right. I couldn't fix every single problem in the world.

I spent the next two weeks licking my proverbial wounds. Kenny hated me, and he was taking it out on Allan. Mom was disappointed in me. I couldn't go to karate because I'd betrayed Sensei Nam by using karate outside the gym. I couldn't go back to the newspaper, because Mr. Jonas only wanted proof for his story, and I had none. Officer Metz probably thought I was using him for revenge.

All of it was for naught anyway. I was no closer to finding Allan's attacker. If anything, I was further away. My top suspects had unassailable alibis. It was over.

Without karate class, I spent two hours a day thrashing the bag in the garage. I did my workouts, including push-ups, sit-ups, arm curls, leg lifts, core builders, and stretches, but faster than usual and with very little rest. When I flexed my biceps in the mirror, the scrawny little nothings had been replaced by golf-ball-sized lumps of muscle.

While looking in the mirror, I set about regulating the swelling in my black eye. I didn't feel any pain from it, but I could see the huge black and blue mark that transformed my eye into a slit. I focused on my aura, slowly changing the abnormal discoloration. After twenty minutes, I felt comfortable with my ability to calibrate the swelling. The exercise was reminiscent of opening cuts on my arms and healing them, or creating the feel of insects on unsuspecting kids on the bus while riding to school last year.

I avoided trips to the library, mostly because I didn't think I could handle Miss Kessler's upbeat personality. I also couldn't bring myself to go back to the police station or the newspaper. I preferred to stew in my juices.

However, Miss Burnell reminded me about my obligation as I returned to class on Monday after winter break.

"How's your civics paper coming along, Hunter?"

"Um, OK," I sputtered. "I talked to one officer, and I have an appointment to see a lieutenant."

"That's a good start. I'd like to see an outline next week, if possible. Remember, it's supposed to be ten pages. That's a lot," she emphasized.

"All right," I said.

"If you need some help, see me before lunch."

She turned to Patty. "How about you?"

"I'm doing great! I have interviews with the representative-to-be, the campaign chairman, and half a dozen others."

Her progress made mine look pedestrian.

I wasn't sure if Mom scheduled an appointment with Lieutenant Herlihy or not, so I'd have to check when I got home. Since I'd made no headway and the teacher wanted an outline soon, I did need help.

In the end, I decided against asking Miss Burnell, because I didn't want her to know how little progress I'd actually made. I'd have to figure something out on my own. Ian had given me some ideas on interview questions, and I could incorporate them when I went back to the police station.

Since my face was completely healed, I returned to karate practice that evening, expecting to be questioned about my absence. However, we'd had a week off after the belt tests, so nobody noticed. As before, practice helped me focus.

Allan made an excuse about wanting to go shopping, so Mom had to drive me. On the ride home, I asked if she could help me again with the civics paper.

"Miss Burnell wants me to turn in an outline," I said.

"Have you figured out what you want the paper to say?" she asked.

"What do you mean?"

"Any time you write an essay or a term paper, the goal is to create a thesis and prove it. I used to write articles for scientific journals, and we always used the same format. Introduction, methods, materials, results, discussion, conclusion. We also had to write an abstract, which summarized everything. For your paper, you only need an introduction, results and a conclusion. But that begs the question: what are the results? What questions are you asking? What do you want the reader to learn?"

After arriving home, we spent another two hours discussing the ideas Ian suggested, formulating an interview. She taught me how to pool the results of multiple conversations into a single story. She was surprisingly helpful. Furthermore, she called the police station and made an appointment for me to speak with Lieutenant Herlihy. She even helped me rehearse so I'd be ready when the time came.

*   *   *

Tuesday after school, she dropped me off at the police station, and I signed in and waited for the woman behind the counter to buzz me in. A tall, blonde-haired man introduced himself as Lieutenant Herlihy, and we proceeded to his office in the back. We walked past Officer Metz's messy desk, and my heart raced as I saw an open file there. Could that be the Highlanders file? I tried to slow the pace and take a look, since Metz wasn't there, but the Lieutenant hustled me past.

"How can I help you?" he asked politely.

I checked his aura quickly and found a genuine, helpful, caring, tough man.

"I'm doing a paper for school, and I was hoping to ask you a few questions," I said, using the opening line Mom helped me create.

"Certainly. Shoot."

"What training did you need to become a police officer?"

"We had a series of tests, starting with a written exam. This was twenty years ago, mind you, so I have no idea what the questions were, but I recall vividly that nearly a thousand people took the exam. Those who overcame that first hurdle, like me, were subjected to a physical assessment. That was basic stuff. Push-ups, sit-ups, a mile and a half run. Then we had an oral assessment. We stood in front of a panel consisting of two officers and one civilian who asked us questions about our moral code. Meanwhile, the department conducted a complete background investigation, including every job I'd ever had before. They talked to my parents and friends. I couldn't believe how thorough it was. We had a regular physical, with a doctor, plus a psychological screen. Once I passed this, I had to meet with the psychologist one-on-one for an interview. By this time, only eighty-six of the original thousand were left!"

"Wow!" I said, suitably impressed. It took me a few moments to remember my next question, as I was so deeply engrossed in his story.

"How long had you wanted to be a policeman, and what made you interested in the field?"

He chuckled. "I remember in second grade when 'Officer Friendly' came to our class. That wasn't his real name; he was the father of one of my classmates. I was enamored with the prospect of wearing a uniform and enthralled with the idea of driving a police car. But as I grew up, I realized that police work and family life didn't mix well, so I decided to pursue other interests.

"While working in a middle management job, I became friends with a Seattle police officer and his family, and they managed to enjoy vacations, barbeques, birthday parties, and everything I wanted in a home life. I wanted to contribute to society and do something my kids could be proud of. I wanted to be able to look back on my life and say that I made a difference."

I was fascinated. This was how I felt about becoming a doctor. I really liked this guy. I gave him Mom's next question.

"Can you describe a day that 'made it all worthwhile'?"

"Oh, I've had a lot of those. I've been doing this for more than twenty years. I've changed peoples' lives for the better on any number of occasions. I think the best answer to your question, though, is my current assignment.

"My job is to remove impaired drivers from the streets. You know, people who drink and drive. You may have heard the TV ads?"

I shook my head.

"Well, anyway, impaired drivers kill or injure hundreds of people in Seattle every year. I have to admit, when I started, I was looking for the best way to maintain my home life as I had a newborn, and some of the detective stories about being away for days at a time frightened me. But as I learned more, I discovered I could make a huge contribution by not only catching DWI offenders, but by revamping the training process. A lot of drivers were avoiding prosecution by exploiting improper arrest techniques. Often they became repeat offenders, sometimes with horrific consequences. I had a knack for processing impaired drivers, and by teaching my fellow officers the tricks, our arrests have increased fifty percent in five years. More importantly, the increased public awareness has reduced fatalities by nearly the same amount. I'm very proud of the work I have done."

His aura confirmed his sentiment.

"That's very cool," I said.

"Do you have any other questions?"

"If you could do it all over again, would you change anything?" I asked.

"I would have started earlier. Right out of school. Instead, I wasted several years doing things I hated. But the bottom line is, I love what I do, and I plan to continue well into the future."

"Thanks so much for speaking with me," I said. He'd given me a ton of stuff that I could put right into my paper. Plus, I'd formed an idea for the conclusion, but I'd need to interview another officer to make sure I was on the right track.

He walked me out, through the buzzing door, and Mom was waiting in the lobby.

"How'd it go?" she asked.

"Great! He answered all the questions, and I got some fantastic information for the paper."

As we headed home, my thoughts drifted to the file on Officer Metz's desk. I needed another interview, and perhaps I could get a look....

CHAPTER 42

THOUGHTS OF Metz's file danced in my brain all night long. I knew my obsession was unhealthy, but I couldn't help it. My best friend had been harmed, and I had the tools to discover the culprit. An idea struck me, and I leapt out of bed, flipped on the light, and rifled through my backpack.

The news stories Mr. Jonas had given me spilled out from beneath my schoolbooks. I'd been so certain I knew the answer, I hadn't even read them.

There were three stories. I scanned the titles. "Mysterious killer strikes again," "Cherry Hill man killed outside his home," and "Quiet neighborhood struck by killer."

I drank in the contents like a man who'd been stuck in the Sahara for weeks.

One article said, "Police investigators believe the killings are linked, based on general location and mode of attack. All four victims to date were killed by head trauma with a blunt object, thought to be a baseball bat. All died in areas normally not associated with murder, generally quiet neighborhoods. And in all four cases, there were no witnesses, despite the fact that the crimes occurred in relatively populated areas."

This was the story that the information guy at the *Times* had been talking about. He'd asked me about a baseball bat. I read through the other two stories, but didn't learn much. Mr. Jonas hadn't written a story about Allan, but perhaps that was because he wasn't killed. Or maybe because he was a minor. The other victims were all adults.

A horrible thought soured my aura. What if Allan *was* hit hard enough to die, and only lived because I healed him? Other than being younger than the others, he fit the pattern of this serial killer. A quiet neighborhood, struck in the head by a blunt object, and, if I hadn't felt the killer's aura and had Mom turn around, there would have been no witnesses.

With all notions of sleep completely purged from my mind, I considered what I knew. The assailant was a member of a motorcycle gang. He'd struck others with a baseball bat in various locations throughout Seattle. There were two possible gang affiliations: the Highlanders and the Low Riders. Many of the prior attacks appeared random.

I'd been sure they'd been perpetrated by someone Allan knew, like Kenny, but that no longer seemed likely. It had to be this "baseball bat assassin."

My breakthrough was simultaneously encouraging and discouraging. Although I had a better feel for the culprit, the number of potential suspects rose astronomically. Getting my hands on the files suddenly became a top priority.

How was I supposed to accomplish that?

After considering the problem for a few hours, I had an idea. After another hour, I developed a plan. It was risky, but I was pretty sure it would work. I only needed Mom to schedule me another appointment with Officer Metz, and I'd take care of the rest. I settled back into my bed. I'd need sleep, and it was already after four in the morning. My mind relaxed now that I had a strategy. In moments, I was out like a light.

*   *   *

The next morning, I felt surprisingly good despite my limited slumber.

"Hey, Mom, can you help me with my project?" I asked her while eating breakfast.

"Ah, got the writer's bug, have we?"

"What?" I asked.

"Never mind. What do you need?"

"I want to interview Officer Metz."

"OK, I'll call the police station while you're at school and set something up."

And easy as that, I was back on track.

Unfortunately, when I returned home from school, Mom informed me that it wouldn't be until next week because the policeman wasn't available.

The disappointment pulsed through my aura so thoroughly that it didn't take a detective to identify.

"Maybe you'll be able to interview someone else," Mom suggested.

I stopped myself before refusing this suggestion. I didn't want Mom to know what I was planning, and giving away the fact that I needed to see Officer Metz would clearly raise her suspicions.

"I don't know anyone else there, but I suppose it wouldn't hurt to explore other options," I conceded.

"Why don't we try to write the outline tomorrow instead? Isn't it due this week?"

"Yeah, you're right," I realized aloud.

"And you have karate tonight and Friday. It sounds like next Tuesday is probably the best time for you anyway," Mom said.

"You're right," I said again. My disappointment was replaced by relief and fear. I'd forgotten about finishing the outline, and I was running out of time. But, I could still see Metz and continue on with my secret plan.

That settled, we had dinner, and I readied myself for karate, again going with Mom because Allan wasn't talking to me.

I immersed myself in the workout for the entire two hours. Even after I had changed into my clothes, sweat continued to form on my face. The temperature had been rising this week, as spring was in full force, but tonight there was a nice breeze that helped cool me down as I walked to the car.

"How was it?" Mom asked, as I jumped into the front seat.

"It was fun! I sparred with one of the brown belts and used one of the moves Dad taught me on him. I'm getting a lot better."

"Fantastic! You'll have to show me some of these new moves," Mom replied.

We chatted on the way home about combination kicks and other feints. As we pulled into the driveway, something felt wrong. My aura tingled with danger. I regretted not bringing my coat with me, because I didn't have any extra food.

Mom parked the car, and we both jumped out. I must have been making a face of some kind, because Mom stopped before walking into the house.

"What is it?" she said quietly.

"I thought I heard something," I said.

Mom's aura blazed and vibrated with accentuated purple coloring, and she stared carefully in every direction. I felt the aura on her side of the car, approaching us. It crackled with a rancid, jet-black streak of malice. The tingling turned to pounding as the danger amplified. The man intended harm.

Somehow, Mom recognized the danger as well, and just in time.

The figure appeared from behind the trash cans and leapt forward. I shouted, "Mom!" as he swung a baseball bat right at her head.

Miraculously, she ducked under the swing, whirled her body around and struck the man in his forward knee with her right foot. She followed this up with a roundhouse kick to his face, which caused him to drop the bat and scramble back behind the bushes.

"Mom?" I said, surprise now dominating both my aura and the assailant's.

"Go inside and call the police, Hunter," she commanded. The golden confidence in her aura made me act quickly to follow her wishes.

As I got to the door, I started to second guess my decision. I could easily stop this guy. All I had to do was yank his aura into the void, and the attack would be over. But then, Mom would see what I could do, and that might be even worse. Besides, Mom had already disarmed him and, from what I'd just seen, I suspected the attacker was more likely to become a victim.

I called 911 from the telephone in the kitchen.

"What's your emergency?" the woman asked.

I stammered. "Mom, uh, my mother, um, there's an attacker!"

"What's your location?" she asked. I told her my house number. "Your name?"

"Hunter Miller."

"Has there been bodily injury?"

I paused, cleared my aura, and felt for spicy redness in Mom's aura, and found none. The attacker was no longer there.

"Sir?" came the voice.

"No, Mom's OK."

"Does the assailant have a weapon?"

"He had a baseball bat," I said. "But Mom knocked it out of his hands."

"A police officer is being dispatched. Please stay..." she said, but I hung up, cutting her off. I ran outside.

"Mom, are you OK?" I asked, despite knowing the answer.

"I'm fine," she said, walking back toward the house.

"How did you *do* that?" I asked, still incredulous.

"Oh, your father's taught me a thing or two," she said, smiling.

"Very cool!" I said. I had a whole new appreciation for Mom's abilities.

$$*\qquad*\qquad*$$

Officer Metz arrived minutes later, his police lights blazing for the entire neighborhood to see. At least he hadn't used the siren.

"Mrs. Miller, sorry to see you under these stressful circumstances," he said, extending his hand for her to grasp, which she did.

"Hunter, right?" he said, looking at me.

"Yes," I answered.

His gaze swept around the driveway and landed back on Mom. "What happened?"

Mom explained. "A man appeared suddenly and tried to attack us with a baseball bat. I disarmed him and sent Hunter into the house to call 911. He took off in that direction," she pointed, "and left the bat. I heard a motorcycle start up moments later, and he was gone."

"You disarmed a grown man wielding a baseball bat?" he asked, the fern-green color betraying his disbelief.

"She smacked him good!" I offered. "Started with a kick to the knee, then a roundhouse to the face. It was awesome!" I couldn't help swelling up with pride at Mom's self-defense tactics.

"I take it you have some training?" he asked.

"My husband is a black belt," she said.

"Hmm. Yes. OK," he said. "And the bat?"

"Right there on the ground. We didn't touch it."

"Good, good," he said. "I'll put it into evidence," he said. He went to his car, retrieved a large green garbage bag into which he placed the bat, and put it into his trunk. He wrote some things on a large sticker and attached it to the outside of the bag.

"Did you get a look at your attacker?" he asked upon returning to us.

"Yes, I did," Mom answered.

"Would you mind coming down to the station and looking at some mug shots?"

"Not at all."

"I'm coming too," I said.

"It's pretty late," Mom said.

"Is your husband home?" Officer Metz asked.

"No," Mom said.

"Then perhaps it's not the worst idea for Hunter to come with us," he suggested.

"Yes, I see your point," Mom said. "We'll follow you to the station. But let's try to hurry this along."

At the station, Mom had to sign the log while the woman behind the counter buzzed us in.

"Why don't you wait out here," Mom said.

"What? Why?" I protested.

"It's safe here. Don't worry," she replied, misinterpreting my meaning.

"No, I'm not worried," I said, pressing the issue. I wanted to ask Metz about the other attacks that I'd learned about from the newspaper articles. Since he was the officer running the investigation, he'd surely know about them. It wouldn't be too difficult to ask about prior incidents, and I'd know if he was lying by his aura.

"It'll go faster. Just wait here," she said definitively, and the two of them went through the door, which closed with a large click.

I took a seat in the waiting area, and about thirty minutes later a tall, thin man appeared in the doorway.

He strode purposefully toward the entrance, but stopped and looked at the sign-in sheet when he saw me out of the corner of his eye.

"Hello, Chief," the woman said. The man ignored this greeting. Instead, he came over to me.

"Who do we have here?" he asked.

I was taken aback. I wasn't used to people I didn't know walking up and talking to me. I stared, open-mouthed, until he spoke again.

"I'm Chief Beurline," he said, extending his hand. "And you?"

I shook his hand, shuddering a bit from the touch of his aura, which was a strange mix of bright gold, sky-blue, and cold brown with a gamey smell. What bothered me most was the damp murmur of greenish suspicion, a combination I'd worked out with Mom during one of our outings.

"Hunter," I said.

"Yes. Hunter Miller. You've been here before, correct?"

I was still reeling a bit from his aura, but I composed myself. "Yes, I have," I answered simply.

"Lieutenant Herlihy said that you were doing a paper for school."

THE TASTE OF DESPAIR   291

I relaxed. "Yes, he let me interview him," I said, relieved at the direction of the conversation. I thought he was going to ask me about Metz.

"Well, who better to interview than the Chief of Police," he said.

"I, uh, what?"

"How would you like to interview me for your paper?" he said, clarifying.

I remembered what Mom had suggested, and thought this would be a fine way to obfuscate my true goal of reading Metz's files.

"That would be great," I said.

He handed me a business card with his name and phone numbers on it.

"Wonderful. Call this number tomorrow morning and ask my secretary to schedule an appointment. I should be free tomorrow or Friday afternoon, whichever works best with your school commitments."

"Thanks," I said.

He nodded and went inside, pausing at the door for the woman to buzz him inside.

About thirty minutes later, the door buzzed again, and Mom emerged.

"How'd it go?" I asked eagerly. Perhaps she'd been able to identify the man.

"Come on, let's go," she replied.

"Did they have a picture of the guy?" I persisted, as we exited the building and walked to the car.

"No," she said flatly. I noticed some small waves, like her statement wasn't the complete truth. Either that, or I was very tired and misreading the auras. I should have eaten something before leaving home.

She had no interest in discussing the matter further, so I let it drop. When I got home, I was so exhausted that I went right to bed.

CHAPTER 43

THE FOLLOWING morning, Mom found the card in my pocket containing Chief Beurline's phone number.

"What's this?" she asked.

"Oh, yes, I forgot. You know how you suggested I should interview another police officer? Well, this chief guy gave me his card and suggested I call his secretary to get an appointment for today or Friday."

"Great initiative," Mom said. "I'll call from work. She's probably not in until nine, so it's too early now, and you won't be able to call from school. Perhaps you could ask your teacher for an extension on the outline. Otherwise, we'll have to finish it tonight after the interview. Friday you have karate, so it's better to do the interview today."

"Thanks!" I said. "I'll see if Miss Burnell will let me turn in the outline Monday."

*   *   *

I managed to catch my teacher before class started, and briefly explained my situation. To my great surprise, she agreed to let me turn the outline in on Monday. I paid attention through the morning lessons to ensure she didn't get angry with me and change her mind.

At lunch, Allan invited me to sit with him.

"You OK?" he asked.

"Yeah," I said. Had he heard what happened?

As if reading my mind, he answered. "My Mom talked to your Mom about driving to karate tomorrow. She said someone came to your house after practice."

"Did she tell you anything else?"

"No, just that someone was there. What was he doing?"

"He had a baseball bat. He tried to whack Mom with it!"

"Holy crap!" Allan said, now fully understanding. "How did she get away?"

"She kicked his buttocks!" I said, using a word Grandpa had taught me.

Allan couldn't help but laugh. "How?" he asked, still giggling.

I lowered my voice, but didn't try to hide my pride. "She kicked him in one knee, then spun and kicked him in the face. I couldn't believe it. She was incredible!"

"Wow, I didn't know your Mom knew karate too," Allan said, amazed.

"Neither did I."

We continued our conversation as though nothing had ever disrupted our friendship, losing track of time and nearly forgetting to eat. We were forced to run back to class so we didn't miss the bell. Despite the cramping in my stomach from the milk, my aura glowed a joyful yellow. I had my best friend back.

✶   ✶   ✶

When I got home, Mom met me at the door.

"Good news. I talked to Chief Beurline, and he agreed to meet you in one hour. You have just enough time to go over your notes and practice the questions once before we have to go."

We reviewed my questions again on the way, and I felt well

prepared as the woman behind the desk buzzed me into the back section of the police station.

"His office is all the way in back," she said, as I passed through the door. Mom signed in my name on the sheet and took a seat in the waiting room.

✱   ✱   ✱

Chief Beurline's tall, thin figure met me in the walkway a few steps inside.

"Hunter Miller," the Chief said, smiling broadly. I noticed there was no yellow in his aura. The smile without happiness confused me.

We walked past Officer Metz's desk, which was empty. I tried to scan it for the gang files, but Chief Beurline ushered me so quickly past that I had no chance. The name on the door said *Captain Beurline*, which I also found puzzling.

"Oh yes. The door. This was my office before I became chief, and things don't happen too quickly around here. I get to keep it until they find a new captain. Having this office means you didn't have to go downtown, which would have been quite a trek for you in rush hour traffic."

I nodded like I understood.

"Let's get right to it, shall we?" he said.

"Sure," I said.

"First, how about telling me what got you interested in the project?"

I'd been ready to launch into my prepared questions, but this threw me for a loop. I decided to go with the truth, since I was pretty sure this guy would be able to tell if I was lying.

"To be honest, I became interested in the police when my friend got injured."

"Oh, no," he said. "Tell me about it."

"Allan was coming home from practice and somebody hit him in the head with a bat, and then rode off on a motorcycle. Allan got a concussion, but otherwise he was fine. Just some stitches and a couple of days off from school."

"And you met a policeman that day?"

"Yes, Officer Metz. He was cool. That's when I got the idea to write the paper on the police."

"Did Officer Metz find the person who attacked your friend?" he continued.

"Uh, no, not yet. Still looking."

"That's too bad. Do they have any leads?"

"They think it has something to do with a motorcycle gang," I said. "They are looking at two of them in the area, the Low Riders, and the Highlanders. Do you know of them?"

"Sure I do. Bad men, these gang members," he said.

I realized I was way off topic, and since the main point was to make this look like I was here to get my paper done, I refocused on the questions I'd brought.

"So how did you train to become a policeman?"

"Ah, yes. Back when I started in Pennsylvania, we only needed an eight-week police academy course. A lot has changed since then, but I was grandfathered in. Do you know what that means?"

I shook my head.

"It means that I didn't have to go through all the new training because I was already on the police force. I was a Sergeant when I transferred to Seattle, and I worked my way up to Detective, Detective Sergeant, and Captain. Last year, I was appointed Chief of Police by the Mayor. It was a great honor, and I'm happy to serve."

"What got you interested in becoming a police officer?" I asked.

"Oh, I remember the exact moment. I was a sophomore in high school, out for a run, and I went by a house fire. There were tons of firetrucks, police cars, ambulances, and people all pitching in to save the lives and property of one of my neighbors. I saw a police officer in the front yard, comforting the child whose possessions were all destroyed in the house behind him, and it hit me like a bolt of lightning. Boom! Right then and there, I knew. I wanted to serve and protect."

"Wow!" I said, impressed with both the story, and the flair with which he told it. I almost forgot my next question.

"Can you describe a day that made it all worthwhile?"

"There are so many. Let's see. Ah, yes, here's a good story," he said, settling back into his chair.

"You have to understand that I consider myself a victim's advocate at heart. As a detective, I always relished the feeling of helping those whose lives had been interrupted by a burglary. Arriving at their homes after recovering their stolen property, seeing their joy, that was special.

"But my best days were those when I protected children from abuse, whether it be physical, sexual, or mental. Sitting in the courtroom with a parent, watching the perpetrator get sentenced to years in prison, that's a feeling you just can't imagine. The raw emotion of a parent crying and hugging me once I'd helped them obtain some semblance of closure after a horrific event. That's one of the most intense feelings I've ever experienced as an officer, or as a human being."

I was captivated. What an amazing man!

"I bet you are the same way," he said.

"What do you mean?"

"You probably want to see justice done for your friend, right?"

"Of course," I agreed.

"Maybe that's why you are so interested in the police, too, eh?" he said, smiling.

I tried to keep my face blank.

"Come on, I can see it in your eyes. You want to get back at the guy. Admit it!"

"I would like to see justice done," I said, carefully phrasing my words.

"Anyone else see it your way? Or does everyone tell you to mind your own business and let the police handle it?"

"Yeah, that's exactly what everyone says. Even Allan."

"But you aren't letting them stop you, are you?"

"No!" I said, immediately regretting it. "Well, yes," I flip-flopped.

"After all, I'm just a kid, what can I do?"

"What can you do indeed," he echoed. "Isn't there anyone who can help you find out more information?"

"Well, my librarian helped me find a guy from the *Seattle Times* who wrote stories about other cases like Allan's."

"Your librarian?"

"Yes, Miss Kessler. She's really nice. Always smiles and everything."

"And who's this reporter? Did he get you any good info?"

"His name is Lloyd Jonas. He's only after the story, though. Wants to see proof of everything before," I said, suddenly feeling a tingling sensation. My aura was telling me that I was about to give up too much information.

Chief Beurline was nodding his head, encouragingly.

"Well, nobody was really able to tell me anything," I concluded.

"And when you were here the other day, do you think that attack was related?"

He was getting too close for comfort.

"I don't know," I said noncommittally. "Listen, I think I have enough for the paper. My Mom's waiting for me so I need to get going."

"Very good. Let me walk you out. I hope I was helpful."

"Yes, it was great," I said, relieved to be leaving. Suddenly I felt like a fly inside a spider's web, as he put his arms around my shoulder and shepherded me past Officer Metz's desk toward the exit.

We proceeded to the giant steel door, waited for the buzz, and I went through.

Mom was waiting on the other side. She offered her hand. "Thank you very much for your time, Chief Beurline," Mom said.

The Chief reciprocated, and they shook hands. "Any time. Any time. Perhaps Hunter here would be interested in joining the force after high school?"

"I want to be a doctor," I said.

"Another noble profession," he said. "Good luck on the paper, and let me know if you need anything else," he added. He waved goodbye as we walked to the car.

"How did it go?" Mom asked, as we jumped into the vehicle.

"Pretty good. He talked about being a victim advocate and how he liked putting away bad guys who abused kids," I said.

"I've been thinking about your outline. Perhaps you should add information about crime rates in the area. Maybe say something about the size of the police force."

She gave me a few other ideas and ways to find the information, but I'd lost interest. I had a skill to practice to execute my plan on Tuesday when I went to see Officer Metz. I was *going* to see those files!

CHAPTER 44

FRIDAY WAS a good day. I loaded up on snacks and took great personal amusement in practicing for Tuesday's interview. My poor classmates had no idea what was going on. I had it down pat after affecting Patty Owens and Kristen Worthy, but just for fun, I inflicted Glenn King, Alan Paul, Christy Johnson and Amy Mullins.

"What is going on with everyone today?" Miss Burnell asked.

I did my best to suppress a smile and hung my face low to make sure she didn't see it. I knew exactly what was going on. I thought of Ian. He'd be so proud.

*   *   *

I went to karate and worked out hard, enjoying the sparring in particular. I was pairing up with the higher belts, even Paul Dooley and Mitch Govell, both of whom were brown belts on their way to black. I watched them carefully as we sparred, and learned more upper level techniques and how to counter them. I could tell from their auras that they were impressed by Dad's moves, and I was excited that I had finally developed an aptitude for something other than dragging people into the void.

We learned the rest of the blue belt one-steps and board-breaking techniques, and since we'd already covered the *kata*, all I had to do to prepare was practice. I figured I'd spend all day Saturday in the garage, honing my techniques.

Allan caught me in the locker room after practice. "Hey, tell your Mom we can bring you next week," he said.

"Cool, thanks."

Our relationship had always been very strong, and I felt horrible having betrayed his trust. But now that I'd been attacked too, he seemed to better understand my need to find the offender. I still didn't talk to him about it, but he accepted my decision. That made it all good.

*   *   *

I woke up early and had breakfast with Mom.

"I'm going to work today," she said. "I'll be gone most of the day, but I'll be back for dinner. You should write your outline, and I'll help you when I get home."

"OK. I'm gonna spend some time on my blue belt stuff too," I said.

"Nice. You'll have to show me when I get home."

Now that I knew that Mom was a stealthy martial artist, I understood why she wanted me to show her what I was doing. I nodded. "You probably know it already."

She smiled as she picked up her keys. "See you tonight."

I went right to the garage and started right up. I began with a callisthenic workout, stretching routine, and *kata*, then practiced the one-step moves. After lunch, I launched into the breaking techniques, and finally, I practiced sparring against the bag.

The workout was intense. I'd completely lost myself in the flow. Punch, punch, punch, dodge back, kick, spin and kick, reset my balance, forearm strike, block a pretend strike from the bag, and counter with another kick. By the time I felt the tingling sensation, it had turned into a pounding. I turned my head from the bag in time to see a man swinging a bat at my head. Then everything went black.

＊　　＊　　＊

The pain burned and throbbed so badly I could hardly stand it. It felt like I'd been in the void for hours. Without my watch, I had no idea how much time had passed since… what?

"Hey, he's coming around," a deep voice said.

"Finally. Jeez, I thought you wanted the kid alive! After all, you're already a full member." came another voice.

"I hardly tapped him."

"He's been unconscious for three hours!"

"Must have a soft head."

"He's got a kid's head. At least he's not dead yet. You can find out what he knows."

I could barely follow the conversation. They were discussing my death as if it were the daily menu at a coffee shop. Whoever these guys were, killing people was part of their background.

"Yo, kid! Mommy's not around to protect you this time," said the man with the deep voice. He was big and bulky, bald headed and stinky. He waved his fist in front of my face angrily. I tried to focus on his aura, but all I could sense was muddled, cloudy redness. And spicy pain. It hurt so badly. How could anyone live with pain like this?

Despite my misery, I did notice something on the man's forearm. It was a tattoo, and a very strange one at that. The picture was a man, sort of. The man had a lion head and lion feet, and he was holding a long sword across his body, with the point touching the ground. Perhaps it was my waning consciousness, but it appeared rather blurry.

"I'll be right back. Wake him up so I can question him."

Water splashed onto my face and I flinched and shook my head, sending water droplets flying onto the man with the tattoo.

"Nice job, Aug," said Tattoo, clearly irritated.

"Well you said to wake him up."

"Yeah, but I didn't ask for a bath!"

"You probably could use one," said the first man, a tall, pencil thin guy with greasy hair and a pockmarked face.

Tattoo grabbed the skinny man by the shirt and flung him several feet into a stack of crates that went flying willy-nilly, creating a loud crash that reverberated throughout the building. The noise echoed in my head for several seconds, worsening the spicy pain.

"Watch yourself Schmidt. I'll plant you in the pit!"

"Sorry, Logan. You smell like a bed of petunias after a fresh spring shower," said the man, who was struggling to stand up amidst the broken glass and spilled liquid that had previously been inside the crates.

It seemed for a moment that Logan was going to follow up on his threat to "plant" Schmidt in the pit, whatever that meant, but seeing the mess, he waved dismissively at him instead.

I couldn't see auras, but I did notice that we were in a massive room, at least a hundred feet either direction. Crates, like the ones Schmidt's body had broken, were stacked in giant mountains along the nearest wall. The floor was a slate grey, smooth and cold. I didn't see a way out. It was dark, dingy, and smelled of motor oil, or worse.

I found myself lifted in the air by Logan and dropped ungraciously into a chair. The drop rattled my head, which pounded with pain. I put my hands over my head to try to squeeze away the pain, but it was no use.

"Hey!" said Logan.

I ignored him and kept my hands over my eyes and ears. I felt a smack across my face, whipping my head sideways.

"Look at me when I'm talking to you!" he demanded.

I could barely focus as it was, and the blow to my face resonated throughout my head. I squinted in his general direction.

"That's better. Now, I got some questions for you. And it's going to go a lot better for you if you simply tell me the truth."

His face faded in and out of focus. I thought it looked vaguely familiar, but I couldn't place him.

"Do you know who I am?" he asked.

"No," I said.

He sat back. "OK, good start. What did you tell the police?"

"What?" I said.

He smacked me hard on the face.

"We *know* you've been talking to the cops. What did you tell them? And don't even try to lie. I can read your face like a book!"

"I'm talking to the police about a paper I'm writing," I said.

Smack! I fell off the chair onto my knees, my ears, head, and face all ringing with pain.

"What's the real reason you're talking to the cops?" he yelled, grabbing me by the shirt and stuffing me back into the chair.

"I really do have a paper," I started.

This time, his fist collided with my mouth, splitting my lip and sending blood flying. The chair almost tipped over backwards, but the other man, Schmidt, caught it before it toppled.

"No point in lying, kid," said Schmidt quietly. "Just tell us what we need to know, and we can get this over with."

"The police. What did you tell them?"

"I didn't tell them anything. I was asking questions. Pretending I was questioning them about the school project so I could learn about who hit my friend," I confessed. I wanted the pain to stop.

He studied me for a moment. "There, that wasn't so hard now, was it? Just tell the truth, and we won't have any need for violence," he said.

"OK," I blustered. Blood spilled from my mouth.

"What do the police know?"

"About what?" I said, shrinking back. I thought he was going to hit me again.

"About who hit your friend?" he asked.

"They think it was someone from a biker gang," I said.

"Aha, now we're getting somewhere. Which gang?"

"They have files on the Low Riders and the Highlanders," I said.

"Have you seen the files?"

"No. They wouldn't let me."

He paused again, apparently reading my face.

"Good, good. Let's see, who else knows about what you're trying to do?"

"Nobody," I said. Before the word was out of my mouth, I was on the ground, more blood coming from my nose.

"What about your librarian friend?"

"Miss Kessler?" I said, completely befuddled. "She's just helping me find newspaper articles. She doesn't know what I'm trying to do."

"And your contact at the *Times*?"

"Lloyd Jonas? He just wants the story. He knows about the different gangs, but he has no idea which one the serial killer runs with."

"Serial killer?" he said questioningly.

"Yeah, Jonas thinks the guy is running all over Seattle, hitting people in quiet neighborhoods with a baseball bat."

"He thinks it's the same guy? Ha, that's rich," said Logan, laughing gruffly. "Is that what the cops think too?"

"I don't know what the cops think. Metz won't tell me anything."

"Well, I do appreciate your honesty. Who else is helping you? Your parents?"

"No, my parents have no idea what I'm up to!" I said loudly. I wasn't thinking very clearly, but I somehow felt that implicating my parents would put them in danger.

"Really. You expect me to believe that you're chasing down a serial killer, and your parents have no idea?"

"I'm good at keeping a secret," I said.

"I highly doubt that. You just think you are. But at least you're not lying." He paused, as if collecting his thoughts. "OK, that's good enough. Schmidt, go ahead and take him to the pit."

"You want me to wax the kid?" he said.

Logan shook his head. I thought his body posture suggested frustration, but without the auras, I couldn't tell for sure.

"No, don't wax the kid, just *take him to the pit*," he said, carefully enunciating each of the latter words. He nodded at me.

"Oh, gotcha. Yep. I'll take him to the pit," he said.

"Now you've got it. Much easier this way. I'm heading out. I'll catch you tomorrow at the meeting."

"OK, see you," he said, as Logan went off toward an apparent exit on the other side of the building.

"Let's go, kid. The pit's out back."

He picked me up by the arm and I stumbled silently along beside him. The building exit on the ground floor opened up into a vast space that led to woods on three sides. We took two steps out into the cool night air, and Schmidt inexplicably toppled to the ground. A gun fell out of his hand onto the ground in front of him.

I was processing events very slowly because of the tremendous pain, but the fact that he had a gun strongly implied that "taking me to the pit" meant killing me. I didn't want to die.

It took a few seconds for me to realize that Schmidt wasn't getting up. He wasn't moving at all. Something had happened to him. I didn't want to wait around for Logan to return and find that job hadn't been completed. I scanned the area for an exit, but other than going back into the building, I didn't see an escape path.

We'd been heading toward "the pit," and I clearly didn't want to go that way. The smell wafting from that direction was awful, like badly overcooked meat. I heard a noise somewhere in the woods on my right, which cemented my decision. I started walking quickly toward the left, following the edge of the building. I came to a break in the trees, leading to a service road. A ratty old bike sat propped next to one of the trees. It wasn't locked.

I hustled over to it, still fighting the severe pain in my head. I jumped on and tried to pedal, although I had no idea of my destination. My only priority was getting away. My feet fell off the pedals several times, and I almost wiped out, but I clutched at the handlebars and slowly began moving. There was only one way to go, so I followed the service road. I hoped it led away from Logan. Everything was dark, and my head throbbed, but I pressed on, making gradual progress.

After what felt like almost a mile, the service road formed a T with another road. In the distance on the right, I saw lights, so I went that way. The source of the light was a twenty-four hour gas station. I pulled up next to the front door, dropped the bike, and went inside.

The guy behind the counter didn't look up right away, but when he did, he gasped. "What happened to you?" he said loudly.

"Got hit in the head," I said.

"You're bleeding," he observed. "Were you in a car accident? Fight?"

"Can I borrow your phone?" I said, ignoring his questions. I was starting to regain my senses. I needed to call Mom and have her pick me up.

"Do you need an ambulance?"

I thought about paramedic Phil, who'd picked me up several times in the past, and decided against it. Once I got control of the auras, I could heal myself. I only needed to get to somewhere safe and eat some food.

"No, I need to call my Mom," I said.

"You sure? I can call 911 for you," he said.

"No, I'm OK," I lied. "Where's your phone?"

He let me behind the counter. Since there were no other customers, he hovered right next to me while I picked up the receiver. I stared at him, pleading silently to give me some privacy.

He got the hint. "I'll be over here if you need anything," he said.

I dialed the number. Mom answered. "Hello?"

"Hi, Mom," I said, greatly relieved. "I got into some trouble. Can you come pick me up?"

"What happened?" she asked, voice pressured. I bet her aura was flashing concern.

"I'll tell you when you get me."

"Where are you?"

I looked around. "Hey, what's the address here?" I called out to the cashier. My voice sounded odd, and the loud sound made my head throb even more.

He told me the street name and number, and I relayed it to Mom.

"Are you hurt?" she asked.

"Not really. I'll be fine."

"Stay right where you are. I'll be there in twenty minutes," she said. She hung up without waiting for a response.

I looked down at my shirt and saw the blood spattered everywhere. I needed to get cleaned up. Mostly I needed to stop this blinding headache.

"My Mom's on her way. Do you mind if I take a few things and she can pay for them when she gets here?"

He eyed me suspiciously.

"She'll be here in twenty minutes. I promise she'll pay."

"All right, but no more than ten dollars' worth. It'll come out of my hide if you stiff me!"

I wolfed down three candy bars from the shelf, washing them down with most of a two-liter bottle of cola.

"Good luck with the diabetes," the guy said quietly.

"Can I use your bathroom?" I asked.

He pointed. "You'll need this," he said, handing me a key. I went into the filthy room and did my best to ignore the horrid smell. When I looked in the mirror, I realized why the counter guy thought I'd been in a car accident. I looked as bad as I felt.

I drank down the rest of the cola, and, my system awash with calories, tried again to access my aura. All I could feel was the same muddled redness, but this time, it came with a sense of familiarity. I'd felt this before.

Allan!

It all made perfect sense. Smashed in the head with a baseball bat, cloudy spiciness, confusion and headache. I'd suffered a concussion. I healed Allan's concussion easily. The problem was, I couldn't feel my aura, only the redness. I sat there for ten minutes in frustration. Mom was coming and she'd freak if I didn't clean myself up, so I gave up the attempt to heal myself, took off my shirt, and used it as a washcloth to remove the blood from my face and arms.

Mom arrived sooner than I expected and knocked on the door to the bathroom.

"Hunter? I'm here. Let's go."

"OK," I answered, and I rinsed off the shirt one more time in the sink and opened the door.

As soon as she saw me, she engulfed me with a giant hug, which hurt my head a little but I didn't mind. She ran her fingers along my scalp, taking note of the bump on the back side. Seeing my naked torso and the stained shirt in my hand, she walked over to a display rack and grabbed a t-shirt that said "AC/DC" with a lightning bolt between the letters.

"Add this to the bill," she called to the cashier while handing me the shirt. On the way out, Mom threw the guy a twenty dollar bill and said, "Keep the difference. And thanks for your help."

We walked soundlessly to the car as I donned the shirt, and Mom drove us home.

CHAPTER 45

I KEPT trying to focus on my aura, but to no avail. Whatever damage the baseball bat had done appeared to be permanent. Panic welled up inside me as I realized I'd grown quite accustomed to using auras, and I'd have severe difficulty without my ability.

For years, I'd considered it a curse. The demons had frightened me into the void on a daily basis. Before I gained control, I'd have done anything to be "normal," even if it meant sustaining a crushing blow to my skull. Now, I'd do anything to get the power back.

We pulled into the driveway.

"How are you feeling?" Mom asked.

"Pretty bad headache," I replied.

"I'll get you some Tylenol," she answered. "Then you can tell us everything that happened."

I followed her inside and slumped onto the couch in the living room. Mom gave me two pills and a glass of water. I downed them.

"Let me get you a washcloth, and we can clean your face properly. You may need stitches. I'll be right back."

I saw a flicker of blue out of the corner of my eye. Except my eyes were closed. My *aura*! I seized on the blue color and focused all my energy on it. Abruptly, I felt the complete picture of my deep blue coloring, compounded by the clouded distortion that once represented my brain, and the spicy redness of the injuries to my face, chest, arms, and legs.

I fixed the cuts on my lip and nose immediately. So much for needing stitches. I didn't remember hurting my chest, arms or legs, but I quashed the spicy redness from those areas just as quickly. Then, I focused on the muddled cloudiness. I was repairing the damage when Mom tapped me hard on the shoulder.

"Hunter!" she said loudly.

"Yeah, Mom, I'm OK," I said.

"Good. I thought you were unconscious again. Let's see that face," she said.

She cleaned off the blood, and, to her shock, found no source.

"Where'd the blood come from?" she asked.

"My nose. But it stopped bleeding on its own," I said.

"How's your headache?"

"Getting better. I think I just need some rest. It started out really bad, and I couldn't even think straight. But over the last hour it's been improving. Probably a concussion."

"Well, aren't you the brilliant young physician," Mom said, smiling.

I smiled back weakly.

"All right, you rest here for a little while."

I returned my attention to my aura, and this time, the blue flooded back to all of the areas of my body that had been injured. I began to rejoice, until I noticed the density wasn't the same. I was still quite weak. Healing the concussion took a lot out of me.

I opened my eyes and called out to Mom. "Can I get something to eat?"

She returned to the living room. "What, you burned off your candy bars and soda?"

Had I not noticed the hint of yellow, I never would've realized that she was teasing me.

"Come on, Mom! I missed lunch and dinner!"

"It's OK. I love a good chocolate bar every now and then too. I made you pasta, it's in the dining room. Let's go."

"Thanks Mom," I said appreciatively.

I felt his aura before I entered the kitchen, but I was still surprised to see my father, who was hanging up the phone.

"Dad!" I yelled. "What are you doing here?"

"Hi, Hunter, how are you doing?"

"Better," I said, unsure of exactly how much Mom had told him.

"Relax," he said. "Mom told me what happened and I'm not mad. But we have to talk. Do you think you're up for it?"

"I really need some food first," I said.

Dad seemed to understand. "Yeah, me too. Eat first, talk later. Good plan."

∗   ∗   ∗

After dinner, I felt much better. My brief span without access to auras frightened me, and I neurotically checked for the cool blueness every few minutes to make sure my capabilities had fully returned. I also took time to study my parents' auras, both of which buzzed with an underlying concern that seemed out of proportion to the current situation. Despite having chocolate bars earlier, Mom let me have ice cream for dessert. Immediately afterward, the questions started.

"Tell us exactly what happened. Start from the beginning," Dad said.

"I was exercising in the garage. Practicing for my blue belt test, which won't be for a few weeks, but I learned all the one-steps and everything, so I was working on them."

Dad nodded encouragingly.

"Well, all of the sudden, a guy appeared with a bat and whacked me on the head. I didn't hear him coming or anything," I said. I should have felt his aura, but for some reason I hadn't. This was disturbing, and my features must have betrayed me, because Dad spoke.

"You're safe now, Hunter. Go on with the story."

"I woke up in a huge building with hundreds of crates stacked against the walls. The Two guys were there. Logan, the guy who hit me, and Schmidt."

"Hunter, we've been over this. Kenny's father wasn't involved. He was in jail," Mom said.

"Kenny's father?" I said inquisitively. Of course. Kenny Logan. Logan was Kenny's father!

Dad raised his hand toward Mom, who was about to speak again. "How do you know the men's names?" he asked.

"They called each other by name," I said defiantly. "They said, 'Watch yourself, Schmidt, or I'll plant you in the pit,' and 'Sorry, Logan, you smell like a bed of flowers,' or something like that."

Dad's aura soured noticeably. Mom's continued to exhibit disbelief.

"Could you describe the one called Logan?" Dad asked.

I tried to grasp at the memory of the event, but the only thing I could remember was the marking on his forearm. I never really felt his aura, and, although I saw his face, the memory of it was hazy.

"He was a big guy with a weird tattoo on his arm, right here," I pointed to the location on my own arm. "It had the head and feet of a lion, but the body of a man holding a sword."

Dad nodded thoughtfully, as though he expected this. Mom stared at him with her piercing blue eyes, trying to read his inscrutable face. It was interesting to watch.

"Did the other man have the same tattoo?" Dad asked.

"I don't know. I didn't see it, but I was a little out of it," I admitted.

"That's OK, you're doing fine. What happened after you woke up?"

I considered for a moment. Mom would freak out if I mentioned getting tortured, so I decided to leave that part out. "They asked me all kinds of questions. They wanted to know who I talked to. They asked about Miss Kessler, the librarian, and Mr. Jonas, the newspaper guy, plus Officer Metz and the police. Lots of questions about the police, and..."

"And what?"

"And you. They asked if I told my parents."

"What did you say?"

"I told them that both of you had no idea. I said I was good at keeping secrets."

"How did they react?"

"Logan laughed. He told me that you knew what I was doing, and I only *thought* I was good at keeping secrets."

Dad nodded.

"But now we *know* Kenny's father is behind this. Can't we call Officer Metz and get him arrested?"

"He's got a point, honey," Mom said. "We have him on kidnapping and assault, and if we search the warehouse and find the bat, we'd have all the evidence we need."

"It's not that simple, Marissa. There's the matter of Schmidt, plus we have to explain how Hunter got away."

"Oh, that was the weirdest thing," I said. "Schmidt just dropped to the ground, like he had a stroke or a seizure or something."

"Was he convulsing?" Dad asked.

"No, I guess not. Maybe a stroke then."

"Probably," Dad agreed, but his aura was gesticulating wildly.

"Anyway, I heard something off to one side, so I went the other way. I found a bike, and took it to the gas station where I called Mom."

"What about the clerk at the gas station?" Dad said, directing his question toward Mom.

"A teenager. He thought Hunter was in a fight or a car accident. I don't think he's going to say anything unless someone asks."

"Hmm. He didn't call the police?" Dad said.

"No. From the looks of him, he's probably had his own run-ins with the police."

Dad nodded knowingly. "That's good. Any other possible witnesses?"

"Hunter, did you see anyone else?" Mom asked me.

"No, nobody. I heard someone in the woods, but I went the other way and don't think they saw me. Other than Logan and Schmidt, that was it."

"Are you sure we shouldn't take him to the hospital?" Mom asked, in a manner that suggested it was the fourth or fifth time she'd made this suggestion.

Dad rose from his chair and came very close, examining my head with his eyes and his hands. He squeezed my neck, back, arms and legs, and then asked me to lay down on the couch so he could press on my belly. He shined a penlight in my eyes, had me watch his finger, and then made me perform the same silly exercises that Dr. Stonington had when I saw him about my headaches.

"He's fine. Definitely a concussion because he got knocked out, but he checks out."

He pressed on my nose.

"Didn't even break his nose," he added. "Besides, Herlihy said there may be someone on the inside, and if we sign him in at the hospital, they'll know pretty quickly that he got away."

This last part piqued my interest. Dad knew Lieutenant Herlihy?

"All right," Mom said. "We'll do it your way."

Then she turned to me. "But you're not going anywhere for a couple of days. Not until we get this sorted out. I'll call Miss Burnell and tell her you're sick. And if your headache gets worse, or you feel sick to your stomach, let me know right away."

"Good plan," Dad agreed.

"So what am I supposed to do?" I asked.

"Take it easy. No karate, no television, no school work. And no leaving the house without me or Mom! Just rest," Dad said. "You got your bell rung. It takes a couple of days to get over that. Trust me."

"Now how about getting ready for bed? You must be exhausted." Mom said.

She was right. After putting on pajamas and brushing my teeth, I climbed into bed and was asleep in moments.

CHAPTER 46

I WOKE up the next morning, entirely unfazed by Saturday's mis-
adventure. My head was completely healed, I'd eaten plenty of food,
and my aura was one-hundred percent back to normal. My memories were not entirely clear, but I did recall a few interesting items.

When Dad asked me to describe Logan, I struggled badly
because I never really focused on the man's face or his physical
features, but thinking back, his build and facial structure reminded
me of Kenny. I couldn't place it at the time, but I found his
appearance familiar, and now I knew why.

He'd made comments about me having a soft head. It felt pretty
firm to me, but it obviously wasn't hard enough to stop the bat
from knocking me unconscious and disrupting my ability to use
the auras. Protecting my head from major blows needed to be a top
priority in case I got into another fight.

The most irritating part, other than the painful beatings, was
Logan's insistence that he could read my face. Mom, Dad, Ian, Allan,
Betsy, my teachers, and even random kidnappers could all tell what I
was thinking by my expressions. Suppose someone asked me if I had
supernatural ability? I'd have to lie and say "no," but they'd see I was
lying. What if it was Dr. Eisenberg? She'd either know my secret, or,
more likely, she'd assume I was nuts and lock me up forever.

It was imperative that I learn to cover up my feelings.

After breakfast, I spent the rest of the morning looking at myself in the bathroom mirror while I thought about various people, like Allan, Betsy, or Kenny's father. I wasn't very good at recognizing facial expressions, so it was nearly impossible to cover them up. At the end of two hours, I'd learned nothing.

Both Mom and Dad checked on me several times, asking how I was feeling or if I needed anything. I wanted to ask them how they managed to hide how they felt, but the obvious implications of me wanting to do the same made this a bad idea.

I continued to ponder this while staying home from school on Monday. I had no aftereffects from the concussion because I'd healed it, but Mom and Dad both thought I needed at least forty-eight hours to recover. I insisted I was fine, but neither would budge, even though they could see in my face that I believed it.

"I guess you won't let me go to karate," I said Monday afternoon. I'd been doing really well, and I loathed missing any practices.

"No, sorry, Hunter. The last thing you want after a concussion is further head trauma. I think you'll have to wait at least a week to go back. But maybe we can talk about school on Wednesday."

"I have the appointment with Officer Metz on Tuesday afternoon. I need to interview him for my paper. It's half of my grade, and I have to get that done," I pleaded.

"I'm not sure. You had a major ordeal," Mom said. She sounded worried for my safety, and her aura confirmed it.

"What's safer than the police station?"

Mom wavered.

"Besides, I promise not to talk about anything but the interview. I swear!"

Mom studied my face. Fortunately, I was telling the truth. Had I been lying, she'd be able to see the waves, or, wait…

The concept struck me like a thunderclap. Waves!

"Hunter, are you OK?" Mom said, reading my new expression with deep concern.

"Yeah, Mom, I'm great. I just had another idea. But can I interview Officer Metz tomorrow, *please*?"

"We'll see how you feel in the morning."

"Thanks, Mom!" I said, now full of excitement at the revelation I'd experienced. I wanted to practice immediately.

*   *   *

I ran off to the bathroom and looked at myself in the mirror.

"I have three heads," I said to myself.

The waves came, as I knew they would, but instead of giant whitewash, it felt more like a tiny rivulet. Having three heads was as far from the truth as I could imagine, but my tried-and-true lie detector barely registered.

I tried another one. "I like Kenny a lot."

This time, I felt a brief yank of current, but the waves stopped almost immediately. I didn't have time to quash them, which was my brilliant breakthrough.

My idea was simple. Remove the waves from my aura. It was analogous to healing by eliminating the spicy redness. If there were no waves, the lie wouldn't exist. I wouldn't be able to detect it, and, if my assumption was correct, neither would anyone else. Absolutely ingenious.

Unfortunately, no matter how many falsehoods I uttered to the mirror, nothing worked. It was as though I knew the lie was a lie, so it wasn't a lie at all. I imagined talking to someone else, and tried again.

"Getting hit in the head with a baseball bat was enjoyable, and I can't wait to have it happen again."

By the time I'd finished the first few words, the waves had diminished to the point of irrelevance. This wasn't working the way I'd planned. I needed to lie to someone else. I remembered something Grandpa told me that seemed fitting.

"You can't tickle yourself."

Apparently you can't lie to yourself either. At least, not for very long. I tried over and over, focusing on my aura, and trying to feel the waves, but I was never able to sustain them long enough to eliminate them.

Eventually I was forced to give up. I thought about trying it on my parents, but that could backfire badly, and so I dismissed that idea. My friends would think I was insane, as would my teacher, or anyone else I could think of. It would have to be a perfect stranger. Someone I'd never see again. Someone I could speak to on a Sunday without violating my house arrest resulting from my concussion. Fat chance. I'd have to wait until tomorrow at the very least.

∗   ∗   ∗

The glaring hole in my theory became evident the very first time I attempted to test it out. I caught the mail carrier making his daily delivery and hit him with a blatantly false claim.

"The sky is a wonderful orange, don't you think?"

"Looks pretty blue to me," he answered. "Here's your mail. Have a great day."

He was already on his way by the time I realized that not only did I fail to suppress the waves from my aura, but even if I had, I wouldn't be able to tell whether he knew I was lying or not.

I brought in the mail and tossed it on the counter in the kitchen.

"Bringing in the mail? That's not like you. What's going on?" Mom said.

"Nothing," I said, the waves pouring out of me. Unprepared for the exchange, I wasn't able to stop them.

"Are you sure?" she said.

"I wanted to talk to someone," I said. No waves. That was true enough.

"I took the day off from work, Hunter. Sit down on the couch and tell me what's on your mind."

Now that I knew talking to strangers wasn't going to work, or, at least, I wouldn't know if it worked, I had to rethink my strategy. There was one person who rarely let me down.

"I'd rather talk to Allan."

"I know you're going through a lot, Hunter, but you have to be straight with me. You've stumbled into something very dangerous, and I don't want you getting hurt. Your Dad and I are only trying to do what's best for you."

"I know, Mom. I promise I'll talk to you after." That would give me a chance to verify the results.

"Allan has karate tonight, and there's no way you're going. But maybe he can come over for an hour beforehand. Would that be OK?

"That'd be great. Thanks, Mom."

Mom called Allan's mother and arranged for him to come by after school. It was ironic, because it had been Allan who helped me discover what the waves meant. I'd asked him to lie to me, to tell me that he had two heads. When I felt the waves, I realized that Mom and Dad were lying whenever I'd felt them. Perhaps every parent lied to their children, but not every parent was a member of a secret organization or trying to hide the nature of their biological father. Now here I was, trying to use the same skill in reverse.

"Hey, buddy, how's it going?" said Allan, when he arrived.

"Actually, I'm doing great."

"How come you missed school?"

"Yeah, about that. I'm not supposed to talk about it. So you have to swear not to say anything to anyone. Can you keep a secret?"

"Sure," he said. No waves. A good sign.

"Even if it's a really big one, something that you really want to share?"

"Yeah, of course. Remember Tommy Lachance?" he reminded.

"Good point. Yes. How could I forget?"

"So what is it?" he asked.

"Here it is. I was kidnapped."

"What? By whom?" he said incredulously.

"This is where it gets really tricky, so you have to swear you won't say anything."

"Come on. Tell me!" he demanded.

"Swear!"

"I swear!" he said, with no waves.

"It was Kenny Logan's father."

"Holy cow! Are you serious?"

I nodded. "It gets worse."

"How could it get worse?"

"He hit me with a baseball bat and gave me a concussion."

"You're kidding, right? Kenny's father? Is he the one that hit me, too?"

"No," I said firmly.

"How can you be sure?" he asked.

"All right, this you *really* can't repeat."

"I won't."

"He was in jail the day you got hit. So I know for sure he didn't do it. But I think he's involved."

"How?"

"I'm not sure. But when he kidnapped me, he tortured me and asked me who I'd been talking to about your injury. He kept punching me and stuff, so I told him everything."

"Like what?"

"That Officer Metz has a file on the two biker gangs. The librarian, Miss Kessler, helped me find articles in the newspaper about them. The journalist that Ian's Dad worked with, Lloyd Jonas, told me there were several others who got beaten up just like you and me, but the others all died. He thought it might be the work of a serial killer."

"Oh my gosh!" was all Allan could say. After it all sunk in, he asked, "How did you get away?"

"I got lucky. The guy called Schmidt had a stroke or something and passed out. I found a bike next to the building and rode away until I found a gas station. Then Mom picked me up."

"Wow!"

"So listen," I said. "I need your help with something."

"What?"

"When the guy was questioning me, he kept saying that he could tell if I was lying. Ian always said the same thing, that my face was an open book. I don't want people to be able to read me like that. That's why I was working with Ian in the first place. I wanted to be able to tell what other people were thinking, but I don't want them to know what I'm thinking."

"What's that got to do with me?"

"I discovered a trick."

"What trick?"

I hesitated. "It's just a trick to help me hide if I'm lying. You know, control my face muscles and stuff."

"OK," he said.

"I need you to tell me if it works or not."

"So you're going to lie to me, and if I can spot the lie, it doesn't work?"

"Exactly," I said, relieved that he got the point without further explanation.

"OK, sure. And if it works, you can teach it to me," he said.

"First things first," I said. I'd never be able to teach him what I was going to try to do, but I'd have to cross that bridge later.

"Well, go ahead then. Lie to me."

I started with the lies I'd told myself and the postman, feeling the waves as they emanated from my aura completely unbidden.

"You're lying," he said. "Whatever you're doing isn't working."

"Yeah, I know," I said. "I need to practice for a while."

"I only have an hour," he said.

"OK, let me keep going."

I lied for twenty minutes, telling every fib I could think of, and feeling the waves tumble over my aura without fail. I finally started to get a feel for them, but I wasn't able to stop them from coming, until I realized a critical point. I was spending all my effort thinking of lies, and I couldn't suppress the waves in time. I needed a different tactic.

"OK, I've got an idea. You ask me a question, and I'll try to lie."

"Mix it up. Sometimes tell the truth. That way, I won't know for sure," Allan suggested.

"Great idea," I agreed. "Go ahead, ask me something."

"What color are your socks?"

I made up my mind to lie. I felt the waves coming before I'd formulated my answer. I reached out and strangled them back to smoothness.

"Black," I said.

He looked at me carefully. "I think you're lying, but that time it was really hard to tell."

I pulled up my pant leg to reveal the white color.

"OK, that was a good start. Let's go again."

He asked another dozen questions, and I mixed up the lies with truth. By the end of the set, he whistled.

"I think you've got it! Let me try one more. Do you like Betsy?"

"Sure," I said. No waves. It was the truth.

"No, I mean, like a girlfriend."

I felt my heart race a little. "No!" I insisted.

"Ahh, liar!" he said.

"No really, I don't."

"Sure you don't," he teased. You're going to have to work on that one. You did great telling me the sun was brown and the toilet water tasted good, but once your emotions are involved, pfft… you blew it."

"I wasn't lying!" I insisted. And there hadn't been waves. What did he see that made him think I was lying?

"I gotta go," he said. "I still have practice. See you in school tomorrow?"

"Probably not. Mom said Wednesday at the earliest. Concussion and everything."

"Yeah, that makes sense. I was out a week with mine. But I was fine after the first day."

I knew that. I'd healed his head the same way I did my own. That was another secret I could never let out.

"Thanks for your help. I really appreciate it."

"Truth!" he said, slapping me on the back.

"Truth," I repeated.

"Wednesday, then." He went downstairs to the front door, said goodbye to Mom, and jogged to the driveway where his mother was waiting.

*   *   *

I carefully considered what happened with Allan. I'd had success removing the waves, but he still thought I was lying about Betsy.

There were two potential reasons. First, I was lying, and I liked Betsy as a girlfriend. I'd never had a girlfriend, and I didn't want one. No matter how much I considered this, I had to reject it.

That left only one option. Allan couldn't actually tell when I was lying. The waves were one-hundred percent accurate. The method employed by Mom, Ian, or Allan didn't always work.

The ramification was obvious. When I hid the truth, in addition to removing the waves, I had to stop whatever else people were seeing.

I also needed to practice more, but that would have to wait.

*   *   *

Mom confronted me before bedtime.

"What did you guys talk about?" she said.

"I told him everything," I replied.

Mom's aura hummed with disappointment and a bit of fear.

"Don't worry. He's not going to say anything. I trust him completely."

"I believe you do, but that knowledge puts him in danger," Mom said.

"He was beaten up too," I countered. "He's already in danger."

"You may be right about that. I'd forgotten. Are you feeling OK?"

"I'm totally fine. My brain is completely back to normal."

"I think we should keep you out of school one more day, just to be safe."

"I can start working on my outline. Then I'll be better prepared for my interview with Officer Metz."

"Why is that interview so important?"

The time to practice came more quickly than I'd anticipated. I considered my answer carefully, seized the waves as they formed, and said, "I want to be number one in the class, and there's no way I'll catch Patty unless my paper is better than hers."

She looked at me carefully, and I could see the disbelief in her aura resolve to pride. She bought it.

"OK, then. I'll plan on bringing you down there tomorrow."

"Thanks, Mom," I said, grinning with happiness.

"Good night, then," she said, smiling back.

"Good night."

CHAPTER 47

I SPENT the day going over my plan. I ate a huge lunch, loaded up my backpack and pockets with snacks, and brought two pencils and a giant pad of paper to take notes. I'd written my questions down like before, but this time, I had enough extra paper to write a novel. I threw in my Rubik's cube in case I needed it.

Mom called the police station to confirm the appointment, and I could barely contain my excitement. I paced wildly around. Mom mistook the reason for my anxiety, which was fine.

When the time came for the interview, she drove me to the station and signed the log.

"Perhaps I should come in with you," Mom suggested.

It took everything I had to keep my aura calm. "It's OK. I'll be fine. I won't be that long, either. I've got a few extra questions, but I shouldn't be more than twenty or thirty minutes, presuming he's ready to see me," I said.

"All right. I'll be here," she said, taking a seat in the lobby area. I felt the relief rush through my aura.

After the buzzing door opened, Officer Metz appeared and brought me back to his desk. I was relieved to see that nobody else was around, which made my plan considerably easier.

"I don't have a lot of time, as there's been some activity on one of my cases, so let's get right to it."

"OK, sure," I said eagerly. "What special training did you have to undergo to be a police officer?"

He told me about police academy, ride-along work, and a course he'd taken in family law. I wrote it all down quickly, while scanning his desk for the files.

"Can you describe a day that made it all worthwhile?"

"There are so many," he said.

"Pick one if you can," I prompted.

"It's all about the kids. You know, Garfield High was part of my beat when I first started, and I also used to visit the younger kids at the elementary schools. I loved to watch their faces light up as I came into the building. Some of these kids have only one parent, or even if they have two, both are usually super busy. Having an additional authority figure in their lives helps them remain focused on their future goals, instead of falling into a gang or something. I'd say the thing that makes it all worthwhile is knowing that I'm making a difference to the children of this community."

His voice faded out a bit as I finally spotted the files on his desk. I looked up as he finished speaking, noticing a faraway look in his eyes. Time to enact the plan.

I tainted Metz's aura with the necessary sensation. His eyes lit up with awareness.

"Um, will you excuse me for a minute?" he said.

"Sure, no problem," I said, fully aware of his need.

He rose from his desk, and started toward the bathroom. He paused, fighting his incredible urge.

"Maybe you should wait outside," he suggested.

I pulled the Rubik's cube out of my backpack. "I promise I won't touch anything or move from this spot until I solve this cube."

I added as much strain to his bowels as I could. His knees began to buckle and he held his breath. I eased up the pressure as he made his decision.

"Fine, I'll be right back."

He ran from the room.

I oriented the cube properly, and performed the same "rotate and turn" move exactly twelve times, and *voila*, it was solved. I had set the cube up with the exact opposite series of moves last night. I could have solved it anyway, but I wanted as much time as possible for the next phase of my plan.

I cleared my aura and made sure nobody was around. I crammed a package of candy from my backpack into my mouth and pulled the top file from its location on the desk. It read "Highlanders."

I opened it up, and immediately knew I'd struck gold. Right there on the first page was an insignia. A man wearing armor, with the head and feet of a lion, and a sword across his body planted on the ground. It was the same as the tattoo I'd seen on Kenny's father!

I worked quickly, scanning through the pages and taking notes on particularly salient data points. There were names of known members, including William "Billy" Logan, Augustus "Auggie" Schmidt, and a dozen others.

There were several addresses, including the home address of Billy Logan, an arcade in Madrona, and a building in the warehouse district near a gas station. I wrote them all down, along with the member names.

When I got to a section marked MO, I stopped. I found a paragraph that said:

The initiation rite involves the member of the Junior Highlander organization killing someone by striking them with a baseball bat. If the initiate fails the task, often times they themselves are killed. The bat sends a message to their enemies...

I stopped reading. Metz *had* known exactly what happened to Allan. He was the victim of a gang initiation. It didn't have anything to do with a serial killer, it was a junior member seeking admission to the club.

My aura started pounding, and I felt Metz returning. I closed and replaced the file, reorganized my notes so the pages I'd just written were hidden, and twisted the cube twice.

"Very well, where were we?" he said.

I twisted the cube in the opposite manner twice, solving it again. "I got it!" I said excitedly.

"Nice job! Those are pretty hard to solve, I hear."

"Thanks. OK, I have a couple more questions, and then I need to go. My Mom's waiting outside."

"Go ahead."

I asked him what made him interested in becoming an officer, and he replied with a story similar to that of Lieutenant Herlihy. A police officer visited his school when he was younger. I also asked him how many people were on the force and the hierarchy. I should have asked Chief Beurline, but I was anxious talking to him, so I'd cut that interview short.

With a complete dossier of information, I thanked him for his time and packed up my notebook and pencils into my backpack. He walked me to the door, and the lady at the desk buzzed it open.

"All set?" Mom said.

"Yep."

"You got everything you needed?" she asked.

"I did. It was very helpful."

"Thanks, Officer Metz," Mom called, as the door began to swing closed.

"No problem. Have a great day," he answered back.

My emotions were pouring through me like a violent hailstorm. I was angry at Officer Metz for hiding things from me, and I couldn't help but wonder if he'd been involved in some way. His aura portrayed the picture of a helpful, good person, but he was skilled in obfuscation.

I was also excited. I'd found out a lot of critical information.

Another memory returned from the night I'd been hit.

"After all, you're already a member," Schmidt had said to Logan. Suddenly that comment made sense. These guys killed people to enter the Highlander gang.

I finally understood the *why* of Allan's attack. He'd be dead if I hadn't been there to heal his head. I also knew something about *who* had been responsible. It was a member of the Junior Highlanders.

I also had an idea how to find which member it was. Ask Kenny's father. He'd said "Your Mommy isn't here to protect you this time," so he knew about the attack on us. Mom didn't recognize his picture in the mug books, so it must have been another Junior Highlander trying to get his wings, so to speak.

The conclusion was simple. Kenny's father knew about the attack on Mom because he was in charge of the Highlanders. The police hadn't figured it out, but I had. He was the man who questioned me, and he knew everything.

He hadn't expected me to get away alive, but I had. His secret was out. I also knew where he was. The warehouse. I had the address from the file. I'd pay him a visit, this time, with my full faculties. He'd tell me who hit Allan, and I'd make sure the guilty person was punished. I could also create a recording of Kenny's father in the process, and he'd go back to jail, where he belonged.

Unfortunately, I'd have to wait until Saturday to accomplish this task. I'd convinced Mom to let me go to school, but she wasn't about to let me ride my bike to an abandoned warehouse. I'd need to practice hiding the truth. I'd have to be a complete expert to fool Mom and Dad.

*   *   *

I was so preoccupied by my own agenda that I'd forgotten about my paper. When I got to school on Wednesday, Miss Burnell reminded me.

"Hunter, do you have your outline?"

"Uh, no, I'm sorry. With all that happened I didn't have a chance to finish it."

I detected a salty onion flavor murmuring from the teacher's aura. It was another one that Ian had helped me figure out over the summer. It meant pity. Fine. It worked for me.

"That's OK, dear. Just finish it this week if you can. Your mother told me about your weekend. I understand."

"What was that all about?" Allan asked, when we broke away for lunch. "Did your mother tell Miss Burnell that you were kidnapped?"

"Mom said I was sick. It was enough to get Miss Burnell off my back."

"Oh, man! I was going to say... jeez! If you didn't even talk to the police about it, how could you tell her?"

"My Dad did talk to the police, I think. He knows Metz's direct boss, Lieutenant Herlihy. But he was concerned that maybe Metz or someone is involved. You know, like Orlando Ryan."

"What is it with the police force here?"

"I don't know," I answered.

"So what are you going to do?"

I hesitated. I trusted Allan implicitly, but I still wasn't sure I could tell him. We went through the line and sat down, away from Brady, Bob, Mickey and the others.

"I know where the main hideout is."

"How?" Allan practically yelled.

"Keep your voice down," I chided. He nodded his understanding.

"I read the file at the police station when I interviewed Metz."

I told him the whole story, including all the information I found in the file.

"Holy cow!" Allan said.

"Mom's got me on a tight leash since this concussion, but I'm going to try to sneak out on Saturday. I found the gas station on a map, and the warehouse is only a mile from there."

"Do you want me to come with you?" he asked.

At first blush it sounded like a good idea. I'd be able to tell my parents I was going out with Allan. Maybe they'd let me leave the house if I went with Allan, say, to the park. He could keep a lookout while I went inside to find evidence. Plus it would be nice to have a friend along.

The downside was equally powerful. If Logan was there, and I had to question him, I'd have to do the same thing I'd done to Ryan last year. How could I explain that? I did trust Allan with *almost* every secret, but not that one.

Also, he'd be in deep trouble if anyone found out, which they eventually would. I didn't want Allan getting punished because of me.

"Hunter?" Allan prompted.

In the end, I decided against it. Too much risk. "I'd better go alone," I said. "But I do appreciate the offer."

His aura belied his relief. I'd made the right decision.

"You heading back to karate?" he asked, changing the subject.

"No, not until next week. Mom's orders."

I remembered to eat my sandwich, and we went back to class.

I made a decision about how I was going to get away. I'd have to sneak out. There was no other way. So I spent Thursday and Friday working on removing the waves. I learned that lying affected my aura in other ways, too. The reaction depended upon the seriousness of the deceit. I experienced a slew of sensations, including a fizzing forest green, a hissing, musty blush, and a fossil-grey slime, depending on how horrible the lie was. I felt a buzzing sensation that smelled like sweat and tasted like peanuts when there was a possibility of discovery.

I rehearsed removing the additional sensations, but I had to be careful. Betsy pointed out that when I cleared my aura too much, my gaze went to nowhere and my face looked vacant. This was as bad as getting caught lying. I needed to return my aura to the pristine blue that represented my baseline state. When I was my proper color, I looked normal.

By Saturday at noon, I was ready for the ultimate test.

"I'll probably spend the day in my room working on my paper," I told Mom. I took away the waves, the sizzling, dry nervousness, and the musty remorse.

Although my aura was completely normal, she remained suspicious. Her aura fizzed with forest-green. I waited while she studied my face carefully.

"All right. I'll come get you when it's time for dinner. Dad should be here to join us."

It had worked!

CHAPTER 48

I ATE as much as I could stomach and pretended to go upstairs, but sneaked into the garage instead. I checked the map one final time, made sure my pockets were packed with my recorder and as much food as I could carry, and mounted my bike. It was over six miles to the gas station, and then another mile to the access road, which wasn't even on the map. I looked to be sure Mom didn't see me, and set off at a brisk pace toward my destination.

After about twenty minutes of pedaling, I made the turn past the gas station onto the access road. I saw the lonely building rising slowly into the foreground. Last time I'd been there, I'd been lucky to escape with my life.

I found the tree where the crappy bike had been, and I wondered briefly who had left it there. I heard a noise, so I dismounted and ran quietly to the side of the building. A car entered the parking lot out front, and William Logan got out. As he went inside, I felt the rancid stench of his aura, which was dominated by a metallic brown. From this distance I could only get a general sense, but it was enough. I'd recognize it again if I felt it.

My blood boiled with rage. Being the head of the Highlanders, he'd been directly responsible for the attacks on Allan, Mom and me. He sanctioned the murders of at least four others, according to the files. Plus, he tried to have me killed a second time. He'd rot in prison for the rest of his life after he confessed to his crimes.

I crept back to the alleyway behind the rear entrance. Last time, I'd been concussed so badly that I wasn't able to record normal memories. I only vaguely recognized my surroundings, so I had to hunt around to locate the door. I hadn't been able to see or manipulate the auras then, either. Unlike now.

I cleared my aura and sought out Mr. Logan's stench. I found it, along with two other men who shared evil character. Sharp hatred, encased in an odor of decay, blurred my aura. I had to clear it away again to focus on the men inside the building. It was a challenge to tell them apart from this far away, and I was wasting energy, so I relaxed. It was time for the next phase of my plan.

I crept into the building through the door, which was so decrepit that the lock didn't function. Inside, I pushed over a stack of crates, creating a commotion. I felt a man's aura light up with confusion, alertness, excitement, and fear. As he approached, I searched carefully for signs of murderous intent, which were absent. I clicked on my recorder and headed back toward the exit, deliberately crossing into the man's path.

"You!" he cried out. "Stop!"

I did as commanded.

"Show your face! Now!"

I turned around slowly. The man's aura lit up with wonder and happiness.

"I don't believe it. You're that Hunter kid! Ha ha!! The chief's gonna love this!"

I made a move toward the exit.

"Don't even think about it!" he yelled firmly. He pulled a gun from a holster near his hip. "Hold still or I'll shoot you in the head!"

I could tell it was a bluff, but the man was pointing a gun in my direction, and it might accidentally go off.

"Walk this way. Remember, I'm holding a gun on you, and I'm not afraid to use it!"

The waves fluttering around his buzzing, sweaty aura confirmed that he was quite afraid.

He spoke quietly into a walkie-talkie. "I've got a visitor."

"Bring him to the holding room," said the disembodied voice.

He led me through the basement door, and up a stairwell onto the ground floor where I felt the presence of another man. Kenny's Dad.

"Well, well, well," he said. "Who do we have here?"

I was right. Mr. Logan *was* the boss of the Highlanders. He'd tell me who beat up Allan and tried to kill Mom and me.

"I knew it was you!" I blustered.

"Ah, Mr. Miller. Such a great pleasure to have you here today," he said politely, flourishing his hands in a grand gesture.

I growled.

"Ah yes. The one who's been such a pain in the butt to the chief. How convenient."

"You're the boss of the Highlanders!" I declared.

He laughed loudly. "Me? How did you ever figure that?"

My aura drenched itself in confusion, but I squished away all of the emotion, and iron-fisted away the waves as I said, "I just know!"

He looked at my face sternly. "What else do you know?"

I played my bluff. "Your son is guilty!" I spat.

"Guilty of being a screw-up!" he answered.

"He bashed my friend in the head!" I said accusingly.

"Sure he did! And he tried to get you and your mother too!"

I hid the shock and confusion from my aura. There were no waves. I'd been right all along about Kenny. I'd expected Logan to confess the guilty kid's name to defend Kenny.

"But he screwed up!" Mr. Logan added.

"What do you mean?"

"You have to *kill* to become a member of the Highlanders."

"What do you mean?" I repeated.

"It's a right-of-passage. You can't become a full member until you take a life."

Officer Metz was right. The head-bashing was an entry exam for the criminal gang.

"But Allan didn't die!" I protested.

"No shit, Sherlock!" Logan said angrily. "A few stitches. That's it. What an embarrassment!"

"So you sent him after me?"

"I didn't *send* him, he took initiative. He wanted to become a full member. Instead, after failing a second time, he was banned for life, thanks to you. It was all I could do to keep the Chief from killing him!"

I remembered the words from the file. *If the initiate fails the task, often times they themselves are killed.*

No matter how much I disliked Kenny, I didn't really want to see him killed. I thought of something else that made no sense. "Kenny doesn't ride a motorcycle," I said.

"What's Kenny got to do with it? He's a pussy. A mama's boy. He couldn't hurt a fly. He'll never be a member of the Highlanders."

"But you said that your son…"

"Donnie, you moron. Donnie's the one who bashed your friend!"

I fought to keep the dumbstruck expression out of my aura. Kenny's brother, of course! I should've seen it before. I knew he had a brother from the newspaper articles. Kenny couldn't have done it, because he didn't ride a motorcycle, but he felt guilty because he knew who did. He was protecting his brother.

"Now's my chance to get even," Logan said. "I'm gonna be the one who brings you to the chief. He'll want to question you before he kills you. He's gonna need to know who you're working with. He was furious when you escaped! He'll want to know who took out Schmidt and helped you get away. You might lose a few fingers in the process. I'm *sooo* looking forward to it. Let's go! March!"

He shoved me forward toward the stairwell.

To the guy who'd found me outside he said, "Call the chief. Tell him we got the little turd he's been looking for, and I'm keeping him in the office!"

Who was this "chief" he kept talking about?

"So you're not in charge of the Highlanders?"

"Of course not, you idiot. You're soon going to meet the man who is. Or should I say, meet again," he gave another surly bark of laughter.

What was he talking about? I already met the… CHIEF!

I stumbled and nearly fell over when the answer hit me like a ton of bricks. Chief Beurline! Of course! He was the inside man. He'd been Orlando Ryan's boss. In more ways than one, it seemed.

I recalled when Pam Winston interviewed Captain Beurline, and she'd been confused as to why he hadn't arrested Ryan immediately. Beurline covered up for Ryan, falsely claiming he was part of an undercover investigation, and telling her they would handle the matter internally. They blamed the ring on Vincent Batapaglia, a known felon.

Fortunately, I discovered the truth about Ryan, but apparently not about Beurline. Pam had been investigating further, and…

This time my face planted into the floor as a new realization struck me.

"Get up, you lazy skunk. The chief's gonna be here in a few minutes and you're gonna answer his questions! Come on!"

I didn't resist as we proceeded to an office on the second floor. I was furious. I'd visited Chief Beurline at the police station and I never once suspected him. He'd asked about my progress on the case, and he learned everything I knew. That's why Logan questioned me about Metz, Miss Kessler, and Mr. Jonas. I'd given their names away myself. I'd been completely outflanked by a master manipulator.

Well played, I thought. Well played indeed. But I had him now. My recorder was still running, and I already had Logan's confession. I'd have Beurline's soon. I had to stick to the plan.

*   *   *

Chief Beurline strode into the office with two beefy goons. Their auras were menacing, but I kept my focus on my own. The stench of sweat leaked out despite my attempt at control. As I considered my next move, I realized showing fear was a good idea, so I stopped trying to suppress the smell.

"Why if it isn't Hunter Miller. Right here in my own warehouse," he said. "Cuff him," he said to one of the goons, handing him a pair of handcuffs.

"My old friend Mr. Batapaglia, may he rest in peace, mentioned that a twelve-year-old boy was giving him trouble. I laughed at him. At least, until I found out you were stalking around the police station. You're either very brave, incredibly stupid, or both."

This was not a helpful development. I said nothing, barely able to control my fear, as they locked my hands in place behind my back.

"I have some questions for you. No need to be afraid. I'm not going to kill you."

I relaxed slightly.

"Yet," he added.

I didn't feel murderous intent in his aura, but my own trembled slightly with danger. I was counting on my ability to detect the change, as I would need to act quickly once he decided to make good on his threat.

"Who knows you're here?" he asked.

"Nobody," I replied. Since this was true, my aura gave away no signs of deceit.

"Very good!" he smiled. "And thank you so much for being honest. I presume Mr. Logan told you about the way we remove fingers from people who lie. I'd hate to have to torture you and make a mess of this nice, freshly cleaned floor."

I tried to maintain my composure. Dad's words came to mind. "Turn your emotions into your ally, or they will get the better of you."

"Now tell me, what do you know about my operation?"

"I know *you're* in charge."

"But of course," he replied. "I am the Chief, after all."

"You had people killed!" I said.

"Tsk, tsk," he said. "To whom are you referring?"

"Orlando Ryan!"

"Ah yes. Guilty as charged. The man had his uses, but when he revealed the existence of the ledger, I realized he couldn't be trusted. There was no reason for it, either. We'd already pinned the entire prostitution ring on Vincent Batapaglia, and we only needed a few weeks to let things cool off before restarting with a new crew. But alas, he betrayed me, so I offered a generous reward to make sure his fellow inmates would dispatch him. They were *more* than willing to comply with my request, let me tell you!"

"What about Pam Winston?"

"The TV producer. Very unfortunate. She started out so helpful, allowing me to proclaim Batapaglia's guilt on television. After Ryan's arrest, though, she kept digging. She was getting too close to the truth. She had to go," he said. His aura displayed a hint of remorse.

"Who else?" I asked. My recorder was still running. Might as well maximize the confession.

"Oh there were so many more, but I have a question for you. Who is helping you? You can't expect me to believe you came here alone. Is it the reporter, Lloyd Jonas?"

"He told me to stop looking into the matter. Let the police handle it," I said truthfully.

"Aha, yes, smart man. What about your librarian friend, Miss Kessler, isn't it?"

I wrenched my aura back to a calm blue. I really liked Miss Kessler, and I didn't want her getting hurt.

"No, she was helping me with my civics project. She doesn't have anything to do with this."

"Really. Well, I can see you're telling the truth, which I very much appreciate. Now I don't have to kill her too. See, this all goes so smoothly if you don't try to lie."

I struggled against my handcuffs. I should have planned for those.

"Then it must be your parents," he continued. "Let's see, there's the mild mannered genetics professor, who happens to know enough karate to disable one of my potential recruits, or your mysterious father, who spends a great deal of time traveling for his job. What is it that he does again?"

I suppressed my aura completely. "He's a professor at the University of Washington. He goes on trips all the time to interview indigenous populations of many countries for his work as a sociologist."

I let no hint of waves escape.

"Really," he said again. This time, seaweed green streaks of doubt flowed through his aura. "So which one of your parents extracted you from my clutches last time?"

"Neither one," I said simply. He stared at me carefully, but since this was the truth, my aura remained a rock of solid blue.

"Either you're telling the truth, or you've somehow become the best liar of all time. Judging from our last interview, I'm going to have to go with choice A. But this leads me to the monster question. How *did* you get away from Auggie? And don't even think about lying, because I'll know!"

"I know karate," I said.

"Do you now?" he said calmly. I could smell a slight hint of fear in his aura.

"And your plan today was?" he asked.

"Get you to confess."

I could feel the man's mind working hard. "And confess I have. But that must mean you are recording the conversation. Do you have a tape machine on you, by any chance?"

"No, I don't. I thought the police would be here by now."

This time, the sticky seaweed was palpable in his aura. I must be letting something slip through.

"Search him!" he commanded.

The goon closest to me rose and approached. This was it. I had enough information to burn Chief Beurline to the ground. Time to get out of here.

I cringed as the gorilla touched my shirt and patted it down. As his gigantic hand reached toward my pants pocket, I grasped his aura and yanked it violently into the void. He crumpled to the ground next to me, unmoving.

"What the heck?" the other goon said. He reached over and felt for the man's pulse. I could feel the confusion and slight fear emanating from both of them now.

I leapt up and axe-kicked the man in the neck, adding enough force to push the man into the void as well. It was more difficult, and I could feel the expense of energy draining my strength.

"You weren't kidding about the karate!" Beurline said. "But let's see how well you can dodge a bullet!"

He pulled his service revolver from its holster and aimed it at my chest. The murderous intent in his aura matched with the pounding of imminent danger in my own. With my energy levels falling, I was too far away to pull him to the void, but I felt inspired by the story of Skeet Metz.

"Wasp!" I yelled.

I poked his left ear with spicy redness.

"Ow!" he yelled, temporarily distracted. He pulled the trigger as I leapt to the side. I felt the spray of fiberglass from where the bullet struck the wall behind me, right where my head had just been.

I struck out again, this time placing the spicy redness onto his right hand, as close to the trigger finger as I could get.

"Ouch!" he screamed, dropping the gun.

"Did you see that wasp?" I reiterated.

"I'm allergic to bees!" he cried. I stung him again in the leg and in the back.

He rifled through his pockets, pulling out an epi-pen. The handcuff keys dropped to the floor, along with several papers, a pen, and several coins. He uncapped the medication and stuck the needle through his pants into his left thigh and pressed the syringe.

I jumped toward him, my hands still cuffed behind my back. He recognized the danger and put up his hands in a defensive posture.

I adopted a fighting stance and put my weight onto my back foot. I sent my right foot in a sweeping roundhouse toward his head. He ducked, setting himself up for the second half of the combination, a side kick to the exposed face. "Thanks, Dad," I thought silently, as my foot crashed into his face. Not willing to make the mistake I had with Kenny, I added enough power to recreate the cloudy grey concussion in my adversary's brain. He, like the others, fell to the ground, unconscious.

I saw the keys on the ground next to the man, and I turned around so I could pick them up. I carefully inched backwards, feeling blindly along the floor for the keys. As I closed my right fist around them, I felt other auras approaching outside the office door.

"Everything OK, Chief?" called Logan.

I calmed myself as best as possible. There were three armed men outside the door, I'd burned a ton of calories dropping the men inside the office, and my hands were in cuffs, so I couldn't get to my snacks. I needed to escape.

I walked to the window, still trying to manipulate the handcuff key into the slot. I was on the second floor, but as long as I didn't hit my head, I could heal whatever injury I sustained jumping out.

If I stayed, these men would kill me. Easy decision. I held on tight to the keys, smashed the window with my foot, kicked away the shards of glass that had remained stuck to the frame, and dove through. I tried to roll forward, the way I'd learned in karate class, so that I'd end up on my feet.

I only made it about three quarters of the way around, and I landed hard on my butt. I held onto the keys, though. I felt the spicy red pain at the point of impact, but I healed it while shuffling quickly to my feet. Raised voices shouted from the window of the room I'd vacated. Without turning to see what they were doing, I took off running toward the woods, clutching the keys tightly behind my back.

Bang! Bang! Bang!

Several gunshots rang out as Logan or one of his goons started shooting, probably at me. Fortunately, I was already out of harm's way. I ducked behind a large tree trunk and tried again to unlock the cuffs. I suddenly felt another aura, very close by, moving quickly in my direction.

Although it contained some black, the baseline color was a deep, tactical blue. And it was familiar. I knew it well. Sharp, cold, salty, and fearless orange. Plus, it was hissing maroon. Angry!

Dad emerged from behind a copse of trees wearing what looked like Army fatigues. "Hunter! What on earth are you doing here?" he half whispered, half shouted.

"At the moment, trying not to get shot," I said.

"Wha?" he sputtered. "Get the heck out of here!"

"Would you mind," I said, still trying to remain as calm as I could while turning around to demonstrate my hands.

"For heaven's sake, Hunter. You've got to be kidding me."

He expertly flicked the handcuffs open, releasing my hands. I waved them around, allowing them the opportunity to enjoy their newfound freedom.

"We'll talk about this later. You need to go, now!"

"Wait! You'll want to hear this! Chief Beurline and Billy Logan confessed!"

I tossed him my recorder. He shook his head disapprovingly.

"Go HOME!" he said firmly. "I'll take care of this!"

And with that, he was off. I caught my bearings, reversed course back toward the building, and found my bike near the back corner. After stuffing my face for a moment with some snacks, I pedaled furiously onto the service road without a second glance back. I wasn't going home, but I wanted to be as far from this place as I could get.

CHAPTER 49

MY NEW destination was several miles away. I'd memorized the addresses from Metz's files, in case Logan hadn't been at the warehouse. He had been there, but I needed a different Logan. Donnie.

As I pedaled and sucked on sour candies from my pocket, I thought about Dad. Why was *he* at the warehouse? Was he on some super-secret mission? And if so, was the Highlander gang at the heart of it? Obviously the police knew about it, but maybe there was more to the story.

I trusted him to take care of it, as he said he would. He had all the proof he needed to arrest the guys inside, including Chief Beurline. One problem might be the other voice on the tape. Mine. How would he explain that?

I decided not to worry about that right now.

After about twenty minutes, I found the correct street, and by checking mailbox numbers, my target. I coasted my bicycle into the driveway of a modest house with cracking paint, shingles falling from the roof, and other signs of general disrepair. I disembarked, leaned the bike up against a tree, and went to the door.

I tried not to think about how poorly my visit here would be received as I knocked on the door.

Kenny Logan answered. "What do *you* want?" he spat.

I picked through his aura. Abrasive, yes, and there was the odor of halitosis (a cool word for bad breath I found in a medical book) which identified him as a pompous jerk. But everything else was more like Dad or Sensei Nam. Medium blue, bright gold, ivory white, and the fearless color of orange, like a tabby cat. Or a tiger. This was not the aura of a person who would bash someone's brains with a club.

"Look, Kenny, I'm sorry I accused you of anything," I said.

His aura swirled in disbelief. Mine made no waves, so I didn't have to change it to make them go away. I really was sorry.

"I'm actually looking for your brother, Donnie. Is he here?"

His aura raged with anger. "No, he's not. And even if he was, I wouldn't tell you!" he spat.

No waves.

I recalled the addresses from the file.

"Is he at Genie's Arcade?"

The waves appeared before he started his denial.

"No. How would I know? I'm not my brother's keeper. Just get out of here already!"

That was all I needed from Kenny. "Thanks. You're really nothing like him, are you?" I added, leaving him in stunned silence.

I hopped back onto my bike, silently plotting a course for the arcade. I made a few wrong turns, getting lost so badly that I had to stop and try to remember the map I'd memorized. My legs were getting tired from biking, as I'd gone more than twelve miles. I rejuvenated with some more snacks before heading off again in the proper direction. Fortunately, it was less than a mile away and I made it there easily.

Genie's Arcade was a popular hangout for lots of kids of all ages. There were dozens of bikes in the rack out front, and I locked mine up in a slot near the edge. I'd been there once with Allan and the guys, before my depression turned me into a social outcast. They had pinball machines and video games, many of which were pretty cool. Mom discouraged me from going to places like this because of the autism, but the flashing lights and sounds didn't bother me as much as the concentration of people in one spot.

As I walked in, I felt the oppression of bodies, or more accurately, auras, all around me. I ate the last few bites of candy from my stash and tried my best to ignore all the human rabble. I belatedly realized that I had a problem. I didn't know what Donnie looked like. I'd never felt his aura either, so I couldn't simply clear my aura and scout through the teenagers inside the arcade.

I was stuck with the worst possible method. I'd have to ask around.

I picked my way amongst the strangers, unable to bring myself to speak to anyone. When I finally overcame my anxiety, the result was less than helpful.

"Um, excuse me, do you know Donnie Logan?" I asked a random kid, who looked to be about my age.

"Never heard of him," he said, turning and walking away.

I wandered among the middle school kids, until I remembered that Donnie was sixteen, and he'd never be caught around these youngsters. I walked past some of the video games toward a room separate from the main hall. I caught sight of a tattoo on an older kid's upper arm, and I tried to see if it had a lion head and a sword.

"What are you looking at?" the kids asked, whirling to face me.

"Your tattoo," I said, retreating slightly to create more space between us.

"Oh," he said, evidently expecting a different answer.

"Do you know Donnie Logan?" I asked.

"What do you want with Donnie?" he asked. Clearly he knew him.

"He's got a tattoo on his arm with a lion head, doesn't he?" I asked, hoping to find a reason for this kid to spill the beans on Donnie's whereabouts.

"Yeah, a bunch of kids have one. What of it?"

"Is Donnie here?"

I felt the waves. He didn't want to tell me.

"You're too little to be a cop," he said.

"I'm not a cop," I reassured. "I liked his tattoo and he was going to tell me where he got it."

"Well that's easy. He got it from Spider."

"Spider?" I asked, trying to keep the conversation going.

"Yeah, sure. That's where I got this beauty," he said, pulling up his pant leg to reveal a full length snake.

This was all fascinating, but I needed to find Donnie. Instead, I felt another familiar aura, one I'd been recently studying carefully. The owner sped past me into a back room.

"That's great," I said, with minimal expression. "Spider, thanks."

The older boy smiled as though he'd given me the key to the city. I turned and followed the path of the younger kid, whose aura I knew well.

Kenny Logan was inside, speaking to a boy with similar facial features and a distinctive tattoo. The aura surrounding him stunk of rancid hatred, and the metallic brown and malicious black combined with a streaky medium blue and bronze. The resemblance to his father was unmistakable. I'd found Donnie.

"Hey!" I yelled.

This back room had pool tables and dart boards, rather than video games and pinball machines, so the underlying mechanical noise level was absent in here. My voice carried and reverberated off the walls, causing a strained silence.

"Ooh, isn't this hysterical," said Donnie, who shoved his brother aside like a leaf in the wind. "I'm going to enjoy this!"

He approached me, carrying a pool cue. Three other boys, also carrying sticks, followed him as Donnie crossed the room. Noticeably, Kenny did not join them. Four on one was much better than five on one.

Donnie stopped several feet away and slapped the pool cue repeatedly onto his left palm, making a characteristic sound that pierced the sudden stillness. The others stopped alongside him.

I noticed the lion-faced tattoos on the arms of the sidekicks, all of whom were most likely Junior Highlanders.

"I've got an idea," Donnie said, and he turned around and walked toward the back of the room, dropping the cue on the nearest pool table. He picked up a baseball bat from the corner, and said to the guys, "Joey, grab him!"

The largest of the boys, who was easily twice my weight, stepped forward menacingly. Instead of trying to seize me, Joey took a swing with his weapon.

It was like a one-step exercise. I ducked underneath, swinging my foot hard into his gut. When he doubled over, I cracked him as hard as I could on the back of the head with both of my interlocked fists. He landed on the ground, sending the pool stick scuttling across the floor. As he started to get back up, I kicked the back of his head, causing his forehead to collide with the ground. He made no further attempt to rise.

I could feel the surprise in the auras of the other two.

"Well, get him already!" yelled Donnie, who was coming over with the baseball bat. Apparently he'd decided that I'd be his ticket to the Highlanders, and he wanted to get a clean shot with the bat so as not to repeat the mistakes he'd made on Allan and Mom.

Spurred into action, the teen ruffians rushed at me, brandishing their pool cues. They struck simultaneously, one on my left, aiming at my head, and one on my right, aiming at my chest. I used a double arm block to the left, breaking the stick and bruising my arms, but protecting my head. The other stick struck my chest unopposed, causing spicy redness to shoot from a pair of broken ribs.

I cried out at the contact, even though I was able to suppress the pain completely. Donnie laughed. "Nice one, Huck! I think you cracked a rib!"

What a psycho.

I didn't have a chance to heal my ribs, as both boys were rearing back for another strike, one on each side of me. Donnie approached from the front, although he kept out of my range, apparently content to have his friends subdue me.

My first priority was to avoid the concurrent blows. A *kata* series from the blue belt test flowed into my brain, and without thinking, I began.

I spun to my left and continued the move with a roundhouse kick that hit home, the boy's face distorting under the blow.

Although he didn't go down, he was now standing between me and the other two, making it a fair fight. He brandished the broken stick in his right hand, and I could feel the anger and pain with varying shades of red coursing through his aura.

He rushed me, exactly what I wanted. The next move in the *kata* was a block, but when he swung the broken cue at me, it was easier to duck. He missed badly, and was off-balance and out of position when I countered with an elbow strike to his ear. This time he went down, howling in pain. As I had done with the first kid, I lashed out hard with my right foot, bouncing his head onto the hard floor and silencing his cries.

The anger flowed through me as wildly as it had through the other boy. I looked up at Donnie. Instead of golden confidence, his aura now smelled slightly of fear.

"Hold on Huck!" he said, as the stick-wielding boy prepared to hit me again. "We need to attack him together. He's pretty good, but if we both attack him at once, he can't stop it."

Huck stepped back, tossed the cue aside and collected something from Donnie. The reprieve gave me time to heal my ribs, which helped, because I couldn't really punch or block with my right hand.

"I'm going to kill you, Hunter. Thank you so much for presenting me with the opportunity to earn my spot with the Highlanders."

Both boys approached, and that's when I saw the glint of metal in Huck's right hand. Donnie had given him a blade. I retreated, but found the solid wall behind me after only a few backward steps.

"Now!" yelled Donnie, and both of them converged on me.

"No!" came a voice from my right, as Kenny grabbed Huck's shoulder, spinning him around. Donnie's bat came at my head, but with Huck pulled aside, I dove forward into the empty space. The bat struck the wall hard, and I rolled forward, this time successfully using the trick from karate to end up standing. I whirled as Donnie took another swing, which I easily dodged.

I approached him, and our positions were now reversed. Donnie had his back to the wall, and I could feel frustration, anger and panic rising in his aura. As he swung the bat, I used a side-kick to ping-pong his head into the wall behind him, dazing him slightly. I swung my left fist at his right shoulder, making him drop the bat. I punched him with my right fist as hard as I could in the stomach, doubling him over. A scream emanating from behind me stopped me cold.

I spun around, seeing Kenny bleeding profusely from his belly, a knife hilt protruding ominously from the wound. I covered the ground between the three of us in two strides and did a flying front kick into Huck's surprised face.

I landed on top of him, put my hand on his face and yanked him into the void. He wasn't going anywhere.

"No!!" Yelled a voice behind me. Instead of picking up the bat and cracking me on the head, Donnie had run to Kenny, whose injured body lay limply on the ground.

At that moment, Officer Metz and Lieutenant Herlihy burst into the room, both holding their service weapons with intent to use them.

"What the hell is going on?" Herlihy yelled.

I realized I'd made a huge mistake. I should have healed Kenny instead of attacking Huck.

"We need an ambulance!" I said. At a nod from the Lieutenant, Officer Metz stepped to the side and made the call.

"You called the police?" Donnie said to Kenny. "How could you? We're brothers!"

Kenny looked up and tried to shake his head from side to side.

"You traitor! I hope you die!"

Herlihy spoke to Donnie. "All right, son, how about explaining what happened?"

"I'm not talking to you, pig!" retorted Donnie.

"Let's go!" Herlihy said, reaching out to pull the boy off his brother. In one smooth movement, Donnie yanked the knife from Kenny's body and struck out at Herlihy's chest.

The sound of the gunshot exploded through the closed room.

Officer Metz's shocked expression and aura made it clear that he hadn't intended to shoot, but had been forced to do so by the actions of the boy. He'd been about to kill his boss.

For an instant, nobody moved. Donnie's lifeless body fell to the side slowly and landed at Kenny's side with a dull thump. I jumped over to Kenny and felt at his aura, disregarding what Metz and Herlihy were yelling.

The wound was bad. Internal organs were damaged. I could feel the effects of the blood pooling inside his abdomen. I found the source of the internal bleeding and, like I'd done so many times on myself, fixed the deep wound by replacing his normal aura.

I found myself forcibly removed from Kenny's unmoving form, but not before I'd done what I needed to. The doctors could fix the external cut easily. They may have been able to repair the internal damage too, but I wasn't willing to take the risk. Kenny had saved my life, and I owed him the same.

"Hunter!" the policeman yelled again.

I turned toward Officer Metz as the paramedics loaded Kenny onto a stretcher and wheeled him away.

"He's in shock," said Herlihy. "You just shot a kid right in front of him."

Others flooded into the room, putting up yellow tape, checking on the unconscious bodies of the other Junior Highlanders, and taking crime scene photographs.

"Let's get out of here," said Metz, who grabbed me by the elbow and escorted me to his car outside.

When I arrived at the police station, Mom was already there. Someone must have called her from the arcade.

"What happened?" she demanded, aiming her gaze at Officer Metz.

"From the looks of things, Hunter and his friend beat up three gang members, but the last one stabbed Hunter's friend and attacked the Lieutenant, so I had to shoot him. We're still processing the crime scene, but that's the picture."

"You didn't try to question him without his parents, did you?"

"No Ma'am," Metz said.

"Can we deal with this tomorrow? He's clearly a wreck and will need time to process."

"We'd really like to get some answers," Metz said. Mom made it clear with her facial expression that she wasn't going to permit any further conversation.

"OK, tomorrow then."

*   *   *

We drove home in silence. My mind reeled. Donnie was dead, but Kenny was alive. I'd accomplished my goal of finding Allan's attacker, but at what cost? Mom and Dad were going to... what? I didn't even know how they were going to punish me. Kenny had nearly been killed. And after all was said and done, I didn't feel any different. There was no great sensation of accomplishment for a job well done. I only felt exhausted.

CHAPTER 50

I SAT on the couch and explained what happened as succinctly as possible while Mom and Dad listened, focusing their attention on my every word.

"So instead of heading right home, like I asked, you went to Kenny's house to confront Donnie. Kenny told you where Donnie was, and you went there, by yourself, to attack a group of wannabe gang members. Is that about right?" Dad said.

I'd had to lie about how I discovered Donnie's whereabouts, or else confess to reading the police files to learn of the arcade. I'd removed the waves so well neither Mom nor Dad noticed.

"It sounds much worse when you say it," I said.

Dad reared his head and laughed loudly, but not in a good way.

"Listen, Hunter, you can't *do* things like this. It's a miracle you weren't killed!" Mom said. "Do you understand what I mean? You could be dead. Gone forever. Existing no more. Do you hear me?"

Mom's aura blasted me with maternal concern.

"I'm sorry," I said weakly.

"You're sorry. He's sorry," she added, looking at Dad. "You just don't get it."

Dad put up his hand and Mom stopped speaking and started pacing.

"There's another issue we need to clear up," Dad said. "You've been keeping secrets from us."

I looked up at him, frozen in terror. He knew.

"It's time to come clean. No more lies."

My aura began thrumming wildly, pounding with danger. I turned defensive.

"Well what about you?" I yelled back.

"Hunter, we've been over this. What I do at work has to be kept under wraps."

"So you say!" I said, standing up.

He put his hands on my arms and looked directly into my eyes. "I am not lying to you. I cannot talk about my work, and that's that. You cannot ask me about it, and I can't reveal a single thing about it. It doesn't matter if you are my son, my friend from high school, or the guy that serves me fries at the local restaurant. *Nobody* can know about what I do. Get it?"

His aura blossomed with deep gold, and there wasn't a single wave to be found.

Briefly mollified, I relaxed and sat back down. "But what about Mom?" I said.

"What about me?" Mom said, stepping forward.

"Are you going to tell me that you are really just a university professor?"

I felt the waves starting. "See?" I said. "You are lying!"

"I didn't say anything, Hunter," Mom said, her aura now blazing in concern and confusion.

I caught myself. "No, I mean you *were* lying. You have no students. You have weird emergencies where you have to go into the 'lab' and do things at all hours of the day and night. You never grade papers or give lectures."

Mom's aura smelled of fear.

"And then there's the big one. About Dad not being my father!"

This time, I was nearly knocked over by the sensations from the auras.

"Of course I'm your father!" Dad bellowed. He nodded at Mom, who suddenly put her hand over my mouth. I was so stunned I didn't know what to do. Should I pull her into the void? My own mother?

Dad ran around the room, picking up objects and looking carefully for something, and then bolted out of the living room. Mom mimed "shhh" with her finger to her lips. What the heck was going on?

Dad returned with a wand of some kind, waving it through and around the clock, lamp, and every electrical outlet. Then he walked meticulously past every wall, window, and piece of furniture, using the device and checking a meter that was attached. When he'd finished, he said, "Sweep's clean."

"Better check the rest of the house, just in case," Mom said quietly.

He went off, presumably to use the apparatus everywhere else.

Mom grabbed me by the shoulders the same way Dad had, gazing directly into my eyes.

"It is imperative that you never repeat what you just said. Ever. If anyone, and I mean anyone, thinks what you said is true, your life, as well as mine and your father's, would be at great risk. Do you understand me?"

Her epic plea contained no hint of untruth.

"No, I don't understand. Why?"

She gave me a little shake. "I can't *tell* you why!" she said. "On this matter, you simply have to trust us. Maybe someday I'll be able to explain it, but certainly not now."

I nodded.

"Good," she said. She sat down next to me on the couch, deep in thought.

"I'll tell you what. We'll come clean about everything we can, and in return, you promise me that you'll stop doing clandestine operations. Is that a deal?"

I thought about it briefly. I'd finally get to learn about Mom and Dad. "Deal!" I said earnestly.

Dad returned shortly after, nodding at Mom. "All clear."

"Hunter has agreed to stop playing supercop if we divulge what we can about our careers," Mom said.

Dad nodded again.

"OK, Hunter. We'll tell you what we can. But if anyone asks, you stick to the story you've been told. Is that clear?"

"Yes," I said solemnly.

"As you are aware, I do work for a government agency," he started. I saw where he was headed.

"Mom's a super spy too!" I spouted.

"An analyst, dear," Mom said quietly. "I don't work in the field like your Dad. It's not really any different than working as a university professor. I do research and try to discover very specific applications."

"I knew it!" I said. "Wait, is that how you got together?"

The both quietly chuckled.

"Guilty," said Dad. "In fact, fraternization between employees was completely forbidden. Fortunately, your mother is literally the only person in the world who does what she does, so they made an exception in our case."

"Well, your Dad's one of the tops in his field too," Mom boasted.

Dad bowed humbly.

"Now listen, Hunter," Mom started. "That's really all we can say. And you cannot repeat it to anyone, even Allan. Understand?"

I nodded.

"Now it's your turn. Dr. Eisenberg told me that you were cavorting with prostitutes. Would you mind telling us about that?"

"I wasn't cavorting!" I protested. "Wait, what does cavorting mean?"

"Just what you think," said Dad.

"I was only talking to them. I was trying to…" I stopped.

"No secrets," said Mom.

"OK. I was trying to figure out who was running the prostitution ring. I thought it was Orlando Ryan."

"And that's why you were running around with Ian last year, creating the story for Ian's father that broke Ryan's case?"

"Yes," I admitted.

"And this year, you spent all that time going to the police station trying to get a look at the files on the biker gangs?" Dad said.

Busted. He'd known all along what I was doing.

"How did you know?" I said.

"It's what I would have done," he replied.

"So you *knew* I'd been doing these things and you didn't try to stop me?" I asked.

"Not at first. When Dr. Eisenberg informed me about your extracurricular activities, you were going through a terrible time, having lost your grandfather. We were afraid to bring it up because you were in such a fragile state. As you regained your mental strength and got back on track with karate, your friends and school, we continued to wait to discuss what you'd done so as not to disrupt your progress," said Mom.

"Then, your mother told me that you were starting to act strangely, with a profound interest in police and a pathologic fascination with trying to stop Allan's attacker. You were exploring gang activity and searching through old newspaper articles. That's when we put the two things together and figured you were trying to repeat what you'd done before," Dad said.

"As long as you were simply doing research, I thought I could keep an eye on you," said Mom. "But you must have found something, because they sent that kid to attack you."

"That's when I took a leave of absence. I looked into the problem myself, called in a few favors here and there, and figured out the gist of what was happening," Dad said.

I considered this. He knew what I was doing. Then something struck me. He *knew* what I was doing.

The bike? Schmidt's "stroke" and subsequent faint? These hadn't been accidents.

"You were there!" I accused.

Dad smiled wryly.

"You did something to Schmidt. And you made the sound in the woods to get me to go toward the bicycle, and you're the one who put it there!"

"I told you he was smart," said Mom.

"Why didn't you just go in and get me?" I demanded.

"Remember I said I couldn't tell *anyone* about what I do? That includes explaining to the local authorities why I was at an abandoned warehouse where people had been found murdered. I needed to make sure you got away safely without being detected. Plus, I had to take care of Schmidt."

"How did you know about the warehouse?"

"I saw the file. Metz documented several known locations. Then I followed you there. That was the first time I realized how much danger you were in, and why we grounded you. But you decided to sneak out and try to trap a dangerous man on your own."

"And you were nearly killed!" Mom interjected.

"I'm still not sure you understand the consequences of your actions, Hunter," Dad said, more calmly. "These are very scary people. The gang members have to kill someone to get in. They buried the bodies in that pit at the warehouse. There were a dozen members listed in the file, so that makes at least that many murders. They wouldn't think twice about killing you."

He was right. Both times, I was nearly killed.

"The worst part was the inside man. It was clear from the investigation notes that details were being provided to the killers. Metz is a good man, and I've known Herlihy for over ten years, so I doubted either of them were dirty. But Beurline? The mayor hand-picked him for Chief of Police. I wouldn't have believed it if you hadn't proved it."

"What happened to him?" I asked, happy for the change of topic.

"We cooked up a story to keep the public out of the loop. The Chief was killed in a shootout while attempting to arrest the head of the Highlanders who, along with several other gang members, also died in the struggle."

It was the same sort of lie that Beurline had used when Orlando Ryan was caught.

"So he's dead?"

"Yes. He didn't care to be arrested and tried to kill me, so I had no choice. Again, I needed to keep my involvement unknown, so I phoned in an anonymous tip with a possible explanation. They used it."

"And people will believe it?"

"They usually do, unless someone can prove otherwise. The only ones who can do that are Officer Metz, Lieutenant Herlihy, and us. Both of them will be promoted, and obviously your mother and I won't be saying anything. I know you would very much like the entire truth to come to light after all your hard work, but trust me, this is the best solution for everyone."

"So Hunter, we have a proposal," said Mom.

"Here it is," said Dad. "From now on, we'll promise to be as open and honest with you as possible, but we ask that you do the same with us. If there is some question we can't answer because of our work, you'll have to trust us."

"And if you find yourself in any kind of trouble, tell us. We may be able to help," added Mom.

"And no more lying to us," said Dad.

"Is that fair?" Mom asked.

"Yes," I answered. They both gave me a giant hug, and I liked it.

CHAPTER 51

MONTHS LATER, we gathered at the end of year assembly. It had special meaning for me this year, my last at Madrona. I'd come a long way since starting in Mrs. Bonefant's third grade special needs class. If it hadn't been for my lackluster performance in French, it would have been me, rather than Patty Owens, with the top overall grades.

I did receive the award for best scores in mathematics. It was not a surprise, because I scored one hundred percent on every single test, including a special placement test for advanced math at Garfield High next year. It was fun to walk to the podium to claim my award while the other students and parents politely clapped.

There was no float or giant spectacle this year. The incident with Tommy Lachance two years ago was still etched in the minds of the teachers and principal. Instead, the event was more subdued, with Mrs. Frechette reading off the names of students and their achievements, and then each eighth-grader walking onstage to receive their diploma.

"Congratulations, Hunter," said the principal, when it was my turn to accept the diploma.

I tried to pull my hand back quickly, like everyone else had, but she held onto it and continued speaking quietly to me.

"You have incredible potential, Hunter. Remember that. Do your best and you'll be destined for greatness. I'm sure of it."

"Thanks," I said, struggling to reclaim my hand.

When I got back to my seat, Allan, who'd seen the exchange, asked "What did she say to you?"

"She said I have incredible potential."

"That's very true, my friend," he said, smiling.

*   *   *

After the formal ceremony, which took forever, we dispersed to our respective parents, families, and friends. The area exploded with whoops and yells. Smiles, hugs, and pictures were the order of the moment. I found Mom and Dad at the outskirts of the crowd.

"We're so proud of you, Hunter," Mom said.

"And we expect many great accomplishments in the future!" said Dad.

"Your grandfather would be proud too," Mom added.

I missed Grandpa, and I knew I always would. But I'd learned to carry him around in my heart, knowing that he'd always be there, whenever I needed him.

I gave Mom a hug, and Dad joined in.

Betsy came over with her mother. "Congratulations!" she said. Her aura was the least depressed that I'd ever seen.

"You too!" I replied.

"This is my mother, Leslie."

"How are you?" I asked.

"I'm doing much better," she said.

Mom reached out her hand, "Marissa Miller. And this is Hunter's father, James Miller."

They all shook hands.

"I've heard so much about you, Hunter," Leslie said.

I didn't know how to respond.

"All good, I hope?" interjected Mom.

"Oh yes. Betsy says that you're wonderful. You saved her life!"

Leslie smiled at me, and I smiled back awkwardly.

"I take it you're heading to Garfield next year?" Leslie asked.

"Yup," I said.

"Good. Betsy will have at least one true friend. She really needs that," she said.

"Mom!" Betsy said disapprovingly.

"Let's give them a minute," Dad said, noticing the angst on Betsy's face.

The adults stepped to the side and chatted amongst themselves.

"Thank you, Hunter. You really did save my life."

I smiled. She kissed me on the cheek, which burned like it was on fire afterwards.

"See you over the summer, maybe?" she suggested.

"Yeah, that would be cool," I agreed.

She smiled, turned on her heels, and walked away, her aura basking in a spectacular yellow.

✶   ✶   ✶

Of all people, Kenny Logan approached me next. We hadn't said a word to one another since the incident at the arcade.

"Hey," he said cautiously.

I stared at him without speaking.

"The paramedics told Mom that you put pressure on my stomach after Huck stabbed me. They said I might have lost a lot more blood and even died if you hadn't done that. I just wanted to say thanks."

It was true. I'd very likely saved his life. But, he'd saved mine too.

"I'm sorry about your brother," I said.

"He was a jerk."

I nodded my agreement. He'd been about to bash me in the head with a baseball bat.

"Thanks for standing up for me, too," I said.

"I guess we're even," he said.

"Yes," I agreed.

"One more thing," he said.

"What?"

"I'm sorry about calling you names and stuff."

His aura indicated that he was conflicted, but not lying.

"Well, stop doing it," I said simply.

"OK. Hey, um," he started, but then lost his nerve.

"What?" I prompted.

"Do you think you could teach me some of those karate moves? Those were really cool."

"Sure," I said.

"You're all right, Hunter," he said.

I smiled, and he went back to his mother, who nodded in my direction.

"What was that all about?" asked Allan, who'd been watching from a few feet away.

"He wants to learn karate," I answered.

"He...what?"

I shrugged.

"If I hadn't seen it for myself, I never would have believed it. You might have a new friend," Allan said.

"Yeah, maybe," I said.

He shook his head and chuckled. "Count on you to do what nobody is expecting."

Allan's comment sparked a memory of Grandpa's first words to me. *You aren't at all what I was expecting.*

Grandpa. I felt a lump of sadness in my throat. I knew he'd be proud of me. I'd learned so much this year. He'd guided me toward a path of helping people in a way that only I could. Travelling this road would be an adventure, and throughout my journey, I vowed to always honor his memory.

I looked at Allan and basked in the purple bond that glowed between us.

"You ready to get out of here?" he asked.

"You bet," I replied.

I was ready to move forward with the next chapter in my life.

ACKNOWLEDGEMENTS

HEARTFELT THANKS go out to Nick Brown who was my sounding board (often during a run) for plot lines throughout this book, then later, an alpha reader for the completed manuscript.

Guiding me toward an authentic story are some real life heroes: Patrick Brady, Pete Metz, Michael Moran, and Jonathon Huber. Thanks for your help!

Research into the field of depression—an integral theme of the book—was as painful as it was insightful. In fact, it added an extra six months to the writing project and, I hope, a new level of understanding of this insidious disorder. Thanks to those of you who bared your souls and contributed your stories so that others may relate to the pain you have suffered.

A special shout out to Jim and Dave Johnson, who know the true meaning of "3:57 AM" from the opening line of the book. Thank you so much for your support!

Thanks to friends and family who provided insight, assistance, support, or all three. They include, but are by no means limited to: Melissa Brown, Alex Brown, Kat Wadiak, Nancy Bocklage, Makayla Brown, Jody Brown, Janel Hansen, Kayla Jones, Heather Williams, Stacey Desjardans, Dave Dunham, Rob Freundlich, Nicola Delorio, Jenny Craun, Peter Waterstreet, Susan Urasky, Tara Mackenzie,

Andrea Libby, Nancy Stone, Bethany Potter, Matthew Peters, Linda Burson, Meils Preece, Josh Snell, and Roger Pierce.

Once again, thanks to my editor, Ellen Ward, and my book designer, Glen Edelstein, for another fantastic job.

And finally, love and undying gratitude to my wife, Dr. Sandra Brown who is a gifted editor, but so much more. You sustain me with your unfailing support and guidance.

ABOUT THE AUTHOR

DARIN C. BROWN grew up in upstate New York, the youngest of seven children. After twenty years in clinical practice as an ER physician, he began writing The Master of Perceptions series. He has written, directed, and performed murder mystery theater shows, comedy sketches, and parody songs. He is an avid runner, and former national champion in master's track. He currently resides in the White Mountains of New Hampshire with his wife, Dr. Sandra Brown, and their many pets.

Made in the USA
Middletown, DE
14 January 2021

30107183R00208